DAUGHTER OF DARKNESS AND DREAMS

DAUGHTER OF DARKNESS AND DREAMS

ANASTASIS BLYTHE

DAUGHTER OF DARKNESS AND DREAMS

www.AnastasisBlythe.com

Hardcover ISBN: 978-1-960606-05-1

Jacket Cover design by Moorbooks Design.
Laminate Cover and Interior Design by Dragonpen Designs.

FOR PENNY, WITH MUCH LOVE AND GRATITUDE.

CHAPTER 1

MEILING'S HEART LURCHED wildly with the echo of the swinging doors. It took everything to not sprint down the polished granite floor into the throne room and throw herself at her parents.

She forced herself to steady her footsteps, to draw herself as tall as she could, and walk with all the dignity of a princess born and bred as the door attendant announced, "Princess Meiling!"

She kept her movements graceful and stately, but inside, she was weeping. After traveling across the empire and being kidnapped by brigands, after being imprisoned in Fang Zedong's fortress, she was finally home again.

When she lifted her eyes, there was Pa sitting regally on his throne. His legs spread wide against the armrests, and his golden robes glittered in the light streaming through the window ceiling. His clothes seemed to only accentuate his size, and she bit her lip to restrain herself from racing into his wide, open arms. She wanted to lose herself in the folds of his robes and hear his gentle coos that everything was all right now.

Despite the sheer magnitude and glory of her father, she couldn't help but notice the new lines on his face, the dark circles beneath his lower lashes.

His eyes widened at the sight of her, his whole body going suddenly taut. At his right hand, the reedy, long-bearded advisor stood with an upturned chin and flaring nostrils, a tablet and quill in his hands—Meiling's reminder that she wasn't approaching her Pa, but the Imperial Emperor. His Glorious Majesty.

"All dismissed." Pa's voice rang out before Meiling was even halfway to his throne, commanding and final despite the edges of emotion. "Send for Her Majesty the Queen."

As one, the line of warriors along each wall turned and marched through side doors. The advisor glanced at Pa, and Pa gave him a firm nod. The advisor bowed, took his tablet and quill, and likewise exited the throne room.

Meiling kept her steps stately, her head lowered reverently. The sounds of scuffling boots echoed through the golden throne room until the last door closed with a firm, muted thud.

And then she was alone with her Pa.

"Meiling!" His raw tone was choked. "Meiling, my girl!"

She couldn't restrain herself anymore. The tears came, swift and salty, and she ran toward those open arms. She didn't run far, because Pa had flown off his throne, scooping her up and hugging her close to his chest.

It was like being swallowed whole by affection, and she happily drowned in it.

Home, home, home.

"Oh, my sweet girl," he murmured, holding her so close she could barely breathe. "I have never known fear like . . ." He trailed off and tightened his grip. "I'm so sorry. It's my fault. I never should have sent you with so few guardians. I should have suspected that he would find out that you'd fled. I'm so sorry, so sorry—"

The imprisonment in Zedong's fortress seemed a lifetime ago. She wanted to lock away the memories of those dark days and endless nights forever. Still, she could never blame Pa, Shang, or even Fen for what happened. There was only one person to blame.

Fang Zedong.

"It wasn't your fault," Meiling said, her arms wrapped around her Pa's neck. Before she could continue, a side door opened, and they both looked up as Ma burst in, her mouth open and one hand pressed to her heart. More tears swelled in Meiling's eyes, and then sobs broke loose as Ma picked up her skirts and ran. Pa opened his arm, and then Meiling was nearly suffocated by not one, but two parents.

It might have been the best moment of her life.

She'd missed them so dearly.

They hardly spoke as they held each other. The words were in the air, hovering above them—declarations of love and affection, so many fears, questions, and even a slow-burning anger.

Meiling could almost hear the faint echoes of her Pa shouting in this very throne room: "How *dare* Fang Zedong capture my daughter?"

She didn't want to think about Zedong right now. She'd rather sink into the warmth surrounding her, the familiar smell of Pa's robes and Ma's spices, the quiet hums of their own tears.

Eventually, the reunion was over. Pa dried his wet cheeks as he pulled her into one last embrace, then released her and marched back up his dais and sat on his throne. Ma stepped to one side of the throne and pulled her face into a serene mask—the one she wore for public events.

Meiling dabbed her eyes with her sleeve, staying where she was, facing the throne.

"Advisor Chong!" Pa boomed, and from the power in his voice, she never could have guessed he'd just been weeping.

The door the advisor had disappeared through opened, and the slim man reentered. With controlled dignity, he took his place at Pa's right hand.

Just like that, the entire air in the room shifted.

Meiling straightened her spine, falling into her own role as a princess of Zheninghai. The Emperor's Guard was not called to return.

"Send them in!" Pa called toward the great, double doors.

At once, they swung open by two guards on the outside.

Three figures stood on the threshold.

The first—a tall, fierce woman with an aggressive stride, wearing robes that could not hide the tone of her muscular frame. It was the first time Meiling had seen her since she'd been lying incapacitated outside of Liafugen. There was stiffness to her movements now, perhaps due to residual pain from her injuries.

Hu Fen.

The second was another young woman. This one not as tall as Fen, with a willowy form, white Academy robes, and quirked mouth. She walked with more of a saunter, her hair loose and long instead of bound. Meiling's one and only true friend: Li Feiyan.

The last figure stood between the two young women, taller than both by a full head. His dark eyes sparked with their characteristic cunning and calculation, his broad shoulders set, his step purposeful and unfaltering. His handsome face was hard as flint, and his dark hair was pulled back in its typical queue. Instead of deferring his attention to the emperor, seated before him on his throne, the young warrior's gaze went straight to Meiling's. His penetrating assessment took her in from head to toe as though reading every thought in her brain. Her stomach flipped despite her best intentions.

Tan Shangdi.

All was silent except the clicks of their boots on the granite floor until they flanked either side of Meiling, Feiyan to her right and Shang to her left.

Princess though she was, Meiling kneeled with them and pressed her palms and forehead into the floor. Cold seeped into her skin. As the highest rank of the group, she tried to speak, but found her voice hiding behind a series of chokes and half-coughs.

"Glorious Emperor," Meiling said. "Honored Queen."

The advisor scratched something on his tablet.

"Rise, Princess Meiling." Pa's voice boomed between the dragon pillars.

Meiling lifted her eyes to Pa's and immediately blinked back another traitorous rush of tears. He smiled softly down at her, his eyes warm and filled with emotion. Usually, he would never dare such a sweet smile for her in public.

Keeping her emotions in check was going to be much harder than she had anticipated. She stood on shaky limbs. Shang tilted his head slightly her way from where he kneeled on the ground. Was her wobble that obvious? She inhaled quickly, exhaled slowly, hoping to calm herself. She squared her shoulders and met her father's gaze. This was no time to lose control. She would be a dignified princess to honor her father. As much honor as possible for a cursed princess.

"Daughter, we are glad you are returned to us safely," Pa said, his tone distant and formal. He glanced back at Ma, who had let a tear escape and run down her cheek. "I am *greatly*"—he faltered slightly here—"relieved that you are safe and whole."

She bowed her head and outstretched her arms again. This act might be the death of her. "Thank you, Majesty."

"All rise," Pa ordered.

Together, Fen, Feiyan, and Shang rose to their feet. Shang moved with enough dignity to be a prince, though the same could not be said for Fen's stiff movements or Feiyan's casual posture that communicated the slightest disinterest in rituals.

Meiling stood silently with her . . . friends? Comrades? It was tempting to scoot closer to Shang and hope some of his confidence and strength would imbue her. She gritted her teeth and kept her feet planted solidly on the ground.

When Pa spoke, it was in his most dictatorial tone. “I require a full report. Beginning from the moment the princess was escorted out of the palace until now. Commence.”

Whether Shang saw how all eyes turned to him or not, he stepped forward, bowed again, and began. He kept his eyes respectfully lowered from meeting Pa’s, his deep voice carrying through the throne room.

It was strange to hear the adventures of their first journey described in such bare, emotionless detail. Shang told the story like it was a distant legend of old, robbed of all color and flavor. Fox spirits, phoenixes, dragons, qilins, brigands. Had they truly fought so many *mó guǐ*? It felt so long ago. He withheld almost any information about Meiling that was not crucial, but he did not hesitate to state outright how they discovered her magic and how she employed it on their journey.

Pa held up a hand and Shang immediately closed his mouth. “Who initiated the investigation into the princess’ magic?”

“I told them, Your Majesty,” Meiling interjected quickly, before Shang could incriminate himself for his role. “I could not hide it anymore, not after how I was in their minds.”

The advisor scratched his quill on his tablet.

Pa’s eyes roved between Meiling and Shang but did not so much as glance at Fen or Feiyan. He looked back at Ma, who stood nearly emotionless at his side.

“Has anyone else heard of this magic?”

“Only the people standing before you, Majesty,” Meiling said. Them . . . and Fang Zedong. She inhaled deeply through her nostrils and met her father’s troubled gaze. He was silent for a long moment. She waited, boldly studying his face and trying to ascertain from the various crooks and furrows of his brows what he might be thinking. What did Pa’s mind look like?

Fen shifted her weight from one foot to the next, keeping her head down. Pa waved his arm for Shang to continue.

When Shang reached the part about their attempted and botched rescue of Feiyan, he worded it carefully. "We stumbled upon the brigands keeping the healer Li Feiyan captive. We battled them, but were unsuccessful in recovering the healer, so we fled with the princess."

No mention of Fen's insubordinate behavior or Meiling's near-capture.

Pa interrupted his steady stream of report with a raised hand. "Who decided to attempt a rescue of the healer?"

Shang swallowed and glanced down. He lifted his gaze, light reflecting off his dark eyes.

Oh no. He intended to take the blame. He opened his mouth—no doubt to save Fen's neck from admitting her fault. Meiling was about to interject that it was at her order, but Fen saved them both.

"It was I, my lord," Fen said, and bowed low before Pa.

Pa tilted up his chin and furrowed his stern brow. "Did you think," he said deliberately, "that I would not send a force of wielders to recover the healer? Did you think I do not protect my own? Especially one as important as the empire's only healer?"

Fen bowed herself to the ground, hands and face planted into the floor. "No, Glorious Emperor. I beg your mercy."

Meiling had never seen Fen so subservient. So docile. It was hard to believe that the one who had been so flippant, so rebellious, so brash, could be this humble. The splendor and majesty of an emperor apparently had this effect. "The healer," Meiling heard herself saying softly, "was close and suffering under the hard hand of her captors. It was a matter of compassion, Glorious Emperor."

When she lifted her eyes to her Pa's, he regarded her with tight lips and an expression of . . . Was he wordlessly telling her to be silent? She quickly lowered her eyes, cheeks heating as her shoulders sagged slightly. She swallowed against the biting sting of failure that hounded her every step.

Why had she just spoken back to him? In front of his subjects and his advisor? Meiling cursed herself inwardly as the weight of her mother's eyes seemed to penetrate her thoughts. She knew better. It did not matter how close the healer had been or how she had suffered; Shang had been right that their duty to the emperor was to stay focused on their individual mission.

Pa waved his hand, and Shang continued the tale with the slightest glance toward Meiling. Of course, he had noted the mute communication between her and her father.

For as long as the journey took to live, it took surprisingly little time to summarize. Within a few minutes, Shang reached the terrible part when they'd crested the hill in full view of their destination, only to be ambushed by the brigands that had pursued their trail relentlessly.

He held nothing back.

Hearing that tragedy falling from his lips, hearing of her own actions to save their lives—it felt like he spoke about someone else. It was not Princess Meiling who stood up to brigands, who offered her life in exchange for her comrades. Who had pressed a blade to her own heart as a threat against her enemies.

She certainly hadn't felt as brave as Shang made her sound. She'd fought to no avail against Fang Zedong, had not been able to keep herself from being used as a tool to reveal countless secrets to their enemy. In the end, it had been Shang and not her that had been the reason for her escape.

Ma's eyes darted back and forth between Shang and Meiling, then down to Fen who stayed kneeling on the floor. Fen, who had been injured almost beyond recovery. Fen, whose performance on the mission had been not so daring and courageous as Shang's.

The shapeshifter stood on far shakier ground than Shang after his brilliant fortress rescue.

When Shang finished his tale, he turned to Meiling and Feiyan to tell of their time as prisoners of Fang Zedong. With far less eloquence and a lot more disorder, Meiling explained what she had endured. As much as she wished to hide her failings from her father, she lowered her eyes and told everything she could remember. The breaking of Zuan Wan, the mind hunting, the illusion of her siblings to threaten her.

She had not told anyone these things. Not in full. Though he didn't look at her, she was acutely aware of Shang's attention as he listened to the tale of her captivity. He probably didn't approve of her choices. He probably thought she'd acted a fool.

Finally, when Meiling had finished, Feiyan had told her part, and Shang had explained his side of the story from sneaking out of Liafugen and joining forces with Lieutenant Jadaala to his capture and subsequent rescue of Meiling and Feiyan, all was silent in the emperor's throne room. Not even the barest shuffle of feet or the rustle of long robes could be heard. For several painfully long minutes, the sounds of Meiling's own soft breathing seemed loud enough to fill the room.

"Tan Shangdi. Hu Fen." Pa leaned forward in his throne toward the two warriors on her left and steepled his fingers. She dared not look at them as they awaited his next words. "You were given an assignment to deliver Princess Meiling safely to the fortress Liafugan on penalty of death."

Meiling's heart faltered.

"I explicitly instructed you that if you failed, your lives were forfeit."

Scratch, scratch, scratch, went the advisor's quill.

No. No, no—*no.* Had Pa not heard what they'd spoken? Did he not see that they had been outnumbered from the start? That the journey was doomed from its conception? Did he not see how much Shang and Fen had suffered and fought on her behalf? Did he not know that, if not for Meiling's intervention to save their lives, she might have made it to the fortress?

Did he not see that her capture was her own choice? Not Shang's or Fen's fault?

He'd even *said* it was his fault for not sending more warriors!

Meiling blinked rapidly at the floor, betrayal filling her as the advisor's quill clinked against the lip of an inkwell.

"Because of this," continued Pa, "you will both stand trial starting tomorrow, after the morning parade beginning the Festival of New Lights. Five days your trial shall run. On the sixth day, the day after the festival is finished, you shall face your verdict and fate."

The blood drained from her face. This had always been their fate, and yet she had *hoped*. She'd believed her Pa would pardon them somehow—despite that power not falling under his jurisdiction, but that of the courts.

Both Feiyan's and Shang's arms darted out toward her when she staggered slightly, but she stepped forward, ignoring them, and all but collapsed to the ground, prostrate before her father. She bowed with her palms out and face flat against the icy granite.

"Glorious Father, please heed my voice," she practically gasped. She pressed her hands into the ground to keep from clenching her fists. Taking a deep breath, she steadied her voice. When she opened her mouth, her words came out less desperate and more composed than before. "These wielders did everything within their power and duty to protect me, even to the point of laying down their—"

"And yet it was *you,* and not them, who was captured." Pa's voice rang out loud in the throne room, reverberating off granite and marble and glass. Suppressed anger thrummed in those echoes, revealing more of Pa's true feelings than he likely intended.

For all he blamed himself for not sending more warriors with her, he was still furious that the warriors he'd charged with her protection had lived while she suffered.

Meiling shut her eyes tightly against the burn in her chest. She sucked in more steadying breaths. Her hair fell down her arms on either side of her like a curtain. A curtain shielding her from whatever reaction the three wielders behind her bore on their faces.

One more breath, then she spoke softly. "I did it to save their lives."

"Speak up, daughter."

His tone was a knife in her chest. She gritted her teeth and repeated louder, "I did it to save their lives, Glorious Father. They would have been killed. My life was never at risk."

"Your life, perhaps. But think of those who died trying to rescue you from the fortress and those that will die because of the information our enemy received when you were captured." Pa's voice grew gentler as he spoke, taking on the informal tone of a father. Still, it bore an edge betraying his struggle to maintain his lofty, revered distance as emperor in front of the three wielders and his chief advisor while interacting with his daughter.

"Meiling," he said, and her name was like a blow to her face.

He's disappointed in me. Frustrated with me.

She could not bear his disappointment and chastisement. Not after missing him, not while she even now longed to fling herself back into his arms after being separated for so long. Not in front of Shang, Fen, and Feiyan.

A tear squeezed through her tightly clenched eyelids. Her lungs tightened painfully.

It was true; she had not considered how saving two lives could cost so many more. Even so, she would have done the same thing again. How could she abandon Shang and Fen after all they had done for her?

How could she *ever* leave someone behind to die?

"They did not accomplish their mission. They may not be fit for service to the emperor," Pa said, resuming his kingly tone. "The courts will decide such."

"Oh, no—Glorious Father! They are most worthy—" The words spewed too quickly out of Meiling's mouth, and the instant she said them, she shut her eyes and let the fire of a horrendous blush overwhelm her face.

Pa said nothing. He should have. He ought to have rebuked her for forgetting her place, for dishonoring him. But he didn't, and somehow that was worse.

Still prostrate before him, still with her face pressed to the floor, Meiling sagged. She could say no more. Humiliation drowned her in a torrent so fierce she could think of nothing. Nothing except how she would rather have the entire empire here to witness her impudence than have Shang standing silently beside her.

Ma must be shaking her head. Was Fen hiding a smirk? Would Pa punish her later? Would he send for her and issue a thorough, private rebuke?

Pa addressed everyone. "Publicly, this journey never happened. Princess Meiling was kidnapped from the palace along with the healer, Li Feiyan. Tan Shangdi and Hu Fen, you both will serve as temporary instructors at the Academy during your trials. The trials will not be public until the conviction. Your appointments are withheld indefinitely unless you are pardoned but I do not guarantee them to still be available if you are indeed acquitted." He paused, and Meiling did not know if he eyed Fen and Shang carefully, if he studied her bowed form, or if he glanced back at silent and stately Ma. "You both know the law; if you flee during the trials, you are forever banished from the empire. You will lose your chance at acquittal and will be dishonorably executed on sight."

There was another pause. At long last, Pa said firmly, "All dismissed."

All. Including Meiling.

She lifted her flaming face but kept her gazed downcast as she slowly rose to her feet. Her eyes betrayed her and snapped to Pa's. Conflict was heavy in his face—and perhaps a plea for her to understand. To understand what? That he had no choice but to punish innocent people?

Something hard formed in her gut. She hoped she *never* understood that.

She couldn't bring herself to look at Ma. Instead, she followed the other three out of the throne room as the Emperor's Guard returned with chunking armor and thick boots.

When she reached the large double doors, she considered glancing back, seeking just a scrap of the warmth she'd been welcomed home with. Pursing her lips, she kept her attention forward and stepped over the threshold. The doors banged behind her.

Life wasn't going to go back to the way it was before her capture, was it?

Fen was already storming away. Feiyan and Shang hung back, but somehow it only made her more embarrassed. Shang's back was to her as he watched Fen leave. Before Meiling could look away, Feiyan reached out and hugged her tightly. Emotion built in Meiling's chest, but she restrained it as Feiyan's healing warmth spread through her limbs.

"I hear work has piled up for me," Feiyan muttered as she pulled away. She rolled her eyes and shrugged. "Apparently, people don't stop getting sick when the healer goes on vacation. Come visit some time if you're in the mood for bodily fluids. It's a little hard for me to get away sometimes." She winked and then strode off down the hallway after Fen. Her white robes moved with her slender form and added a little more breadth to her slightness.

Meiling would always envy Feiyan's confidence and strength.

Shang's back stayed turned against her as he gripped his wrist behind him with his feet planted wide. She hesitated. He must want to speak with her; otherwise, he would have rushed already after Fen and Feiyan. But what could he want to say? The last thing she wanted was his condolences for her humiliation. Oh, how much worse it would be to have him turn, fix those cool black eyes on her and say, "You lost control of yourself." Or even worse, "I'm sorry."

Could she slip down the other hallway? Away from him? No, he would simply walk after her.

Meiling ducked her head and made to walk past him. He said nothing as he slipped into stride with her down the hallway lined with more guards. His robes swished with each purposeful, silent step. She kept her head lowered and clasped her hands tightly before her. Once, she stole a glance at him, but his face was set down the hallway and line of guards.

This might be worse than verbally acknowledging her error. It burned in the air between them until she was weak with shame. But what could she say? *"I know I was an idiot in there."*

Shang sighed.

Was it a sigh of pity? Of exasperation? Frustration? She stole another look and was rewarded with the same impassible face and unreadable expression he'd worn the entire journey back from Zedong's fortress. It felt like ages ago that he was warm and open with her.

An urge to break into a run and race down the hallways of the palace to her room plucked at her limbs. But she was a princess, and she intended not to embarrass herself any further by forgetting that. They passed the last set of guards. She could breathe a tad bit easier without their witness to her struggle for composure.

At last, Shang tilted his head toward her but did not look at her fully. "Don't try to save me." His tone was distant, formal.

Decorum might be the death of her.

Meiling turned away from him, glancing down a corridor they passed as an excuse to avoid facing him. Too soon, she had to pull her eyes forward once more. She wished she could trail her fingers along the beaded curtains lining the wall and listen to their familiar clicking. Wished she could stare with her neck craned backward at the ceiling artwork portraying battles of wielders and *mó guǐ*. Wished she could let her eyes feast on the bright colors and be happy to be home.

Shang cast a sidelong glance at her when she said nothing. He probably saw every thought that raced through her mind—probably even saw the clenching of her stomach and the dizziness behind her eyes.

He lowered his voice, and just *maybe* there was a layer of feeling in his tone that hadn't been there before. "I mean what I say, Highness. I know you, and I know you will want to intervene, but I would like you to stay out of this. I can save myself. And if I cannot, perhaps the emperor is right. Perhaps I am unsuited for this work."

"Unsuited?" Meiling cried, whirling to face him. He met her gaze and cocked an eyebrow. She ignored his expression as her pent-up frustration and hurt gushed out in a stream of words. "You are the most capable wielder I know. You are the most principled, honorable, and clever person I know. Fathers, you rescued me *on your own*. You're smarter than anyone else I've met, and you're so strong and powerful and . . ."

When her mind caught up to her words, she clamped her mouth shut and turned away. How many times must she disgrace herself? Was she tired from their journey? Was that why she kept losing control of her mouth? Meiling had never struggled with thinking before she spoke. Of all her siblings, she had been the one who guarded her words best. So why was this trial of Fen's and Shang's what made her tongue come unhinged and speak out of turn?

Unfortunately, her earlier embarrassments did not temper the rushing heat to her cheeks. Her breath snagged in her lungs, and she clenched a fistful of long sleeve in her hand. She had stopped walking and wanted to lean against the wall—and perhaps hide behind a curtain. Why could Shang not see that she wanted him to leave her alone? "I simply mean," she said, attempting to regain her composure, "that you are suitable for the work. Anyone who disagrees is wrong."

He stopped beside her, close enough for his warmth to caress her back. Then, so gently she barely felt it, he brushed two fingers against her elbow and said softly, *"Meiling."*

She did not look back at him.

"If I am all of those things," he continued quietly, "then the judge will let me live. Either way, you should probably meet some other wielders." The last words were spoken lightly, as if with a smile.

Meiling did not need to meet more wielders to know how capable he was. She dragged in a long breath, determinedly set her face, and finally turned around. He remained unreadable, but not so stern as before. He regarded her seriously for a minute, and then he began walking again. She hesitated for a split second before continuing alongside him.

Would he die in seven days?

She simply could not think about that. Refused to consider the possibility. Surely there was something she could do to prevent it from happening—

As though guessing her thoughts, Shang gave her a sidelong glance.

If he thought she was going to sit by and let him and Fen die, he was wrong.

CHAPTER 2

SHANG CURSED EVERY pair of servant and guard eyes, cursed every inch between him and Meiling. It had been hard enough to keep his distance on the journey back from Fang's fortress, but it was even harder when she was so obviously upset.

It went against every instinct to restrain himself, to not comfort her.

He'd much rather draw her into his arms and ask her to name every thought and emotion she struggled with now.

Instead, he walked beside her, his fingertips buzzing from the barest slip of contact with the sleeve of her elbow. He tried not to look at her too often, lest she sense it. She was still too thin, her skin a ruddier hue from the travel, and while her mouth maintained its sweet tilt, her eyes didn't glow with the same bright innocence they'd once had. Instead, something else sparked there. Something stronger, more defiant, more stubborn. She was different—changed.

They both were.

The Meiling he'd escorted out of the palace gates would never have spoken back to His Imperial Majesty. For all her flushed embarrassment, Shang liked her better this way. But if he told her he was, in fact, *proud* of her determination to stand up to anything she perceived as an injustice, he'd only draw attention back to the event that had flustered her.

Besides, there were eyes and ears covering this palace from foundation to the tip of the flag flying in the highest tower.

Not to mention . . . he really should keep his distance. He wasn't her bodyguard anymore. He had no claim to her, not to protect her or to comfort her. They weren't in imminent danger now—not *yet*, at least—and she wouldn't be cursed to sleep, in need of his kisses to wake.

And then there was his potential execution to consider.

Shang's gut sank lower, and he ran a hand through his hair.

Nothing was guaranteed. The courts could still pardon him, despite the very clear mark against him. But Fen? She wouldn't survive the week without a miracle.

A wave of sickness hit him, and he quickly pulled his thoughts back under control. The week wasn't over. Better to savor this moment walking beside Meiling, this little indulgence in the pleasure the sight of her brought. This could be the last time they spoke. The last time they even saw each other. Did she know it?

For just a few more minutes, they were . . . more than nothing. Soon, he'd be a wielder on trial for his life, and she'd return to her role as princess of Zheninghai. They'd have about as much familiarity as he had with the Butagin soldiers he'd killed to save her.

It felt wrong after everything they'd been through together.

For now, he stole another glance at her, at the frown she tried to hide, and savored her nearness.

Another time, he'd ponder over the wildly odd stipulation of His Imperial Majesty that Shang and Fen spend the week training students at the Academy instead of chained in the dungeons. The only valid reason Shang could think of was that the emperor knew Meiling's capture wasn't truly their fault.

They rounded a corner, and he inched closer, opening his mouth—

At the other end of the hallway, dressed in Academy robes, was a young girl about eleven or twelve years old. Shang recognized her immediately as Princess Hou. She shared Meiling's same large and expressive eyes. That was the only resemblance between the sisters. Princess Hou took after the harsher features of her father, whereas Meiling was a near replica of her mother.

Shang had already instructed Princess Hou here and there at the Academy through the years, and she had the wild temperament of a shapeshifter despite her fire magic. The girl's scowl lifted suddenly and her eyes widened like saucers. She raised her arms and her long white sleeves flapped like bird wings as she broke into a run.

"Mei!" Princess Hou cried.

Meiling gasped, and she flung aside her careful posture and controlled elegance, breaking into a run. The two sisters met in a great big hug in the middle of the hallway, Meiling's tear-choked laughter ringing out as she buried her face in her sister's hair.

Shang stayed where he was, a storm of emotion swelling inside him as he watched their reunion. *She's home. She's safe. She's back with people who love her.*

She's not mine anymore.

Meiling's muffled voice reached him, despite the distance. "I'm so glad you're safe, sister."

Shang's jaw twitched. He knew why she said that—why she was thinking of Hou's safety at all. Because that dragon-cursed Fang had *threatened* Meiling with illusions of her siblings. Hearing her say that in the throne room, along with so many other horrible things she'd endured in Fang's fortress, had made his blood boil then, and it boiled again now.

Fang Zedong wouldn't accept his loss. If Zheninghai didn't prepare its forces properly, Meiling wouldn't be safe from him much longer.

"I'm so glad you're back," Hou responded without releasing her bearhug. "They told me you were just sick and could not leave your room or have visitors, but I knew better than that. I knew you left. I'm so happy you're here. Can you come to my arena battle at the end of this week? It's the day after the festival ends."

The day Shang could be condemned to death and executed.

Meiling froze, as though realizing the same thing, but managed a tight nod. "Of course, Hou. Of course I'll be there." She twisted to look over her shoulder to where Shang stood. Her eyes were red and puffy, but it was the spark of determination that concerned him.

Don't get involved, Meiling, he wanted to say yet again. If she wasn't careful, she'd reveal her magic, and then she'd be even worse off than him. She'd sacrifice anything to save him and Fen, and that was what scared him.

She'd sacrificed enough.

He should leave them to their—

"Who is that? I've seen him before," Hou whispered, apparently thinking her voice was quieter than it was, the side of her head pressed against Meiling's chest. "He is very handsome."

Well, now he *had* to stay for Meiling's response.

She cast an awkward wince over her shoulder at Shang, and his lips twitched in a barely contained smile. *It's alright, you can agree with her. I won't be mad.*

Not mad at all.

Meiling bit her lip and hugged her sister tighter, her face pinched as she tried to come up with an answer. She settled on a noncommittal, "He went with me." Then she pulled back and frowned. "When did you start noticing boys? I thought they were all gross."

Hou giggled. "Maybe not *all* of them . . ."

Fathers spare them from children who decide they're old enough to fall in love.

Meiling rolled her eyes and groaned, but smiled anyway. "How was your last battle?"

"Oh! Mei! I have to show you what I learned to do." Princess Hou pulled away and stepped back a few paces. Her eyes glittered and her brow furrowed by habit, but she grinned as she raised her arms. "Watch this—"

"No fire games in the palace," a loud, masculine voice came from further down the corridor. Crown Prince Yun.

Shang had stayed too long. He was already slipping down the opposite hallway when the sound of Meiling's gasp and scrambling footsteps reached his ears. The prince's warm laughter followed his quick strides.

It was just as well that he didn't get to say goodbye to her. He might have been tempted to say or do something he would regret.

Everything had changed in that dark room in Fang's fortress when he'd kissed her again and again. There was no more hiding, no more denying, no more pretending.

Shang loved her.

He loved her more than he had ever loved anything, and there was nothing he wouldn't give for her to have a chance at freedom and happiness. If it meant he lost this trial, if it meant he and Fen had to die to keep her magic a secret, he wouldn't hesitate.

But his death would mean nothing if Fang razed this place shortly thereafter.

Shang navigated through the palace complexes past sets of guards and flurries of working servants, one minute inside breathing the subtly spiced aroma, then outside in courtyards perfumed with the first blooms of bright yellow wintersweet, then back inside until he finally reached the door nearest the bridge to the Academy grounds.

He spotted Fen marching down the portico beside the red-painted ornamental railing separating classrooms from the pits where students were almost always practicing combat. She met his gaze and tipped her head, stopping to wait for him to reach her.

She should still be resting and recovering, but it was a relief to see her back on her feet again.

"Coming to the headmaster to report for duty?" she asked, matching her stride with his.

"You go first; I'll be in to report shortly."

She glanced at him, a knowing look in her eye, but mercifully didn't ask questions. "I'll let you know how it goes."

Shang gave her a nod as they knocked the sides of their fists together in quick, silent camaraderie. Then he peeled off, cutting through one of the boys' empty dormitories to get to Master Dong's office. There was a chance his old mentor wasn't teaching a class. Shang reached the familiar wooden door in the corridor of offices and knocked. A firm, decisive sound.

"Not now!" called the voice from inside.

Shang turned the latch and pushed open the door.

"I *said*, not—*Shangdi*! By the fathers!"

Master Dong, a portly man with a shaved head, immediately set down his quill on the short desk he sat before. He leaned back on his heels, his gaze sharpening as it ran over Shang from head to toe, taking in his travel-worn appearance.

Shang shut the door behind him. "I need to speak with you. About Fang Zedong."

CHAPTER 3

MEILING COULD HARDLY believe it was her brother grinning at her. She tripped as she scrambled into a run, leaving Hou whining behind. She flung herself into Yun's broad arms and he laughed, hugging her back—though not near as crushing as Hou had—while she swallowed more tears. They would only make Yun uncomfortable. Instead, she grinned like an idiot and refused to let go when he stepped backward.

He is safe.

And she was home.

"Enough, enough!" he cried, reaching behind him to unwind her arms from around his waist. "You're too clingy for a princess, sister."

"Are you happy to see me?" She beamed up at him, her grin taking on a mischievous glint as he pried away from her grip.

He was dressed in Academy student robes, but his were more rumpled and dirtier than Hou's. His topknot was falling and a few rebellious strands stuck out at ridiculous angles. His eyes shone with an alertness that she recognized from her travels with Shang and Fen.

"Who were you battling just now?" Meiling smiled and reached up on tiptoes to tuck a few of his wildest strands back.

Yun batted away her hands with a cringe. "Only a feral wielder."

"Then why are you so tousled?"

He glared at her, and she burst into laughter. Hou came running up behind them and flung her arms around Meiling's waist. "I'm *so* glad you're back."

"Where did you go?" Yun asked with a frown. He folded his arms across his chest and leaned back against the wall in his typical attempt at over-confidence.

Meiling pursed her lips and shrugged. "Long story. How did you both get away from the Academy for so long?"

"I finished my battle. They gave me a break and Ma sent a servant, telling me you were *better*." He rolled his eyes and spread his mouth in a wide, thin line. "Said I should come say hello."

"I'm glad you did." For a moment, they were back to the carefree relationship they used to have—before pesky things like curses and magic invaded the simplicity.

They turned to Hou for her explanation. She narrowed her eyes, her lips pulling back in something that might be a grin or a snarl. Planting a hand on her skinny hip, she faced them. "How I got away is none of your business."

"Hou!" Yun exclaimed, face suddenly serious. "Did you sneak out of your lessons again? Do you want to get sent to detention??"

"I'm a princess; they can't send me to detention," Hou returned flippantly, tossing her hair over her shoulder and fixing Yun with a pouting glare. "Besides, it was so *boring*. When will I ever need to know who all the guardians are?"

Meiling met Yun's eye over Hou's head. He looked momentarily at a loss, but turned back down to Hou, frowning sternly. "Back to class, sister," he said and pointed down the corridor. "Before you get in too much trouble."

Hou rolled her eyes and hugged Meiling again. "You cannot tell me what to do."

Meiling closed her eyes and smiled. Then, she drew herself up seriously and pushed Hou away with a firm grip on her shoulders. "Our brother is right. You ought to go back. It's not a good appearance to have the princess disregarding her studies."

Hou stared up at Meiling for a long moment, as though testing if she was serious. Evidently, she determined she meant her words. She sighed like she was a long-suffering martyr. Then she puffed the hair out of her face and raised a hand in a disinterested farewell as she moped off to her studies.

Meiling bit back a grin and turned her attention to Yun. He pushed away from the wall, rattling the beading on the tapestry of Zheninghai countryside as he did so.

"I should follow," he said, nodding after Hou's retreating form. "But I'm happy you are back and safe. If anything had happened to you, I would have personally hunted down every last offender and burned them to a crisp."

She laughed and rubbed her arms. "I have no doubt. You'll have to tell me everything that happened at the Academy while I was gone."

He started nodding and continued nodding—as if he didn't know what to say next. "Well . . . I suppose . . . I'll see you tomorrow. For the parade."

He surprised them both by reaching out, grabbing her shoulders, and leaning in to kiss her quickly on the cheek. He cleared his throat and strode down the corridor without a word.

Meiling stared after him, lips parted in surprise and heart ready to burst. A little curl of smoke escaped Yun's hand, but he quickly suppressed it.

So, he was just as happy to see her as she was him.

Had he ever kissed her? Likely not, since she was a baby. Meiling stared after his departing form much longer than necessary and reached up to touch her cheek softly.

"Fang has armies," Shang said urgently, keeping his voice low as he pointed to the map Master Dong had spread across his desk. "Both forces from Butagin, and an entire brigand army."

"Who leads the brigand army?" said Master Dong, serving two cups of tea they both promptly ignored.

"Shi Yong—I saw him at Fang's fortress when they took me to and from the dungeon. I couldn't confirm what networks were involved, but I know for a fact that a significant amount of them were Hidden Ones. The only tattoos I saw were nine-tailed foxes."

"I *knew* that Shi family was leading the Hidden Ones," Master Dong growled. "I just couldn't prove it. No one could. Not even Lieutenant Jadaala, and he's been dogging their trail for over a decade now. Every time we captured a brigand, someone broke them out before they could be questioned. It didn't matter if guards were posted. By morning, they were always gone."

It was nearly impossible to track down an evanescer committing a crime, much less an entire family of them. But Shang had a suspicion about who'd been breaking them out of the Suguan incarceration unit: Yong's younger brother, Shi Kai, who enjoyed pretending to be a worthless idiot.

Shang had never liked either Shi son, and he didn't have proof beyond a few notable instances of Kai's absence. "I don't know which members of the family are involved, but Yong seemed to be the only one at the fortress."

"The younger one better not be involved," said Master Dong with a rueful twist of his lips. "Since he's in the Secret Service."

Shang had just taken a sip of tea and nearly spat it back out.

"What?"

"Shi Kai is in the Secret Service. He and two others—Lian Delan, one of the more reliable investigators in the Secret Service, and another fresh graduate, Sun Aranya—were instrumental in proving the trail of the missing wielders did, indeed, trace back to Fang."

"Sun Aranya, the partial shapeshifter?" Shang could hardly believe his ears. He made it his business to know every graduate in his year and their appointments—had worked hard to learn the names and abilities of every student at the Academy. "She was assigned to Zushui as a warden. What do you mean she is in the Secret Services?"

Master Dong lifted both hands and shook his head. "Something strange happened. I haven't been able to figure out what. But word has it they were part of the sacking of Fang's fortress following your escape, along with Jadaala's forces."

He wasn't going to waste more time on the partial shapeshifter. She wasn't the pressing concern here. His inclination was to be skeptical of Shi Kai's loyalty, but as he turned the facts over in his mind, he couldn't come up with a reason why Kai would directly contribute to a major defeat of his benefactor unless he wasn't actually involved in Shi Yong's schemes. "So, Kai might be a traitor, but it—"

"It doesn't seem to be the case," Master Dong finished. "Fang's fortress fell to Zheninghai only four days after your rescue."

Because Meiling freed those phoenixes.

Shang buried the warm burst of pride in his chest. "But most of his forces weren't even stationed there." He tapped his finger on the map, then trailed it between the mountain markings. "He could regroup at this fortress, to the east. And this pass—"

"Goes straight to Suguan," said Master Dong, his face grim.

Shang worked his jaw, hoping he was wrong, knowing he wasn't. "It's almost as if he *wanted* this fortress to fall. To lull us into a false sense of victory while he's already prepared his escape plan, which puts him in an even better position to attack."

Master Dong studied the map quietly for several long minutes. His years as one of Zhenighai's top military strategists were obvious from the keen light in his eyes. Those eyes snapped up, pinned Shang in place. “Does he have enough strength to take the city? From what you’ve seen?”

Shang ran a hand through his hair, gritting his teeth. “He could take all of Zheninghai. We don’t have the manpower—not since we only employ wielders in our military. Our forces are specialized. Based on what I saw in his fortress, combined with the intelligence you’ve heard, it’s obvious he outnumbers our military five to one. Even if powerful magic isn’t common in Butagin, *some* of those soldiers will have magic. They won’t be trained like they would have if they’d been raised in Zheninghai at the Academy. But it’s another element of surprise against our soldiers. We need to do something, or our home is gone.”

“But you can’t do anything—not while you're on trial.”

Ice ran along Shang’s skin, his sense of the air’s moisture prickling in response as his hands turned cold. “If I do nothing, this place is going to burn.”

And Meiling with it.

CHAPTER 4

THE EVENING WAS alight in dying fire.

Meiling pulled her shawl around her nightclothes as she stood by her window, staring out at the sprawling city as it swallowed the ocean shoreline. Midnight darkness crept up from the horizon to envelop her, and the little pinpricks of torchlight flickered to life in the city.

How long had it been since she last stood here? Over two months. She leaned forward on the sill, sticking her face out into the stiff wind. Tomorrow was the first day of the Festival of New Lights, but to her, celebration seemed impossible.

It felt like a façade. A pretty lie to soothe them all to sleep.

She sighed and slouched against the stonework. Her cheek brushed against the heavier curtains she should probably draw closed to keep out the chill.

She did not care what Shang said, she would do whatever she could to save him and Fen. After all, was she not a princess? Surely there was something she could do to help. Any unbiased court should see that they had not set out with enough wielders for their journey. In the chance that this trial went south, she intended to intervene as necessary.

Her maids had left not long ago to stand outside her room until after dark, awaiting her beck and call. At this moment, she heard the shuffling of their bows and murmurs of deference.

Ma must be coming.

A conglomerate of anger, humiliation, and exquisite joy battled for ascendancy in her mind. Her fingernails dug against her windowsill, her knees locking up tightly. She held still and did not turn as the door opened and silk rustled.

The door closed. The rustling stopped.

"Meiling," Ma whispered. Tears choked her voice.

Meiling could not bear it any longer. She whirled and ran to embrace her mother. They held each other tightly and their tears mingled in a wet, salty mess across their faces. It was this morning all over again.

Eventually, Meiling pulled away and stepped toward her bed. Like she had done a thousand times before, she slid onto the firm surface and pulled the quilt up to her chin. Ma sat near her feet and, by habit, her hand reached out to trace along the fabric.

"I have an idea to help the war," Meiling blurted.

Ma's eyes shot up, and a frown puckered her beautiful features. "War? My dove, you must not concern yourself with the war. Your father has been meeting with his strategists much of the day for that purpose. You're safe now. If you want to talk about anything that happened, I'm here."

Meiling did *not* want to rehash anything. Not her journey, her captivity, and certainly not this morning in the throne room. She wanted to move forward, and she knew things about Zedong that no one else knew. "As you heard earlier, when Fang Zedong imprisoned me—"

At those words, Ma looked away. Meiling shut her mouth, instead studying her mother's profile and clenched jaw. Her puckered brow. The mingling of fierce anger and sorrow.

He actually meant something to her. Perhaps not romantically, but . . . Zedong's affection had not been as entirely one-sided as she had originally expected. The thought made her heart clench painfully, and she ripped her eyes away from her mother and stared down at her hands squeezing the edge of the quilt.

She didn't want to think of Ma caring about someone who had tortured and tormented her.

"He used my magic to hunt through prisoners' minds and give him information about the empire that he could use against us," Meiling continued without looking up at Ma. "I could do the same here. Any prisoners or even people who are not prisoners but who might be withholding secrets from the empire—I could infiltrate their minds. I can do it stealthily; no one would know."

She could have cut the shock of that silence with a knife.

"Mei," Ma said with quiet fire, "you cannot help with the war. Your magic is unsanctioned."

"Cannot Pa sanction it? Grant me an honorary title?" Meiling pressed. "I know I could help; there are so many things I could do that could aid the empire in the war. Even scouting for Zedong's brigands—"

Ma shook her head, and Meiling's chest constricted in dread. "Your father cannot sanction your magic, my love. It is too late; to do so would incriminate him of treason against the empire. You understand what would happen, Mei? Our entire family would be executed."

Meiling flung back the covers and shot to her feet, striding to her window and thunking her elbows down on the sill. "Then *why* was this not sanctioned years ago? When I could have learned to use my magic, gone to the Academy, and not lived this qilin-cursed life of a cursed princess!"

"Lu Meiling, your language!" Ma rebuked sharply. "Control your temper."

Ma had never told her to control her temper. That rebuke was saved for her two fiery siblings. Meiling sagged, the edge dissipating off her anger. But not entirely. She still had many questions she needed answered.

Why could she not have been a fire-wielder like Hou and Yun and Pa? Or even a low magic seer like Ma? Anything but what she was.

She turned around to face Ma. In an even tone, she asked, "Why is my magic a secret? Why would you and Pa make me keep a secret that could destroy our entire family? A secret that is bound to come out, eventually."

Ma's gaze sparked with that subtle ferocity. "Do you know what happens to wielders with your kind of power? Exactly what happened to you in Zedong's fortress. You find yourself asleep for your entire life and you are little more than a slave to the empire. And what if your power falls into the wrong hands? Like it did? That level of power equips tyrants to become the terrifying rulers they are. We were protecting you—but not *only* you."

Meiling fell silent. She thought of Feiyan, who had—in some ways—preferred her captivity.

Ma's voice quieted. "You think you are the only wielder in the empire who keeps their magic a secret? Do you know one of the reasons healers are so rare?"

Surely Ma wasn't implying . . .?

"Are there more healers besides Li Feiyan?" Meiling asked, incredulous.

Ma shrugged and drew her knees up onto the bed. "There is evidence to suggest there might even be entire lineages of healers who have kept their magic secret for hundreds of years. The only healers, then, are the random ones that seem to come out of nowhere. Their parents, excited to have such a powerful wielder, immediately send them to the Academy."

And then they end up like Feiyan. Little more than a commodity.

Meiling shifted her weight to raise her hand and rub the bridge of her nose. All this time, she had misunderstood so many things . . .

"We did not want that life for you," Ma said softly. "You know we would give anything to offer you more than life as a cursed princess, but we wanted you to live your life rather than be chained away in the dark. We wanted you to experience life, love, a family, freedom. Things you could never have as a wielder."

Several sharp remarks crossed Meiling's mind—remarks about how difficult it was to find love when everyone believed her curse, how she wanted more from life than redeeming her shame through children. But she could not bring herself to say any of them as a picture suddenly flashed through her mind.

She saw herself sitting here, her arms full of a cooing bundle. Instead of Ma perched on the end of her bed, it was Shang. Tall, long-legged, handsome, grinning down at a toddler in his lap. She saw him look up at her, and the image of that smile and the happiness on his face was enough to make her insides turn to water.

Meiling pivoted on her elbow so she could stare out the window—away from Ma's knowing eyes. Away from that image that was forever impossible, especially if he was executed in a few days.

"So, my magic must remain a secret I carry to my grave," Meiling said at long last. "Not only for my sake, but for my entire family's sake."

"Yes."

"This is why I cannot help fight Zedong? Why I cannot use my magic to help defeat the one who imprisoned and tortured me?"

Silence. Then, a hesitant and trembling, "Yes."

Meiling left her window and climbed back onto her bed. For a long minute, she met her mother's gaze and saw so many things that terrified her. The implications of this reached farther than she could even imagine. She would *forever* be viewed as cursed—to her dying day. She could never, ever be herself. Her very existence was a lie, a lie she and her dearest loves could die for. Shang, Fen, and

Feiyan all knew her secret. Their silence was treason. *They* could be executed too.

She would never be seen. Never understood.

And if she was, it would cost her everything.

Ma stood, her fingers lingering only for a second on the quilt. "Your father is doing everything he can to protect you. He will keep you safe. Please do not concern yourself with the matter. You've been through so much and you need time to *rest*. Think instead of the festival this week. I know you love the fireworks."

Meiling nodded, tight-lipped.

Ma bent forward and planted a soft kiss on Meiling's forehead. As she did, a shuddering breath escaped her and a tear landed on Meiling's nose. "I am so relieved you are home safely, my love."

"Me too," Meiling said as she wiped away Ma's tear from dripping off her nose, then hugged the quilt with both hands under her chin.

Ma rose, made her way to the door, but stopped with her hand on the handle. She looked back, as though knowing Meiling wasn't placated, as though knowing there was a mountain resting on her shoulders that she couldn't move.

Suddenly, Ma's eyes flew wide.

Her brown irises twisted. Purple light flared out of her eyes, straight toward Meiling.

"Ma!" Meiling leaped out of her bed and rushed to her side just as she collapsed against the wall. "Ma! *Ma!*" She slid her arm under Ma's shoulders and heaved her toward the bed. As she did so, Ma began struggling violently. Her limbs flailed, fighting Meiling's hold. "Maids!" Meiling screamed. "Hurry! Help the queen!"

The door burst open. Maids rushed forward just as Ma twisted and swiped her nails at Meiling's face, only barely missing. The purple light faded until only her eyes glowed that strange hue, but her face was devoid of her own personality and consciousness.

"To the bed!" Meiling shouted as maids circled her and grabbed at Ma's floundering limbs. Carefully, they laid her on her back as

Meiling ordered them to hold her down so she didn't hurt herself. Her heart threatened to beat straight out of her chest.

A scream tore free of Ma's throat.

Those doe-like eyes were white-ringed and unseeing, filled with purple. Her mouth hung open and her body writhed under the restraint of half a dozen maids. Her head swung wildly from side to side.

Meiling had heard the stories of visions coming over seers, but in all her life, she had never seen one happen. It was far more frightening than she had imagined. "It's alright, Ma," she said through gritted teeth as she held down Ma's surprisingly strong left arm. "It's alright."

After an eternity of thrashing, the purple light finally faded from her eyes.

"Ma?" Meiling gasped, tentatively releasing her grip on her arm. "Ma? It's me, your daughter."

Ma blinked rapidly and her eyes swiveled in their sockets to Meiling. "My dove?" Her voice quavered sharply.

"All dismissed!" a loud voice boomed from the door.

Meiling straightened as Pa stormed into the room through a flood of ducking and bobbing maids. After slamming the door shut, he ran to kneel by Ma's side.

"Liena?" he asked, his voice breaking slightly. "Can you hear me?"

Ma rolled her eyes over to him, smiled, and nodded. "Yes, I can hear you."

Pa spewed a sigh of relief and gripped Ma's hand. "I came as soon as the servants said you were having a vision. I'm so sorry I wasn't here when it started."

"No need." Ma whispered quietly through a scratchy throat. "Meiling handled it very well."

Pa looked up from Ma to Meiling and his face melted from strain to pride. Gone was the tension from earlier. He smiled at her and reached across the bed to squeeze her shoulder. "My good girl."

Meiling ducked her head and nodded mutely. She returned her attention to Ma, who endeavored to sit against the bedframe. Pa eased her up, making her look uncharacteristically frail. She quickly came back to herself, however, which made Meiling's rapidly pounding heart slowly ease.

Pa's mouth was tight, but he smiled at Ma anyway—perhaps to comfort her. He kept his hand in Ma's and his thumb was busy stroking her knuckles.

"What was your vision?" Meiling asked.

Ma turned her head from Pa to Meiling, and when their eyes locked, her lips parted and a gray cast fell over her skin. She pressed a hand to her stomach. "Nianzu, I'm—"

Pa yanked off his cloak, stuffed it in Ma's lap, and rubbed her back as she leaned forward and retched. His attention flicked to Meiling, and the look sent a sharp bolt of worry through her. He called for the maids to return. They hurried in with more bows as he wrapped up the soiled cloak and ordered them to change the bedclothes, just to be safe. Then he eased his arm behind Ma's back to lift her upward into a sitting position.

Ma glanced at Meiling, and almost immediately bent over and dry heaved.

Somehow, Meiling knew this wasn't a normal part of having visions.

Pa bent down and swiftly scooped Ma up into his arms. He looked just as alarmed as Meiling felt. At the same time, he and Meiling both opened their mouths. She immediately shut hers, her eyes falling from Pa's to the long streaming of Ma's silk robes hanging to the floor.

"She will be fine shortly." He nodded at Meiling, his face softening just slightly. "I love you. I would have burned this whole world down to get you back safely."

Then, looking down at Ma in his arms, he strode out of the room as servants opened the door for him. They shut it behind him and barely avoided snagging Ma's shawl in the process.

Once her maids had made quick work of changing the bedclothes, Meiling fell heavily upon her bed and laid in stunned stillness for a long while.

That had been fear in Ma's eyes. Ma was never afraid.

Did she see something about Zedong? Something about him taking the city? About him taking her captive again? Meiling's gut roiled at each new idea until she was so sick, she nearly retched on her new quilt.

CHAPTER 5

WHEN SLEEP CLAIMED her at long last, Meiling rose out of her body with profound relief. She hesitated only a moment, hovering in the darkness of her room long after the last light of day had faded. Then, shooting like a fire star, she tore through her window into the sky.

There were things she needed to do tonight, but first . . .

She soared through the streets of Suguan, surrounded by the cacophony of the stars overhead. *I missed you all too,* Meiling told them with a smile. Though they were the same stars that had traveled with her long and far, it felt different when they sparkled over her home. Here, she could almost believe she'd never left.

She flew past flickering torchlight and the dying din of people in the streets finalizing their preparations for the Festival of New Lights. She could have exploded from the bursting emotion at these familiar sights.

Meiling hurried onward and her gaze snagged on her destination, looming high ahead. *Almost there,* she whispered with a sudden surging of longing. One last burst of speed, and she reached her favorite cliff overlooking the moonlit ocean. She paused as white caps bobbed below her and the grass waved under the cold night wind.

She slid down into a puddle on the grass. Flinging shadow legs over the edge of the cliff, she leaned forward and stared out at the far reaches of the ocean.

I'm home, she said with a sigh that sent her soul sinking to the ground. *Home.*

In some ways, home was the most terrifying place to be.

Meiling had not wandered the Academy at night for a very long time. She'd had this irrational fear of being discovered by so many magic-wielders in one place. Tonight, it was bright with multicolored glows shining out of windows. It was a large complex, and depending on which measurement was used, could be considered larger than the palace. The buildings created a crescent moon shape around the training grounds, with the gardens behind the buildings. No one practiced so late at night, as they always did their training first thing in the morning.

Instead, the students still awake must be the ones with their noses glued to parchments and ink wells and books. The students studying for their exams.

A memory that she had seen in Feiyan's head flashed across her mind. One of Feiyan and Shang studying together silently in one of the libraries by candlelight. The night Feiyan had tried to kiss Shang, only to have him storm away in anger, books bundled under his arms.

Was Shang still awake at this hour? It must be long past midnight. It was a wonder that any of the students remained awake. What about Feiyan? If she searched in the libraries, would she find her friend half asleep after a full day of healing, trying to catch up on her studies?

Meiling lowered herself out of the air, nearer to the ground. One of the multi-leveled buildings with pristine red paint seemed to glow brighter than the other buildings. She floated forward, trailing dissolving spirit behind her. When she reached a window, she tried to look through it, and ended up melting through the wall unintentionally. Startled, she pulled herself back.

She floated near a long hallway. When she came closer, glancing this way and that, she found it divided into two long stretches of dormitories. Within the thin paper walls, dozens of sleeping souls glowed the colors of the rainbow.

Backing away slowly, she flitted through the walls again until she flew suspended in the air above the training grounds. Something familiar caught in the corner of her vision, and she whirled at the sight of an ice-blue glow.

She was not fast enough; that ice-blue glow disappeared through a door just as she turned its way. Growling soundlessly, she flew forward to the building on the far side, where she had seen Shang enter.

When she burst through the walls after him, she wheeled to a stop.

Before her, in a surprisingly opulent and spacious Academy master's chamber, Shang sat on one side of a desk, engaging in a quiet, but forceful conversation with an older man in black master robes that matched Shang's. The ice-blue glow emanating from Shang's soul mingled with the golden glow of the master. Some brand of feral magic, then.

"We have forces at these checkpoints along the route to Suguan," said the master, pointing at the map spread between them. "At least when Fang moves, we'll know. They'll send messengers—"

Shang shook his head. "Fang knows about the checkpoints. He could—"

"How does he know? These aren't public knowledge!"

Meiling's heart dropped, and she hung back against the wall, dread washing over her like water. *She'd* uncovered that knowledge in his mind. Because of her—

"He knows because I knew," Shang said, voice hard as ever. "He took the information from my mind."

The master cursed viciously, shaking his head. "This isn't going to help your trial!"

Shang's soul-glow pulsed as his brow narrowed. "Forget the trial. There are bigger concerns here. What if Fang takes the checkpoints before they have a chance to light the signal fires? Then we *won't* know when he's advancing. He could be at our doorstep before we ever knew he'd left Butagin. He could be halfway here already! You need to take this to your former colleagues in the strategist department. If they're not ready—"

"I can't tell them this information without jeopardizing your trial and piling evidence against you! They'll want to know *how* you know classified information; they'll blame the loss of our warriors' lives on you. They'll see it as your failure to get the princess to Liafugen that led to the events of your capture and Fang getting ahold of the classified information you shouldn't have known. Shangdi, you'll be condemned *before* week's end." The master spewed the words out in one breath, holding out his upturned hands, as though pleading with him.

Meiling pressed a hand to her chest as she sank lower and lower toward the ground. She'd known the situation was bad, but she hadn't realized the full extent of disaster. Even now, when his life and empire were on the line, he *still* protected her, still guarded her secret.

Shang—oblivious to her presence—leaned forward, planting his large, square hand flat on the map. He enunciated each word carefully, his mouth set like flint. "Tell. Them. Anyway."

"Shangdi—"

"I don't care!" Shang snapped. "The trial *doesn't matter.* Zheninghai matters. The people in this city matter. If you care about my life, then help me get this information to the people who have the power to do something with it. Because Fang is coming. He will sack this city. And he knows me. If I am still alive when he comes, he will hunt me down and kill me—in a way that would make any Zheninghai execution look pleasant. This conquest of his is about settling scores, and he has a score to settle with me."

He didn't even know how right he was. Zedong never forgave.

If Meiling was in her body, she might have thrown up.

The blazing force of Shang's will clashed with the master's own will, their gazes locked and unfaltering. At last, the master sighed and ran a hand over his shaved head.

"At least it seems like the emperor is on your side. He did not have to give you a trial, you know." He shook his head. "That Hu Fen. I told them! She's too careless. She is strong and talented and always worked hard. But I knew from when she was a mere toddling babe she did not have the attention to detail nor a full scope of understanding to succeed in a setting like that. She's powerful, they said! What could go wrong if she was paired with you to balance out her fire? Harumph! I could have picked one or two partners for you that would have made the difference between success and failure for this mission. But do they care about my opinion? Absolutely not!"

Shang said nothing.

"And now you, my brightest student in years, are paying the price." The master continued shaking his head. His forehead wrinkled more with each shake. "Bureaucracy is a mess wherever you go."

Meiling's tether burned with anger. She stayed where she was, in the corner, watching the two of them at the low table, but she couldn't help the fury coursing through her. Good wielders like Shang shouldn't have to pay the price for bureaucracy being a mess. Strong, principled, brilliant wielders like Shang shouldn't have to *die* via execution while giving their all to save their empire.

It was wrong, and she wasn't going to stand by and let it happen.

The master rose, revealing that his robes were ever so slightly too long on his short frame. He walked around the table to where Shang stood. They faced each other for a long moment—Shang, mostly expressionless, and the master with a tight jaw—before the master reached out and embraced him.

Meiling jerked back again, and this time did pass through the wall into the darkness outside. Quickly, she floated back through in time to see Shang return the affection.

"I will plead on your behalf for a miracle. Perhaps the fathers will be merciful," the master said, pulling away swiftly and returning to where he had been sitting before. "Get some sleep before tomorrow."

Shang bowed. "I am in your debt."

The master waved his hand dismissively and Shang strode out of the room. Meiling hurried after him, but kept her distance as trepidation thumped through her spirit like a heartbeat. Ahead, the wind caught on the long strands of his black hair and blew them away from his face. He walked purposefully by the light of the sconces, not knowing everything around him was illuminated in white-blue light.

As much as she wanted to continue following him, she'd invaded his privacy enough tonight. Tempting as it would be to slip into his mind, to read whatever thoughts floated through his mind, she didn't want to wield her magic—her *power*—that way. It wasn't for satiating her curiosity, or even for dulling the ache of missing him. She stayed where she was, floating on the covered portico as his glow grew more distant and less vibrant, and finally as it disappeared behind the resounding thud of a wooden door.

One thing was certain: Shang didn't intend to win this trial. Which meant if there was any hope of a pardon for him and Fen, Meiling had to be the one to fight for it.

She turned on her heel and flew back the way she'd come. She planted herself on her favorite cliff overlooking the starry sky as it met the ocean's edge to think of exactly *how* she'd go about trying to save Shang and Fen.

When Shang settled into his temporary private chamber at the Academy, he was surprised to find he already had a missive waiting for him from his father. He'd spent hours with Master Dong, discussing the movement of Fang's troops. They'd been interrupted by Master Dong's regular class schedule, during which Shang presented himself to the headmaster for duty. The headmaster had an expression that communicated without words exactly how strange he thought this arrangement was.

"It's even stranger than you think," part of Shang wanted to remark.

It was back to Master Dong's office after that. By the time Shang pushed open his door and lit a few candles, the sun had been set for hours.

The room wasn't much—a cot to one side, a low desk to the other. A basin for washing and shelves along the far wall. It was still far more space than he was used to having at the Academy, so he should be glad for it.

Instead, he missed the comforting sounds of Renshu readying for sleep and the crackle of a fire out in the middle of the wilderness when Meiling had always been nearby.

Renshu might be dead.

He tried not to think about it. He doubted he could handle a loss like that any better than he handled Meiling's almost-loss. If he'd known in advance that Renshu was in that dungeon with him, he could have thought of an escape that involved him. He could have freed Renshu first before he even went to wake Meiling. But by the time he'd known about his friend, it was too late to change plans.

All they knew about Fang's fortress was that it had been sacked just a few days after he'd gotten Meiling out. Fang had fled with his forces. No word had come of survivors or casualties, either from dungeon prisoners or Zheninghai's attacking forces. He had no idea when he would learn if Renshu made it.

Shang eyed the letter, his name written in his father's precise script. He didn't really want to open it. Fathers knew he had enough things to worry about as it was. With a tight exhale, he flicked his finger, coating it in long, razor-sharp ice, and sliced open the seal.

He skimmed it, discarding the subtle barbs and passive-aggressive comments about how well Shang had better do in his new appointment, until he found the important part. His stomach sank.

Arrangements are underway for your marriage. It took me some time to dig into her lineage, to ensure the strength of the ice magic, but the young lady is nearly a purebred ice-wielder. One of her elder sisters is married to a feral wielder in the Secret Services, so even though they are not especially noble, it is still a reputable match that will preserve the bloodline and elevate the Tan line. Negotiations are in progress, and I will take care of everything. You need only to show up for the wedding once we've set a date.

The Shang from hardly a few months ago wouldn't have hesitated. He would have nodded and said, "Yes, Father." He wouldn't have cared. This had always been the plan.

He held the corner of the parchment in the flame of the nearest candle and watched as flames licked over the words and devoured them whole. "There is only one woman I would take for a wife," he muttered under his breath. "And she sure isn't a qilin-cursed ice-wielder."

His vision blurred along the edges, a reminder that he was long overdue for rest. It would be an early morning and a *long* day tomorrow—but maybe he would postpone writing back to his father. Just until after he'd slept so he could think carefully about how to respond instead of acting rashly.

He prepared for sleep, and it was the mundane motions that allowed space for thoughts of *her* to invade his mind. Was she asleep now? Did she fly around the palace or the night sky at this very moment? She had such immense power, power he knew exactly how to wield to accomplish his goals. With magic like hers, he could have traded in secrets to lie, steal, and manipulate his way to being emperor.

But she was probably using it to admire the stars.

For the first time in hours, Shang's lips lifted in a small smile.

And that was why he would hazard everything he'd spent his life pursuing for her.

CHAPTER 6

MEILING MOVED SLOWLY to not upset the headdress fastened with a thousand pins into her hair. Her heartbeat was unusually fast this morning as her maids dressed her in white robes printed with blue flowers and fastened a gold sash around her waist. Now, whenever she moved her head, crystal beads rattled and swung. She had much practice wearing such ornaments, but today's seemed unusually tall and made her feel like if she cocked her head the slightest bit, the whole thing would come tumbling down.

Paint covered her face. Not so much as Ma's, but it was probably enough for twelve princesses to be sufficiently decorated. If she smiled too wide—as was expected at festivals—it flaked around her cheeks and the corners of her eyes.

She dismissed her servants and stood for a minute longer in her chamber. "Just smile," she whispered to herself as she tried not to fiddle with her sleeves or the hem of her sash. "That is all. It does not matter what they think of you."

Taking in a deep breath, as if the air itself could give her courage, she opened her door and stepped out into the hallway. Her maids were waiting, accompanied by two guards. Together, she and her entourage paraded down to the lower levels of the palace where her family would ride through the city streets, welcoming the festival.

When they reached the lines of fidgeting horses outside, Meiling forced a smile and turned to find her family. They stood nearby, similarly adorned. Gone were Hou and Yun's white Academy uniforms. Hou looked even less comfortable than Meiling, but her head was suspiciously barren of ornaments. That must be why she smirked.

Ma wore white with gold brocade and a headdress twice the size of Meiling's. She smiled slightly at something Pa said and managed to make climbing into a litter look graceful. No one would suspect she had been screaming and thrashing last night. Before the curtain was pulled closed, however, she glanced out and saw Meiling. Instantly, her eyes clouded and her lips parted.

Something was wrong.

Pa stepped in after her.

Meiling pressed a hand to her stomach, attempting to settle its sudden roiling. Ma saw something—something horrible. It didn't mean it *would* happen, only that it could. But she appeared to have no intention of telling Meiling. She probably didn't want Meiling to worry; she wanted her to rest instead.

It only made her worry more.

She stared at the back of the litter until a footman bowed in front of her. She raked her attention away from the knots of dread filling her. Right now, she needed to focus on getting through this parade without humiliating her father.

Later, she would worry about . . . everything else.

"May I assist Your Highness?" the footman asked, gesturing toward a black horse's saddle not far behind her parents' litter.

At the sound of rattling beads and the shifting weight on her head, her hand darted up to touch her headdress. *It is fine,* she told herself. Wild stallions could not rip it off her head. Hopefully.

It only *felt* like it was going to fall off.

"Yes, thank you," she managed.

She tried not to think of Shang when the footman bent to offer his hands for her foot. Tried not to think of his tall frame as the footman tucked her shoe into the stirrup. Instead, she twisted to look behind her as Hou was helped in her saddle.

"I can mount a horse just fine," she growled.

"It's a little tall, Highness—"

"Nonsense."

The stars and sun and moon could not keep Hou from doing what she wanted to do. With strength that belied her short, twig-like frame, she heaved herself up into the saddle with a face that seemed to say, *"Watch me."*

There was no need to inform Hou of Meiling's own struggles to mount. The thought made her simultaneously want to blush and chuckle. Let Hou think Meiling only accepted the help to be the dignified lady she was.

Yun rode ahead of her. His posture—back ramrod straight, shoulders wide—reminded her so much of Pa. He looked like Pa too, though not *quite* so tall and wiry where Pa was burly.

Shortly, all was deemed ready. The horns blared, the gate opened, and together they rode out to take their place in the parade. Mounted guards surrounded her and her family. Two members of the Emperor's Guard flanked her, and she spared a prayer for Cao Renshu's safety.

Once they eased into their place in the parade, Meiling looked backward—cognizant of her headdress—and found horses and people for what seemed to be dozens of li. Where was the end? She could not find the beginning either.

Not for the first time, Meiling wished she could be a regular person in the crowd, free to delight in the parade's entirety, rather than experience only the tiny bit she was part of. Somewhere in the line would be men on stilts, fire-breathers, the dragon dance, and beautiful, exciting music.

Their entrance into the streets of Suguan marked the beginning of the Festival of New Lights, and the roar of the people welcomed them.

Meiling shoved her lips up in a smile as they rounded the bend.

The street crested before descending into the main thoroughfare of the city. Her horse clip-clopped at its leisurely pace, making her sway with the motion. A gust of chilly wind sent her heart leaping and her hand flinching to brace her headdress. Just in time, she stopped herself from reaching for it.

A sea of people stretched as far as she could see. The sight of so many cheering people and the power of their uproar took her breath away, like always. Gooseflesh rose on her arms, and she nearly forgot to smile.

Another step, and they plunged into the midst of the people.

Her breathing went shallow in awe. Their energy and thrill for the festival was contagious, and she found her smile growing more and more natural. People garbed in their finest, most colorful clothing flung themselves to the cobblestones before the royal family.

It was the first day of the festival, which meant people were here for more than celebrating. They shoved themselves forward from the back, and the shouting became discernable words.

"Bless my daughter's marriage!"

"Bless my son's match!"

Hands were raised and flailing toward her family. The guards on foot grimaced as they fought against the swell of people seeking a blessing. Yun reached out two fingers and began pointing at people as they passed. Once they were blessed, the people fell to their knees and bowed in gratitude.

Such a simple thing, and yet it made Yun seem the most benevolent crown prince.

Ma and Pa were doing the same thing, and if Meiling turned, she knew she'd find Hou stretching her fingers out, tapping the air.

Meiling's hands, however, stayed in the saddle, clutching the reins. She fought to keep her smile from faltering.

A woman burst through the guards and fell precariously close to the hooves of Yun's horse. "Bless my son's marriage, crown prince!" she shouted, prostrate on the ground.

It was too loud, and Yun's head was turned in the other direction. He did not see or hear the woman and his horse passed her by. Meiling nibbled her lip, watching the woman cry and reach out toward Yun. She was obviously poor by the state of her garments, and this was likely the only chance the woman had for a blessing. Despair overtook her face as the guards pushed the woman back into the crowd.

Meiling's two fingers twitched. She wasn't cursed, even if everyone thought she was. Besides, those who danced around her shadow were those of high rank and birth. This woman was a commoner.

It would be easier just to let the woman be forgotten.

Just like Meiling had always been forgotten.

Coming to a decision, she met the woman's gaze and reached out her fingers. "May your son be blessed."

The woman's eyes went wide in horror. "She's cursed my son!" Her shriek turned into a wordless wail of mourning.

Meiling drew back as though stung. It had always been silent. She had felt it, but never had she been publicly called disgraced, shamed, or humiliated. It was unspoken; tangible and real, but never *this* real.

Commotion formed around the woman until the guards lining the streets escorted her away from the street as she wept. There were a few shouts, and someone was knocked to their knees as confusion mounted. More guards dispatched to restore the peace, but nothing could ease the sudden tumult of her stomach.

She rode past the scene and tore her eyes away, facing forward with flushed cheeks and a pounding heart. Never had she been so imprisoned in a parade before. She had never loved these sorts of events when the eyes of the world were upon her, but she had never felt so lost. Never wanted so desperately to be anywhere else.

Instead, she sat up straighter in her saddle and forced a smile back on her face. As people crushed in close for their blessings, she kept her hands lowered. She was stronger than this. Had she not stood up to brigands and Fang Zedong? She would not be waylaid by the cold looks in the people's eyes.

She was a princess, and her magic was more powerful than most here could dream.

The knowledge felt hollow.

Shang didn't have time for the parade. He'd risen before dawn, written his father back, asking if he'd come to the capital for visitation this week so they could discuss marriage arrangements, dressed, and readied himself for his trial.

He should already be in the courtroom, waiting with Fen just in case the judge decided to start early.

Instead, he'd slipped out of the Academy grounds, past the palace gates, and climbed the steps to a covered portico outside a line of shops. The whole place was bustling, crowded to the gills with festival goers. Shang worked his way up another stairway to a balcony tearoom. The owner was busy shooing away people who just wanted a good view and no tea, so Shang took a seat as close as he could get and set a few copper tangus on the table. A smiling girl in colorful robes came by with a tray of tea and set it before him.

He poured himself a cup but didn't drink it, only let it warm his cold hands. His eyes were glued to the shut gates, waiting for the moment they opened.

He just wanted a glimpse of her.

Was it foolish? Absolutely. Did he care? Not a whit. Even if he did, there wasn't anything he could do, not when he needed the sight of her like he needed air.

He wanted a lot more than just to look at her from afar, but that couldn't be helped.

At last, the gates opened, and the peoples' cry went up. Steps pounded up to the balcony, and even the owner's shouting couldn't deter bodies cramming against the railing for a better view. Shang was forced to stand and thanked the fathers for the view his height afforded.

Most of the parade meant nothing to Shang. While children shrieked at the shooting columns of flame from the firebreathers, he kept his gaze focused on the gates. Waiting. His eyes glazed over for the dragon dance. He'd seen it all many times before.

Then, *at last,* the Emperor's Guard came into view. Shang's heart quickened. The cheering throng doubled their volume as the royal litter became visible through the gates. He didn't care about the queen and His Imperial Majesty, though. Leaning forward, he craned his neck, searching.

There she was.

Looking breathlessly beautiful in her gown of white . . . and also very uncomfortable. Shang's lips tilted up at Meiling's tense posture on the horse, likely due in part to the headdress she wore. It was lovely and regal on her, but for all her royal elegance, she had such simple preferences.

She smiled at the crowd, and it was almost believable.

Shang's own smile slipped away, replaced by a cold anger that only increased when people began calling for blessings from the royal family, and Meiling was the only one who kept her hand lowered.

She's not cursed, you fools, he wanted to snarl. *A blessing from her is worth twice that of anyone else's.*

He would carry her secret to his grave, but this was the only reason he regretted it. They should know her. They should know her worth went far beyond her magic. She might die before anyone realized she was the best person among them.

To think he might never have seen it himself.

He saw it now.

She was grace, beauty, goodness, indomitable fortitude, quiet strength, and so much more. Anyone who didn't see it was a blind fool. And though she was right before him, near enough he could call out to her, an ache built in his chest.

Too soon, she rode out of sight, and the crowd swallowed her.

That is going to have to be enough, Shang told himself as he gave up his spot and climbed back down the stairs to head to his trial.

CHAPTER 7

ALL SHE KNEW was that the trial was set to happen sometime after the parade and, presumably, before the feast tonight. When Meiling returned to her room after the parade, she called her maids to unfasten her headdress. Four of them, dressed in their gauzy pink, bent over her and hunted for pins.

She touched her face and her fingers came back powdery white. She wished she could wash it away for now. Could she? The maids could reapply it before tonight, surely. The last thing she needed was to attend the trial with a face painted beyond recognition.

Shang's warning words not to intervene wafted through her mind, but she pushed them aside.

Like she was going to stand aside and let him die.

Her maids rearranged her hair much simpler at her request and promised to dress her up again before the feast. Their titters were unmistakably disapproving, but she ignored them as they wiped the paint off her face, revealing dry skin beneath the caking layers.

She replaced the gaudy gold sash with a more muted, blue one that matched the print on her robes. After enough fidgeting to make her go mad, she was finally presentable enough to leave.

What if she was late?

"Thank you," Meiling breathed as soon as she was ready, leaping up from the stool and whirling toward the door. "You are dismissed."

In a flurry of silk, she hurried into the hallway and cast sideways glances at the extra guards flanking her doorway. They had not been there before the incident with the evanescer months ago.

She ought to take her maids with her, and they waited at attention next to the guards. She pursed her lips and shook her head, forcing another smile. "No need to follow."

The maids bobbed, poorly concealed curiosity painted across their features. The guards made no reaction. Satisfied, Meiling turned and scampered down the hallway as quickly as she could. Servants and guards were everywhere outside her wing. Their eyes burned into her as she hurried to the nearest staircase and struggled to keep her steps small and dignified. They dared not challenge her, but their unspoken questions were almost audible.

What could the cursed princess be doing now? Should she not be resting or preparing for the feast tonight?

Meiling had far more important things to do.

She had never been inside the courtroom before, but she knew where it was. When she slipped between complexes, she wished she'd brought a warmer shawl to ward off the cold. At last, with numb, shivering fingers, she entered the court complex. Guards greeted her at the carved, red-painted doors to the main courtroom. When she reached for the handle, their spears crossed in front of her. She looked up, frowning.

"Court is in session, Highness," the first guard responded carefully. "It is not open to the public."

Already started? Her breath snagged in her lungs, and she shoved away the growing sense of panic in her breast. "I am aware," she said, lifting her chin. "I assume entering now would be disruptive?"

"Indeed."

Meiling paused for a moment, quelling her frustration. She looked at the guard fully in the face, noted his unusually wide nose and mouth. "There is a balcony, correct? For viewers?"

"This trial is not open to viewers."

"This trial involves me. I may be called as a witness. As your princess, I ask you to lead me to the balcony."

The guards exchanged glances and then the closer one stepped away from the door. "This way," he muttered.

Hardly believing her luck, she followed him down the corridor to a side hallway. The sconces were not lit here, leaving it a small, dark corner of the palace. He paused before the nearest door and stood at attention. "Here, Highness."

"Thank you!" She didn't wait for the guard to retreat before turning the knob carefully. Her heart pounded as she pushed it open and was met by a staircase. The guard was gone when she poked back out the door before she closed it.

Quiet as a mouse, she tip-toed up the wooden stairs, desperately careful to keep them from creaking. At the top was a railing that mostly concealed her. To her left was the viewing gallery. She ducked her head low as she slipped behind the railing and took a seat along the front row of benches.

She poked her head over the top enough to peer down into the courtroom.

Less than ten people occupied the large space below her.

She spotted Shang immediately, seated beside Fen, to the left of the judge. Someone stood to the right and read from a very long parchment in a language Meiling did not understand, but recognized as an ancient dialect used in some official or religious settings. It was said that their founding laws—some as old as the mountain behind the city—were written in this ancient dialect. At least, that was the explanation Meiling received for why it was sometimes still in use today.

The judge wore long, heavy purple robes edged in silver. He sat sternly on the dais overlooking the room. His long black beard trailed down the front of his robes and settled on the edge of the table. There were only a handful of people on the benches below, viewing the trial.

Meiling lifted her elbows onto the ledge and settled her chin on them, hoping enough shadow shrouded her presence that no one would look up and see her. Her gaze strayed to where Shang sat as though carved from stone. His face was utterly unreadable, his hands unmoving in his lap. Fen, on the other hand, fidgeted and readjusted her position. She scowled sourly next to Shang's mask of nonchalance. She leaned over and elbowed him softly, trying to say something. His head moved in an almost imperceptible shake, and she retreated. Her scowl deepened.

The man droning on in the unfamiliar language set the first parchment down, took a swig of water, lifted the next parchment, and began reading aloud.

"Hu Fen, shapeshifter, you are accused of treason against the crown of Zheninghai through neglect and incompetence on the first assignment of your career. If you are found guilty, you will be sentenced to death by hanging or beheading as the judge sees fit. Tan Shangdi, ice-wielder, you are accused of treason against the crown of Zheninghai through neglect and incompetence . . ."

Meiling's mind reeled in disbelief as the words hummed in her ears. Treason? Neglect? Incompetence? Even Fen could not possibly be guilty of such heavy charges. She wanted to be hopeful; if the charge was too severe, surely it was more likely that they would be acquitted. Right?

There was no space for hope around the dread that sank to her toes like a rock in the ocean. She could hardly hear the following words around the buzzing of those first few—

Treason. Neglect. Incompetence.

Hanging. Beheading.

She remained frozen as the man continued, but everything inside her raged like wildfire. Heat flooded each of her limbs, down into her fingers and toes and up to the tips of her ears. Her breath came in short, soft gasps.

"Hou Fen, what do you plead against these charges laid before you?" asked the judge, turning his deep-set eyes on her.

"Innocent," Fen snapped.

The judge frowned at her but moved forward. "Tan Shangdi, what do you plead against these charges laid before you?"

Shang looked up at the judge and said without expression, "Innocent."

"Proceed." The judge waved his hand to the man, who sipped his water and reached for the next parchment.

His hands fumbled with the paper, his cup clinking when he set it down. With each movement, her heart clenched tighter. She stole another glance back at Shang.

He was looking straight at her, eyes wide.

Meiling gasped and ducked her head beneath the railing. Had he seen her enter? How did he know where she hid? She pressed her cheek against the plastered wall of the railing, its coolness seeping into her skin as she clutched her hands to her chest and drew her knees close.

Was he angry?

She decided to wait until her breath calmed to poke her head over again. But as the man began reading aloud again, her breathing only grew more rapid. Her ears went hot at the mention of her name.

"The assignment in question involves a secret mission to escort Princess Meiling, no magic, from the palace of Suguan to the fortress Liafugen."

The judge's voice boomed, "Hou Fen, do you affirm this?"

"Yes."

"Tan Shangdi, do you affirm this?"

"I do."

This went on for some while, setting the facts and particulars of their mission before the judge. Every few minutes, the judge asked Shang and Fen for their affirmations. As the minutes passed, Meiling's will to rise from her hiding place fled her. Instead, she listened with nausea to the proceedings beneath her.

"Where did you first encounter the brigands claimed to be attempting a kidnapping of the Princess Meiling?"

Claimed? The word made Meiling bristle until she was drawing breath between barred teeth.

A small, unexpected hiss cut through the silence. She looked up toward the ceiling, where she thought it had come from, but there was nothing.

"The village Wunghai," Shang responded.

"It was at the village Wunghai that you were first attacked by the brigands you claim worked for Fang Zedong, formerly mind-magic wielder and apostate Academy student?"

Shusss.

This hiss happened again, but it seemed to come from the far wall. Meiling crawled forward to look, but there was no movement in the gold and silver woven tapestries hanging from the ceiling. She frowned.

"It was," came Shang's voice from below.

"What magic abilities did these brigands possess?"

Scuttling. That was the sound. Like a crawling bug or a skittering rodent. Meiling looked the other way, furrowing her brow tightly. She should not be afraid of bugs, but if one startled her, it would give her place away and she might not be allowed to return. She tried to ignore the sound and focus on the words wafting up to her ears.

But she couldn't ignore it. It went quiet, only to sound again at random intervals, always from a different place than before. Each time, her indignation at the trial faded a little more, replaced by a heavy unease.

The sound . . . was *familiar*.

Try as she might, however, she couldn't place it.

The trial was over surprisingly quickly. Perhaps they only meant to establish a broad overview of the journey today. Even now, she dared not peek over the balcony to watch what happened as papers rustled and feet shuffled. It sounded like everyone was leaving.

Still hunched too low to be seen, she half walked, half crawled to the staircase. She waited at the top for a minute, as the unintelligible murmurs slowly came to a crescendo after a door closed. Then, carefully, she crept partway down the stairs. She would need to wait a little longer before venturing out of her hiding place, in case people walked by the hallway as she exited. She tried not to grow impatient as the courtroom continued to hum softly with life. Her hands found the edges of her sash and she wound and unwound it around each finger in turn. She pulled hard on the sash until her poor index finger swelled and darkened to red. As she released it, the color immediately faded.

The door at the bottom of the staircase opened, and a dark figure stepped inside.

Meiling scrambled to hide but froze. *Shang*. Her hand stayed on the banister, her back arched away to flee—her sash still caught in her grip. She released the sash when Shang's black eyes fixed on hers from below.

Her lips parted, but no sound emerged. Nothing but the softest gasp.

He jerked his head, beckoning her to come down to the landing. She hesitated. He remained silent.

Slowly, step by step, as her heartrate picked up, she descended the rest of the stairs until she stood on his level, looking up at him now in the narrow space. He propped one of his legs on the first stair and crossed his arms. When he spoke at long last, his voice was a whisper.

"Please do not watch these trials."

There was nothing warm in his posture, nothing warm in his words. She swallowed, too aware of the gallery's shadows that fell around them. With his eyes so intently on her, she found it hard to collect her thoughts into words, resulting in her saying the last thing she intended to—

"Are you angry that I came?"

Shang released a soft exhale and glanced back toward the door. He seemed to listen for a minute to whatever was outside and then looked back at her. "I wish you would not come."

Which was not the same as being angry. Her tightly clasped hands relaxed enough to fall to her side. She turned her gaze down to the floor, to the edges of their opposite-colored robes. "If I do not come, I will never know what happened. You know very well that no one will tell me."

He tilted his head to one side, glancing away. "*Please.* It is . . ." He heaved a quiet sigh, and pain overtook his features. "It's disgraceful."

Several replies clambered at her lips—*Do you think I care about what is disgraceful? It's not your fault that you are here. Disgraceful or not, I want to make sure you and Fen are tried fairly.*

Instead, she said, "I want to watch. You said yourself that you do not want me intervening—"

"And this will provide ample temptation for you to intervene."

"I only want to know what happens! If worse comes to worst . . ." Meiling stopped, her own fear reflecting in Shang's eyes. She drew in a fortifying breath and continued. "I do not want to be in the dark forever on this. If I do not see it now, I'll never know."

"You do not need to know."

"That's what everyone says and I'm tired of it!" she growled, louder than she intended. She gritted her teeth, her jaw going rigid. She stood up straighter and leveled a glare at him. "You cannot stop me from coming."

Shang blinked slowly, giving her time to realize the petulant tone infiltrating her words and manner. She scowled and looked down at her slippers peeking out from beneath her robes. Memories of this morning's parade and the woman's shrieks made her close her eyes, trying to shut out the words. They only grew louder.

"You are free to do what you wish, Your Highness," he said at last, his voice removed and impersonal. "I will not stop you."

The formality, the brusqueness, the dragon-blasted *title*—it was like a slap to the face. So when Shang uncrossed his arms and turned to leave, she'd had enough.

In two steps, she cut him off, planting herself firmly in front of the door, and fixed him with her sternest glare.

His eyes slid from the door behind her down to her face. Maybe she was insane, but she could have sworn his gaze trailed to her mouth before coming back up. A muscle ticked in his neck. "Highness—"

Her anger softened to a plea, her fists unclenching until she held out both hands toward him. "*Shang*. Surely, we needn't be so formal when it's just us."

He closed his eyes, his chest expanding with a breath, as though he warred with himself. "It's better if we keep our distance."

"No, it's not."

Shang's brows rose, and she wasn't sure which of them was more surprised by her vehemence. But she meant it, and she wasn't about to take it back. Instead, she lifted her chin, daring him to challenge her. "I have been to *diyu* and back with you. You are one of the only people in the entire world who *knows* me. I have been in your mind—*I know you*, Shang." Emotion threatened to make her voice break, but she wasn't done. "It is *not* better for you to be stoic with me."

He studied her for a long, quiet minute. She didn't retreat from his scrutiny. She met it head on, and that was how she caught the subtle shift in his expression—a layer being shed. They were already close in the narrow space of the landing, but he seemed to lean almost imperceptibly closer.

"Do you think I *want* to be stoic with you, *Meiling*?" he whispered, emphasizing her name in a way that sent thrill all the way to her toes.

He took a full step closer, tilting his face down toward hers. "Do you think I want that?"

The back of her head hit the door when she looked up at him. Her words came out a tinge breathless. "Sometimes I'm not sure what you want."

His forearm landed on the wall above her head, coming near enough that they breathed the same air. "I don't think it would be a good idea for me to tell you what I want."

Blood pounded through her veins, yet somehow, she managed to beam at him. "I'm all ears."

His lips parted as he stared down at her. Then, mutely, he shook his head.

"Shang—"

"You were the one who said it didn't matter what you wanted when there was no chance of you having it," he said, clenching the hand above her head into a fist.

"And you were the one who made me tell you my secret dreams, anyway!"

"We were never going to see each other again."

"And this is so different? We're living on borrowed time as it is. I know Zedong is coming."

Shang went rigid. Every last shred of softness—*gone*. "How do you know that?"

So . . . maybe she shouldn't tell him about her eavesdropping last night. "I spent a lot of time with him. I know it won't be long before he attacks again."

Shang's jaw worked, his gaze fleeing from hers. His voice dropped. "If he manages to get to Suguan, he will kill you. You know that, right? He won't take you captive. He will *kill* you. And he won't make it quick."

She studied his profile, her heart never once letting up its rapid pace. She knew what he said was true, of course. And yet . . . "Why are you telling me this?"

"Because you are wasting your time with me and this trial. Don't you see that it's *your* life at risk here?"

She couldn't think when he fixed her with a look that intense. She lowered her gaze to his chest as it expanded and contracted. What she wasn't prepared for, however, was Shang cupping her face and lifting it back to his. His touch was there and gone in an instant, but the gentleness of it seared forever into her skin. She stared up at him, wide-eyed.

"Meiling," he whispered, almost *pleaded*, "you need a plan to escape the city if it falls. That is where you should be spending your energy. Not on me, not on this trial. It means a great deal that you care, but don't let your sweetness be what gets you killed."

He thought she would *run away* while everyone else was slaughtered? Did he think so little of her? Meiling narrowed her brows at him, trying to decide which argument she wanted to hurl into his face.

She wasn't about to just *sit by* while Zedong destroyed her home.

Shang leveled an equally stubborn look back at her, apparently reading the thoughts swirling in her mind. "I can go back to titles and formality if you want. *Or* you can put up with this version of me—"

"The version that believes you're the only one who fights and makes sacrifices?"

"No," he growled, bringing his face close to hers, his teeth flashing. "The version that cares about you and is *sick* and *tired* of watching people hurt you."

His words stunned her speechless.

But he wasn't done.

"I have watched you be an exile among your own people for most of my life. I tolerated Fen's cruelty toward you for far too long—*contributed* to it—even though I saw what it did to you. My own anger and resentment blinded me, and I tried so hard not to care. But you didn't complain. You didn't break. You stayed strong, even though we treated you *despicably*."

Meiling's lips parted, emotion filling her dry throat. Tears prickled behind her eyes, and she fought to keep them at bay.

Shang leaned even closer, resting his forehead on the door above hers, his lips hovering near her ear. His voice turned husky, but the anger didn't abate. "I watched them take you, strike you, shove you to the ground. I saw what they did to you in Fang's fortress. Do you think I've forgotten what it was like to be shackled and restrained while I watched him lay his hands on you? I will *never* forget, Meiling."

Her lashes fluttered shut, a tear slipping free to slide down her cheek, and at some point, she realized her hands weren't at her sides, but resting on his heaving chest.

"You've endured enough," he whispered. "You've sacrificed enough. I know you, and if I stand by and allow it, you will bleed yourself dry for those who despise you. Zheninghai doesn't deserve more sacrifice from you. Zheninghai *owes you* its sacrifice."

He said this as if he wasn't the exact same way—as if he wasn't actively sacrificing his life to an empire's perverted sense of justice. "Sacrifice isn't about fairness," Meiling whispered back, her voice breaking as she swallowed. "If sacrifice was only left to those who deserved it, no one would do it. And where would we be then?"

"*Meiling—*"

"Maybe Zheninghai is worth sacrificing for—not because it has no grievous faults, but because there still is enough goodness to fight for. Maybe if we survive this war, we can make a difference. We can *be* the difference."

He pressed in closer to her, his warmth a shroud around her. His voice was rough as he punctuated every syllable. "How many ways must I say this? Let me be clearer. *I don't want you to die.* Do you understand now?"

It was hard to think with him so close, with his heart pounding beneath her palm. Did she understand *what* now? Of course he didn't want her to die. He would have to be a monster to want that—and Shang wasn't a monster.

"I need to get to the Academy for my assignment," he said, without moving an inch. "If I stay much longer, I'm afraid I'll kiss you. And I don't need to give His Imperial Majesty more reason to kill me."

Meiling's eyes flew wide. "What?"

Shang pushed back from her, and though his mouth twisted in a rueful smirk, the intensity in his irises never abated. "I can't use the Yanzhao Technique as an excuse anymore."

"Excuse?"

"Do you require an escort, Highness?"

"What?"

"Do you need me to escort you to your next destination?"

She shook her head to clear her mind of the sudden confusion that his blatant declaration brought. Only once she'd slid away from the door, backing herself against the staircase and wrapping one arm around her middle, did she realize she'd accidentally declined a few more minutes with him.

It was just as well.

Shang grasped the handle, but paused. It was hard to make out anything in the shadows but the outline of his black robes and his tied queue. He lifted his head, seemed to move it slightly in her direction. "Wait a minute after I am gone before leaving." Then he flicked his wrist—and extended his hand toward her.

She stared in confusion at his palm until something caught the light. *Ice.* She hesitantly took the two frozen discs, even more confused. He twisted the knob and pulled open the door. Black robes fluttered behind him as he slipped out and shut it behind him.

His gaze darted up to hers for a split second just before the door closed. In that tiny span of his attention, memories flooded her mind—memories of a dark chamber, his arms around her and his mouth kissing hers like he'd longed for her those weeks they were apart. Memories of him holding her while she wept, drying her tears and whispering sweet, gentle things in her ear. Memories that belonged to lifetimes ago.

He shut the door.

The silence left behind in his wake swelled around her like a tidal wave, nearly swallowing her as she stumbled onto a seat on the stairs. She needed to stop being so . . . *affected* by him. She needed to focus her mind on the problems of Zedong and this trial—*not* on a stupid, desperate hope he would stay a little longer and do exactly what he left to avoid.

Instead, she had to sit here until her flaming cheeks cooled enough that their color wouldn't betray her.

Oh.

She lifted the twin discs of ice in her hands and discovered they fit almost perfectly to her cheeks. Shutting her eyes, she pressed them to her face and muttered, "Dragons curse you, Shang."

CHAPTER 8

SHANG'S HEART DIDN'T stop pounding for hours.

He threw himself into instructing a group of sixth year students on wielding their magic in battle and honing their intuition on when to use weapons instead of magic.

It wasn't enough.

He could still feel her, smell her, see the moment her face had split into that brilliant, beautiful smile in his mind's eye.

This morning, it had been easier to try to convince himself of the lie that admiring her from afar would be enough for him. That he could easily deny himself of her just like he'd denied himself of every good and pleasant thing his entire life.

Watching her from a distance would *never* be enough. And the few moments she *was* near did nothing to satisfy his longing—it only increased it.

"Fathers curse me," he muttered under his breath, then brought up his wax wood staff in a quick defensive maneuver against a student. "Again! But *faster*! Harder!"

Tonight was the one night a year Meiling's family ate together—just them. Still, she was expected to be as grandly arrayed as she would be for a full court feast.

Her thoughts buzzed around her brain as she sat in a half-aware fog while her maids clucked and poked at her, applying careful paint to her face and re-affixing her headdress to her hair.

Six days, including today. Then Shang and Fen would be executed if they were not proved innocent. *Six days.*

By the time the sentence was passed, it would be too late. There would be no time to think or do anything. It was straight to the executioner after that. She ought to prepare herself for that probable outcome. She ought to prepare herself to see Shang's neck stretched out on the chopping block, taut and vulnerable.

Her stomach heaved.

She couldn't.

She held herself together through her maids' ministrations, despite her hands going clammy and her chest clenching so tightly she could barely breathe.

Before long, she found herself standing outside the feasting hall, followed by a dozen maids in pink and flanked by two guards. Such an arrangement was too conspicuous for Meiling's comfort; it drew attention and proclaimed the passage of a princess. She preferred to slip in and out of places unnoticed.

The door opened for her, and her name was announced. "Princess Meiling."

Meiling entered the hall, leaving her maids to flutter away. It was not a very tall room, with dark beams lining the ceiling and corners. The floor was polished to such a sheen that it reflected the carved gold *mó guǐ* decorating the walls and inlaid into the ceiling beams. In the center of the room was a low table surrounded by colorful, plush cushions and covered in bowls of steaming cuisine.

Pa sat at the head of the table, cross-legged on a cushion. Ma sat next to him, and Yun was across from her. A smile broke out on Meiling's face and she hurried to sit next to Ma like always, leaving the seat next to Yun open for Hou.

As she sat, she immediately felt the change in Ma's demeanor. It was more of a sensing than observation, but Ma's warm smile faltered ever so slightly. Meiling's movements slowed in hesitation, and she uneasily settled herself on the cushion. Her eyes flicked up to Ma's, and Ma offered something meant to be an encouraging grin but considerably fell short.

Meiling's mouth went dry, and her rumbling stomach twisted at the sight and smell of so much food.

"Princess Hou."

All eyes turned as Hou entered while trying to control a wicked grin. Meiling's attention snagged on the dirty hems of her gown. And Hou had thought she could get away with it without notice.

The girl needed a lesson or two on subtlety.

A quick sidelong glance revealed Ma had noticed too. She said nothing except smile in a greeting. When Hou came to sit down, Yun shook his head.

"You're dirty. Don't sit close to me."

Meiling looked down into her lap to hide her smile.

It seemed only a few minutes later that a servant entered with an announcement. It must have been hours; the food was half-eaten and cold, and Meiling's belly fought the restraints of her sash. Her mouth hurt from smiling so much, and Hou had fallen over once or twice in laughter. A spilled bowl of roasted vegetables next to her cushion evidenced that.

Pa made more jokes during the feast than all the year prior. Meiling's theory was that he saved them up for tonight as they occurred to him during the year. Once, he and Yun even got up to have a fire-wielder's equivalent of an arm-wrestling match. Pa won, of course, but Yun gave him a good challenge. Hou leaped up after they finished and demanded her turn, refusing to be left out of the competition.

Ma did her best, clearly fighting the preoccupation of her mind. A few times, though, she did seem to be drawn into the evening fully. Those were the moments that her beautiful eyes would sparkle with an otherworldly light. The moments that she seemed utterly satisfied with life. One of those moments, when Ma was laughing and her eyes were shining, Meiling swore Pa did a double-take.

"It is time for the lantern lighting," the servant said.

Meiling sighed and looked around the faces of her family and was relieved to see she was not the only one disappointed that the best part of the entire festival was already over. Tucking her chin and suffering to stand from her mat, she followed behind Yun out of the feasting hall. Had he grown since she had left? He seemed taller. A little broader too.

Something jabbed into her waist. Without turning, Meiling rolled her eyes and braced herself against Hou's teasing pokes. "Shhh," she chided.

Only a giggle answered her.

Guards lined the stretch of hallway until the double doors. Her heart beat faster as they approached, no one making a sound, except Hou's clumsy shuffles. Two guards bowed and opened the doors—

A dark sky, lit by millions of stars above and thousands of lanterns below, met their eyes. Filing solemnly onto the large balcony with her family, Meiling situated herself slightly behind Hou and Yun. Better not to be in a prominent position.

Even though this scene had unfolded before her countless times in her life, it never failed to steal her breath. They stood above silent crowds, illuminated by the floating lanterns they held. Salty sea wind swept with the winter chill, balm and cold together. On the balcony railing, one lantern was tethered. It was orange, painted with the designs of multicolored, flaming dragons. Fire, for her family. It was already lit, casting dancing shadows over the serious faces around her.

Pa approached it. With three purposeful strides, he stood in front of it, his bulky shoulders almost entirely blocking it from Meiling's view.

"Good people of Zheninghai," he bellowed.

"May balance be restored by the new lights," Meiling whispered, joining her soft voice with the multitudes below and her family beside her.

Pa released the lantern. It wafted high in the air, at first alone, then surrounded by lanterns as unique as each person forming the crowd. It was a beautiful scene. Cheers erupted. She found herself grinning, gaping with neck craned at the star-like lanterns filling the sky.

Was that what the stars were? Lanterns hung in the sky, never burning out?

Meiling tossed her smile to the one person of her family she knew appreciated this beauty to its fullest—and found Ma staring at her with tear-filled eyes. She froze, her smile vanishing. Ma immediately looked away.

A thick lump formed in her throat. Beautiful as the lanterns were, dancing in the night sky, beautiful as the joyous music drifting up now as people began to dance, she could see none of it. Not around the dread tightening her lungs and threatening to cut off her breath.

She was almost too terrified to imagine what Ma saw in that vision.

One step behind another. Meiling slowly backed away from the scene, away from her family's distracted eyes, away from the people who would most likely be happy she was gone, anyway. She turned, and slipped silently out of the balcony, through the line of guards with cocked eyebrows.

As soon as she reached a separate hallway, she pried off her headdress, stuffing it behind a curtain. This done, she heaved a sigh as her hair tumbled free around her face.

She burst into a run. There should be no worries about someone seeing her; all the servants who could be spared would be watching the lantern lighting and dancing with merriment.

So, she ran down ornate halls, past windows full of lanterns glowing against midnight, her feet falling softly on woven rugs. Her breath came in gasps, but in a good way. The passages grew darker, lit only by sconces along the walls. Shadows fell—

Crrrsh, crrrsh.

What was that?

She slowed, then stopped at the apex of four hallways. She knew where each led—the royal family's complex, the throne room, the main entry of the palace, and the feasting hall she had just come from.

No sound met her ears. The only movement of shadows came from the flickering sconces. She peered down the half-lit abandoned hallways surrounding her, her brow wrinkling. She had probably only heard her own movements.

Dignified this time, she walked through the hallway she selected. If there was one person who would not be at the lantern lighting, it was the person she desperately wanted to see. She tried not to let her eyes wander to the strange shadows on the ceiling, which seemed to make the *mó guǐ* come alive and battle in murky, dreamy movements near the trim. She tried to keep her eyes firmly fixed ahead, on her goal. Tried not to let the hair raise on the nape of her neck.

Crrrsh, crrrsh.

There it was again.

Meiling spun, lifting one hand unconsciously to her lip. She bit hard. The silent walls betrayed nothing. No signs of life flickered beneath the closed, darkened doorways. Even the candlelight seemed to behave, taming the shadows.

She was being ridiculous, right? This was only her tired, spooked mind inventing every manner of fear. But who could blame her? Ma had seen *something* in her vision, something that terrified her, and she hadn't told Meiling.

It was night, too. Darkness could make cowards out of the bravest.

She didn't want to turn her back on any direction, certain the moment she did someone would leap out from behind a curtain and grab her. *Irrational fear.* She faced her destination again, but this time she walked faster than before.

Meiling stopped again. "I know you're there," she hissed.

Her voice echoed in the hallway, bouncing off qilin horns on the ceiling and a tapestry woven in the design of lotuses. This time, the candles flickered faster. Dangerously.

"Stop hiding from me." She tried to growl, but it came out more like a squeak. Holding still and slowing her breathing, she waited. Her eyes darted over every inch of the passage. Despite her wild urge to whirl and ensure no one approached her from behind, she stayed where she was. Listening.

Crrrsh. Shhhh.

There it was again. Scuttling. Faint, but distinct. Like . . . like in the courtroom.

Was there a palace bug infestation? Cockroaches, perhaps? Bugs shouldn't make her so uneasy. Or was she even more skittish and afraid than she believed?

She broke into a run. The scuttling grew louder, more insistent, dogging her footsteps. The louder the scuttling, the faster she ran. The faster she ran, the louder it grew. By the time she burst outside through a side door, ignoring the guards eyeing her oddly, she could hardly breathe around the exertion and the fear choking her.

She ran into the night, blind to the sky full of lanterns. All she could see were the shadows hounding her. She raced down the colonnade and bridge that connected the palace complex to the Academy. As she expected, it was only *mostly* abandoned.

She calmed her pace and drew herself up like a princess, despite her sweaty, clinging garments and smearing makeup. Almost instantly, the shadows surrounding her receded. The scuttling stopped.

Meiling choked on a cry of relief.

What an embarrassing thing to run from nothing. And yet, she couldn't shake the strong notion she *had* been followed.

Zedong isn't here, she whispered to herself. *He's in Butagin. He's. Not. Here.*

She folded her hands into her sleeves like a demure little princess and walked along the training grounds, hugging close to the buildings she had no names for. While she did not know where many things were, she knew where the library resided.

Redoubling her pace, she hurried and ignored a few white-clad students' sidelong glances. Could they tell in the dark who she was? If they could, they would not want her near them. She lowered her head, letting her hair fall into her face and shield her.

The library was darker than she had expected. In the entire place, only one candle glowed. It flickered and bounced, illuminating a low desk topped with parchment, ink wells, trimmings, and the profile of a half-asleep, frowning face.

"Feiyan!" Meiling breathed, closing the library door and hurrying forward.

Feiyan jolted in surprise, whipping her head up. "I'm awake! I'm awake!" Her gaze cleared. "Meiling! What are you doing here? Come to punch me awake at my studies?"

Meiling smiled, relieved beyond words at the sight of her friend. She slid onto the cushion next to Feiyan, crossing her legs and folding the embroidered edges of her robes over her feet. "I just . . . I wanted to see you. And find out how you were doing. I know festivals are busy times for Academy students, and I thought it was probably especially busy for you." She stopped, then quickly added, "Of course, you must send me away if you are too busy to talk. I do not want to add to your strain or stress in any way."

Feiyan chuckled and dropped her quill to the table. She turned, situating herself so she could lean her elbows back on the desk and fling her legs out straight. "I dare not be too busy to talk to a princess."

Meiling snorted. She leaned forward, propping her face up with an elbow planted on the wood. "I thought you might miss the lantern lighting."

"Pfft—I've missed it every year. Favorite day ever. Yes, I heal all day, but the masters aren't there to hound me about anything, so I get to do *whatever* I want when the sun goes down."

Meiling glanced at the textbook opened in front of her, the several stacked next to it. Studying was most *definitely* not Feiyan's idea of a jovial way to spend her free time. Exhaustion lined the healer's face, evident despite a saucy crooked eyebrow.

"Since you asked," Feiyan continued, flopping one hand about in an odd gesture. "Ever since we got back, I cannot think straight. My thoughts are fogged and jumbled. Makes this—" she smacked the textbook, "—so much more difficult. I think my brain hasn't caught up to my body after getting back."

Meiling sighed. "Same. We're supposed to go about ordinary activities as if everything *is* ordinary." As if their entire home and way of living wasn't on the brink of collapse.

"It feels ridiculous," Feiyan agreed with surprising forthrightness.

Feiyan didn't even know the extent of the ridiculousness. Meiling chewed her lip, debating whether to tell her what she knew.

The healer's attention sharpened. "What?"

"Shang thinks Zedong is going to take the city," Meiling blurted in a quiet rush. "*Soon*. And I have no idea what to do!"

Feiyan gave a sudden wince and pressed the heel of her hand to her temple.

"Feiyan? Are you alright?"

"Just this qilin-spawned headache." She squeezed her eyes shut. "It comes and goes in waves. But have no fear, gentle princess. It'll fade."

Meiling laid a careful hand on her friend's shoulder, concern drawing her brow into a tight knot. "You need to rest. Let me send for a peppermint tonic and some ginger tea. That should help with—"

Feiyan was already shaking her head. "I'm already behind as it is. And see? The headache is already abating." She flashed a lopsided, unconvincing grin.

The healer was going to run herself into the ground if she didn't rest. But Meiling couldn't make Feiyan do anything she didn't want to do. Slowly, she got to her feet, trying to ignore the droop of her friend's shoulders and the heaviness of her head.

"I'll leave you," Meiling whispered. "Drink the tonic when it arrives. And please, try to get some sleep."

"I'll sleep when I'm decapitated."

"Please sleep before then."

"Absolutely not."

"Feiyan."

"Fine. *Maybe*. And I'll drink whatever you send, so long as it doesn't taste disgusting."

"Do you like honey?"

"Lots of it."

Meiling's lips twisted up in a rueful smile. "I'll make sure they put plenty of honey in."

Feiyan tilted her head upward to peer at Meiling, still sprawled in her half-seated prop against the desk. "Next time you get stabbed or shot with an arrow, come see me." She winked, but her eyelid was slow to raise again.

"Will do." She reached out and gripped Feiyan's hand tightly, giving it a squeeze. "I'll see you again soon."

Feiyan saluted her, a lazy half-grin spreading across her face.

Meiling hurried out of the library but paused on the threshold. She glanced back to see Feiyan's head fallen low against her chest. Asleep? Heart clenching in her chest, she left the room.

Now that the lanterns were released, more students were returning to their dormitories. At least, the ones who wouldn't spend the rest of the night celebrating with their visiting families. Meiling folded her hands in her sleeves and bowed her head, slipping into the main hallway leading out of this building. She hoped few people recognized her.

A familiar stride coming toward her, however, made her whip her head upward.

Entering through the sliding door ahead, was a tall form she knew better than her own face. Meiling's steps halted, her mouth going suddenly dry.

Shang looked up. He froze just inside the doorway. A stray student glanced sidelong at him, and Shang stepped out of the way so he could slip outside.

"Meil—Highness," he sputtered, even more shocked than her. He cast a covert glance around to be sure they were alone, then dropped his voice. "Meiling."

"Hello Shang."

Drawing his composure quickly around him, he crossed the distance between them and offered a short bow. Meiling's lips parted, an urge that he never bow to her on her tongue, but he stopped her with a polite, "May I escort you to your destination, Highness?"

That's when she heard the soft footsteps coming up behind her. *More students.*

"I . . . yes, thank you." She hoped it didn't sound as awkward in his ears as it did in hers.

He held out his arm to her. He still wore the black robes of an Academy master, but they did nothing to conceal the corded muscles of his biceps and forearm when she slid her hand into the crook of his elbow. Without asking where she was going, he drew her outside to a covered portico. On the other side of the railing were the pits for combat practicing, and this was one of the few times they were empty. A tantalizing thread of his masculine scent mingled with the cold night air. If she closed her eyes, she could almost paint an entirely different circumstance for their current situation. One where everything was right with the empire, she wasn't cursed, and he wasn't condemned to die.

A world where the distance between them didn't feel like hundreds of li.

When they were far enough away from any prying eyes, Shang's muscles tightened beneath her fingers.

"What are you doing?" he whispered, not harshly, but with a tinge of urgency. "Where are your guards? Your maids?"

"I was only visiting Feiyan. I don't like being followed by a parade."

"Meili—"

"No," she said firmly, pulling them both to a stop. "Don't rebuke me about not being safe. Not right now. Please."

A muscle rippled in his jaw, but he didn't argue. They kept walking, and Shang still didn't ask where he was taking her. In fact, it almost seemed intentional when he guided her away from the palace.

"What were you on your way to?" Meiling asked, breaking the silence.

"I was going to meet with my former advisor."

"Oh! I didn't mean to take up your time! We can go back to—"

"It's fine."

"I know, but—"

"Meiling," he said, his mouth quirking. "I said it's fine. How was Feiyan?"

Meiling sighed. "Not well. She's working too hard."

"She's always been that way. Hasn't had much of a choice in the matter."

"How many hours a day does she heal?"

Shang shrugged, guiding her around the back of the Academy complexes, until they walked down a vacant portico beside the gardens. These gardens weren't as expansive as the palace's, but it was still a beautiful shade of silver in the moonlight. Her fingers and toes were slowly freezing into useless icicles.

She couldn't care less.

Not when Shang's low, rhythmic voice was warm beside her. "Almost sunup to sundown, as far as I'm aware. She has her full Academy course-load on top of that."

"It's wrong," Meiling gritted out between frozen lips. "They'll work her to death like that."

"Yes, they will," Shang replied. He eyed her sidelong. "They would have done the same to you."

Meiling's gaze shot to meet his. She wasn't a healer. People didn't rely on her for their very lives. "What do you mean?"

Shang stopped walking, turning toward her, his head tilted downward as she stared up at him. That dark, glittering gaze of his ensnared her like a rabbit in a trap. "Fang isn't the only person who would spell you to sleep and make you serve his purpose. The difference with him is that you fought it. Would you fight it here, Meiling? When it was your people who needed you? Who enslaved you? No, you wouldn't. You would submit to the very same treatment."

Something cracked inside her. "What?"

He sighed, his face softening as his voice lowered. His free hand reached up, his knuckles a featherlight touch beneath her chin. "Meiling. This isn't as simple as hero versus villain. Those labels are rarely made of truth—only perception. To those in Butagin who were displaced from this land, Fang is a hero. He gives them hope."

"He lies to them."

"Yes. But it's not all lies, is it? Neither is Zheninghai all truth or all good. If you think this empire wouldn't drain you dry, then look at Feiyan. Look at what your own father risked protecting you. He didn't rashly choose to hide your magic." His words were achingly gentle. A stark contrast to the passion with which he urged her earlier this afternoon to not watch his trials. He didn't want to hurt her.

The words hurt anyway. She didn't want to think of her home this way. It was her *home*. She'd grown up here.

"I suppose that is what you learned?" Meiling asked, trying to deflect the conversation away from her. Away from the sensation of her gut rotting away inside her. "From your preparation to be a military strategist? That corruption is everywhere?"

"Corruption and injustice, yes. Though I learned as much just from being the son of a general."

"A general?" Her interest sparked, and she was glad for the distraction. Her eyes widened suddenly. "How did I not realize that you're former General Tan's son?"

Shang smiled, and the world tilted on its axis. Just slightly. "You didn't know?"

"It wasn't as if you *told* me!"

His smile widened. "If only I shared a surname with my father and inherited his ice magic."

She didn't think. She just reacted—and that reaction was a playful whack against his arm. "Don't tease me! I don't know many people! How was I supposed to make the connection?"

Shang was fully grinning now, and it was the most dazzling thing she'd ever seen. It gave her enough distraction to not be utterly mortified that she'd just *hit* him. Then he gave her another distraction: his arm wrapped around her waist, dragging her flush against him. "I'll tease you if I so please," he replied as warmth flooded her. "*You* didn't tell me your father was the emperor, and yet I—"

"It is not the same!" Meiling cried, smacking his chest with the side of her fist as she twisted to disentangle herself from him. "You're intentionally provoking me!"

His grip only tightened, his pleasure radiating from his beaming face. "Of course I am. And I'll keep provok—"

Footsteps. Voices.

They both went deathly quiet. Shang's arms were still around her, and her palm was upraised to whack him again. Their gazes locked, but it wasn't urgency in his dark gaze. If anything, it was amusement mingled with something else she couldn't name.

"We've got to hide!" Meiling hissed, pushing against his chest.

"Why?" His arms didn't loosen a fraction.

"Because!" she gasped, growing more frantic as the voices grew louder—about to come around the bend ahead. "We can't be caught like this! Let me go!"

"Why can't we be caught like this?" That was definitely amusement tugging at his lips.

"Because I'm cursed! Your reputation will be ruined!"

At that, his eyes darkened, the amusement washing away as though from a tide. "You are *not* cursed."

"Everyone thinks I am! And if they see you with me . . . like *this* . . . they'll think you're cursed too!"

Stubbornness flexed in his jaw, and he only pulled her closer, sending her thoughts scattering with the wind. "Then let them see."

"*Shang!*" she pleaded, bouncing on the balls of her feet as shadows appeared at the bend ahead. She flung out the only argument that could possibly work against him. "My father will kill you if word gets back to him! It'll hurt your trial!"

Shang let out a long, growling sigh, but looked one way, then the other, as though searching for a place to hide. His eyes fixed on hers, sharp and bright. What did that look mean?

She didn't have time to wonder. He scooped her up, ignoring her squeak of surprise, and set her on the railing overlooking the garden. "What are you doing?" she hissed, panicking as the first swish of white robes became visible around the corner.

"Hiding in plain sight," he growled back, eyes flashing as he closed the distance between them. He filled every inch of her vision as he bent over her and splayed one hand between her shoulder blades, pulling her against his chest. His back shielded her from the gazes of the students who came around the corner, chatting and laughing among themselves.

This wasn't going to work! And even if it did, how was she supposed to think straight with him touching her, holding her so close that his familiar scent of a clear winter day filled her nostrils?

How was she supposed to *breathe*?

He caught the side of her jaw, lifting her face to his as he whispered, "Pretend you're enjoying this fake kiss."

His lips grazed the corner of her mouth, so soft, barely there, as he positioned his hand to block the view of their mouths.

So the students didn't see that he only nuzzled her face instead of actually kissing her.

Her heart was a wild, thundering animal in her breast, but she was a bird soaring above the stars, a song twining with the disappearing lanterns. *I'm going to die,* she thought, half-deliriously, half-miserably. Why didn't he just kiss her outright? Why didn't he say the words she dreamed hovered on his tongue?

"Oh!" one of the students blurted.

"Oh!" the other one echoed. "Sorry, brother! We'll go the other way."

And with that, they turned and hurried back the way they'd come. Leaving Meiling where she was on the railing, her face hot as an oven, as Shang went still where he was, his slow smile curving against her cheek.

"And you didn't trust me," he teased.

"They apologized to *you*," Meiling breathed, not a single muscle moving except the rise and fall of her chest for air.

Shang's fingers flexed on her back as his smile grew. "Of course. It's common courtesy not to interrupt another man having a . . . *moment*, shall we say, with his darling."

His darling.

The young men were gone, and there were no more sounds of approach. No voices, no footsteps. Just the peaceful burble of gently flowing water and the chirp of songbirds mingling with the distant noise of festival celebration.

But Shang didn't move.

He inhaled and exhaled slowly, his mouth dangerously close to hers. He didn't let go of her jaw, or unwind his other arm from around her.

Out of nowhere, the urge to cry barreled into Meiling. They were so close in this moment, and either of them could suddenly break. He could turn his head a mere inch and claim her lips. She could reach up, wrap her arms around his neck, and pull him closer.

They were *so close*, and yet it was like they were further away than they'd been when he was at Liafugen, and she at Zedong's fortress. The world was falling to pieces around them, and in this moment, it seemed like there was nothing they could do to prevent complete and utter disaster.

She just wanted to lay her head against his chest and believe everything would turn out fine. But she couldn't. It was too obvious a lie for even her hopeful heart to fall for.

She swallowed hard to keep the tears from falling.

"I should take you back," Shang whispered, his exhale a caress against her cheek. "We don't want the palace in an uproar because no one can find you."

"N-no, we don't," Meiling replied stupidly, shakily.

As though hearing the unshed tears in her voice, Shang drew back slightly, tilting her chin up so he could run his eyes over every inch of her face. As though reading each thought she tried so hard to hide from him.

His fingers brushed a strand of beads hanging from her hair. "I'm not going to tell you lies when you know as well as I that Zheninghai is in dire straits. I will tell you this however: you might not be my charge anymore, but I will spend the rest of my days working to ensure your safety . . . and your happiness. Understand?"

She nodded, and the welling tears slipped free, sliding in twin trails down her cheeks.

His brow creased, and he bent down toward her again, softening his voice even more as he whispered, "Hey, hey. It's alright. Come here."

He pulled her against his chest as he'd done once before, and she clung to his robes as she wept quietly. Once upon a time, she'd wanted nothing but to be alone, to be left with her own mind and her own thoughts, and to escape the constant pressures and anxieties she experienced around other people. But now she didn't want to go back to her lonely room. She didn't want the company of her own mind.

She wanted to stay here.

With him.

"Do you want to tell me what is on your mind?" Shang asked. When she first met him months ago, with his icy demeanor and cold streak of ruthlessness, she would never have dreamed him capable of this softness.

Part of her wondered if he *hadn't* been capable of it then.

She shook her head wordlessly. How could she explain to him what she wanted? It wouldn't be fair to either of them to speak such things aloud.

So, she tried to ignore his strong arms around her, the steady beat of his heart, and focused instead on composing herself. He held her tightly while she sniffled and hiccupped, and didn't pull back until she'd been quiet for several minutes. "Ready?"

She nodded, shivering in the cold as he released her before offering his arm to escort her back to the palace.

They said nothing more as the frosty night wind whipped around them. Shang led her back the way they'd come, walking her over the bridge to the palace complex. She didn't know if she slowed her steps the closer they got to the warm yellow lanterns hanging outside one of the palace's side entrances, or if it was him. It didn't matter because they still reached their destination too quickly.

Shang handed her off to the guards, and with a deep bow said, "Goodnight, Highness."

She didn't have a chance to reply before he was gone.

CHAPTER 9

THE AIR WAS so much colder after Meiling was gone. Shang welcomed it, letting the icy wind blast his face. There was no way in the seven valleys he was going to fall asleep tonight. He was going to lie awake, staring at his ceiling, fighting against the memory of each moment with her, and all the times he could have kissed her. All the times he'd barely held himself in check. He would struggle in vain against imagining exactly what it would have been like to let his control snap.

It wasn't fair to her if he kissed her and told her everything that was in his heart. He was going to *die*, one way or another. Meiling was too good, too sweet, too precious—and even if she didn't care about him romantically, which he was almost certain she did, she still cared about him. She cared about everyone, and she was right: he knew her. She knew him. Perhaps in a way neither of them had been known before. There was a bond between them he couldn't deny and couldn't resist.

But that bond was the dangerous part.

If Shang told her the truth, that she was his sun and moon and stars, it would only crush her that much more when he died.

He didn't want to do that to her.

If he truly loved her, he wouldn't break her heart.

I should have kept my distance.

Shang raked a hand through his hair, not sure how he was going to pull his composure back together before visiting Master Dong. The older man had always been able to read him better than anyone.

"*There* you are!" came a familiar, roughened female voice.

Shang turned around to find Fen walking stiffly toward him.

"Dragons, it's miserable out here," his friend growled. "How are you just standing here? Don't tell me you're an ice-wielder. We both know that doesn't make you immune to cold."

"Are your injuries bothering you?" he asked, frowning at her gait.

She waved her hand dismissively. "It's the end of the day. I'll feel better tomorrow. For the fathers' sake, come inside before I freeze my backside off."

Fen had never been adept at reading him. Times like now, that was a relief. He followed her while she muttered complaints about the cold and led them inside. When they'd shut the door behind them, and the cold was nothing but a draft, she turned to him, her face going fierce.

"I've been thinking through this," she whispered. "I can get a few of my old masters to say something to the judge. I know someone who has a connection to him, and she would be willing to arrange introductions tomorrow night at the banquet. Even just an off-handed comment could—"

Shang was already shaking his head. "It's too obvious, and it wouldn't work, anyway. The trials are a secret. No one is supposed to know."

"Well, what other options do we have?" she snapped, flinging her hands wide. "We're dead by the end of the week if we don't find some way to work this trial in our favor."

"It's a *trial*. What are we supposed to do? It's out of our control."

"Says the man who *broke out of Liafugen* and *into* an enemy fortress!"

"That was inside my control."

"How is this any different?" she demanded.

"Because this is a civil court case. You don't win by killing people or outsmarting your opponents. That judge has control over the outcome, and even the emperor cannot gainsay it without risking being deposed by the council."

"Then get your father to bribe the judge! My family obviously doesn't have the money."

"*Bribery,* Fen?" Shang lowered his brows. "Would you also like to flee the empire and face dishonorable execution on sight?"

Fen's harsh expression slipped into something far more desperate. She reached out, grabbing Shang's forearm—hard. Her eyes pleaded with him.

"You might be fine, but *I will be dead* if something doesn't happen. They'll kill me, Shang! They'll kill me! What will happen to my family then? How will my mother and siblings have anything to eat to survive the winter?"

Shang's eyes shuttered, the weight of the entire world pressing heavily on his shoulders. He couldn't do it all. He couldn't protect Zheninghai from Fang and keep Meiling safe, much less save his own life and Fen's.

Blood was going to flow. Death would strike. That was the reality. He didn't need a seer's foresight to know that.

"My father won't bribe the judge," Shang said quietly, and the words were almost physically painful. "If he knew . . . everything, he'd kill me himself."

Tears welled up on Fen's lower lashes. Until the journey with Meiling, he'd only seen Fen cry once. That was when they'd become friends, actually. It had cut him then to see the vulnerability behind the constant aggression, and it cut him again now.

He reached out, clasped her forearm. "We will ask the fathers for a miracle."

"You don't have enough money to bribe the judge yourself?"

She was grasping at straws. He hated seeing her like this, reduced to begging for her life. "Of course I don't. Not until my father dies and I receive the inheritance. But chin up. I believe the emperor is on our side. He is a fair and just man. For all we know, His Imperial Majesty is working for us to have a pardon. Don't give up hope yet."

He gave her arm a squeeze, and she swallowed her tears, nodding. "You're right. I mean, why in the seven valleys are we here at the Academy instead of in the dungeon?"

"Exactly." Shang forced what he hoped was a reassuring smile. "Get some rest. Tomorrow is another long day. Don't overdo it training tomorrow."

She huffed. "And give those students a break? I don't think so."

His smile turned genuine. There was the Fen he knew.

She cocked her head, her sauciness fading away. "Your father didn't come to visit you tonight? Even my Ma made the trip."

"I only just wrote him this morning that I was back in Suguan. I imagine he'll come tomorrow or the following day." Shang hesitated. Then, dropping his voice even lower, he whispered, "He . . . um . . . he's in the middle of arranging a marriage for me."

Fen winced. "Oof, that's awkward. Are you going to tell him? About the trial?"

Shang let out a long exhale. "Yes."

"Double oof."

"Indeed."

"I'll plead to the fathers on your behalf."

Please do. "I'll be fine." He squeezed her arm once more and let go. She did the same. "Goodnight, shifter."

She rolled her eyes. "Goodnight, Ice Man."

The moment he walked away from Fen's welcomed distraction, fresh memories of Meiling assaulted him. He could have kissed her—

Stop, just stop, he pleaded with himself.

Did she have any clue that she drove him to the brink of insanity?

Floating in a sea of lanterns was not quite so ethereal as it used to be. In years past, Meiling had twirled among the lanterns, reading the riddles written on the side and trying to guess the answers. She'd spent hours delighting herself in each unique, beautiful design until the lanterns floated out of reach.

Now, she sat on her windowsill instead, shadowy legs hanging over the long drop to the ground beneath her.

Don't go back to the Academy, she told herself over and over again. *Don't follow him around like you're some puppy starved of attention. Have some respect for yourself!*

She tried to distract herself by mulling over her many problems. Feiyan. Zedong's impending conquest. Ma's vision. Shang and Fen's trial. Her own reputation. Never would she have thought that there were aspects of living as Zedong's captive that she missed.

She missed having her magic known.

But the more Meiling thought about her time in his fortress, the more certain she became of several fledgling ideas. Things she had not quite fully grasped at the time.

When Zedong marched on Suguan, he would not be the same person who had run away from the Academy all those years ago, and not even the same person she had escaped from. He was growing stronger. His black magic was strengthening. That last stretch of time she'd been imprisoned, when she'd been asleep, was mostly a fog, but she hadn't forgotten that he'd made her look into *how* the magic of his different prisoners worked.

She leaned forward, glaring at the rising lanterns.

Well, sitting here pouting was certainly useless.

Maybe she *would* follow Shang—no. She would check on Feiyan and make sure she received the tea and tonic she'd sent. Yes. This would be a good thing for her to do.

She slid off the ledge and flew toward the Academy.

She definitely was *not* going to hover near the spot overlooking the gardens where Shang had held her earlier and relive those moments through her imagination. Definitely not.

Meiling wandered past the training grounds, which were still mostly abandoned by the celebrating students and masters. A few people lingered, but not many lanterns had been launched from here, making this area bereft of the glow.

When she headed toward the library, an unfamiliar glow broke through the surrounding darkness. She wheeled in the air, trying to get a closer look.

The glow was pure silver.

She'd seen thousands of soul-glows in her life, nearly every color of the rainbow. None, however, had been this bright, star-glittering silver.

Something was wrong.

Her rational mind spun, cobbling together all manner of excuses to fight the sudden sinking of her soul. It was only a unique magical ability she'd never come across before. She wasn't seeing clearly. The light was coming from something else.

But when she lowered herself, coming closer to the silver glow, there was no further denial. The creature took the form of a woman, but not a youthful, fair woman. It was a middle-aged, slightly plump woman, with hair knotted for function rather than beauty, clad in a plain robe. She smiled, and held her arms out to a child—probably eight or nine years old—on the other side of the training grounds, wearing white.

It was impossible for a nine-tailed fox spirit to be roaming the Academy grounds.

Impossible.

With so many wielders around—*impossible.* But most of them were gone, and the ones that remained were only students.

There was no way this was possible . . . unless Fang Zedong was behind it.

The child gasped. "Ma? Ma! You came!" His dark blue glow pulsed brighter, and he broke into a run.

Meiling screamed voicelessly.

There was no time to find Shang and tell him about the fox spirit.

She did the only thing she could do.

She dove straight into the fox spirit's mind.

CHAPTER 10

MEILING BLINKED.

She stood, wet and salty and steaming, braced in a defensive stance. White fluttered around her eyes, the sultry sweet smell of sweat and the bitter grit of dust cloying in her nostrils. Just in time, her leg shot up—seemingly of its own accord—and kicked a blow aside. She breathed through an open mouth, shuffled bare feet in dirt, opposite a girl in white.

This felt very different from every other mind she'd been in.

The girl's braids flew in the air as she launched another attack at Meiling.

"Strength is not the only weapon. Use your enemy's strength against them," a voice called from behind her. "Do not show hesitance or reluctance."

The girl barred her teeth, bursting with feral strength. Her training kicking in, Meiling watched the girl's eyes, not her movements, to betray her next move. The girl lunged to Meiling's right, and Meiling snatched her chance. Instead of trying to strong-arm the girl, she used the girl's momentum to propel her forward, to whirl her around and slam her into the ground, straddling her and yanking her head up to expose her throat. The girl gasped.

"Well done, Princess Meiling," the master in black said. "Well done."

Meiling stood, wiping her slick hands on her white uniform. She bent and held out her hand to the girl, who accepted it with a rueful smile.

"For one without battle magic, you are accomplished," said the master. "Master Uru is awaiting you for your magic tutoring."

She could not help her smile as she bowed. "Thank you, master." The smile remained pasted to her face as she strode out of the training grounds, head high and back straight, gliding with the grace of a princess and the prowess of a warrior.

Why couldn't she frown? Why couldn't she stop her feet from moving, one in front of the other? Why did she feel like she occupied the body of another as she was dragged through this mind?

Why did she feel like a puppet?

The boy.

She had to save the child, had to get out of whatever this was and find a way to save him before it was too late. She tried to rise into the air and fly, but her feet remained solid and dirty and callused against the sand of the training grounds. This was . . . *solid.* Real. Despite how her mind thrummed with panic, how she struggled to make the smallest muscle obey her, she remained smiling and walking toward her next Academy lesson.

This was very, very wrong.

Her insides hollowed out, her heart nearly bursting out of her ears. Each elegantly shaped foot stepped firmly out before the last, and her lungs screamed at the precise, practiced slowness.

The midday sun beat hot and heavy upon her shoulders, her brow, her plaited hair.

The boy, the boy, the boy.

How much time did she have left? Was she already too late?

One of the doors opened in front of her, and an icy hand closed around her wrist. Her mind wanted to fight, to twist and break his hold, but her body let herself be drawn into the room as the door closed behind her.

It was a dimly lit scribal chamber. It smelled of dried ink and dusty parchment, crisp papers and bookish dryness. Unoccupied.

"The princess is early for her next lesson," rumbled a deep voice she knew like her own.

She bashfully lowered her gaze, even while her mind nearly lost itself in a frenzy. She did not have time for trysts in abandoned rooms! The boy was going to die if she didn't get away!

Shang smiled down at her, his handsome face softening and brightening at once. "You have no explanation."

"The master is waiting for me." The words poured from her lips, trembling and hardly her own. *Let me go! I know you're not real; I know you're only a vision.* But though her thoughts scrambled and banged against her throat, only a gasping half-breath escaped her. "Shang."

His grip on her wrist tightened. Warmed. Light flared in his eyes, bright and full of promise. Her mind faltered. Was she sure this wasn't real? Even if it was only a vision . . . Her heart pounded, lips parting, hands quivering.

The strength with which she had just now overcome a classmate in battle fled her limbs.

"The people adore you," he mumbled, pulling her closer. "You saw how they clambered for your blessings today during the parade. Even more than the Crown Prince. Your magic is like nothing else in this world, Lu Meiling." His words were whispers, honey-sweet and silk-soft.

Save the boy. Save the boy. Save the boy.

"Please," Shang rasped, "let me kiss you."

Alarm bells rang in her mind, and terror pounded in and out of her lungs. She wanted to break free of his hold, to turn and run, to race for freedom.

Please don't be too late to save the boy.

He pulled her into his arms. Physically, she gave only token resistance, her traitorous heart pulsing with more than fear. In her mind, she screamed. She wheeled and banked and scrabbled and yanked. It was useless.

Shang's arms were no longer icy, his touch no longer frozen. His skin warmed and warmed until it burned into her, into her back and her arms. His fingers burst into flame, and he carved a searing, burning caress down the side of her face, from her temple to her jaw.

He changed.

His butter-soft smile shifted into a leer, his teeth growing longer and sharper. His nose melted into a long, silver snout. Black-as-night eyes turned to gleaming, hungry diamonds. When he spoke, it was not Shang's voice that emerged from between fangs and snarling black lips—

I will have you instead of the child.

Flame engulfed her, choking smoke, her own shrieking fear. Nine silver tails, tipped in white, whipped around with the excitement of a hunter cornering his prey.

Idiot, idiot girl! She should have known better than to enter the mind of a fox spirit. Should have known—should have known!

The fox spirit opened its gaping maw, and its teeth came for her neck.

CHAPTER 11

MEILING KNEW NOTHING but the agony of flame and tearing teeth. She had no power here. No strength to resist as fangs ripped into her soul, shredding her to pieces like a tiger mauling its prey. There was no refuge to be found in oblivion.

She couldn't even scream.

There was no room for cohesive thought, not even for the realization that this was her horrible, wretched, anguished death. Soon there would be nothing left of her to devour.

But then—

The faintest voice.

Calling to her.

Reaching for her.

Teeth tore into her soul again, but Meiling latched onto that voice. It became her lifeline, and the tiniest refuge from the torment.

Suddenly, something caught her, wrapped around her, and shielded her. The consuming fire was gone, the snarling jaws snapped shut. She lay in vague awareness, still unable to move or make a sound. Pain pulsed through every part of her mangled soul—what was left of it.

But she was held. She could endure this.

Hold on Meiling, the voice called to her. *I've got you.*

So Meiling held on. Slowly, bit by bit, the pain ebbed. A river of gold threaded with emerald wound around her, knitting back the pieces of her that had been torn away.

Keep holding on. We're almost there. I've got you, friend. You're going to be alri—

Meiling woke as the faintest light of dawn melted on her face like a first snowfall. Warmth coursed through her veins from a hand holding hers. She sighed. Opened her eyes.

"Feiyan?" she croaked, blinking against the dimness and the bobbing of a nearby candle.

Feiyan lifted her head from the edge of the bed, her eyes bloodshot and half-closed. Her gasp echoed around the room.

"Meiling! Praise the fathers!"

She peeled her gaze away from Feiyan, moving with sluggish effort toward Ma's pinched and drawn face hovering so near her own. Two warm hands claimed her free hand. Pa leaned over her, his skin a ghastly pallor.

She frowned. Looked down to find herself tucked safely in her bed, just like she had been last night. Her gaze traveled the breadth of the room again, pausing on each of the three faces. "Why are you all here?"

A confused, almost awkward pause filled the room. Meiling knit her brows and pulled her hand free of Ma's so she could scoot into a sitting position.

"Your guards heard you screaming," Pa said eventually.

Now that her sleep muddled brain was clearing, she noted the wetness of Ma's face, the sheen over her doe-like eyes. The nightclothes her parents wore, the knotted and disarrayed state of Feiyan's hair.

"Screaming?" Meiling repeated. Vague vestiges of a nightmare, of fire and teeth and unimaginable pain, scrabbled at the edges of her awareness. If she tried too hard to remember it, it vanished altogether. Why was Feiyan here just for a nightmare?

She sat up straighter, suddenly more alert. How could she have had a nightmare? She hadn't had dreams since her magic developed.

"When they opened the door, you were covered in burns. You had one here," Ma traced along Meiling's cheek. A flashing memory of Shang drawing her into his arms, tracing his finger exactly the same way assaulted her, and Meiling jerked away. Ma's hand froze in midair.

Not a nightmare. Not a nightmare. Something happened—something *real*. Something that was both real and not real.

"Where's Shang?" she blurted, her heart racing. And then it came back: *the fox spirit*. She tore her hand free from Feiyan, flinging her legs over the side of the bed. "The boy! Pa! Hurry! There is a fox spirit—"

Pa placed a square hand on her shoulder and pushed her back down onto the bed. Ma shuffled aside so he could kneel next to Meiling and envelope both of her hands in his. "Meiling, the fox spirit has long been killed. Hours ago, by Hu Fen. One of your former protectors. The fox spirit harmed no one."

Meiling tried to process this information, tried to reconcile it with her hazy recollection of last night. A blush seeped into her cheeks at the memory of Shang's words, his insistence as he drew her into his arms.

Everything she saw in that vision was a mirror of herself. What she wanted. She closed her eyes, fighting tears. Fighting shame. To think that the boy's life could have been lost because of her vanity!

Finally, the rest of last night came back. The excruciating pain as the *mó guǐ* devoured her. The moment a shield had wrapped around her, protecting her as she was restored. Pa released her hands, and she dropped her face into them.

There was a whispered, "You may leave," followed by a muted shuffling on Meiling's left. Her head shot up.

"Feiyan!" she cried, reaching out toward her friend. "You . . . You saved me. How?"

Feiyan pursed her lips, glancing quickly at Ma for permission to answer. Ma nodded once, tightly. Feiyan turned her sagging frame to Meiling, and it was like all the light had fled her face.

"I was summoned immediately, and I barely reached you in time. I thought it was too late . . . The fox spirit had consumed parts of your soul. It took all night, but thankfully you have recovered."

She had been awake through the night, healing nonstop.

When Ma dismissed her again, Meiling did not protest. She was too shocked to even utter the smallest of thanks. Instead, as soon as the door was closed, she sputtered, "Pa, you must send for her masters and tell them that she must rest today."

"The healer cannot be spared that long," Pa said, shaking his head.

"What?" Meiling cried, trying again to leap out of bed and was again restrained by her father. "But you saw her, she'll be ill! She cannot—"

"You ought to have considered that when you foolishly entered a fox spirit's mind!" he snapped, fire burning brightly in his pupils. He immediately lowered his head, breathing deeply through his nostrils, trying to regain his composure.

She fought tears.

"Meiling," he said, much gentler. "Fox spirits devour body and soul. You know this. By entering its mind, you let it devour you soul-first. I know your heart, my sweet girl." He reached out, gripping her knee under the quilt. "I know your good nature. You cannot watch suffering—this is good. I do not wish you hardened. But your goodness must be paired with wisdom. You must not rush headlong into situations you are unequipped to handle."

"You would have me stand by and watch people die?"

"I would have you not pay a price you cannot afford."

Dawn bloomed pink through her window, catching on the lines of Ma's face. The fear in her eyes reflected the sunlight. Meiling averted her attention to the back of Pa's hand on her knee. She picked at the embroidery of the quilt.

They did not have to say it. She understood what Pa was trying to tell her. By attempting to save the boy, she cost the empire's one healer her few hours of rest. Her impulsiveness required Feiyan's bone-deep exhaustion and sleep deprivation, or the deaths of the people she would have healed if she could sleep today. The cost was greater than only her life or the boy's life.

Yet she would do it again. She could not stand by and watch the boy die.

Bile rose in her throat—brackish, bitter, and salty.

"You called for Shang," Ma said. "Your other protector—Tan Shangdi?"

Meiling nodded mutely.

"Why did you call for him?"

She looked down at the silk nightdress she wore. Not the white Academy training garments she'd worn in the nightmare. How real Shang's touch had felt—her wrist seemed to throb and freeze where he had snatched her and dragged her into the scribal chamber.

"I thought he was in danger," she lied. She hated lying to her parents.

"Meiling," Pa said quietly, taking one of her hands again. His tone was even more serious than before, making gooseflesh raise along her arms and the back of her neck. "There's something we need to tell you."

Meiling stiffened instinctually, fighting the urge to pull her hand away as she glanced between the intensity lining Pa's face and the tears filling Ma's.

Pa drew a deep breath. "Your first night back, when your mother had a vision . . . it was about you."

Ma's face crumpled. Her shoulders shook with quiet sobs. Pa's gaze shifted to her, pain wracking his features, but he continued relentlessly, his voice only barely quavering. "She saw your body. On the floor of the throne room."

Alarm ripped down Meiling's spine. "My body?" she repeated, almost stuttering. "My . . . *dead* body?"

Pa's hand was almost crushing hers. He opened his mouth to answer, then closed it—as if he couldn't get the words out. He only nodded. She stared at him in shock, waiting for him to continue, to say anything at all.

"It might not come true," he said, finally. "But it *could* come true."

"Have Ma's visions ever not come true?" Meiling asked, her voice surprisingly steady.

Pa glanced at Ma, his jaw flexing. "Very few haven't."

"I know you feel suppressed," Ma interjected suddenly, and there was an underlying thread of ferocity in her voice, despite the tears. "But there are so many forces at work against you. We are fighting for a chance for you to *live*, Meiling. That's why we hid your magic, why we still hide it. It's not because we don't believe you are capable of incredible things—we *know* you are. You've already performed shocking feats of skill without any training. But we want you to *live*, my dove."

Meiling bit down hard on her lip. She hated herself for the scraps of resentment she'd carried toward her parents for choosing this path for her.

"We thought you deserved to know about the vision," said Pa, lowering his voice. "We don't want to frighten you, but it is your life. You should know. You should also know that we love you so very dearly, and there is nothing we want more than your life and happiness. There is very little we wouldn't sacrifice for that."

His words hit her harder than she expected, a resonance of Shang's words to her last night. So many people despised her. It was a crushing burden she'd borne most of her life. And yet . . . the people who mattered saw her, loved her. Maybe she'd been so caught up in the opinions of strangers that she'd failed to see how deeply her own family loved her all along.

So Meiling threw herself into her father's arms, burying her head in his shoulder, but her words were for both of her parents: "Thank you for working to keep me safe. I love you."

Shang forbade himself from attending this morning's parade. He'd managed enough sleep to regain a fraction of his senses after the commotion of Fen killing a fox spirit on Academy grounds, and those senses told him he ought to renew his commitment to keeping his distance from Meiling. That started with not ogling her during the parade.

Even if it took every ounce of self-control to keep himself firmly occupied at the Academy, training a few students who'd rather practice their combat than join in the festivities.

It would be better if he focused his energy on the puzzle of last night's fox spirit invasion. How had such a thing *happened*? Was it just coincidence? Or had Fang expanded his *mó guǐ* control to include dragon-blasted *fox spirits* along with the phoenixes? How in the seven valleys was it possible to trap a fox spirit?

Then again, he'd once believed it impossible to trap a phoenix.

After nearly two hours of grueling training, the sun crested the horizon. The students asked for a water break, and Shang obliged. He took a long draught from his waterskin, then pressed an ice-cold hand to the back of his sweaty neck. He didn't even have to use his magic—his hand was already freezing from the cold. His toes were numb, too, and he hardly cared.

He was taking another drink, about to order the students back to work, when a curiously familiar figure walked across the bridge from the palace complex, her steps heavy.

What was the healer doing at the palace so early?

"Oh, fathers," Shang breathed, hoping the sudden pounding of his heart was just his paranoia.

It could have been anyone that needed healing. The younger princess could have burned herself on her own fire. The emperor could have fallen ill, or perhaps his queen had. The prince could have injured himself doing something stupid.

But despite her slumped shoulders and the haggard circles around her eyes, Feiyan walked straight to Shang.

His gut plunged into the earth. He had already pulled away from the students, grabbing his tunic from the railing bordering the pits and pulling it over his sweaty torso, when she reached him and said without a single note of her characteristic sarcasm, "I need to speak with you."

Shang's heart nearly stopped at those words. "Tell me she's alive," he demanded.

"She's alive."

He closed his eyes, running a hand down his face. He cursed under his breath, then fell into step beside the healer. They walked in silence down the covered portico until they reached a deserted stretch, far enough away from those with both normal and augmented hearing abilities.

Shang's patience nearly snapped. Somehow, he maintained control. Part of it was due to his pity for the bone-weariness of the healer's movements. She might normally find immense satisfaction from tormenting him, but right now, he couldn't maintain his usual frustration with her.

"Meiling is alive. She is in full health, and is completely fine," said Feiyan as a preface.

That only served to make his dread sink deeper.

"The fox spirit last night . . ."

"What?" he demanded.

"She went into its mind."

Shang's world stopped. One instant became a hundred, then two hundred. A thousand. All while his entire being screamed internally: *No, no, no, no.*

"It almost killed her."

She didn't have to say the words aloud, but they struck him like blows, anyway. He staggered to the wall, caught himself, and slid to the ground. He ran his hand through his hair, then grabbed a fistful of it.

"The little boy that was almost caught by the *mó guǐ*—the one that Fen saved? I believe she was trying to save him."

Shang let out a growl, something akin to rage pulsing beneath his skin. Of *course* she was trying to save the child. Of *course* she nearly threw her life away doing it. Of *course* she didn't stop and realize the consequences—or the alternatives. Obvious alternatives like entering the boy's mind instead. "What was she *thinking*?" he growled, even though they both knew exactly what she was thinking. That there had been someone in danger, and that Meiling would never stand by while someone died.

Even if it sometimes made her make the absolutely *stupidest* decisions.

"How bad was it?" he asked, terrified of the answer he already knew. Feiyan was just now leaving the palace and Fen had killed the fox spirit over seven hours ago.

Feiyan was silent for a long moment. Then she gave a single, nondescript answer: "Bad."

Shang groaned, pressing the heel of his hand into his eye socket. The next time he saw Meiling, he was going to strangle her.

"But she's fine now. I was able to mend the damage to both her body and her soul."

Body and soul. How had she not realized that she'd handed her soul over to a predator when she'd entered its mind? He tried to tamp down on the rising fury and sudden panic. *She's fine. She's fine. Meiling is still alive. She's healed.*

“I’m sorry,” Feiyan whispered. “I was ordered to secrecy, but . . . you needed to know.”

“Thank you,” Shang croaked, and wished he had more to give to her in thanks for what she’d done. “Thank you.”

“I didn’t do it for you.”

“I know. But I thank you anyway.”

Feiyan’s heavy footsteps thumped away, giving Shang privacy as he wrestled his composure back under his control. Then, with a growling curse, he shot to his feet, not caring to change out of his tan-colored training clothes for his full black robes.

By all the fathers, he was going to the parade again. He had to lay his eyes on her, just once, to prove she was alright.

So he did. He didn’t find nearly as good of a view as yesterday, but his height continued to lend him the advantage. When the palace gates opened, and the royal family finally emerged, there she was. Sitting straight in her saddle, her face an elegantly serene mask. She was beautiful, as always, with not the barest trace of what she’d endured the night before.

He sagged in relief and coaxed his heart back into its normal rhythm.

His darling was fine.

CHAPTER 12

MA WASN'T PART of today's parade. Instead, she was spending the day with her elderly parents, as custom dictated, for the second day of the festival. Meiling's mind spun as she let herself be aided onto her horse, puzzling over last night.

Was there a way she could enter a fox spirit's mind without endangering herself? Or rather, was there a way to not be ensnared upon entering? There would always be danger, but could she work her way around it—remain unscathed?

It was a difficult thing to test.

She plastered a smile on her face, thanking the fathers for the eighteen layers of paint she wore, but couldn't forget the vision in her mind. The memory of the unabashed praise, her triumph over her classmate in a battle. Shang's words of the people's adoration as he pulled her closer.

Folly.

Her mind had betrayed her. Her secrets and her faults stared back at her, unrelenting.

It was only when the gates opened, as the people cheered, as her horse put one clopping hoof before the next, that the engulfing cries of the people distracted her from her thoughts.

"Bless my baby!"

"Give my firstborn your bountiful blessing!"

The throng pressed harder than yesterday, holding out swaddled newborns dangerously close to the road. Her eyes roved over the people, but her hands stayed fixed in her saddle as her siblings and father blessed the babies thrust in their faces.

Next to a ragged, dirty woman holding out her baby stood a man in fine, tailored robes holding his own child out. The desire for blessings transcended rich and poor, honor and dishonor.

She kept her smile pasted to her face and wondered if tomorrow she could convince her maids to paint a smile on her face so her mouth wouldn't hurt so much after the parade. Her eyes rebelled, and she found herself scanning the crowds for a tall form. But Shang was nowhere to be found—not that she *actually* believed she could find him in a crowd this big.

Her smile slipped for one instant when she spied a hunched, cloaked figure ahead, pressing to the front with the young parents. Why did her hackles rise? Why did she suddenly hear that scuttling sound again? Her hands went clammy on the reins, cold and slick.

She rode past the hunched figure. As she did so, the head lifted, and beneath it shone eyes hardly visible between the folds of a crinkly smile. A long, white beard. Missing teeth. He looked straight at Meiling.

Why did she feel like she'd seen him before?

She passed the man. When she twisted to look back, he'd been swallowed by the sea of people stretching for miles through the city's winding streets.

Shang kneeled on the woven mat in the courtroom as the scribe droned through the traditional prayers. Fen sat beside him, her features arranged in a scowl most wouldn't recognize as her resting face.

Today, the real investigation would begin.

He stuffed any trepidation down deep inside himself—stuffed *all* emotions down where they wouldn't show on his face.

The scribe finished his prayers, rolled up the ancient scroll, and adjusted his spectacles. Judge Lin's small, piercing eyes shifted to Shang, then to Fen.

The interrogation began.

"Hu Fen," began the judge, "do you confirm that while you were injured, Princess Meiling, no magic, was captured by Fang Zedong?"

The first question confirmed it: they'd need a miracle for a pardon. Shang kept his face expressionless as Fen frowned, but answered, "Yes."

"Tan Shangdi, do you confirm that while you were distracted fighting, Princess Meiling, no magic, was captured by Fang Zedong."

He was as good as dead. What kind of question was that? He hesitated, turning the words over in his mind, then answered, "Yes?"

A black-haired head poked over the edge of the viewing gallery.

It was a very subtle movement—so subtle no one but Shang noticed. And he only noticed because he'd been watching for it.

He shut his eyes and exhaled. For all her sweetness, Meiling could be stubborn as a mule.

At least she was alive.

"Hu Fen, do you confirm you broke protocol not once, but twice when you left Princess Meiling alone and unprotected outside the village Wunghai?"

Fen shifted, protests bubbling up on her lips. She restrained them—thankfully—and merely answered, "Yes."

"Do you also confirm that you broke protocol when you attempted a rescue of Li Feiyan, healer?"

"Yes."

Shang had known from the beginning that decision would cost them both.

"Tan Shangdi, do you confirm you broke protocol by leaving Princess Meiling alone and unprotected to go after Hu Fen?"

His shoulders rose and fell with a deep breath, even as his jaw clenched. That hadn't been an easy decision, but even *with* Fen, they'd been outnumbered. Shang had gone after her because if he hadn't, Meiling would have been even more at risk. But there was no room to say any of that. He could only give a single, emotionless, "Yes."

A second movement from the balcony drew his eyes. Only this time, it wasn't Meiling failing to stay hidden. A second head, this one concealed with a hooded cloak, poked over the edge of the railing.

Shang's blood turned to ice.

Meiling slid her fingers onto the railing and slowly lifted her face until she could see over the edge, down into the courtroom. Everything looked the same as yesterday, with the judge seated upon the dais, a man standing to his left by a pile of scrolls, and Fen and Shang seated on the judge's right. The viewing gallery remained mostly empty. She hated being late, but it couldn't have been helped—not with how late the parade had gone.

It was good to see Shang again, with his severe stoicism, and remind herself that the version she'd seen of him in the fox spirit's mind wasn't real. Still, the questions being hurled at him and Fen made her fists clench around the railing. They were asked as though the nuanced answers were completely black and white. Even the questions directed at Fen were unfair. Fen hadn't abandoned her outside that village; she'd left first to scout the area for *mó guǐ*.

That was *protecting*, not abandoning. She left the second time to burn the fox spirit's body, which was arguably not the smartest decision, but she did it so the smell wouldn't travel into the town and give away their presence to the villagers.

And Shang's questions were far worse. *Distracted* by fighting? Her blood boiled. Shang went after Fen because she was outnumbered and would have been killed, and if she had been killed, Meiling would have been at more risk than before.

Protocol was shortsighted. And stupid.

The door opened behind her. The voices droned on below, but she spun as a hunched form hidden beneath the folds of a black cloak, his long white beard the only distinguishing feature. She recognized him immediately as the man she'd spotted in the parade—the one who had raised her hackles.

She stayed where she was, kneeling on the floor, but planted one foot firmly on the ground—ready to flee.

"Ahhh! The Princess Meiling!" croaked the old man, lumbering up the stairs faster than he should be able to. He smacked his gums, smiling with three teeth. "What a lovely spy you make."

"Stop where you are," Meiling hissed, rising but staying crouched beneath the railing. "I'll scream if you come closer."

He gave a wheezing excuse of laughter. He held up both hands in a placating gesture. "Forgive me. I forget myself. Please, may I join you?"

She was silent, still poised for escape, still tense as a deer cornered by a hunter.

He grinned. "I suppose I have not introduced myself, now, have I? I'm Hu Fen's grandfather. Word reached me of her trial, so I came to watch like you. Are you related to her partner?"

She did not respond, still eyeing him warily. Grandfather? He certainly was old enough. Was that why he struck her as familiar? She'd encountered him at some point, not realizing who he was?

She doubted it.

Taking her silence as consent, the old man wheedled his way up and plopped himself on the bench, leaning on the railing like Meiling had done yesterday. He did not bother to fling back the hood of his cloak, but just stared between his wrinkled skin at the scene below. He smacked his gums happily, like this was some game.

Her rational mind told her nothing was wrong. It was only an old man. She could definitely outmatch his faded strength. So why did gooseflesh erupt on her arms? Why did the hair on the back of her neck rise?

She should focus on the trial. She was missing important information.

"Tan Shangdi, do you confirm—"

"Honored judge," Shang shot to his feet, bowing deeply with his arms outstretched. "I request a five-minute recess."

Meiling's breath caught, her attention darting between Shang and the frowning judge. The frown turned to a scowl as the judge regarded Shang, still bowing.

"The audacity," the judge spat, his old, withered hand quivering.

Shang's words were cool. "Is it not correct that each defendant may request one recess at any point in their trial?"

His words hung in the air.

"Recessed," the judge growled. He leaned forward, shaking his finger at Shang's face. "You are not helping your case, boy."

Shang bowed again, ignoring Fen's gaping mouth, and strode quickly out of view.

Meiling's held breath spewed out. Questions whirled in her mind. Shang, who was one of the most professional and collected people of her acquaintance, had interrupted the judge?

Whatever for? Was he so bothered by the questions that he needed to leave?

That did not sound like him at all.

"Strange," the old man cooed. "Strange boy, strange boy." He wheezed again, making a loud sucking sound. She wanted to urge him to be quiet, but her throat was dry and no sound would come out.

The door opened.

She twisted away from the railing. Her eyes widened when it was Shang pulling the door shut, a stormy expression on his face. He took the stairs two at a time but did not look at her even once. His gaze was fixed on the grinning old man.

"Out," Shang growled, nodding with his head toward the door. "Out before I drag you down the stairs."

The old man's white eyebrows shot high on his forehead. "Aw, boy, I'm just here to support my granddaughter Fen—"

"Leave."

The man sighed, the air seeming to rattle around his lungs. "Youth these days," he grumbled, getting to his feet and eyeing Meiling. "They're all paranoid idiots. Won't give an old man any respect."

She looked back and forth between the man clambering down the stairs, muttering as he went, and Shang, who stood low enough on the stairs that he wasn't visible to the judge. The muscles of his jaw flexed tightly.

Finally, the door closed behind the man.

Meiling lifted her eyes from where she sat on the floor behind the railing.

Shang turned from staring at the exit to look down at her. She drew her knees up to her chest, wrapping her arms around them. Her thanks wouldn't leave her tongue.

"Fen has no grandfather," Shang said, black eyes piercing. "Do not let him come near you again."

"Who is he?"

"I don't know."

She couldn't deny her relief that the man was gone. Her shoulders dropped a little, and finally she managed a quiet, "Thank you."

He stayed silent for a moment, even though he must only have had two or three minutes left before he needed to return to the courtroom. She racked her brain for anything more to say, but could think of nothing except insisting that the trial was being unfair. Which he already knew.

Shang climbed the stairs back up to her and sat on the top one, only a foot or so away from her. Close enough that he could reach out and touch the tips of her slippers peeking out from her silk. His gaze never left her face.

"Why did you enter the fox spirit's mind last night?"

She stilled. "Who told you?"

"Feiyan told me."

Feiyan? How had she had the time to do so? Pa would have sworn her to secrecy, so why had she told Shang?

He lowered his face for a breath. "She thought I should know. She said it almost . . ." His eyes snapped to hers, burning black. "How could you be so careless?"

She drew back, her face hot. Her arms tightened around her legs, as if it could make her smaller and disappear. Her gaze fell from his face to his hand, planted on the floor, splayed out wide.

"I could not let the boy die," she mumbled.

"Meiling," he whispered urgently, leaning forward. "You are noble—the most noble person I know. But you cannot afford to be stupid. Understand?"

Her heart caught on the word *noble,* and something burst like a hundred butterflies from their cocoons in her stomach. But her mind caught on something else.

"Stupid?" she cried in a low voice. "How could I have known what would happen?"

"By simple deduction. If a fox spirit can devour a soul—and it can—then it can devour your soul entering its mind." His lips pursed tightly, his gaze flicking above her head to the railing, as if counting his seconds left. He blinked a few times, drew a deep breath. Exhaled. His gaze returned to her. "Promise me you will never enter another fox spirit's mind again."

Her brow furrowed, and she tilted her head to one side. "Promise? I cannot make such a promise. There must be a way around its enchantments—"

Shang reached out, pried one of her hands free of her knee and gripped it hard. She instinctively jerked back, but he tightened his icy hold. "Promise me," he pleaded urgently. "I need you to promise me, Meiling."

She stared at him, mouth agape.

Shuffling from below met their ears, mingled with the impatient grunt of the judge.

"I have to go," he growled, letting her hand drop. "I don't care who you're saving. Don't enter a fox spirit's mind. You cannot win."

He drew himself to his feet without another glance toward her and hurried back down the stairs, as fast as he had climbed them. Silently, he shut the door behind him.

Meiling stayed where she was, staring with parted lips at the empty stairwell.

CHAPTER 13

FORMER GENERAL TAN sent word of his arrival in Suguan, and Shang obtained special permission via Master Dong to leave his students early and visit him.

In many ways, this seemed a truer trial than the one he'd already attended. For his entire life, his father's approval had meant everything to him. He'd done *anything*, sacrificed anything, just for the chance of a warm word or the tiniest shred of a smile.

But then Meiling happened.

His perfectly ordered life had crumbled to pieces.

Now?

There were things he wanted that he was willing to sacrifice his father's approval for, and in that knowledge, Shang discovered that approval hadn't been worth much in the first place.

Still, it was a challenge to keep his heartrate steady as a servant let him into his father's Suguan mansion. He had to keep a rein on his emotions and focus on his goals: stop the marriage arrangements before they got too far and explain that he was going to be executed in a few days for failing a special mission from the emperor.

This wasn't going to go well.

General Tan was taking his afternoon tea in an outdoor pavilion, despite the cold. Shang kept his face blank as his father's ramrod-straight back came into view. Gray hair streaked the older man's long hair and beard, but at sixty-five years old, he was still as tall and strong as ever.

He didn't smile when Shang bowed and sat on the cushion across the low table. He didn't offer a greeting as the servant bent and poured Shang a cup of tea. It wasn't until the servant was finally out of earshot that the former general settled his penetrating gaze on his son.

"Why were you so late in responding to my letters?"

"I was not in Suguan, my lord. I responded once I returned."

"Why were you not in Suguan?" the general demanded, small but potent shards of anger in his tone. "Your appointment is in Suguan. Where else could you have been?"

Shang kept his voice neutral and calm, his expression blank, and his emotions detached. "I was on a personal errand for the emperor."

"What errand?"

"I am not at liberty to say."

The general's brows narrowed. "Are you telling me you got involved with Secret Services?"

"No, my lord. It was a personal errand for the emperor, not for the Secret Services."

"I don't like that patronizing tone, Shangdi. It was a fair question."

Well, Shang didn't like the general's tone either. He didn't offer an apology, instead leaning forward and letting just a touch of coldness into his expression. "I didn't come here to be interrogated, Father. I came because I am delivering news, the first of which is this: you must cancel the marriage arrangements. I won't—"

The general's hand slammed onto the table. "Cancel the marriage arrangements? They're all but finalized! Is it the girl? I don't see any objection to her! I've seen her myself and she's a pretty little thing. Smart too, with a pure ice lineage. There's nothing—"

"I'm sure she's wonderful, but I—"

"Then marry her! Don't tell me you've gotten some foolhardy notion into your mind about securing your own marriage. I've told you since you were a child that I would be arranging it and you've never had an objection your entire life!"

Shang dropped his voice, leaning forward onto the table, and said with deathly calm, "Let me finish."

The general's mouth dropped open, shock almost immobilizing him. Shang had never talked back or interrupted. Even now, it went against every instinct inside him, which told him to placate his father, to show respect and obeisance.

"I will explain everything if you would let me," Shang continued quietly, taking advantage of his father's shock before he recovered enough to explode into anger. "I have many reasons for refusing this marriage, but the one worth mentioning is that I . . ." He swallowed, his composure fracturing just a hair. It was easier to think the words than say them aloud. "I am to be executed after the last day of the festival."

Sure, there was still a chance he'd be pardoned, but after today's trial, it appeared less likely than ever.

If the general had been shocked a moment before, now he was completely stunned.

"The errand was a failure," Shang continued, gentling his tone. "It was not my fault, but the cost of failure was our lives. The emperor has put us—me and my comrade—on trial. We do not anticipate being acquitted."

The general's teacup rattled when he set it down, orange tea sloshing over the sides.

Shang had never pitied his father until this moment. "I'm sorry to be the bearer of such ill news. You understand now why I must reject the marriage arrangement."

A broad, muscular forearm swept across the table, smashing teacups, saucers, and teapots into the pavilion wall. "Understand?" the general bellowed. "I understand nothing! What do you mean, this errand was a failure? What do you mean, it wasn't your fault? If it wasn't your fault, you'd be acquitted already!"

"You know that is not how it works."

"Do I? Do I, Shangdi?" He shot to his feet, coming around to Shang's side of the table as though to grab him. "I ought to kill you myself!"

Shang darted out of the way, lightly stepping out of the pavilion, and noted his retreat options if his father decided to execute his threat. "I gave everything," he shouted, despite knowing nothing would convince his father. "I broke out of Liafugen without getting caught. I fought in Butagin. I escaped Fang Zedong's own fortress dungeon with two of his captives. *By myself.* But you would say—"

"It is not enough!" The general filled the entrance to the pavilion, ice gleaming in his fists. "You should have fallen on your own sword instead of coming back here in disgrace! Does the Tan name mean nothing to you?"

Why did Shang even bother? He should have just let his father discover with everyone else that his only heir was being executed. The marriage arrangements would have been halted naturally.

He'd *known* this was how his father would react, and yet it cut like shards of ice into his chest. Maybe part of him had hoped he'd been wrong, that his father loved him more than his reputation after all. That he wasn't just an heir to continue the family lineage, but a dear son.

Well, he had his answer now. Despite that, he hated how they would end their last time seeing each other, Shang was glad he knew the truth. And he was glad that, for once, he hadn't bent his knee to someone who didn't deserve it.

Shang turned his back on the general and marched away. "Goodbye, Father."

"Stop right there—or you're no son of mine!"

There was the inevitable disinheritance. Shang didn't stop.

"The errand had to do with the princess, didn't it?"

Shang stopped. Slowly turned. The general still stood in the pavilion's entrance, his severe face a thunderstorm. "I told you, I'm not at liberty to say."

"You rescued her from Fang's fortress, didn't you?"

With a long exhale, Shang ignored the general's question and kept walking. His father had always had his own spies around the palace. It was no surprise he'd heard of Meiling's capture and subsequent rescue. He'd known about all the missing wielders when so few people did.

"You escorted her back to Suguan, didn't you? And you didn't keep your proper distance, *did you*?"

Don't let him provoke you. Nothing he says matters. Nothing—

"No wonder you've lost everything for our family! She's brought her curses down on you. She's a witch, that girl, and she's going to—"

Shang's control snapped. He whirled on his heel. "Princess Meiling is the daughter of your sovereign, and deserves your respect, *Father*."

"Respect?" the general bellowed, storming down the steps of the pavilion toward where Shang stood his ground on the walkway. "That little minx should have been cast out a decade ago when her magic didn't develop! It's her curse that is bringing the barbarians down on us!"

Shang's voice lowered to a lethal snarl. "Princess Meiling is the best person I have ever known, and she might be the only truly innocent person in that palace. I will not tolerate you speaking ill of her."

The general stopped, shocked for the third time. He recovered quickly, shaking it off and replacing it with menacing fury as he growled, "She has *bewitched* you, boy. You've fallen under her thrall. No wonder you're not yourself—you're not seeing clearly!"

There was no reasoning with him. No understanding. It had always been orders that Shang was expected to follow. There was no point in arguing further. He'd accomplished what he set out to do. So he left, his father's angry tirades slamming into his back, as he muttered under his breath, "I've never seen clearer in my life."

If the first night of the Festival of New Lights was Meiling's favorite, the second night was her least favorite.

Painted and arranged until her maids clucked with satisfaction, Meiling rose and looked at her face in the mirror. Red dots lined her brow, reminiscent of the queen who wouldn't be in attendance tonight.

She drew in a deep, fortifying breath, her hands trembling slightly. She wasn't ready for the stares and whispers. The people who shuffled out of her way, fearful of her shadow falling upon them.

"It doesn't matter," she muttered to herself, straightening her shoulders. Her maids trailed by twos after her as she glided out of her bedroom and through the palace hallways. She had faced brigands and Fang Zedong, *mó guǐ* and hard journeys on unforgiving terrain. She'd been on the brink of death several times now. A few courtiers were nothing.

So why were her palms so dragon-blasted sweaty?

The doors opened before her.

"Princess Meiling," the crier announced.

Meiling smiled, swallowing her blanch at the sight of the room. This was the same feasting hall from last night, but the silk partitions were tied back, leaving the room vast. Doors opened into the night, giving guests the opportunity to meander through starlit gardens and admire the moon reflected in gurgling fountains and lily-filled pools.

So many people.

Robes of all colors glittered under a thousand candles. Brilliant sashes gleamed. Chatter filled the room as Meiling slipped inside and searched for a familiar face.

Pa was seated on the dais toward the far side of the room, visible to everyone. He sipped from a goblet, his attention diverted by a few fancy-dressed courtiers who dared approach him. She longed to join him, perhaps even take Ma's empty seat, but she restrained herself. Princes and princesses must socialize.

Except no one wanted to socialize with Meiling.

Where were Hou and Yun? She found herself backing into a wall, trying to find a niche to snuggle into. Why was she breathing so hard? Unconsciously, she fidgeted with her sash, but stopped herself the moment she realized what she was doing. Her stomach churned when Pa's eyes flicked toward her, his brow furrowed slightly.

She was being a terrible princess.

There was Hou, dressed in a soft pink lined with beads and silver thread. She kept glancing down at her robes, tugging on her sleeves, and moving too fast for her headdress, making it rattle precariously. But she stood with several guardian daughters her age, chatting happily. Meiling drifted closer as she complained, "All this fancy getup is making me want to just rip it off. How am I supposed to fight in this?"

"You're a princess," laughed one of the girls. "You can hardly rip your ornaments off during a banquet."

Hou raised an eyebrow. "Watch me."

Meiling hurried forward, stepping next to Hou and trying to ignore the other girls casting her strange looks. "Sister," she said with a smile. "You look lovely. How was your combat class earlier?"

"Oh hullo, Meiling," Hou said, taking her hand away from her headdress, not noticing at first how her friends immediately tensed at Meiling's presence.

Meiling glanced quickly at the girls, and her heart dropped when each one bowed and made an excuse to take themselves off to another part of the banquet. It wasn't a surprise, but that sense of lostness returned to settle on Meiling's shoulders.

A familiar movement caught her eye, and she dragged her attention from the fleeing girls to find Shang dressed in a well-tailored, fine robe of dark blue, leaning against the far wall next to several other young men, goblet in hand, gaze flitting between Meiling and the girls.

Her stomach flipped over itself from the sudden influx of embarrassment and thrill. Shang's gaze met hers suddenly and fled away just as quickly. As though he hadn't meant for her to see that he watched her. He took a draught of his wine, then interjected something in the conversation. The other young men laughed in response.

"You scared them off," Hou said with a quirked eyebrow. "Not that I'm disappointed. Maybe I should bring you with me to the Academy. There are a few people I'd like you to scare off for me."

Meiling tore her gaze away from Shang. "Oh, well . . . I'm glad to help." She swallowed thickly. How dry her throat felt! "I can assure you I'm quite good at that."

Her traitorous eyes peeked at Shang again, who was looking down and smirking as one of the other men seemed to tell some story, waving his hands about in apparently funny gestures. Why was he even here? She assumed he would share only in the duties of the Academy masters, not also the honors and privileges.

Apparently, she was mistaken.

"Oh, look, it's that man from the other day," Hou nodded toward Shang, tossing a mischievous grin up at Meiling. "Fathers, but he is *so* handsome."

Meiling gave a little laugh, hoping Hou would not notice how forced it was, and rolled her eyes. "You're eleven."

"What? You're saying I'm too young to know when someone's pretty or ugly?"

Meiling shook her head, smiling.

Hou narrowed her eyes into a glare, daring. Challenging. Meiling laughed outright. She glanced at Shang as she did so, and his head jerked her way at the sound of her laugh. She immediately looked away. "Hou, what do—"

"Oh! I need to talk to that girl over there. And the boy I'm going to marry is next to her. Here, give this to a servant, will you?"

"The boy you *what*?" Meiling hardly had time to catch the sloshing goblet of punch thrust toward her before Hou scampered off, abandoning her in the middle of the room. As soon as Hou departed, the lightness in the air dissipated, and the world closed in around her.

So many people. So many faces—many she recognized, none she dared approach—all swarming about and laughing and socializing and doing *people* things.

Her breaths came shorter and shorter. She drifted toward a corner, depositing Hou's goblet on a servant's tray as she whisked past. She counted the minutes until the earliest possible moment of escape.

There was Fen with a rare smile on her face. She sidled up next to Shang, and the two began conversing. Even from where Meiling stood, hovering listlessly by the tapestries lining the wall near the door, she could see the way Fen's smile quickly vanished, how Shang's lips pursed.

She needed air.

Clear, cool, starlit air would open her lungs and prevent her from suffocating.

She stepped away from the wall she clung to, dodging around fluttering servants and trying to ignore the sideways glances and quick sidesteps out of her periphery. She gritted her teeth, focusing on her destination: the wide-flung doors open to the moon-bathed gardens.

Being born without magic was no crime. Unless one was a princess. Then it was a crime above all crimes.

Sticky, flowery perfume cloyed in her nostrils, and her robes clung to her skin in the oppressive warmth of several hundred bodies pressed close together. She stepped faster than she ought, evidenced by the clinking of the strung beads on her headdress. Perhaps she was swallowing back tears; she was too angry to notice.

If only they knew.

She should be thankful, should enjoy the happy laughter surrounding her. Had she heard such a joyous sound in Fang Zedong's prison? She should feast her eyes on the beauty of the bright, illustrious colors of the palace, filled with the loveliest shades from the occupants' robes. This place was alive, good. The very opposite of that rotting dungeon.

What was wrong with her?

Why could she not be happy with this beautiful life of hers?

It was because she was tired of being looked upon like a plague. A curse. She could never hurt any of the people in this room. Though she possessed the ability to enter their minds, harvest their secrets and shames—she could *ruin* these people with the secrets she unearthed—she would not do it.

A blast of chilly wind met her as soon as she reached the doorway. The chill prickled her neck and cooled her hot cheeks. She stepped through the line of guards, lifting her robes just slightly so she could step over the threshold into the fresh night air beyond the clogged room.

She drank in the stillness.

It was not entirely still, however. Whispers, scuffles of slippers and boots, and the trees and shrubs swaying in the wind filled the garden. The nights were growing colder and colder, and she wrapped her arms around herself, hugging in her warmth. Her teeth chattered.

It would not look good if she went and lost herself in the depths of the garden, hiding from the festivities. But no one wanted her here, anyway. They only *expected* her to be here.

She would tarry outside a little longer.

A set of stone stairs descended into the garden. As she took a step, the first notes of a flute from inside wafted out to her, above the laughs and conversation buzzing in the air. It swelled louder, and the further Meiling wandered down the pathways splitting around the large reflection pool, the clearer it sounded over the din.

The reflection pool was not large, but it was stuffed to the brim with lilies and lily pads. She chose the seat furthest from the colored paper lanterns hung around the garden. She leaned over the edge of the railing and touched the soft edges of a blooming white flower.

Voices carried to her ears. Male, edged with courtly refinement, mingled with battle hardness. Meiling sat up straighter, casting a quick look down the lane of budding cherry trees.

"It was successful, yes."

"And they are returning?" a second voice queried.

"Indeed. Tomorrow. It is a quiet reception, but the families of the captured have been informed. They are to be received around mid-afternoon, so the report said. Behind the palace, near the west gate."

"After all these years . . . Some of them will likely not be recognizable." There was a faint tsking sound, then a deep sigh. "Hearing the guardian had died was quite a blow. I still cannot believe it. The Zuan Wan I knew would never . . ." The voice trailed off, as if he was not quite sure what he intended to say.

There was silence for a long while. Meiling held her breath, her hand still hovering over the flower. When the voices resumed, they were too far away for her to understand. She strained, half-stood, considered going after them, but stopped at the sound of another voice. This one, from behind her. And too familiar.

"Eavesdropping?"

CHAPTER 14

MEILING'S BREATH WHOOSHED out of her lungs as she whirled. "Shang! You startled me."

The light from the palace was behind him, so it was hard to discern his exact expression—he was mostly a lump of formless tall shadow—but she got the impression that her admission pleased him somehow.

He leaned on the ledge of the pool, a good three feet or more from her. "You do a lot of sneaking these days. Figured I should keep up."

"Like you ever needed practice sneaking," she muttered, rolling her eyes.

A flash of white teeth in the darkness. Light caught on his profile, illuminating his smirk. Her throat suddenly went dry, and her chest constricted again like the air was suddenly thinner.

Was he teasing her?

She ducked her head. "Why have you followed me out here?"

"Followed you?" He raised his eyebrows, as though rebuffed by the suggestion, but the twinkle in his eye belied his words. "I merely came to catch some fresh air. And saw you crouched as though in wait for prey. It would be rude of me to not address the princess."

"Startling me can hardly be considered an address."

He grinned, returning his attention to the cherry trees. "Perhaps if you didn't react, I'd be less tempted."

She rolled her eyes and huffed.

"The second princess is lively," he said, changing the subject. "Not so much like you."

She laughed, tucking her icy fingers into her sleeves. They froze the flesh on her arms. "No. Not like me. We are all three very different. Apparently Hou has already decided who she's going to marry."

"Oh? Did you get a look at him? What is he—ten years old?"

Another laugh bubbled up in her throat. "I didn't, sadly. The crowd was too thick. I'd rather the boy be ten, because I have a suspicion this boy is probably closer to my age than hers."

"She should be careful," said Shang, picking up a stray twig and twisting it between his fingers. "She doesn't want to get caught up in some whirlwind romance with a young man of questionable intent. Many people will want her hand in marriage, and not for the right reasons."

"Pa has already gotten deluged in marriage proposals. For Hou. Yun looks out for her at the Academy, though it's usually more in a futile attempt to keep her out of trouble." She paused, then peeked sidelong at him. "What is it like to not have siblings?"

He tucked his chin into his chest, like he was looking at the ground, before lifting it up again. His nostrils flared in the darkness. "Stressful."

She remembered the memories she had uncovered in his mind, of his father's high expectations. Failure was not an option for him, and until her, he had never failed.

"I visited my father today," said Shang suddenly.

Meiling tilted her head, waiting and listening.

He sighed, then ran a hand through his hair. "I told him about the trial. Just so that he would have some warning before . . ."

Her stomach twisted into knots, and she was glad she hadn't eaten. The last thing she needed to be doing right now was vomiting into her lap.

"He was also arranging a marriage for me."

"What?" Meiling blurted, spinning in her seat toward him. The moment the word was out, in that horrified tone, she regretted it. *How obvious do you intend to be?* she rebuked herself. It shouldn't be a shock; he was of marriageable age. He could have been in a betrothal this whole time and she wouldn't have known—hadn't thought to ask.

His face was mostly shadowed, but there was just enough moonlight reflecting off the water to illuminate his single lifted brow.

"Would you congratulate me if I was to inform you of my impending nuptials?" he asked, and while the question was obviously intended to be playful, part of it felt . . . serious.

"I . . ." Meiling blinked, reaching up and twisting a strand of beads hanging from her hair. "Why—yes, of course. I would always congratulate you on . . . good . . . news. Now I might be concerned about the choice of pursuing a betrothal in . . . your current situation, but other than that . . ."

"You wouldn't be jealous?"

"Jealous? Wh-when did I say I'd be jealous? Why would I be jealous? It's your duty to marry your father's choice. Even better if you have some acquaintance and mutual respect for the young lady." Flustered, she folded her arms across her chest and glared into the dark expanse of the gardens.

"Oh?"

"Is this your way of tormenting me instead of simply telling me whether or not I am to congratulate you?"

"Is it truly a torment to not know if—"

"That's not what I meant, and you know it!"

Shang slid closer to her on the bench. "Then what did you mean?"

He had one arm on the back of the bench behind her shoulders, his knees tilted toward hers as he leaned in. For a moment, all rational thought left her mind, and she scrambled for some semblance of an answer. "I only meant that I was merely curious."

"Merely curious?" He studied her for a moment, and she could have sworn he was fighting a smile before she went back to glaring at the cherry trees. "Well, in that case, you'll be disappointed to learn I have no betrothal."

She spun toward him. "You don't?"

"I told my father to cancel the arrangements. For obvious reasons. Come now, you look very relieved after just declaring that you would be glad to congratulate me." His knee nudged hers while his lips twisted in a teasing smirk.

"No matter what I say, you're going to somehow twist my words back on me."

"Only because you're a delight to tease."

Heat rushed to her cheeks, and not even the freezing wind could calm their blazing fire.

"It's also a delight to watch you blush," added Shang, apparently in the mood to drive her to the absolute brink of her composure.

"I'm not blushing!" cried Meiling, hoping her vehemence would make up for the obvious lie. "And if I was, you wouldn't be able to see it, anyway. It's too dark. You're purposefully trying to rile me up. I know your ploys and they're not going to work."

He gave her chin a gentle chuck, making her stiffen. "Listen, I think I deserve the opportunity to tease you after you scared me out of my wits this morning."

"You weren't supposed to know! And I didn't *know* it was going to go so badly. I promise I wasn't trying to scare anyone, especially not you."

"I'm glad I know."

"I'm not."

With those declarations, they fell silent. She groped for more scraps of conversation to offer, but could think of nothing. Not while he sat so close, with the possibility of contact buzzing between them. When several minutes had gone by and neither of them said anything, she expected him to push off the ledge, tip himself in some distant bow, and stride off to somewhere else. Yet he stayed. She forced her eyes away from trying to read his profile to staring up at the stars. The night was much darker than last night, devoid of thousands of floating lanterns. She could see the stars, could make out a few constellations.

"Did you know the stars whisper?" Meiling asked.

He tilted his head her way. "I beg your pardon?"

She smiled, returned her gaze upward. "The stars. They talk. I assume to each other, though I cannot understand them. When I am asleep, I can hear them."

She'd never told anyone this. Not even Ma.

Shang's neck craned as he stared at the blinking stars. "There is an ancient legend that speaks of the stars." His voice was quiet and low, but tinged with a new tone she had never heard before. Could it be awe? "I figured most of it was not true, being passed down through thousands of years. People love to indulge in fanciful thinking and exaggeration. But . . . it said a man named Zhou was . . . They called him a dreamwalker. He walked among the stars, said they spoke in a language unlike any he'd ever heard, yet he could understand them. Legend says he became something like a god himself; knowing the deepest secrets of man and heaven alike."

At his words, her heart seemed to catch fire and burn within her breast. A dreamwalker? To walk among the stars . . .

Shang was looking at her. She couldn't look at him. Instead, she twisted and stared into the reflection pond, where the stars twinkled on the surface of the water between white lilies. "My tether is too short." Her voice sounded thin to her own ears. "I cannot get close to the stars." It felt like admitting a fault.

His chest rose and fell with a soft breath. "You might be the first in millennia to hear the voices of the celestial beings." He shook his head, suddenly smiling. He seemed to want to say more, but he only shook his head again. In—*disbelief*.

Meiling stared at him, and sunshine burst in her heart. Perhaps it was hope. Or maybe something else entirely. She could no longer feel her fingers or toes, but she didn't care. She was too warm to be cold.

Laughter burbled up from nearby, and she startled. Shang said nothing, but she could have sworn another smile tugged on the edge of his mouth. It was nice to pretend for the span of this conversation that his trial and Zedong's conquest didn't exist. For a beautiful moment, it was just them. Just Meiling, sitting with the best man she'd ever known.

"Let me bring you inside," he said, pushing off the ledge. "You look cold."

"Inside?" She drew back. "I'm not *that* cold."

"The more you hide from them, the more it will confirm their belief of what you are. You need to make them forget why they ever avoided you."

He said it so simply, but she didn't believe him. Fathers, the *effort* it would take to do such a thing! But she didn't want to argue with him; didn't want to explain why she could never fight their prejudice.

Instead, she stayed where she was and asked, "Can you get cold?"

Shang raised an eyebrow. "Yes, I can get cold."

"How do your hands not freeze off? Or get frostbite? Or turn black?"

He smirked, stood, and slipped her arm in his. She blushed, suddenly entirely without the will to protest further as he pulled her to her feet. "You cannot dissuade me by distracting me. You're shivering, and we're in public, so I cannot put my arm around you. Come inside."

Put his arm around her? She cursed everyone in the nearby vicinity for making the gardens *public*.

"Will you not answer my question?" she managed around the roaring of blood in her veins and the sudden muddling of her brain.

"My hands can tolerate extreme freezing temperatures. It's part of my magic. But it's only my hands. Very similar to your fire-wielding family members."

A good warrior will never tell you his weaknesses, Fen had said so long ago.

The flute carried through the open doors, warmth and light following it. Dread knotted in her stomach. The sound of rambunctious laughter—only a little tamed by the palace grandeur—drifted to her ears.

She pulled Shang to a halt, grabbing hold of his elbow with her other arm. He glanced down at her as she blurted, "We can't go in yet! I have more questions! Are there ever wielders who have abilities they cannot use because their hands—or whatever—cannot withstand the strain of their magic? Like if your hands couldn't tolerate the cold?"

"I've never heard of such a thing. Now quit stalling." He stepped up the first stair, giving her arm an insistent tug.

"Please don't make me go back in there," Meiling begged, surrendering to her desperation.

The lightness abandoned his expression, leaving nothing but sternness and a flexing jaw. "Why?"

"Because they don't want me! I don't belong in there—"

"You *do* belong in there," Shang growled, the muscles of his arm tightening against her fingers.

"Haven't you seen—"

"Belonging is about perception. As long as you believe you don't belong, you won't. But if you decide you *do* belong here, that this is your home and these are your people, eventually others will believe it too. Your perception shapes your reality. So choose what you want to perceive. Choose to believe you belong here."

With that, he dragged her up the stairs, not letting her savor her last bit of clear air before she was forced to choke on perfume, spices, and sweat, and pretend she didn't notice the judgmental stares in her periphery.

She looked up at him, but his gaze was set forward on the throng of people they approached. Warmth blasted her in the face when they reached the top step, surrounding her and making her numb fingers clench on his arm. She gave one last effort to slow them down, but he pulled her alongside him and stepped over the threshold.

Did the room go a little colder when they entered? Did the laughter die a fraction? Like a dozen candles went out in a flicker of smoke? She lowered her head instinctively, pretending to focus on holding her robes so she would not step on the hem.

"Lift your head," Shang whispered. "You listen to the stars sing while they sleep."

Meiling's breath caught in her lungs, but she obediently lifted her head. She met the eye of the master she had spied talking to Shang. Then she met the gaze of a guardian and looked his daughter straight in the face. She was one of the girls who had been talking to Hou earlier. They all looked away, but she kept her head up. It took effort, but she did it.

A thrill of determination snaked straight to her core. Maybe Shang was right. Maybe she didn't have to be a victim of what her people thought of her.

She could carve her own path.

"Let me introduce you to Master Dong," said Shang, moving just fast enough through the throng that courtiers couldn't dodge Meiling's shadow. By the time they'd reached the older master in black with a shaved head, one of the middle-aged ladies had tripped over her own robes in her haste. Shang had only barely restrained his smirk. Meiling could almost hear him mutter under his breath, "Serves her right." Then he bowed to Master Dong, who in turn bowed to Meiling. "Master Dong, may I present Her Highness, Princess Meiling."

"I am honored, Highness," said the master with a warm smile.

Meiling nearly gaped like a caught fish. This Academy master was *speaking* to her? Smiling at her? Giving her obeisance? "The honor is all mine," she squeaked, barely recovering herself.

"Master Dong took me under his wing many years ago," said Shang, pleasure radiating from his face as he glanced between them, pointedly ignoring the evil eyes from those around them. "He was the one who encouraged me to pursue a career in military strategy. You should ask him about his travels. Before he was a military strategist, he was an emissary."

"An emissary?" Meiling said, her interest immediately piqued. "Where have you traveled, Master Dong?"

"Oh, many places! Too many to name. But my favorites by far were the tropics. The Southern Isles—"

"You've been to the Southern Isles?" blurted Meiling, unable to help herself. "What were they like? I've heard they don't even have winters there!"

The portly man laughed, the skin around his eyes crinkling. "Indeed, they do not. They have rainy seasons and dry seasons instead. It's warm year-round. And I won't lie; every time our winter rolls around, I crave another visit to those sunny shores."

"Oh, I'm sure! They sound delightful!"

"They certainly are. The water is crystal clear as far as you can—"

"Crystal clear? Could you see fish?"

"We absolutely could. Whenever we sailed those waters, I spent hours leaning over the boat, watching the colorful fish below. Turtles, dolphins, stingrays, even sharks, too."

Meiling pressed a hand over her mouth, trying to stifle the urge to make an unladylike sound. "Oh, I would *love* to see that some day! It must be so beautiful!"

"Master Dong!" came a new voice. "It has been a long time, my old friend!"

Meiling turned as a stocky, middle-aged wielder with a close-trimmed beard and dressed in an unadorned set of robes approached them.

Shang gave a gentle tug on her elbow. "Let's go speak to Fen and see if she'll behave herself, eh?"

"Don't run away with the princess just yet," interjected Master Dong, after clasping hands with the newcomer. "I ought to introduce both of you to Lian Delan, federal investigator. Delan, this is Tan Shangdi and Her Highness, Princess Meiling. Highness, I thought you might be interested in meeting one of the people who had recently aided you in a significant way."

It took her a minute to process what the master was implying, especially since she didn't recognize this man. He meant that he'd played a role in her rescue. What role, she didn't know. Either way, she turned her attention to Delan. "I am gratefully indebted to you."

"I only wish we could have done more, Highness," said Delan, giving her a low bow. Why wasn't he recoiling from her? Did he know about her magic? He spoke with her like she was a regular princess. "I also wish I could introduce you to my two colleagues, but alas, one of them lives in Zushui right now and the other is supposedly in attendance tonight, though I haven't seen a speck of his sorry hide. He's probably too busy writing a sappy letter to his girl."

Meiling couldn't help her little giggle. "He sounds very sweet. Please send him my sincere thanks."

With that, Shang succeeded in dragging her away from the conversation. "Don't you know that when you are in social gatherings like this, you're supposed to talk to as many people as possible, say nothing of significance, and only feign interest in other people's conversation?"

He was teasing her again. Though his face was mostly controlled, she could feel his radiating pleasure, which in turn sent happiness to her toes. "Your mentor seems so interesting! I want to talk to him for hours about the places he's been to! It's a shame we were interrupted."

"See, you're breaking the rules. If you show this much genuine interest, you'll become a magnet for the people who love the sound of their own voice, which is a very dangerous place to be."

Meiling laughed outright. "Oh, come now, I don't mind so long as it's interesting!"

Her laugh seemed to ring through the banquet hall, bright and clear. Her neck prickled with sudden awareness, as though a dozen pairs of eyes snapped to her. She glanced up, found Pa's stare settled upon her from the dais.

He wasn't frowning. If anything, there was an unexpected lightness in his expression. His mouth softened. When Meiling's gaze met his, he smiled warmly at her.

She couldn't help but grin back.

Pa's attention shifted from her to the young man whose arm she clung to, and thoughtfulness pinched his brows. She looked away, cheeks heating. Was she being too obvious? She hadn't meant to forget herself, but she'd just talked to *two* strangers, and neither of them had treated her like she was cursed.

"If you keep smiling like that," Shang whispered, leaning down toward her ear, "I will have much more competition for the honor of being your escort."

"Don't be such a tease!"

"I'm only telling the truth."

He wasn't, and they both knew it, but the flattery pleased her, anyway.

They reached Fen, who was still standing against the far wall with a handful of young people who seemed to be former classmates. She was dressed up for the first time since Meiling had met her, though not in anything extravagant. She wore light paint, dark red robes, and a lovely carved wolf's head hairpin. When Meiling and Shang approached, she shifted from the conversation happening around her and actually *bowed* to Meiling.

"Highness," said Fen, with only a tiny thread of annoyance.

"Fen! I didn't have time to speak with you the day we arrived back, but I'm so glad to see that you have recovered well," said Meiling, inexplicably glad to see the grouchy shifter.

The young people flanking Fen mumbled excuses and started to wander off, which was more of a relief than embarrassment at the moment. Meiling's shoulders loosened.

"Highness, let me make introductions," said Shang sharply, and rattled off the name of each person trying to make their escape, forcing them to stop in their tracks. They hesitated to meet Meiling's gaze, but they bowed and offered respectful mutterings of, "Your Highness."

It felt like standing there while a parent forced their child to apologize. Meiling tried not to let her hands twist into her sash, nodding at each person and repeating their name back to them with a gentle, "It is a pleasure to meet you."

Shang released them, and then it was just the three of them. Like old times.

To Meiling's surprise, Fen was almost laughing. "They're still so scared of you," she said, and it wasn't clear which of them she addressed.

Shang's face had shifted back into his typical hardened mask, the remnants of a scowl edging his expression.

"So, you're doing better?" Meiling asked Fen tentatively.

Fen gave a shrug, growling, "As better as I can be."

"The students are giving her a difficult time in combat," said Shang.

Fen's head whipped to his, thunder immediately gathering on her brow. He only gave her the tiniest smirk back. Her glare soured. "Considering the circumstances, you're in an awfully chipper mood."

"He certainly has been," replied Meiling with a bright smile up at him.

Now it was Shang's turn for the merriment to wipe off his face, and in an instant, he was transformed back to the taciturn warrior who escorted her across Zheninghai twice now. She nearly giggled.

"But seriously," said Fen, forcing Meiling to swallow her giggles as she turned her attention to Shang and dropped her voice. "Have you thought of anything?"

Meiling's stomach immediately twisted.

Shang's biceps flexed beneath her fingers. "We discussed this last night."

"And you had nothing but prayers. What good is that brain if you don't put it to good use? Where did all your cleverness go?"

Shang's tone lowered to a simmer. "We *discussed* this."

Meiling translated this as: *Stop talking about this because you'll make Meiling worried and then she'll do something stupid in an attempt to save us.*

Just like that, the reality of their situation, the impending doom of Zedong's conquest, and the full desperation of this trial hit Meiling like a blow to her sternum. She managed to stay upright, to not visibly flinch, but Shang must have sensed her sudden trepidation, because he bid Fen a goodnight and escorted Meiling off in another direction.

Toward the exit.

"You've fulfilled your obligations tonight," Shang whispered. "You can flee now, if you so wish."

Moments ago, she wouldn't have wanted to leave. Now, however, the air closed around her lungs once more, the stink of perfume clogging her nostrils, the heat making her skin itch and crawl. She needed to get out of here so she could fly away.

She merely nodded, not trusting words to come out of her tight throat, and Shang took her straight to the doors guarded by a line of warriors. He summoned her waiting maids as her new escort.

Then he stopped. Looked down at her. His eyes ran over every inch of her face, coming to settle on her painted lips. His warm hand pressed on top of hers for a heartbeat, then unwound it from his elbow.

Meiling didn't know why her heart ached as he bowed and spoke with the same distant formalism she'd come to despise so vehemently.

"Goodnight, Highness."

CHAPTER 15

WHEN MEILING WAS back in her room, restlessness plagued her. She tried to calm her swirling mind by going to bed early, but she couldn't fall asleep. She *never* struggled with falling asleep. So to lie awake now, staring at her ceiling, unable to find the freedom she longed for each night, drove her nearly out of her mind.

All she could hear was a deep, rhythmic voice repeating over and over again.

Lift your head. You listen to the stars sing while they sleep.

She didn't just miss him. She *craved* being near him, and the night stretched so long before her. Despite her magical capabilities, she never wanted to invade Shang's privacy. She'd tried to keep herself from following him like a devoted puppy, prying into his conversations and thoughts.

But for all her noble intentions, she could hardly bear the separation.

The time they'd shared this evening wasn't enough. She wanted *more*. More time, more words, more gentle touch.

More of his smiles.

"There are so many bigger things to worry about," Meiling whispered to herself, careful to keep quiet lest one of the feral wielders guarding her door heard her. "But all you can think about is *him*. You're a fool. A stupid fool."

Feiyan would call her a fool. And yet, despite her own words, despite how stupid and pitiful she felt, Meiling didn't actually think she was a fool.

She was just a girl. A girl with feelings she didn't know what to do with, feelings that swallowed up everything else and left her tossing and turning in her bed. Frustrated tears built up behind her eyelids.

"You're so far away, but I want you closer. I just . . . I just want to talk to you." Quiet sobs shook her shoulders as she curled tighter into a ball. "I just want to talk to you."

But she couldn't leave her room now. It was too late at night. Her only option was to fall asleep, find him, and speak to him in his mind. Which, the last time she'd done that uninvited, he'd been furious.

Would he be furious now?

She sat upright, her tears staunched, and wiped the sleeve of her nightgown across the wetness of her cheeks. She didn't think he'd be angry now. Their relationship was a far cry from what it had been then. And if he wasn't furious, then *could* she speak with him? Could she relieve this ache in her chest?

Maybe he missed her, too.

"He might be angry," Meiling breathed quietly. "And if he is, then at least I'll know that I've been misreading him these last few days."

Her fingers trembled with nerves. Did she miss him enough to risk breaking her heart for a chance to be near him again? Another tear slipped down her cheek, but she dashed it away. Her heart was already breaking. There was little enough she had to lose.

There. She decided. If she could fall asleep, she would go find him, and if he was awake, she would go into his mind and see if he wouldn't kill her for it.

She laid back down, and as though by magic, was asleep in seconds.

"No one knows where Fang's army is," said Master Dong, gesturing at the map laid between him and Shang. "I met with the current strategists for hours yesterday, and they're operating as though blind. Not a single scout or spy has seen hide or hair of the army."

Shang rubbed his chin, his brow pinched. The flame from the flickering candles arranged on the desk cast alternating bursts of light and shadow on the map he studied. "Surely they're not suggesting that Fang is still in Butagin?"

"Oh, no, they know he's in Zheninghai. This is the unsettling part. While they cannot find the army, several abandoned campsites have been discovered. Well disguised, but for an army that big, they cannot perfectly cover their tracks."

A chill ran down Shang's spine. "Where was the last of these campsites?"

Master Dong pointed to the map. Right off the main pass leading to Suguan from the southeastern Butagin border. Just as Shang had predicted.

"I don't understand how we've lost his entire army," Master Dong growled. "The campsite suggested numbers very close to your estimate. Tens of thousands. You don't just *lose* that many men off the face of the map."

Shang steepled his hands, his vision blurring as he focused on his thoughts. "He has a powerful illusionist with him. Not one powerful enough to disguise an entire army, but Fang has learned to wield black magic. Princess Meiling has expressed concern to me that Fang was increasing in his ability to wield it even in the weeks she was his prisoner and was teaching it to his brigand army to expand their natural abilities."

"I never thought I'd see the day someone actually learned to master Wungfao." The older man shook his shaved head, tension lining his bowed shoulders. "It was banned for good reason. You sacrifice your soul and sanity for its power."

Shang's father had sat him down when he was but eight years old and explained to him everything he knew about the dark arts of Wungfao. He said the Academy would never teach him about black magic, and that it was imperative Shang knew of its existence.

But when Shang asked where black magic had originated, the general hadn't been able to answer him.

"So," Shang said, keeping his voice measured despite his erratic pulse, "Fang's army is confirmed to be on Zheninghai soil, marching toward Suguan. But no one can find it—we can only learn where it *has been*—and thus no one is confronting him."

"The emperor is readying his troops and increasing the city's fortifications. His bureaucracy isn't celebrating the festival at all but working tirelessly to prepare for battle. That was part of our meeting yesterday—discussing where to focus the city's fortifications."

"I hope they're not leaving the water unguarded," Shang interjected quickly, bending over the map again and pointing to a stretch between mountains, tracing it to the coast about a thousand li north of the capital. "There's a pass here that Fang could take that would cut east to the ocean. If we focus our efforts only on protecting our northern city borders, we'll be left vulnerable if he chooses a water attack."

"That's what I told them, and that's what they're doing."

There was an unusual note in the older man's tone that Shang had rarely heard coming from him. *Resignation.* Ice burned along his fingertips, responding to the cold knife of fear stabbing into his chest. "You don't think there's anything we can do except fortify the city and wait for Fang's attack?"

Master Dong let out a frustrated puff of air. "What are we supposed to do: attack an invisible army? The emperor has increased pass patrols, watches, scouts, and spies. If that doesn't help locate the army, then nothing will. And until we know where he is, we cannot find him."

Meiling could find the army.

The thought came unbidden, and it was more of a hunch than anything. But the more he thought about it, the more it made sense. In her body, she was susceptible to illusions just like the rest of them, but when she was using her magic, could she see past illusion? He bet she could.

But Meiling could only go so far from her body. Which meant if they were to find the army, they would have to set out on yet another journey. Shang couldn't go with her—not with his trial. And if Shang couldn't go with her, then who would? Almost no one knew about her magic. Would the emperor himself and Meiling travel together unprotected through the wilderness of Zheninghai, hunting for the missing army?

He dismissed the idea with a shake of his head. "Maybe we don't need to know where he is now. We know where he's going. We can set a trap."

Master Dong was already shaking his head, a bead of sweat sliding behind his ear, despite the cold. "There isn't enough time. If we had weeks, we could set an effective trap, evacuate the non-wielders via the sea. But we only have *days*. It's a race to fortify the city."

I need to get Meiling out of here. He raked a hand through his hair, cursing under his breath. She wouldn't flee with him. She'd insist upon staying, and he'd simultaneously admire and hate her for it.

"Well," said Shang, breaking the silence after several long minutes. "Thank you for the update."

"I wish it was a more pleasant one."

"That makes two of us," Shang muttered, getting to his feet.

"Now, just a minute there. You cannot leave yet."

Shang paused, knees bent, then slowly extended his legs, so he stood to his full height. That was yet another unusual tone coming from Master Dong. His hackles rose, but for an entirely different reason than before. He knew exactly what his mentor was about to bring up. "Yes?"

"No one thought to inform me what a delight the cursed princess is," said Master Dong, a knowing glint in his eye.

Shang bit back a retort.

"She's a pretty little thing. Has a lovely form, too."

Shang clenched his jaw, calling moisture in the air around his hands and freezing it subtly against his palms. As if that would cool his face, his hot ears. *Keep your composure. Keep your composure. Don't reveal anything on your face.*

He didn't want to listen to anyone comment on Meiling's physical appearance. As if she wasn't so much more than that. As if he wasn't already *very thoroughly* aware of her beauty. It had been hard enough to note the many young men in the room taking notice of Meiling tonight for likely the first time. How could they not? When she forgot herself, when she was just the lovely, interesting, engaging, and personable woman she was, she wasn't so easily overlooked.

Shang had been sure to shoot a potent glare at each and every young man giving the princess a once-over. They couldn't spurn her and then suddenly decide her beauty outweighed her curse.

"Thank you for putting her at ease," he said, shoving aside his stronger emotions in turn. "She doesn't usually enjoy social settings."

Now it was time to leave, before this conversation took a tur—

"I saw how you looked at her."

Shang halted, halfway to the door. *Spitfire.*

"You didn't break out of Liafugen, travel all the way to Butagin, and go through the seven layers of *diyu* to rescue her so you would have more clout in your trial."

Shang didn't answer.

"I'm glad for it," Master Dong rumbled. "I always feared you had too much of your father in you. Are you going to tell her you love her?"

"No," he said quickly, too quickly.

"Why not?"

"Because I am going to die. One way or another."

The older man shook his head, a huff escaping his fat nostrils. "How about you find a way to live?"

Shang turned slowly. "Are you suggesting I flee Zheninghai?"

"Suguan might not be standing in a fortnight. You could take your princess to the Southern Isles and let her feel the warm sand between her toes."

Could you see the fish? Oh, I would love to see that some day! It must be so beautiful!

Shang shook the memory of Meiling's voice out of his mind, hardening himself. "You think Fang will be content once he's conquered Zheninghai?"

"No, but Zheninghai is a big empire. It'll keep him occupied for a while, I think. Even if he has a vendetta against you and the princess, he likely wouldn't be able to pursue. You could settle somewhere. Marry the girl. Have a few children."

The back of his neck turned the temperature of a furnace, even as his heart wept with longing, and his mind conjured visions of white sand beaches, Meiling as his wife, having *children* with her.

If they fled, there would be no return. Even if Fang didn't succeed, if Suguan didn't fall, fleeing meant giving up his chance of pardon. Without a pardon, anyone could execute him on sight.

Meiling might harbor some affection for him, but would it be enough for her to give up *everything*—her home, her family, her future, her people—for them to start afresh in another land?

"I'll consider it," Shang said briskly, then bid a hasty goodnight and strode out of his mentor's office before the man could fluster him any further.

Biting winter met him as he made the trek to his room, his mind a thunderstorm he tried to calm with even breaths. He focused on the cold gnawing through his robes, the wind whipping at his hair, the sound of creaking wood beneath his boots. Now was not the time to let his imagination, his personal desires, get in the way of thinking clearly. He forbade himself from thinking about Meiling, replaying any moments with her over in his mind, or imagining new ones. He needed to recover his composure.

Fen. He should think about Fen. About her plight, her family's plight if they lost her.

Maybe if he fled to the Southern Isles with Meiling, he'd need to bring Fen along. What a trio they'd make again!

There, that calmed his imagination down. Sticking Fen right in the middle of his fantasy of Meiling and their children on a faraway island beach definitely cooled his blood and helped his mind to dismiss it.

Focus on the icy wind. My breath, slow and steady—

Shang? came a sudden, squeaking voice in his mind.

He nearly leapt out of his own skin. Outside, he didn't flinch a muscle, but inside, panic flooded him like a tsunami. Meiling was in his mind. Oh fathers, Meiling—

Sorry, sorry, sorry! she gasped in a rush. *I'm so sorry—please don't hate me!*

I don't hate you. Of course I don't hate you, Shang assured quickly, half-terrified by what she might have already seen in his mind, half-terrified she might misinterpret the frantic upswell of emotion in his mind. He needed to breathe, to focus on his breath, on the wind, the cold. *What are you doing?* he demanded, trying to keep his tone from being too sharp. *What's wrong? Are you alright? Are you hurt?*

Nothing is wrong, she said quickly. *I'm fine. I just wanted to talk to you.*

Talk to me? he repeated, swallowing hard and stuffing down his emotional response to those simple words. It had always been unnervingly intimate to have someone in his mind, able to read his thoughts and search through his memories. But usually, those moments had been desperate moments of high stress. Moments when they had a problem they were working together to solve. Moments when he wouldn't easily betray his inner thoughts and feelings.

I . . . yes, she replied hesitantly, doubtlessly reading his balk at the idea of having a regular conversation in his mind. *I can't leave my room,* she protested quickly. *Otherwise, I would have. If this makes you uncomfortable, I can—*

I'll come to your room, Shang replied.

You—what?

I'll come to your room. We can talk there. Leave your window open and have a blanket ready for me. A blanket—to conceal what they could of his scent. *You have two feral wielders guarding your door tonight, right?*

I . . . yes.

One with augmented smell, the other with augmented hearing, right?

How did you know?

Shang smiled despite himself, fighting to keep his heart from skipping a beat as he veered off course, heading toward the palace instead of his room.

I don't know why you still surprise me, Meiling said with an adorable huff.

The traitorous thought was out before he could stop it. She went so quiet in his mind, if he didn't know better, he might have thought she'd left. This wasn't fair—her being able to hear his thoughts while he couldn't even read her body language for cues of hers.

I'll wait for you, she said, and he could almost hear the blush in her voice. *Are you sure you won't get caught?*

I won't get caught. I'll be there shortly, he promised. It might still take him a few minutes to time things right with the guards, but he didn't anticipate it being long.

I'm leav—

Her voice cut off abruptly as she left, and Shang nearly slumped with relief. Hopefully, he hadn't given too much away. If he was going to tell her his feelings, he wanted to do so when they were together in person—not her accidentally stumbling across it in his mind.

Not that it would come as a shock either way. Surely, it was obvious to her by now that he was hopelessly in love with her.

Shang quickened his step, even while this eagerness was tempered by the rational side of his mind. If he was caught trying to sneak into the princess's quarters, this would be it for him. He'd be cut down without a thought.

But Meiling wanted to talk to him.

And Shang wasn't going to get caught. He was a dead man walking, anyway.

It was *absolutely* worth the risk.

CHAPTER 16

MEILING HAD NEVER agreed to anything more scandalous in her entire life. She woke herself in a flurry of giddiness, realized she was in her nightclothes, and nearly had a seizure trying to decide if she had enough time to dress—or if so much movement would alert her guards.

In the end, she opted to put on two dressing gowns, one over the other, because that felt just frumpy enough to not be completely clandestine.

She pulled a quilt out from under her bed and carried it to the window. She usually slept with the window open, but it had gotten cold enough that it was shut most of the time these days. With shaking fingers, she worked the latch and pushed open the shutters. Cold air rushed in to swallow her whole. She bounced on the balls of her feet, considering donning one more dressing gown, and stared out her window. Each movement made her heart leap, be it tree branches rustling in the wind, a patrol's shadow, or a drunken courtier finding their way home after a long night of celebration.

He was so stealthy she didn't spot him until he had climbed halfway up the wall to her room. He stayed completely in the shadows, utterly silent, and didn't even use a rope to aid his progress.

The moment one powerful hand clamped down on her windowsill, fear shot through her. This *was* Shang, right? What if she'd just stood here while an intruder—

He hauled himself up into a crouch on the sill, filling the space with his broad shoulders. With the moonlight at his back, he was nothing but a silhouette. A warrior made of shadow.

Meiling's lips had parted at some point. She didn't need to hear his voice or see his face. Every last misgiving fled her. She was left with a beating heart and a sudden, unexpected shyness.

He'd come. He was here.

And this was *so* clandestine.

Meiling held up the blanket with stiff arms. He took it with a silent nod and wrapped it around his shoulders as he eased his feet to the floor, not making a sound, and ducked out of the window's view. He slid into a seated position, stretching his long legs in front of him, and silently beckoned Meiling to sit too.

She sat cross-legged, facing him with her back against her bed. Her knees were only a couple of inches away from his feet. His *bare* feet. Weren't they cold? "Do you—"

Shang made a sharp motion, cutting her off. He leaned forward, his handsome face illuminated in silver. He pointed to his lips and mouthed: *"Don't talk. Guards."*

Oh. He was right. Her guard might overhear whispers with their feral hearing abilities. She scratched her head, suddenly nervous. Then she pointed to his feet. *"Cold? Need stockings?"*

A smirk twisted the corner of Shang's mouth. He shook his head.

She flashed him a dubious look, then, too quick for him to stop her, she poked his foot. His leg gave a small, surprised jolt, but she was too busy glaring and waving her finger at him. *"Your feet are ice!"*

He rolled his eyes, shaking his head, the tiny smile still there.

No one can make him smile like I can, Meiling thought with a burst of pleasure.

"Maybe you should warm them," Shang mouthed, cocking one daring brow.

She wrinkled her nose in disgust. He grinned. But his grin slipped just slightly when Meiling took the edge of her extra dressing gown and draped it over each of his feet. *"There. Now you won't get frostbite."*

His gaze shifted from studying her mouth to her eyes. He didn't respond to her teasing, only tilted his head to one side. *"What is on your mind? You said you needed to talk."*

"Oh. Yes." She found herself fiddling with the sash of her topmost dressing gown. She'd been bold enough to go into his mind. Couldn't she at least have the guts to be honest about why? She squeezed her eyes shut, then peeked one open hesitantly as she blurted, *"It's nothing important. I just missed you . . . Sorry."*

Shang stared at her. A furrow appeared between his brows. *"What?"*

He hadn't understood her? Of all things for her to have to repeat! *"I missed you."*

The furrow deepened. He shook his head once, then leaned forward, tapping his ear. *"Try whispering it very quietly in my ear."*

In his ear? It made sense.

But that involved getting very, very close . . .

Biting her lip and shoving away the thundering beat of her heart, Meiling got to her knees and carefully, quietly, scooted closer to him. He bent forward, tilting his ear toward her, but she nearly lost her balance trying to lean close enough. She caught herself with both hands on his chest, and when he didn't react beyond his ribcage expanding with a deep breath, she just pretended she didn't have her hands on him as she leaned the rest of the way to his ear. As quietly as she was able, she breathed, "I missed you."

When she pushed back enough to see his face, there was color in his cheeks, but he was still frowning. Had she whispered it *too* quietly? Dragons blast those guards and their stupid hearing abilities. She leaned forward once more, opened her mouth to whisper, and that was when she felt it: his heartbeat slamming against her palm.

"Shang!" she hissed. "You heard it the first time!"

A slow grin split his face as the color of his cheeks brightened. He wrapped a muscular arm around her waist, pulled her against his chest, and buried his near-silent chuckles in her shoulder.

"What are you doing?" she whispered, hardly daring to breathe as his other arm wrapped around her.

He lifted his head, bringing his mouth to her ear. His low voice tickled down her spine. "I'm flirting with you. I think it's only fair, considering that you dragged me away from much-needed sleep to risk my life so you could ask me if my feet were cold."

"That is *not* a fair characterization!"

He chuckled silently, and it rumbled from his chest into hers. "Would it satisfy you to know that I missed you, too?"

"You did?"

His ribcage expanded with another deep breath that stirred her hair when he released it. "I miss you even now, Mei, and you're still right here."

The nickname, whispered so softly, struck her so hard she couldn't cobble together a response. In the wake of that shock, she slowly processed the rest of his words. Strangely, she knew exactly what he meant.

So she reached up, wrapped her arms around his neck, and buried her face in his shoulder. He tightened his grip in response, breathing harder, and slid one hand to cup the back of her head. Freezing wind filled her room, ruffling curtains and bedsheets and silk partitions, but she had never been so warm in her entire life.

"You're driving me mad." A growl edged his low, nearly silent voice. "From the beginning, you've driven me to the brink of my sanity. I'm losing my mind, Meiling, and the fathers know I don't want it to be found again."

"I'm . . . sorry?" she squeaked.

A huff of amusement escaped him, and he twisted his head toward hers. His lips pressed against her temple in a brush of a kiss. The world seemed to halt—neither of them breathing. Neither retreating. Maybe he was as desperate as she was for this little pocket of wonder and perfection to last for hours. With more purpose, he kissed her forehead. A shaky, half-stunned breath escaped her.

"Would you come with me?" he asked. "If I left Zheninghai?"

She froze. Every ounce of heat leeched from her body. Was this about the trial? It didn't sound like him at all. "You're leaving?"

"I might—but only if you came with me."

She didn't want to leave. It felt like giving up, like stepping aside and allowing Zedong to ravage her home, her family, her people. But also, if Shang was condemned to execution, fleeing was his only hope of survival—and if he wouldn't go without her, then her choosing to stay was choosing for Shang to die.

How was she supposed to answer him?

He shifted slightly, but didn't ease how tightly he held her against him. "Don't answer that. It was selfish of me to ask."

"I'm sorry. I would need to think—"

"Shh, don't make yourself anxious about it. Forget I said anything."

This didn't seem like the Shang, who was always angry at her for risking her life. Why didn't he plead with her to stay safe, to run away with him where she'd be safe from Zedong?

She saw your body. On the floor of the throne room.

Dead.

She shivered. "Shang? What's wrong?"

His response was an almost inaudible groan, and his head slumped against hers, his mouth resting against her ear.

"What's wrong?" she demanded, her fear making her voice just a hair louder than it should be.

"Everything." Shang's words came out in a rush, as if he'd longed to confide in her for weeks. "I feel like the entire world rests on my shoulders, Mei. This trial has barely begun, and it's going even worse than I expected. Even if my life is spared, Fen's won't be. Her family is dirt poor and relies almost completely on the money Fen sends back. If she is executed, they will be destitute. Fang is coming straight to Suguan. No one is stopping him. Few people know just how dire the situation is, but it is dire indeed. There's nothing I can do in my position. And my father—my *father*.

"He flew into a rage today when I refused to go through with this marriage and told him about the trial as my excuse. He has always been a difficult man, but he rarely loses his temper like he did today. And then there's *you*. You and your absolutely infuriating determination to get yourself killed—all for good reasons, of *course*. You and your utter disregard for your own safety. Then there's your secret and the maddening way everyone treats you as though you have the plague. There are those idiots at the festival tonight, my own father's ignorant and degrading comments about you, and so many more.

"I have always believed in taking matters into my own hands," he continued, nearly breathless, agony painting the timbres of his voice. "But there are many things outside of my control. Things I can do my best to affect, but that ultimately aren't in my hands. Like *you*. Like this trial, Fen's family, my father, Zheninghai. *I can't save everyone*, Meiling, and it makes me feel like a dragon-blasted failure."

She understood. Far better than he probably imagined. She knew those tangles of helplessness deep within her own heart. And she understood better than almost anyone what it was like to be too small for the problems of the world.

Words of reassurance seemed too paltry a comfort. Instead, Meiling offered what was more honest. She tilted her head just a fraction, enough to press a kiss to his jaw. What it lacked in duration, it made up for in earnestness and sincerity.

Shang's fingers dug into her scalp. "You're not helping me resist the temptation to spirit you away from here—against your will, if I must."

"Oh Shang, you don't—"

His body went taut as a bowstring. Then, quick as a flash of lightning, he scooped an arm under her legs and deposited her on the floor. He was on his feet the next second with a glance toward the door. Lungs squeezing, Meiling scrambled up beside him.

He caught her face between both hands, his black eyes seeming to swallow her whole. *"Tell them you were talking to yourself. Leave the window open for a few minutes."* With that and a last, unexpected kiss to her forehead, he unwound the blanket from his shoulders and wrapped it around her shivering frame. He hopped up on the windowsill, jaw clenching as he studied the ground below, waiting. Waiting for a guard to continue his patrol? His gaze shot back to her door, as though measuring what time he had left.

Silent as a panther, he swung himself over the edge. He shot her one final look, a look that rooted her in place and refused to let her breathe.

Then he was gone.

The door of her chambers swung open, and Meiling feigned surprise as she turned toward her two guards. "Is something wrong?"

"Are you alright?" the younger one demanded, his companion sweeping the room for threats. "I heard voices."

She swallowed the rock in her throat. "Oh, sorry. I was just talking to myself. I didn't mean to cause any alarm."

Their doubt was written across their faces. They were good men. Good guards. They knew her voice from another's, her scent from another's. But she was also their princess, and they dared not question her. Even if the window was open and had turned her chambers to ice.

She lifted her chin and said more forcefully: "I couldn't sleep, so I opened the window. Thank you for checking on me. I'm sorry again for causing alarm. You are dismissed."

She left no room for them to ask further questions, and since she was obviously hale and whole, the two men retreated, shutting the door with a firm thud behind them. Once they were gone, she pulled the blanket tighter around her shoulders and peered out the window.

There was no sign of Shang.

She let out the breath she'd been holding and shut the window. She made her way back to bed but didn't set the blanket aside. It smelled like him now. Like winter and warmth. She wrapped herself up in it and for the second time in years, didn't use her magic when she fell asleep. Dreams caught her up like a boat on a sea of oblivion and she let them rock her gently until dawn.

CHAPTER 17

SHANG SHUT HIS door and leaned against it, finally letting out the long, low groan he'd been holding in for what felt like ages. He'd almost told her everything. The admission of his love and affection had been on the tip of his tongue.

But then she hadn't been able to answer his question.

Even though she was so desperate to save him from the doomed outcome of this trial, she had hesitated when given the option to run away with him.

She'd *hesitated*.

An understandable reaction, considering the sheer magnitude of what she would have to give up. He would never blame her for hesitating.

That didn't lessen its sting.

Have I misread her so egregiously? Have I completely misinterpreted her partiality toward me?

He might have feared that her care was more platonic, but she hadn't rebuffed him at any point. Not when he flirted with her, touched her, or even when he'd kissed her tonight. She'd sought him out because she'd missed him after spending over an hour almost exclusively in his company. That meant something.

Perhaps she just didn't love him as much as he loved her.

The thought nearly broke him into pieces. He closed his eyes, returned his focus to his breath. Whether his affection was returned, either in part or in whole, didn't change anything. There was nothing he could do but continue loving her with what little time they had left.

If she decided she wanted to run away with him, he'd be waiting with open arms.

Otherwise, he'd take his stand in Suguan.

And die.

There was no parade on the third day of the Festival of New Lights.

Meiling, wearing black with a gauzy veil over her face, followed Pa, Ma, and Yun up the stairs toward Suguan's pagoda. Hou trailed behind her, stomping louder than a princess ought. Louder than a warrior too, for that matter.

She did not want to stare, but her neck craned upward anyway at the towering eaves jutting out from the building. It was beautiful, like the palace.

But unlike the palace, she only came here once a year.

The city was quiet.

Guards lined the stairs, and silent crowds arrayed in black watched their sovereign climb to the door of the pagoda.

Today was the Day of Cleansing. Today was for the penance of sin, for making anew. Later, the people would throw themselves into a frenzy of cleaning. The palace was always a busy place on this day, with servants crawling in every nook and cranny.

A cold wind gusted from the mountain and blew the edges of her robes, veil, and sleeves, but she kept herself from rubbing her arms to keep warm. She maintained her posture, kept her head lifted.

Something plucked on the edges of her senses, shot down her spine, and raised the hairs on her neck. She fought the urge to crane her head, to look for something she could not name. She exhaled impatiently; of *course* she was being watched.

But why was there this niggling sense that it wasn't the crowds that watched her?

She was only nervous. Everything was a little strange on the Day of Cleansing, anyway. When one was expected to reflect on all their sins of the past year, to conceive of brilliant plans to be a better person in the coming year, how could one not feel a little strange?

This day, the sins she must atone for were far worse than the sins of any year prior.

Gooseflesh raised on her arms. Her eyes darted to either side, as far as she could without tilting her head. Nothing.

It felt like the night she had visited Feiyan and had wandered down the deserted, darkened passages of the palace alone. Like something crawled on the brink of her senses, perhaps something not entirely physical.

Guards flung open the double doors, and she stepped inside behind Yun, keeping in file. She dared not turn to look at Hou. Pa went forward, striding forward into the golden room toward the brasier in the center. He took the torch from where it lay next to the brasier and lowered it to light the incense.

Spices and perfume filled the air. It was a mostly pleasant smell, rich with cardamon, myrrh, and frankincense. But at the very end of each inhale, a trace of repugnance wrinkled her nostrils.

Black-robed priests with shaved heads chanted something in a language she did not understand, and habit made her sink to her knees on the reflective gold floor. When she looked down, she was met with a visage of her black veil. She looked like a phantom.

Meiling bowed her head with her siblings, but something caught her vision.

She poked her head up toward the brasier. The flames licking up the incense flickered low, vanishing into black smoke.

A face appeared in the smoke; a twisted, mangled smile and maniacal eyes. The gasp was stolen from her lungs as the face vanished. Orange flames burst forth again, hungrier than before.

She cast a glance to either side of her and found her family still keeping their heads down respectfully. They hadn't seen it.

Had she seen it?

She swallowed, lowered her gaze. Stared down at the veiled face in polished gold. She shivered. The cold was why she trembled, why she wanted to huddle deeper into her cloak.

Her heart never slowed. Not until they had finished their penance and retreated from the towering pagoda. Not until she tore out of the clinging black garments and dressed herself in something warm and colorful.

Her mind was probably still processing the trauma of her captivity. That was why she kept seeing strange things. It was only her mind, playing tricks on her.

That was why she'd seen Fang Zedong's face in that brasier.

"Was the paint truly necessary under the veil?" Meiling scowled, scrubbing away the morning's paint. It would be simpler to leave it when she went to the trial, but it felt about as strange and cumbersome as a tottering headdress. Truly, as a princess, she ought to be used to these things. But she only wore them for the festivals, and a handful of scattered fancy events throughout the year. All in all, it was only a few weeks per annum.

Every moment delayed was a moment she missed of the trial. Everything she missed was forever lost; no one would deign to enlighten her.

Lift your head. You listen to the stars sing while they sleep.

You are driving me mad, Meiling.

Would you come with me if I left Zheninghai?

"Stop *thinking* about that." She scrubbed harder at her face, trying to shove away the dread roiling in her gut with her frustration. "It didn't mean . . . He wasn't . . . I cannot let this make me think . . . I would never want to presume . . . What am I saying? I'm a blubbering idiot!"

She scraped her cheek raw, wresting with the paint. Curse her trembling hands!

Fine. She summoned her maids, and they chittered into the room, pinching their lips and sucking in gasps at the mess she'd made of her face.

"I know," Meiling whispered, slumping onto the cushion and closing her eyes against the ministering hands. Far more proficient, gentler hands than hers. She breathed in the fresh linen scent on the clothes of the maids bending over her.

She'd just wanted to be alone to compose her fraying nerves before she attended another trial and saw Shang again. "Are you done?" she prompted. "Can I go now?"

"Almost, Highness."

Her fingers nervously found the tail of her sash, twisting it between her fingers and tugging it tighter. An impatient huff whooshed through her nostrils. Each moment was slipping by like sand between parted fingers, like her shadow through stone.

"There. You are finished, Highness."

"Thank you!" Meiling gasped and leaped to her feet. Hardly ladylike. Even less princess-like. She did not care as she threaded her way through fluttering pink robes and long, silky black hair, hurrying toward the door. When she opened it, her guards' eyes swiveled down to her. Not the same as her guards from last night, but it was enough to remind her not to sprint through the palace.

Her legs ached to run, and though she primly tucked her hands into her sleeves, she plucked at the inside seams.

When she rounded the corner, her eyes widened, and the air fled her lungs. Fathers above, she'd already forgotten it was the Day of Cleansing. Everywhere she turned, servant girls crouched under tables with rags and buckets of water, scrubbed at windows, dusted the *mó guǐ* statues in corners. Manservants carefully dismantled centuries-old tapestries to be borne with gloved hands outside for cleaning.

Ma would be everywhere today, overseeing the cleaning and the preparation for tonight's feast. And if Ma found out what she was doing, she would forbid her from going near the trial ever again.

Most likely.

The thought of disobeying her parents' expressed wishes . . . She did not want that strain between her and them. That would leave her twiddling her thumbs uselessly in her room while Shang and Fen were condemned to death. Better that Ma and Pa did not find out and couldn't order her to stay away from the proceedings.

Somehow, rebellion only tasted strong and heady on her lips when it was against people she did not care about. She wanted no rift between her and her parents.

Her best hope was to slip through unnoticed.

Taking a deep breath into her constricted chest, she stepped out into the hallway. Immediately, the maids and manservants stopped what they were doing as she passed, bobbing and bowing and mumbling, "Highness."

She swallowed, walking faster as more servants stopped to acknowledge her. She gave distracted smiles, mumbled, "No need, continue your work." But they were insistent, chiming louder and pausing and bowing.

One voice stopped her.

"Princess Meiling, is there aught we can do to help you?"

She halted, turned. A short, sweet-faced maid bowed and looked up with earnest, concerned eyes. Meiling blinked at her. Did she look so distressed that a maid intercepted her? Now that she stopped, she realized her brow *was* furrowed tightly. That tension *did* squeeze her shoulders. Her lips parted, as though to speak, or smile reassuringly, but then a familiar voice startled her.

"Very well, very well. Tell them the substitute will be fine. No one will suspect the mishap," said Ma briskly. "Send some of the servants from the back wings to focus on cleaning the feasting hall and palace entry. The guests will not be hunting through closets; I daresay it is fine to not devote so much time to them."

"Of course, Honored Queen. But—forgive me—would it not be bad luck—"

"Nonsense. The only bad luck is if our guests find a speck of dust in the places they see."

Meiling barely contained her gasp and shoved past the concerned maid. She ought to offer some reassurance to the kind girl, but she fled down the hallway, hoping Ma would not pass this way.

How odd the servants must think her. If she didn't take care, she'd confirm her reputation. She pressed herself into the shadows, blood roaring in her ears.

Please do not stop, Ma. Keep walking. Please don't see me.

The voices grew louder, peppered with little orders from Ma to the servants. Meiling shut her eyes, trying to calm her heaving lungs. How much had she missed of the trial? It was already the third day of the festival; only two more trials remained after today.

Eventually, Ma continued, her voice growing fainter. The chorus of "Honored Queen" from the servants moved down the corridor. Further away. Meiling could hardly breathe easier; she was nearly frantic to reach the courtroom.

But if the servants saw her running through the palace, hitching her silk robes, someone would surely alert Ma. Moving as dignified as she could manage, she hurried past the cleaning servants and ignored their mumbles of "Highness," and bows.

For the sweet-faced maid, she stopped. She forced a smile onto her face, hastened to say, "I am well, thank you for your concern," and tore off again.

By the time she shut the door behind her to the balcony of the courtroom, she was certain her panting gasps and pounding heart would be loud enough for everyone to hear. She clambered up the stairs, crouching at the top and sitting her trembling body onto the bench to peer down into the room.

Everything was as usual, except Fen sat with the strangest, perplexed look on her face. And Shang did not sit, but stood with his hand over his heart. Testifying. Fen must have already finished.

She fisted her hands in her skirts. She had missed much then. Her insides dropped with dejection.

"Do you, Tan Shangdi, admit that you were careless in disguising your campsites, making it easy for the brigands to track you?" asked the judge.

Absolutely not. He had been meticulous about it.

The word seemed to sputter on his lips, but it came out clear and loud. "Yes," Shang answered.

She drew back, away from the railing. *What?* She leaned closer again, her gaze roving the length of the courtroom for some clue about why Shang would lie. He had always been careful with his answers, careful not to reveal her magic to probing questions. But this had nothing to do with her magic, right?

"Do you, Tan Shangdi, admit that you neglected the care of your wounded partner, Hu Fen?"

"Yes."

"No, no, no," Meiling growled under her breath.

"Do you, Tan Shangdi, admit that you bartered with the brigands for your own life, handing over Princess Meiling to their clutches?"

"Yes."

She gasped aloud. How could . . .? How was it *possible* to so misconstrue the events to such a distorted representation of what transpired? And why was Shang *admitting* to these falsehoods? Phoenixes burn everything—why in all the seven valleys did he lie?

She leaned farther over the railing, angling to get a clearer view of Shang's face.

He looked up, straight at her.

His face was in utter bewilderment. Black eyes wide, mouth partially open, forehead knit. She had never seen him looking so lost, so confused, and the sight made her stagger against the railing. She gaped back at him until he tore his gaze away and answered "Yes," to another falsehood.

Scuttling sounded from her left. Then much closer, right behind her. She whirled—thought a shadow melt into the wall—and gazed at nothing. A shudder ran down her spine.

Something was desperately wrong. But she couldn't begin to guess what.

Had Fen admitted to lies as well? She bore a similar expression to Shang, so it seemed probable. Meiling, still staring at the empty benches and wall behind her, slid to the floor and leaned her head back against the whitewashed plaster. She kept her eyes wide open, darting over every inch of exposed space for a hint of what could be making the scuttling sound.

On and on, the trial dragged below her. On and on, Shang's voice, low and strong, said firmly, "Yes." She drew her knees up to her chest and wrapped her arms around them. Each breath shuddered in her lungs.

How could they hope for pardon if they admitted to all these lies?

"I won't let them die," she growled under her breath as a tear slid down her scrubbed and scraped cheek. The salt burned. "I *won't*."

She would do something. If only . . .

Meiling sat up straighter and bumped her head on the lip of the railing. If she could testify, then she could set the records straight. She could explain the truth—make everyone understand. Her fists relaxed, and bunched silk fell smoothly to the floor.

She just had to find a way to get them to let her testify. And she needed to convince her parents to allow it. Which meant she needed to speak to Ma. But she wasn't going to hunt Ma down while she was so busy with overseeing feast preparations and palace scouring—especially because Meiling had another important appointment.

She was so lost in her plotting, the end of the trial came upon her rather suddenly. The rustling of papers, the susurrus of silk, the low chatter, rose from below. She kept her head bowed as she made her way to the stairs. She paused halfway down, a sudden thought making her heart leap.

Would Shang come to see her here?

She waited, breathing through her open mouth. Waited, *hoped.*

Minutes passed. The courtroom quieted, and with the sound of a few small puffs, darkened. The stairwell was even darker, and she sat in the stillness, refusing to move the slightest muscle.

He didn't come.

Meiling swallowed the emotions and thoughts that flooded her. She had other things she needed to do, anyway. She could not be distracted. What if she was already late?

It was a good thing he had not come.

She crept down the stairs, steeling her mouth into a firm, thin line. She paused for only a second at the door; everyone must have already left. One fortifying inhale later, she turned the knob and opened it.

She peered out into the hallway, and her hands drooped on the knob in relief when no one was there. Relief or disappointment—sometimes it was hard to tell which. She had to get to the west gate.

CHAPTER 18

THE CAPTIVE WIELDERS arrived as Meiling scurried up to the gate. Her step faltered when Shang was already there, a tall, severe silhouette waiting with a collection of guards and people who must be the families of the captives.

Well, if he was here, she could demand that he explain what happened in the courtroom. Once they greeted the captives.

Some of these captives had been prisoners for nearly her entire life. Those who had children . . . She glanced sidelong to find a few young men and women near her age among the reception. Some younger, some in white Academy garb. A pang darted into her heart. Some of these captives had missed their children's youths.

Other prisoners had been captured when Pa had sent a force to rescue her from Zedong. Shang had been one of them, and Meiling slipped quietly up behind him as he watched the line of horses and riders come through the gate.

"Are you here for Renshu?" she whispered to him.

He startled slightly, turned, and looked down at her. The alarm on his face was not what she was expecting. "Meili—Highness! What are you doing here? This isn't . . ." A muscle worked in his rigid jaw, and the stern warrior returned with a cold, "Go back to the palace, Highness."

She swallowed as her chest constricted, but she did not move. "I knew them too."

He exhaled. Lifted his face away from her and set his hard gaze toward the approaching caravan. He gripped his left wrist tightly with his right hand behind his back. Tension rippled through his shoulders as one particular young man entered the gate, alive and well. Shang's hand squeezed so hard that his poor fingers turned red.

Collective chatters and gasps burst from the group as recognition hit. Two of the wielders she had discovered in Zedong's dungeon, Liuxian and Tao, rode through the gates. There had been more captives from that failed mission than she realized, but overall, it was hardly more than thirty people. She recognized every single person who came through the gate, as she'd been in all their minds.

She didn't even intend to speak with any of them. Her only desire was to see that they were safe and welcomed them home with a smile. Perhaps she also wanted to prove that Zedong didn't have the last word. Wanted proof that the fortress he'd imprisoned her in had been breached.

The freed captives began dismounting, and the little crowd of welcoming family members burst forward. She had to swallow the lump in her throat so her own tears did not escape at the sight of forlorn spouses finally reunited, of children seen and held and beloved. Tears flowed, laughter bubbled, and despite her attempts at control, she was weeping with them.

Shang strode forward, and his cloak flipped into her face at the movement. He marched toward the largest man of the group—a tall, handsome young man built like a boulder—as he dismounted from his horse. Cao Renshu looked exactly as Meiling remembered, with fire in his eyes and strength in his step. Only he looked weary. Whether from Zedong's torments or the grueling return journey, she did not know.

A broad grin broke out across his face at the sight of Shang. Wordlessly, they clamped each other's hand, seeming to communicate worlds without words. Then Renshu reached out, and they embraced each other so tightly that Shang gasped. His face split into a smile, and he laughed.

"Phoenixes, brother, but you have not lost one ounce of your strength!" Shang wheezed. "Lay off."

Renshu grinned and released him. A memory of dark, strangely lit labyrinthine hallways rife with claw marks flashed through Meiling's mind. She remembered sensing that feral, otherworldly strength flowing through his body, chained by Zedong's dark magic.

Her attention was torn away from their reunion by the approach of a new figure. "Liuxian!" she gasped.

He was little more than a rack of ribs and sagging skin, his jutting brow still hiding his eyes, his beard whiter than she had last seen. He had been a prisoner for so many years. His face was mostly blank, and she figured he might still be in shock. Was his family here? She looked around but saw no one reaching for him.

"I am so glad you are back safely," she said, smiling despite her sadness. "You will be able to rest and recuperate."

He lifted his face, enough that she could make out twin beads of dark staring back at her under pale eyebrows. "Princess Meiling," he rasped.

"Liuxian," she replied with another smile. "You are safe now."

He held her gaze for a long moment, making her smile falter slightly. She forced it back up, fuller than before. She almost opened her mouth to say something but could think of nothing besides another version of assuring him he was safely home.

Where was the snarky and bitter Liuxian she had encountered in the dungeons? Why did he stare at her so intently? Was she the only person he knew in this crowd?

Something scuttled behind her. Instinctively, Meiling turned to catch a glimpse of it. Why did that distinct sound follow her *everywhere*? It was almost like . . .

It was like the sound in Zedong's mind.

The sound of black magic.

Liuxian lunged.

She saw it in her periphery. Heard the sudden shouts of the people around her. Something gleamed like metal in Liuxian's hand.

He punched her hard in the side. So hard she stumbled back. Ice swept her from head to toe, and then warm water soaked through her robes, dripping down her legs. Tingles and numbness followed.

"MEILING!" Shang screamed, lunging for her.

It was just a hit. She'd been hit before. This wasn't even the worst hit she'd taken. He didn't need to scream like that.

She looked down—

—just as Liuxian wrenched a knife out of her side.

Red blood. Everywhere.

It was getting on the ground. This was such a mess. And on the Day of Cleansing! The servants had already spent so many hours today cleaning the palace. Getting blood out of pavement was going to take so much work.

She staggered.

The ground came rushing for her.

The rush of air stopped, but the ground still embraced her. Her vision turned foggy, but she knew it was Shang with his knees on either side of her hips, his hands fussing at her waist. That was his voice shouting. Screaming echoed around her, like flies buzzing in her ears.

When she tilted her head, someone else held a long white beard pinned to the ground. Renshu?

"This is going to hurt, but stay with me, Meiling. *Stay with me.*"

Those words made her turn her head back to Shang. He had her sash knotted around her torso, beads of sweat dripping off his nose. Then he pulled—

Pain like nothing she'd ever known devoured her whole. Blackness seared her vision.

Then the light returned, but the pain didn't ebb. Everything was blurry. The ground moved away at last, and there was blue sky ringed in darkness. She closed her eyes. Fathers, she was so tired and the *pain*, oh, the pain. She leaned her head against something that thudded loudly in her ear.

"Meiling? Meiling! Can you hear me? Wake up! Don't go to sleep, understand? Meiling! *Meiling*!"

Someone moaned. The sound was distant, detached. It seemed to come from everywhere and nowhere. It was joined by frantic, punctuated roars.

"Feiyan! Where is Feiyan? Where is the healer? Someone find the healer! *Now!* The princess has been stabbed!" This was followed by a low voice growling, "Spitfire, spitfire, *spitfire*!"

She opened her eyes. Her gaze clarified for a moment, and she smiled. "Hello, Shang." She choked, coughed, and a wave of agonizing pain shot through her body. She gasped, let out a cry that swiftly morphed into a moan. The world grew dark again, but it stayed loud.

The arms holding her tightened.

"*Feiyan!* Meiling, don't worry, just stay awake for a few more minutes. *Feiyan!* I'm taking you to the healer. You'll be all right. Just don't fall asleep, understand? *FEIYAN!*" The roar choked out at the end.

Distantly, she thought he was running, and that was why she was jostling so much. That was why shooting lightning bolts of lancing pain kept sweeping through her body and soul.

The blue in her vision went black, but not utterly black. An unfamiliar ceiling shuddered above her. Was she dying?

It was a strange thought.

Perhaps she ought to panic, but she was too tired to panic. Besides, she was supposed to die in the throne room. Maybe she was being carried to the throne room so she could die in her proper place.

"I've got you. I've got you. Just hold on for me, darling. Hold on for me. *FEIYAN!*" The voice strained to breaking. Was someone carrying her? Was it someone she knew?

Screaming and shouting and moaning.

"Too loud," she mumbled.

A new voice and smell and sight filled her senses.

"What happened?" a feminine voice gasped.

"No time!"

She flew through the air, found enough strength in her arms to flail them weakly, and everything stopped moving. Something warm touched her side, and then a golden river rushed into her. She sagged.

"Is it too late?" Shang's voice broke. Something cold brushed against the side of her face. Ice pressed into her throat. "She still has a pulse," he gasped.

"We are just in time," the girl responded. "Barely."

The warm, golden river kept flowing. Flowing from her side to her toes, through to the ends of her hair. The pain eased. She could breathe without choking. Ice stayed on her face, pressed into her throat below her jawline. Her heartbeat pulsed against those cold fingers.

Slowly, oh so slowly, thought clarified.

She was inside. The pain subsided moment by moment, from sharp agony to a dull throb. The lower half of her body lay on something hard and firm. The floor, she realized. Her eyelashes fluttered but wouldn't open. Aside from the chilled hand on her face, heat surrounded her upper body. She recognized the hands pressed into her wounded side as belonging to another person. A girl. The golden river flowed from her.

But the heat came from elsewhere.

She blinked.

Shang's black eyes were widened to an impossible size, hovering near her face. She blinked again, realizing that she half-lay in his lap, her head held against his thudding heart, his fingers never leaving her pulse. She held something cold in one hand. And Feiyan was bent over her, brow knit in consternation and focus.

"Meiling?" Shang rasped.

"I . . . I . . . H-h-hello, Shang. What . . .?"

"Oh fathers above, Meiling," he gasped, clutching her face tighter to his chest. "You're going to be all right." His voice cracked slightly. "Feiyan is healing you."

Her head was so heavy. She tilted it even so, away from Shang to find Feiyan. Sweat dripped off her nose, and her shoulders shook. Her eyes were squeezed shut in concentration.

"What . . . why am I . . . how . . .?"

"Do tell," Feiyan managed between clenched teeth, looking up from her work to narrow her eyes at Shang. "What happened?"

"One of the recovered prisoners stabbed her."

"What? Why in all the worlds and wildernesses would one of the prisoners stab her?"

The cold thing in her hand clenched tighter, sending ice shooting through her veins. She chattered and looked down to see Shang's hand holding hers. Quickly, she pulled her hand free and tucked it against her side. He blinked at her, and she smiled weakly. "Too cold." She tried to shrug her face free from his chest and sit up, but both Feiyan and Shang restrained her.

"A little longer," Feiyan murmured, and glanced over her shoulder. Meiling strained—wincing at the pain—to see where she looked. Her eyes widened at the long line of people beyond Feiyan facing an empty chair. All those people stared at her lying on the floor. The room was dark, with only thin windows along the high wall trim to illuminate the place.

Was this hovel where Feiyan spent her days healing?

"Meiling? Do you know why he stabbed you?" Shang asked, the cautious gentleness of his words at complete odds with his widened, raw eyes and his heart pounding against her ear.

She frowned, racked her brain. Winced. "I . . . No. I do not know. I heard . . ."

"You heard what? What, Meiling? What did you hear?"

She shook her head. When she opened her eyes, two extra heads sprouted from Shang's shoulders. Dizziness pounded hard, fighting against the sweeping torrents of Feiyan's healing magic. "A sound. Like a bug."

Feiyan's eyebrow shot up. "He was probably trying to kill the bug."

"Now is not the time for jokes," Shang snapped. He turned back to Meiling. "What sound? Tell me more about the sound."

The sound?

Already, its memory seemed to fade, confusion muddling her thoughts. She'd realized something about the sound, but now she couldn't remember what. "It was . . . It was nothing."

The last bit of the pain vanished like a resolving chord. She gasped, sagged against Shang as the tension washed away. His heartbeat lurched against her ear, and his hand moved away from her face to support her shoulders as Feiyan drew back.

"There. She is recovered."

Meiling almost started when Shang's other hand darted out and gripped Feiyan's elbow when she tried to stand. She froze, her full lips parting. His face held the most vulnerable expression Meiling had ever seen.

"Fathers, Feiyan, you are a miracle," he whispered thickly, his voice catching.

Feiyan stared, utterly dumbfounded. Her mouth gaped, and one eyebrow twitched. Was it the darkness of the room, or did her cheeks flush?

She nodded crisply and stood, pulling herself free and stepping away. She drew a deep breath. "I am honored to serve my princess."

When her back turned, her shoulders slumped. She stopped at a table where a basin rested, next to a towel, and washed her bloody hands before returning to her chair. Meiling's gaze lingered on her, even as Shang shifted.

She turned to face him just as he swept his arm under her knees and lifted her up. "Shang!" she gasped, immediately struggling against him. "I can walk—I am perfectly—"

"Hush."

Chastened, she bit her tongue and went rigid in his arms as he carried her out of the room. She assumed he would set her down once they left the room, or the building, but he didn't. Light greeted them, bright and glaring, as the sun descended into late afternoon. What was she supposed to do with her hands? Fold them up?

She strained to look where they were going, and blanched. "Shang! You cannot carry me into the palace! It's the Day of Cleansing and servants are everywhere—"

He grunted as he moved to kick open the door, but servants rushed forward and opened it first. He stepped over the threshold, and dozens of pattering footsteps filled the air. Not knowing what else to do, she reached up, wrapped her arms around his neck, and hid her flaming face in the collar of his robes. His jaw tensed.

"Highness," came the echoing murmurs as Shang carried her through the hallways of her home. How incessant they were! How numerous! She wanted to crawl into a corner and die.

"Shang, please," she whispered. He either didn't hear her, or he simply did not answer. Her blush grew hotter. She almost asked if she was too heavy, but caught herself just in time. He would probably think she insulted his strength.

He took the stairs, and she clutched his neck tighter, willing herself not to be afraid of being dropped, willing herself to shut out the relentless addresses from the servants.

"My rooms—" she started.

"I know where your rooms are."

There was no point in arguing that just because he knew where her window was wasn't the same as knowing how to find the door. She gave another half-hearted effort to scramble out of his grip, but he tightened his arms. "Be still. We're almost there."

After a thousand more steps of embarrassment making her blood run hot, a familiar chorus of addresses burbled. Her head snapped up, and she craned her neck as her maids rushed to open her door. The frenzy of fluttering and clucking maids immediately enveloped her.

Shang strode into the room, and the maids parted before him. "Draw back the bedclothes. Fetch hot water and prepare a bath," he instructed, as though giving orders to soldiers under his command. "Arrange new robes for her. Send for the emperor and queen if they have not already been informed."

"Shang—"

He set her down on her bed. When he did so, she got a clear view of her own garments. They were torn and completely covered in blood. Her torso was drenched, her sash having been wrapped tightly around the wound—to staunch the flow. A gasp escaped her lips. She quickly sat up.

He placed a hand on her shoulder and gently pushed her back down onto the bed. "Lie down. You need to recover."

"I am recovered!"

He met her eyes, and it was enough to make her swallow her protests. Then her gaze lowered. Widened. The front of his robes was crimson, soaked through and sticking to his torso. His long sleeves were stained, spatters and drips falling to the hems. Those strong hands were bloody, and even his face was smeared. His gaze was hard.

"You don't want to go into shock," he said, turning his attention toward the end of the bed. Before she realized what he was doing, he gripped her ankle and slid one slipper off her foot.

She startled, pulling back. "Shang!"

He ignored her protests and tugged off her other slipper, tossing both to the floor where a maid swept them up. "It was a traumatizing event. In the span of half an hour, you went from full health to near death, back to full health again." He lifted the quilt and spread it over her, gently tucking it under her chin as she lay rigid. He pulled his red-stained hands away, straightened. His black eyes met hers. "You need to rest and give your mind time to catch up."

Her lips parted as she stared at him and gripped the edge of the blanket. Her gaze tailed down from his face again. How was it possible all that blood came from her?

Shang turned toward the maids. "Once the bath is drawn, make sure she has all the assistance she needs. It is not good for her to stay in those bloody clothes."

They bobbed.

Noise behind the door made Meiling jerk upward to prop herself up on her elbow. The door burst open, and Pa stormed into the room, followed by Ma.

"Meiling!" he gasped, rushing forward and grabbing both of her shoulders. "Are you well, my love? Are you well?"

She only had time to nod before Pa pulled her into the tightest embrace of her life. She melted into his arms and tears pricked the corners of her eyes.

Just as suddenly, he pulled away and turned. Ma nearly fell over herself coming to hug her, but Meiling's attention was not on her Ma's anxious embrace or the way her nails dug almost painfully into her sleeves. She watched Pa's gaze rove the length of Shang's blood-stained garments as he bowed.

"Tan Shangdi," Pa's voice deepened, bore a husky edge. "You saved my daughter. You have my eternal gratitude."

Shang bowed again, this time lower than before. "It is my honor to serve her Highness and your Imperial Majesty." He straightened, and without waiting for a dismissal, strode toward the door. Pausing on the threshold, he turned back, his eyes flicking to Meiling's over the shoulders of her near-frantic parents. He held her gaze for the briefest of moments.

Then he left the room.

CHAPTER 19

SEVERAL PEOPLE TRIED to stop Shang, to ask what had happened. He shook them off, his jaw clenched so hard he half expected it to snap in two at any moment. He didn't trust himself to say a single word, and he didn't feel an ounce of pity for their morbid curiosity.

Instead, he went straight to his room in the Academy complex, ignoring the stares at the blood covering him.

He shut the door behind him. Shut out the light of day as muted darkness filled his room.

He collapsed to his knees, buried his head in his hands, and wept.

CHAPTER 20

AFTER HER PARENTS had left, after her maids helped her bathe and redress, Meiling slid back into her bed. She pulled the quilt up to her chin. It was not the one that Shang had tucked her in with earlier. The bedclothes had been changed and discarded.

Already, shadows filled her room. The feast would be starting soon. Thankfully, her parents had given her leave to rest and not attend the feast. She didn't know if they intended to hide the incident. It seemed rather impossible, considering the trail of blood she must have left on the newly polished floors in front of hundreds of servant's eyes.

Her plans were foiled. She had not been able to ask Shang about what happened in the trial. She had not been able to ask Ma for her help in finding a way to testify in the trial.

The days were slipping by. Only two more days remained, only two more trials. She could not keep cowering up in the balcony, listening to her friends be slandered and forced to admit to lies. She also could not afford to keep getting injured. Was this now the third time Feiyan had brought Meiling back from the brink of death? Two of them in the last three days.

Perhaps her parents were regretting bringing her back to the palace. Perhaps it was not safe here for her, after all.

She needed to speak with Shang. And not while she was half dead and both of them were covered in blood. She doubted that he would have a serious conversation with her tonight, even if she managed to slip past the extra guards posted at her door. He would tell her she ought to rest. She puffed a frustrated blast of air out of her mouth.

He had been so worried . . .

But that didn't matter. Saving him mattered. Finding out what had gotten into Liuxian mattered. The Liuxian she had known in the dungeons would not have stabbed her. Verbally thrashed her, perhaps, but in the end, he had not been antagonistic toward her. Not enough to murder her.

She could enter his mind and figure it out herself. Maybe if she entered Shang's mind, he could tell her where Liuxian was. Then she would not have to waste her time hunting in the dungeons for him.

She rolled to her side, staring toward the window that looked out at her city, her ocean. The window Shang had come through only last night. It was shut now, of course. She snuggled deeper into the quilts, frowning.

That hadn't been Liuxian who had stabbed her. She was sure of it. It was not of his volition. Not his idea. What if he was as innocent as Shang and Fen? What if . . .

An image flashed across her mind. A fiery, magma-filled mind of a phoenix. A cursed, bound, imprisoned phoenix who acted on the command of Fang Zedong.

Was it possible? Had Fang Zedong implanted curses in his prisoners before they escaped? Had he cursed Liuxian to stab Meiling when he saw her? What if the other captives were just as dangerous as Liuxian? What if they also harbored hidden compulsion curses?

Meiling sat bolt upright in bed. What if the people below at the feast were in danger?

Renshu . . . *Shang.* If Renshu was cursed, would he hurt Shang?

She immediately fell back onto her pillow. She was most helpful—and the least helpless—in her spirit form. She needed to fall asleep, find Shang, enter his mind, and tell him her theory. Needed him to act on her behalf and ensure the prisoners did not hurt others. At least until she could enter their minds and search for a curse.

Falling asleep while her heart pulsed with stress was not the easiest thing, but she'd fallen asleep in much more stressful and uncomfortable situations than lying quietly on her bed. Besides, she *was* tired. Maybe Shang was right; even though she was healed, she still needed to rest.

She closed her eyes, calmed her breathing as best she could, and eventually her exhaustion claimed her.

The palace was aglow with the wielders attending the feast. Light beamed out of the windows, especially at the feasting hall. But though Meiling searched the feast, though she found her family members all glowing orange except Ma, she couldn't find Shang.

There was no sign of Master Dong. No sign of the returned wielders at the feast, either. She floated toward the Academy. Over the training fields, the dormitories, the classrooms, everything. She flew to the gardens, hunting for a flash of ice-blue light.

At last, she found Shang seated in a pavilion. His master was with him, his steady golden glow pulsing in time with Shang's. *Scorching phoenixes,* she'd have to wait until they were finished before entering Shang's mind. Flitting across the bridge, she approached slowly.

He still wore his bloodstained garments from earlier. They were stiff by now. He sat on the bench, his knees spread wide, and he wiped his hands down his face, covering his eyes. His shoulders were slumped—trembling a little?

Master Dong was still across the pavilion, sitting on the opposite bench. His hands were interlaced on his lap as he studied his former pupil. Shang's voice cut through the silence of the night.

"I almost let her die."

"You saved her, Shangdi. You acted fast, with good instinct, and you didn't lose your head. No one could have handled the situation better."

"But it was almost not enough! She was bleeding so badly, even after I bound up the wound. Had I forgotten where Feiyan heals? Had I stumbled while running—*spitfire?*"

"You've had close calls with her before. You watched her get kidnapped by brigands," Master Dong reminded him, raising an eyebrow.

Shang spread out his arms, frustration making his voice louder. "This was different! I was *right there.* I should have considered the possibility of something happening; shouldn't have let her get so close to them. What was I thinking? I told her to leave, but I was so caught up in seeing Renshu again and making sure he was all right. And do you really think I have forgiven myself for letting her get kidnapped? I almost let Mei—the princess die before my eyes!"

Master Dong leaned forward. "I know you're shaken. I've known you since you were a child, and you've always had a singular focus and a will of iron. You've always known what you wanted, and you never rested until you had it. Until this week. Until *now*. The Shangdi I knew before would have done exactly what you did when the princess was captured. You didn't panic. You didn't lose control of yourself. You didn't *break*. What did you do instead? You planned, planned, and planned. And then you executed the most daring rescue I've heard of. But now, you're faltering. Why, Shangdi? Either you don't know what you want, or you don't believe you deserve what you want."

"I want her to be *alive* and well."

Master Dong steepled his fingers, narrowing his keen eyes. "Why?"

The words shot out of Shang's mouth, vehement and startling to Meiling. "Because she is dear to me! I will content myself with distance from her if I must, so long as she is alive and well."

Because she is dear to me.

"Why?" demanded Master Dong.

"Because she is *good*, and—and—"

"And you are not."

Shang went silent, turning his face away. Were those tears leaking out of his shut eyes? Meiling's heart wrung out.

"You've spent your life believing that you are a failure, that you are inadequate, despite succeeding with such aplomb at everything you set your mind to."

"I am on trial for my *life*," Shang growled. "Don't try to tell me I'm not a failure."

You're not a failure, Meiling said aloud into the ether, and if she possessed physical eyes in this form, tears would have been streaming down her cheeks.

"I won't tell you that you're not a failure. You wouldn't believe me if I did. So I will tell you this instead: I saw how you looked at the princess last night—"

"So you have already informed me."

"Let me finish. I didn't just see how you looked at her. I saw how *she* looked at *you*."

Meiling jolted in surprise, whirling toward the older man even as Shang's attention was equally arrested.

If that man *dared* to—

"When she looked at you, she wasn't looking at a failure. She was looking at a hero, Shangdi. *Her* hero. There was nothing in her eyes but admiration when she looked at you."

Meiling ran a hand down her face, her insides relaxing even as warmth filled her soul. He hadn't exposed her completely to Shang, and he was correct in her characterization. Shang *was* her hero, and she wasn't ashamed of it.

"That is because Meiling sees good wherever she looks," said Shang, not bothering to continue using her title. "She is good, so she sees the goodness around her. I'm not like that. I see corruption, double-crossing liars, crooked ambition, and conquest. Because that is who I am, who I am willing to be if I must."

"Do you see corruption and conquest in the princess?" the master demanded.

Shang pulled back, clearly affronted.

"Is the princess hard on herself?"

"Yes, very much so," answered Shang.

"Do you think she is lacking in the ways she believes herself to be lacking?"

He shook his head vehemently, and something about it made Meiling's shadow lips fall open. "She lacks nothing. Except common sense when it comes to self-preservation. But even that is another of her virtues I cannot help but admire. It isn't that she's lacking sense, but that she values others so highly she won't consider her own detriment." Then Shang's brow puckered, and he shot a finger out toward Master Dong. "Don't you dare tell her I said that. She'll take it as permission to continue throwing herself into dangerous situations."

The full reality of her eavesdropping slammed into Meiling. She flew backward a few feet, shame making her reconsider listening to the rest of the conversation. She should give them privacy—that was what she would want.

It was so strange to hear Shang speak of her this way, of all her so-called virtues, especially when she was invading his privacy even now.

But then Master Dong was speaking again as Shang dropped his head into his hands, and she couldn't resist drifting just a little bit closer . . .

"You're holding a double standard. I will not sit here and attempt to assure you that you aren't the failure you believe yourself to be—only you can truly decide to let that identity go. But I will urge this of you. What the princess sees in you is what I see in you, too. If you won't believe me, then consider believing her. I spoke with her for five minutes, and that was enough for me to see her genuineness. She isn't lacking in sense, and she's not a liar. Her admiration isn't patronization. Maybe—*just maybe*—what she sees is really there. Maybe what she admires is truth. And if it is truth, then why are you going to keep sitting here and moping? Find that iron focus of yours. Find that well of strength inside you. Be the force of nature that you are, Tan Shangdi. You weren't made to be broken."

At those words, Shang's ice-blue glow shuttered. Meiling stiffened as a bolt of fear pierced her. Glows only did that when the wielder was wounded or dying. Could glows dim from soul pain, not just physical pain? Was he—

His soul pulsed, and then, as though the sun had reappeared from behind storm clouds, the glow magnified. Meiling's lips parted as she watched, dumbfounded, as Shang's soul glow tripled in strength, becoming a blinding aura of almost pure white.

Slowly, Shang lifted his head.

His black eyes shone like distant stars. There was something different about the way they glowed. As though he'd just released a mountain he'd carried upon his shoulders. As though his inner fire had just been reignited.

"You're right," he said simply. "Thank you."

With that, he rose and strode purposefully out of the pavilion, the brilliant blue-white of his soul a beacon to his path.

"And for the fathers' sakes, get out of those bloody garments!" called Master Dong after Shang's retreating form. He gave his head a shake, a long sigh escaping him, and Meiling wondered if he had any clue how deeply his words had affected his mentee.

She watched Shang disappear, taking her heart with her. And yet, despite the fact that she hadn't discussed the things she needed to with him, she felt lighter than she had in months. She trusted Shang with her life—she always had—but she'd never trusted him with his own.

That might have just changed.

While she was floating there, pondering what she'd just witnessed, a glow of orange drew her gaze back to the pavilion. Lian Delan, whom she'd met tonight, was joining Master Dong in Shang's absence. He pulled a canister from his robes and wordlessly offered it to the older man.

"Yes, please," said Master Dong, grabbing the canister and taking a large swig. He winced, then took another pull. "I needed a drink. Giving counsel to lovelorn young men is above my paygrade."

Delan blew out a long stream of air and took his own pull. "Here, here."

"Were we ever that stupid?"

Delan winced on his last sip, then screwed the lid back on and replaced the canister in his robes. "Definitely not."

Meiling decided to leave them alone. She wasn't sure she could take overhearing anymore about the impending war just now.

First thing tomorrow, she'd speak with Shang.

CHAPTER 21

SHANG SHOULDN'T HAVE sent a request to the emperor for a private audience in the middle of the night. He also shouldn't have utilized his special connections to ensure the emperor received said request first thing upon waking up. And the emperor shouldn't have granted that request and sent notice of it at fifth watch, long before the sun was up.

But here Shang was, walking through the doors held open for him by the Emperor's Guard, entering His Imperial Majesty's private office.

The emperor was seated at his desk, an untouched tray of steaming tea beside him as he scribbled away feverishly at a piece of parchment. He looked up at the sound of Shang's footsteps. Even in his middle age, he was a striking man. Strain and weariness lined his face, but the flash hadn't left his gaze and strength emanated from his core.

Shang had always found His Imperial Majesty deeply worthy of his respect. Seeing him close and personal like this only emphasized the power and conscientiousness with which he ruled.

Shang bowed deeply.

Emperor Nianzu leaned back, setting his quill back in its inkwell. Unlike Shang, he wasn't dressed for the day, but instead wore an emerald green dressing gown belted at the waist. His voice was gravelly when he spoke, and there wasn't a hint of ire in his tone at Shang's inappropriate request. "Tan Shangdi. I was intending to send for you today, so this works well for me. I've been informed of the trials."

Shang only nodded.

Emperor Nianzu steepled his fingers and leaned forward, eyes flashing. "I have no intention of letting you or that shifter be executed."

Not many things surprised Shang. This, however, made his composure frisson just slightly. He blinked twice and fought to keep his mouth in a straight line.

"I want to give you every chance at a pardon," the emperor continued. "If I declared you pardoned myself, the council would come for my throat and my throne. Any other time in my reign, I would have considered fighting that battle because you have proven your loyalty to Zheninghai and to my beloved daughter in a way that I have rarely seen. I have no intention of allowing an execution to be my thanks for what you've done for Princess Meiling. But *right now*, with Fang about to attack, I don't have what I need to win a long, arduous fight against the council to keep your life and my throne. Zheninghai won't survive against Fang's armies if I am forced to abdicate. So, forgive me for valuing the lives of this city and empire above your pardon and freedom, but that is what I must prioritize."

Shang had been right. Emperor Nianzu didn't blame him—hardly even blamed Fen—for the failure of their mission. As for the difficult dilemma, Shang agreed easily with his decision. The fate of the empire was far more important than his acquittal.

Still, if the emperor couldn't fight for Shang's pardon, but wouldn't allow them to be executed, what other option was there? Only one.

Fleeing Zheninghai.

Without Meiling.

His chest tightened, and not even his careful breathing could ease the ache.

"I've already arranged an escape for you and the shifter," continued the emperor. "You can leave now, or you can wait until the verdict is announced. It is up to you. Perhaps you still might be pardoned. But if not, I'll make sure you get out of the city before the execution. Anything you need, it's yours. This is not the honor I want to bestow on you, as thanks, but I'm afraid there's little else I can do before Fang comes."

Shang bowed. "You are far too generous, Glorious Majesty."

Emperor Nianzu's gaze narrowed at him thoughtfully, and even though Shang fought hard to keep his face from betraying a single thought or emotion, the emperor said, "Something is troubling you. What is it that you would like to request? If it is within my power, I will grant it."

Shang's jaw worked as he glanced away. *Now or never.* Yesterday, he wouldn't have had the courage to make such a bold request, but now determination bubbled within him. He knew what he wanted, whether in Zheninghai or far away, in some other remote corner of the world. He lifted his head, met the emperor's gaze with the force of his own. "I want Princess Meiling. I want your daughter for my wife."

Shock pulsed through the room. The emperor recovered quickly with a rueful chuckle. "At last, a man who isn't a blind fool. My suspicions were true, then. But despite my respect for you as a warrior and the debt of gratitude I owe you, I'm not keen on giving my daughter to be the wife of a fugitive."

Shang didn't want that for Meiling either, but he was a selfish man.

The emperor let out a deep exhale, and a little bit of his fire seemed to extinguish into melancholy. Resolve quickly hardened his brow. "I will leave the decision in Meiling's hands. It is high time she had a say in her future. I've done everything I can to protect her, but she is a grown woman now. If she will have you, then she is yours. I will consider my debt to you repaid."

A beaming smile he couldn't contain burst across Shang's face. He dropped to his knees, bowing in obeisance. It gave him a chance to swallow the unexpected emotion clogging his throat.

It seemed he wasn't the only one fighting for composure. The emperor's voice was thick when he spoke again.

"I won't tell you to take good care of her. I already know you will. *If* she'll go with you. I'll admit, it'll save me from the worry of her magic being discovered and the things I'd have to do to protect her in those circumstances."

Shang was well aware that Meiling might refuse him. This would be the hardest decision of her life. But now this was a firm option. An option to spare both their lives, to give them a future together. He wouldn't try to influence her decision. He'd respect her choice.

Still, for the first time in so long, he burned with hope. And in this moment, an unexpected bond and camaraderie forged between him and Emperor Nianzu. It felt so tangible he could almost reach out and touch it. A bond woven through their shared love of Meiling. Few people knew who she truly was, but Shang and the emperor would rip apart kingdoms—the entire *world*—for her sake.

So when Shang lifted his head and met His Imperial Majesty's heavy gaze, he did something he never would have dreamed of. He reached out his hand.

The emperor clasped it in return.

I may not be worthy of her, Shang whispered in his mind. *But I have loved her with every fiber of my being, and I will never stop loving her.*

I'll kill you if you break her heart, Nianzu's eyes seemed to say in return.

Shang's lips quirked. *Noted.*

They released each other's hands, and just as Shang was turning to leave, the emperor cleared his throat and shuffled through the papers on his desk. "I didn't say you were dismissed."

When Shang immediately spun back around, the emperor pointed a large, rolled parchment at him.

"Take that," Emperor Nianzu said, back to business. "It's a map of the city fortifications. I want you to study them when you're not attending your trial. Tell me if you find any weaknesses."

Shang bowed crisply and accepted the map, his stomach flipping over itself as he restrained another smile. "Yes, Your Majesty."

The emperor lifted one eyebrow. "*Now* you're dismissed."

"Why are you following me?" Meiling whirled, brow furrowed up at the guards and maids moving to walk after her.

"Emperor's orders," one of them obliged. "Your Highness is never to be unattended."

Her stomach dropped. Dawn light crept through drawn curtains, staining the floor a soft gold. She sputtered momentarily, glancing from between her army of maids to the six armed guards.

An emperor's order must never be crossed.

She spewed out a breath of resignation and then spun on her heel to walk down the corridor. Behind her, fluttering maids shuffled and guards stomped. She winced. How was she to slip out of the palace early to speak with Shang if a tromping parade followed her?

Gritting her teeth, she folded her hands into her long sleeves and tilted her head back. Like she was a gracious, elegant princess on her way to teatime, where she would nibble crumpets and sip slowly enough that her tiny teacup would last long after the tea had cooled.

Doubtlessly, the guards and maids were raising their eyebrows at each other. What was the princess doing awake so early?

Another huge gust of air left her nostrils. They would find out soon enough.

To her surprise, when she crossed the bridge to the Academy, drawing her cloak tighter around her shoulders to ward off the morning cold, the practice grounds were alive and full of clattering weapons, striking and dodging students, and shouting masters. The sun was not half risen, and by the looks of the students, they had been practicing for some time.

Could this be any more public? Meiling pursed her lips and did not falter her pace. Behind her, guard boots rattled the bridge. A little snicker from one of the maids made her whirl and look sharply at the offending maid. She almost asked what was so funny as the maid suppressed her merriment, but the answer was probably herself. Swallowing, she looked around and was surprised to see a tiger battling a lad of probably fourteen years. Was the tiger Fen?

Next, she spotted Feiyan. Gripping a quarter staff with both hands, the healer fended off attacks with shocking agility from a girl who was . . . flinging rocks? Sweat dripped down Feiyan's face, making little flyaway hairs plaster to her forehead and cheeks.

She held her own. But she looked exhausted.

Last of all, Meiling found Shang on the other side of the practice field. He squatted by a few children younger than ten years old. He was telling them something, pointing and gesturing as he did so. The hard lines were gone from his face.

He stood abruptly, motioned for one of the boys to join him in front of the other students. He did not wear a master's black robes, but a simple light brown tunic, functional trousers, and a belt instead of a sash.

Shang demonstrated a series of parries and thrusts with a wooden sword, using the boy as an example opponent. As Meiling approached around the edge of the practice field, her parade in tow, the children each picked up their own swords and practiced the movements as Shang did them.

Soon, she was close enough to hear him say, "Good! Don't let the blade fall. Keep up your energy, Jing. Movements like that will show your enemy weakness. Once your enemy sees that you are tired, they will work that advantage. Understand?"

Shang looked up. He froze mid-parry demonstration, making the children twist over their shoulders to see what spectacle captured his attention. She swallowed again when all those little eyes rounded in horror.

What tales had these children heard about the cursed princess?

It didn't matter. She smiled at each child in turn before lifting her gaze back to Shang. When she expected his flexing jaw and impassive brow, she was surprised to instead receive a gaze like warm honey. Her stomach flipped over itself.

"Keep practicing," Shang said, setting down his sword. "These movements need to be as familiar as breathing."

Once he'd finished leaving instructions to the group, he strode quickly to meet her, bowing low when he arrived. He was quite sweaty, confirming her suspicion that they had been training for a long time already.

Shang's eyes darted from Meiling's to the guards and maids following her, then back down to her. His cheeks were flushed from exertion. "Princess Meiling. How may I serve you, Highness?" The words were formal, but there was something gentle about the way he said them. As though he was very, very glad to see her.

She shifted, glancing back at her entourage. "May I speak with you? Somewhat . . . privately?"

He glanced again to the guards and nodded, his face falling into his typical seriousness, reading the concern in her tone. "May I suggest the Academy gardens, as they are usually empty at this time?"

She nodded mutely, and he led them away from the training. They reached the garden, and a pang shot through her chest at the golden light seeping through the tree boughs, turning the leaves orange and glittering on the burbling stream. The pavilion was ahead, where Shang and Master Dong had spoken. Her steps faltered slightly when he led them straight there.

As they crossed the bridge, she turned and smiled uncertainly at the guards and maids. Fourteen people in all. "Would you all . . . wait here, perhaps?"

The guard who had spoken earlier answered. "The maids may wait here. We must encircle the pavilion."

She glanced at Shang, who shrugged. He held out his hand toward her when she reached the steps. Morning light did nothing to ease the intense blackness of his eyes.

The guards posted themselves around the pavilion as she took his proffered hand and allowed herself to be helped up the two tiny stairs. He led her to the bench where he had been sitting last night, set her down upon it, and then retreated with his hands clasped behind him. At attention.

Right, because there were guards and maids craning their necks from the bridge to catch a look at the secret rendezvous that was turning into quite the public event.

"Please sit," Meiling urged, sweeping her hand to the pavilion. She hoped he would choose to sit beside her so they could keep their voices low enough that the guards would not hear.

He sat across from her. His eyes asked his questions.

She took a deep breath, lowered her lashes, and spoke to the floor. "Thank you for receiving me," she started, and immediately felt another blush overtake her face. Of course, he received her. He had to.

Why was everything suddenly so dragon-blasted *awkward*?

"I am very glad you are recovered," he said. It was spoken with an underlying thread of deep honesty, even if it was still so dragon-blasted *formal*.

This would not do.

"I have a theory," she blurted, throwing aside ceremonies. "I believe I know what happened yesterday."

The air quickened between them. He sat up a little straighter, his dark eyes sharpening. He looked as though he had something to say, but held it back. She waited. He said nothing.

She continued, lowering her voice. "I believe he was acting on the impulse of an implanted curse thread, like the phoenixes at the fortress. Not his own volition." She paused, studying his expression carefully and noting his swallows, blinks, and breaths. He was otherwise still. She lifted her chin, met his gaze. "I suspect he is not the only one with a curse."

He turned his head away. He must be thinking about Renshu.

"Where are the captives?" she pressed. She quieted even more, casting a glance over her shoulder as she whispered, "I could enter their minds and break the compulsions." As he snapped his head up toward her, furrowing his brow, and opened his mouth, she rushed forward ruthlessly. "I could do it quickly. No one need know! Then they could go back to their families. They've been separated for so long."

"You cannot help them," Shang whispered, and then with a surreptitious glance toward the guards, crossed the pavilion to sit next to her. The guards eyed him suspiciously but remained at their posts.

"You cannot help them," he repeated, voice low and earnest. His attention entreated her so intensely that she looked away. Her fingers strayed to her sash. "It would be useless for you to intervene. No one could know of your intervention." His voice was so quiet she struggled to discern the words. "You are not alone in your theory; the captives have been sequestered for this very fear. They are already being investigated for any trace of lingering magic or compulsions. You could rid them of the curse threads, but until they are investigated, they cannot be released. And if they find no curses, then Du Liuxian must be tried for treason."

A helpless "Oh," escaped her lips. She half-slumped against the bench, half retained her prim posture. She covered one cheek with a hand as the realization sunk deeper into her stomach. "Oh."

"I heard talk of them calling in Feiyan to heal away the curses. Or a curse specialist. Your way may be the most efficient way, but there are less risky ways that will work. *If* the issue is a curse."

Meiling sat still, his scrutiny burning into her as she studied the rosebud embroidered hem of her robes. Her lips parted, her mind scrabbling for alternative options. She wanted to cry out in frustration that she was not a useless, helpless princess. A nothing. She could *help,* she could do things.

Was her lot in life to watch by the side as all she loved burned?

She lifted her gaze to Shang's and found him looking back and forth between her face and fingers twisting in her sash. She forced them to lie still.

"What happened yesterday, in the trial?" she asked, fixing him with her most pointed look. "Why did you admit to the lies?"

Something like a fog passed over his eyes. Something . . . *muddled.* Iron hardness replaced it. "I didn't lie."

Now it was her turn to study him so closely that he turned away. "Shang?"

He tilted his head toward her, and something vulnerable flashed in his expression. "Yes, Meiling?" His eyes drifted to her lips.

For the briefest second, she forgot what she was going to ask.

"You admitted yesterday to bartering with Fang Zedong's brigands for your life in exchange for mine."

A scuttling nearby made her jolt. Shang reacted, stiffening.

"What?" he whispered tightly.

"Did you hear that?" she asked, turning this way and that for the source of the sound.

"Hear what?"

"That . . . that *sound.* I keep hearing it everywhere."

He looked alarmed even as he shook his head. "Describe it."

"It's like a bug," she said, arching her neck to try to find where it'd come from. "But different, and . . . Oh, you will think this very silly of me, but it always makes me . . . I don't know. It's like fingernails down my spine. It gives me the shudders, and it is *everywhere* and I cannot find what is causing it. I feel like I recognized it once, but now I cannot remember."

"A bug?" Shang lifted an eyebrow, but not in mockery. "I heard nothing. You mentioned it yesterday—"

"Princess Meiling."

She barely restrained herself from shooting to her feet at the sound of her name. Instead, she straightened her back, folded her hands in her lap, and turned her face toward an approaching attendant. "Yes?"

The man bowed and kept his eyes fixed on the ground. "His Imperial Majesty summons Your Highness."

"The emperor?" she blurted and then clamped her mouth shut. She paused, taking a deep breath. "Where shall I meet him?"

"His private study, Highness."

She nodded and dismissed the attendant with a flick of her wrist. Her brow knit tightly as she frowned.

"You seem . . . disconcerted," Shang said as they both stood.

"I am only surprised," she managed, attempting a half-smile. "The emperor . . ." She caught herself before she called him *Pa*. Caught herself before she admitted Pa had only summoned her a bare handful of times in her life, and never to his private study.

She could have sworn Shang's face turned a shade brighter, despite his gentle reassurance. "I'm sure there is no cause for worry, Meiling."

There was just something about the way he said her name without her title that forever undid her. As though she were something dearly precious to him. As though if people did not surround them, he would take her into his arms and kiss her for hours.

She wished he would.

She swallowed, hoping her face wasn't turning a different hue, and drew another breath. The sweet scent of lilies tickled her nostrils. "I suppose I shall find out."

Shang offered his hand to her, and something shifted in his expression. As if he asked for so much more than to escort her out of the pavilion. When she placed her cold fingers in his, his thumb swept in a caress over the back of her hand. She looked up, finding his gaze heavy upon her. Overwhelmed, she quickly looked away.

Her slippered feet found the ground. Shang released her hand as her guards gathered around her and her maids fluttered to their places.

Meiling glanced back toward Shang, still standing on the pavilion, bearing no expression save for his glittering eyes. Her blood pounded in her veins as she said, “Thank you.”

Something flashed across his face. It was too fast for her to read.

She turned and hurried away from the garden.

CHAPTER 22

"YOU SUMMONED ME, Glorious Emperor." Meiling bowed herself to the floor, forehead touching golden tassels on a scarlet woven rug.

"Stand, Daughter. There is no need for formality here."

Pa's back was to her, his hands behind him as he stared out of the windows flanking his desk. Like her, he was not yet arranged for this morning's parade, but still was dressed in fine, ornate robes. His wide shoulders lifted and lowered with a deep breath. He rolled a tongue of fire around on his knuckles. He extinguished it and turned as she got to her feet, keeping her hands clasped in front of her.

"I summoned you to tell you that I have employed extra measures to ensure your safety. If I must move you to my own chambers and keep you by my side, I will not hesitate. The cause of yesterday's calamity is being thoroughly investigated." Then, much quieter, "I do not wish for you to feel unsafe."

He turned away again, his fist planting firmly on the window trim. The barest wisp of smoke escaped between his knuckles. He clenched his fist tighter.

"Thank you, Pa." She took a step closer, eager to soothe the lines of worry between his brows. Even if she *did* hate the extra guards. "I know how hard you work to keep me and our people safe."

His loud exhale filled the room. He seemed to give in to his emotion, opened his palm, and a fireball hovered above his skin. It grew by the moment. He clenched his jaw and snuffed it in a flurry of smoke and fist.

Was this her chance? Maybe if Pa gave her his sanction . . .

"I can help," she began, and did not stop when he whirled to face her. "It would not endanger me—I promise! I could enter the prisoners' minds and find out if they were cursed. I can break their curses, Pa. I could do it very quickly, I think. Then we wouldn't have to be afraid of them doing something in the future."

Pa was already shaking his head viciously, his eyes burning like twin balls of fire. "Absolutely not. This would endanger you more than anything. If I allowed this, your magic would no longer be a secret. I could not protect you from the law then. Not if the council discovered you have been exercising your magic all these years independently."

Each lungful of air was more painful than the one before. Tears burned in her throat. "I don't want to be useless," she said, and threw aside all restraint and ran to wrap her arms around Pa's waist. She buried her face in his chest as his arms encircled her tightly. His robes muffled her pleas. "I want to help. I'm tired of being the one everyone else is protecting. I know I have no Academy training, but I've learned to wield my magic through practice. There is so much potential in it. Pa, if you would only let me, I could do so much for you, for Zheninghai, for—"

"I know you are capable of so much. But my first priority is to keep my family safe. I cannot . . . You must not plead with me like this." He unfolded one arm and used it to tilt her chin up to meet his eyes. Now it was *his* turn to plead with her. "Meiling, my sweet girl, I *want* you to use your magic. I want to see what you're capable of. I know you could be the sharpest weapon in my arsenal. But Meiling, there is no undoing the past. For good or for evil, we kept your magic a secret. If we announce it now, *you will be killed*. I will be dethroned and likely executed, too. I don't want to think what could happen to the rest of our family. You cannot ask me to let you use your magic. Not now. We will uncover what happened yesterday, and it will never happen again."

"But Pa—"

He pressed one finger to her lips, his brow hardening with sternness. "We will purge the prisoners of any lingering curses without risking your life."

"Pa—"

"Meiling, I love you. I know you. I know you willingly gave yourself up to the brigands to save your protectors. This is what I love about you, and this is what worries me so much that I cannot sleep at night. All night I stare at the ceiling and I think—" He stopped himself abruptly, letting out a growl.

She froze, searching the earnest gaze of her father. Something akin to helplessness flashed across his face, and it reminded her of Shang's expression yesterday after she had been stabbed. Her protests died in her throat. She lowered her head into the folds of his robes and hugged him tighter. "I love you, Pa."

She meant it. Truly.

A part of her still died with those words.

Her magic would always be a secret, then.

"Now go," Pa said as he stepped back away from her. "We must ride out soon. Prepare yourself." When she started to bow, he waved his hand dismissively. "Enough of that. Be quick."

When she had left the study, she was followed by her entourage of endless guards and maids back toward her room. She'd hardly gone a few paces before someone tromped loudly down the intersecting hallway and into view.

"Yun?" Meiling startled, drawing back slightly. "Why are you here? Has Pa—His Imperial Majesty, I mean—summoned you?"

Yun shook his head, coming toward her and reaching out to take her hands. "No, but I heard you were here, so I came—"

She jerked back. "Ow! Your hands are so hot!"

"Oops." Yun grinned, quickly looking down. "My mistake. Here, they should be fine now."

"Why are you holding my hands?" She tried to pull back again, yanked harder when he got down on one knee. "Yun, what in all the qilin-cursed seven valleys are you doing?"

Both of Yun's eyebrows shot up. "Don't let Ma hear you talk that way."

"You're not answering my question."

He shot to his feet and dropped both her hands in an exasperated gesture. "Look, I was only trying to ask you to accompany me to the Academy dance tonight. I thought I would do it properly, but you won't have it. I know I should have asked you earlier but—"

"The Academy dance?" Meiling breathed. "You want . . . you want *me* to come with you? Yun . . . Why . . .?"

"Because you're a princess and Hou is too young for me to take."

"You have never asked me to come before."

"This is my last one as a student! Good grief, you're making this weird. I'm allowed to bring a guest and I want you to come with me. Will you? Tonight?"

She blinked back tears, nodding as a grin broke out across her face. "Of course, Yun! I would love—" She stopped herself, afraid of sounding too eager. She lowered her face and nodded again. "I would be honored, brother."

"Good. I will be by tonight to escort you." Yun grinned and waved as he ran off to finish getting ready for the parade.

Meiling stared after him, her feet grown like tree roots into the ground. Yun wanted her by his side tonight? Despite . . . despite everything? She never would have imagined—never would have dared to presume—that he would want her to attend his last student dance with him. Yun, who by virtue of being tall and handsome and the Crown Prince, could have asked any one of the pretty Academy girls his age.

"Highness?" a maid chirped from behind her. "Ought we hurry to your chambers? The parade . . .?"

Meiling blinked. "Oh, yes, yes. Of course. Forgive me for delaying."

She did not have time to do anything more than rip her headdress out of her hair before she ran out her chamber doors to make the trial. Tomorrow was the last day of the festival. The last day of their trial. She needed to speak with Ma *today* to find a way to testify in the trial tomorrow. Surely her words could sway the judge. Whatever nonsense had been happening previously could be ended.

She opened her door and froze.

Fourteen guards and maids blinked at her expectantly.

"Dragons," Meiling growled under her breath. She stood up taller, leveled her shoulders, and fixed the group with the most potent princess look she could muster. "I will be back shortly."

"We must accompany you, Highness," the leading guard said as she tried to walk past him. "The emperor made no exceptions."

She gave no response. Not wanting to waste any more time, she lifted her chin and strode down the hallway. They followed. Could she lose them along the way? It wasn't like she could crowd fourteen people onto the balcony without notice. She highly doubted she could convince the guards to stay quiet and keep their heads low.

She glanced back at the dutiful guards. If she evaded them—which was highly unlikely—what would that cost them? Would they be punished? Doubtlessly. Her maids, too.

Very well. She would have to take a different approach.

She walked straight past the hallway with the door leading to the balcony stairs. Straight toward the guards standing at attention at the main entrance to the courtyard. She flashed her best smile. The guards stiffened, eyeing her entourage. "Court is in session, Highness," the first said curtly.

She lifted her chin. "Then try to announce us as quietly as possible."

"It is not open to viewers—"

"Wonderful. It is a good thing that I am not a mere viewer. Hurry now." The words burned her lips, but she would not back down. "Open the doors," she demanded, firmer.

The guards looked at each other, then over Meiling's head at the guards behind her.

"My guards are not giving the orders," she snapped. She'd never thought her voice could come out so harshly.

The first guard swallowed and bowed. "Very well, Highness."

The doors opened, and blood roared in her ears as she stepped across the threshold and stopped. A long aisle unfurled to the judge seated on the dais. From here, she could only see Shang and Fen's torsos and heads from where they kneeled at the judge's right hand.

"Her Highness, Princess Meiling," the guard cried, his voice catching at first. The dread on his face confirmed his embarrassment.

The anxiety roiling in her gut confirmed her own embarrassment. But she could not retreat now. Trailed by guards and maids, with every pair of eyes lighting on her immediately, she fought to keep her steps even as she walked down the aisle.

The judge scowled, like she had just pounded him awake with a sledgehammer in the middle of the night. The announcer on his left looked more confused than anything, shuffling through papers as his eyes darted between Meiling and the judge. Fen's eyes were rounder than dinner bowls, her jaw gaping open. And Shang . . .

She refused to look at him.

"This case is not open for viewers!" the judge shouted, slamming his fist down on his desk. "Not even for the first princess!"

Meiling swallowed, fighting the urge to turn and run back down the aisle. But *no*. She widened her stance, as though bracing her legs could make her seem bigger and more intimidating to the judge. "This case—"

"What? Speak up!"

She met his gaze, willing her mounting fury to pierce him. "This case, Honored Judge, is about me. I request"—she stopped, inhaled—"I *demand* to sit as a witness." She couldn't look at Shang, but she did peek at Fen. The shock had melted from Fen's face, replaced by something else . . . *Respect?* She faced the judge again. "I am the subject. I was present for all of it."

The judge studied her from beneath hard brows.

Perhaps he was not the type to be won over by power demands. Perhaps . . . perhaps he preferred pleading. Well, it was too late; she had already demanded. She could only stand tall beneath his scrutiny.

The judge leaned back and waved his hand, closing his eyes. "Guards, escort Princess Meiling out of here."

"Honored Judge—"

"You have no power here! This is my domain, and I decide who stays and who goes. You will go," the judge snapped. "Take her away, guards. Immediately."

She gasped when a firm hand gripped her elbow. Gentle, but insistent and strong. She looked up to see her headguard pulling her away from the judge. She growled, her mind scrambling for what she ought to do. Should she wrench free of his grasp, throw herself before the judge, and plead to stay?

Would that be enough to save Shang? And Fen?

Or ought she to let herself be dragged back to her rooms, maintaining as much of her injured dignity as possible?

She was furious enough to leap up to the dais and do . . . something. But in the moment, she could not begin to guess what would be most helpful for Fen and Shang. So she stood where she was as her guard tugged harder and harder on her arm.

With an inaudible moan on her lips, she dragged her eyes toward Shang.

She expected that flash of disapproval across his handsome face. Instead, his lips were parted, his eyes full of understanding. Quickly, almost imperceptibly, he jerked his head toward the door. Telling her to leave. Probably telling her to stop trying to help.

Very well. She'd leave.

She let her guards escort her out the way she had come. Humiliation burned her cheeks hotter than Pa's fireballs. The anger coursing through her veins was enough to make her almost whirl and scream, *"This is all wrong!"* But she kept her composure.

There was nothing she could do to salvage this now.

As soon as the courtroom doors closed behind her, she yanked her arm free of her guard's and threw discretion to the wind. She broke into a run and tore through the palace corridors, little caring about how her guards and maids ran after her until they must have looked utterly ridiculous.

She slammed her bedroom door shut on all fourteen of them and flung herself onto her bed, burying herself in sobs.

CHAPTER 23

A KNOCK ON her door made Meiling jolt, but she did not sit up. She was too enraged, too despairing, too terrified. After everything she had done, tried to do, after all her unique magic that thus far had only existed in legends, she was useless after all.

Too small. Too little. Too weak.

The door opened, and she knew without looking up that it was Ma. *Wonderful*—word must have been sent of her display to her parents. Now she must bear a rebuke on top of everything else. No matter. What was one more thing?

Ma stood quietly beside the bed for a long time, so long Meiling suffered to raise tear-streaked cheeks up toward her.

"I know, I know, I *know*," she growled before Ma could say anything. A few months ago, she would never have dreamed of addressing her mother so, but many things had changed since then. "You don't have to tell me my faults; I'm acutely aware of them. I only . . . I just cannot let them die."

Ma lowered herself to sit next to Meiling's curled body. She laid a warm hand on her shoulder. "Oh, Mei. You've gone and fallen in love with the boy."

Meiling shot upright, yanking herself free of Ma's touch.

"There's no use denying it," Ma said with a rueful smile. "I've known it for some time now."

"That's not—I am trying to save them *both* because they are innocent! I spent weeks with them; I know them. They are *both* far from perfect, but they are innocent of what they are accused. And if I do nothing, they will be executed in only two days. I could not bear the injustice of it!"

Ma gently pushed Meiling's raised hands down, a silent bid to calm herself. Meiling huffed and bit hard on her tongue.

"It has nothing to do with love. I'd try just as hard if I didn't—" Meiling stopped herself and turned her flushing face to her lap. Her nails dug into the soft flesh of her palm. Then she looked up into Ma's soft eyes, liquid with understanding.

She gave up. She flung herself into Ma's arms and broke into a fresh wave of sobs.

"I just want to save them. I know my feelings are ridiculous. I know I wish for the impossible, but I could be content if I only knew they were saved. As long as they are alive and happy. I know I made a fool of myself in the court." At Ma's look, Meiling sighed. "And the throne room, and other places. But I cannot let this run its course. Everything about this trial is wrong and unfair. I've heard it, and I think if I could just speak—"

"Mei," Ma reached out and grasped both of Meiling's hands, rubbing her thumb against her knuckles. She looked down, then up again. When she spoke, her voice was so, so soft. So gentle. And racked with pain. "Mei, my dove, your words have no weight."

Meiling drew back, her mouth falling open. "But this all surrounds *me*. How can my words have no weight?"

Ma's eyes shimmered with unshed tears. "You are a princess with no magic."

Everything came back to that. Her *curse.*

Meiling threw aside the bedclothes and stood. She stumbled to her window, hardly able to see out of it through a sheen of mist. She squeezed her eyes shut around ragged breaths, and fat tears dripped down her cheeks.

"Let me be Feiyan," she choked. "Let me spend my life exhausted and serving. You and Pa took away my life when you took away my magic. You wanted me to be able to experience the joys and wonders of life, but how can I when no one will marry a cursed princess? You have made me a *useless* princess."

She could not look back at Ma, could not see anything for her tears. Could hardly breathe around sobs. "You thought you were giving me your life. Your life of marrying the most distinguished man in the empire, of having powerful children, of overcoming every obstacle. But you gave me something far different. A life that prevents me from doing anything to overcome, a life where I can do nothing to protect those I love. Instead, I stand by and watch it all die."

Her last words tasted bitterest of all: "Maybe Fang Zedong was right."

"Enough!" Ma demanded, her voice breaking.

Meiling buried her head in her palms as her elbows collapsed onto the windowsill. Silent sobs wracked her body as she tried to restrain her tears. Fresh ones poured free anyway.

"Whether we made the right decision by you has yet to be determined," Ma said, and there were tears in her voice. "But you, of all people, should know everything we do is out of love. To protect you."

"I know," she gasped. Somehow, that made it worse. She couldn't resent them like she wanted; she could not make them the scapegoat of her fury and grief. If she had been in the same position, she probably would have done the same thing.

"Right or wrong, the decision has been made. We can only consider our options from here and make the best decision based on the information we have." Ma stood and folded her arms across her chest, ever practical. "Dry your tears and let's discuss the situation."

It seemed like something Shang would say, which made her want to cry harder. But she tugged a handkerchief free of her sleeve, wiped her nose, dabbed her cheeks, and drew a deep breath. Hysterics would save no one. She sat herself down on the bed, trying not to let her lungs shudder with every breath.

"You believe your friends are innocent," Ma prompted.

"If you had known we would be hunted, would you have sent more wielders with me?"

Ma nodded before adding, "We probably would not have sent you in the first place."

Meiling tossed up her hands. "Exactly. So they were not equipped for what we faced. Considering that we *almost* made it, I think that alone proves their valiance and loyalty and dedication. Yet the trial is full of outright lies and nonsense."

When Ma asked what she meant, Meiling explained in detail everything she had heard and seen. She ignored the look Ma gave her when she described sneaking into the courtroom. "I know you said my word doesn't matter, but surely if I were to testify in court, they would believe me. I do not know of another way to stop their executions."

"You cannot testify," Ma insisted. "Your testimony will not help them."

She lowered her head. Ground her teeth hard, so hard her jaw might break. "There must be *something.*"

Ma stood, lifting herself off the bed with such regal grace it made Meiling swallow. "Let me think about it. I will see if there is anything that can be done."

She swept out of the room, leaving Meiling feeling . . . empty. The tiniest bit hopeful, but confused, and still burning from her earlier embarrassment. And like she shouldn't let her hopes rise too far, coupled with a fierce determination that she would *not* let Shang and Fen be executed.

But what could she do?

She left the bed and stood by the window, leaning against the wall and staring out at the city. Afternoon sunshine took the edge off the winter cold, and the streets were full of merrymaking. How odd the distant laughter sounded in her ears.

Was Fang Zedong right?

His promises were alluring. More alluring than she wanted to admit. They had settled like a dormant parasite into her mind, just waiting to feed on any seeds of doubt.

But just because Fang Zedong had correctly diagnosed flaws in their world, their society and social structure, did not mean his solution was correct. Zedong was a man who had threatened her with the blood of her siblings, who had decimated a man with phoenix fire at the snap of his fingers. Who had beaten her nearly to death.

"You're coming, aren't you?" Meiling whispered as the breathiest strains of a flute wafted through the window to her ears. "You're coming to conquer us. You are coming to lay claim to the power you believe is rightly yours. Well, useless princess or not, you can be sure I'm not going to let you take this land. I've seen who you are. I *know* what you're capable of. And as desperately flawed as this empire is, as much as I hate its faults, *you cannot have it*."

She stopped, letting the sound of her own exhales fill the room. The pulse of her heartbeat echoed in harmony.

"It's your fault my friends are on trial. It's your fault I ever had to leave the palace. Everything is your fault. And I'm not going to let you get away with it, Fang Zedong."

At the mention of his name, something hissed behind her.

She whirled, nearly tripping over herself in fright. "Who's there?" she called, moving around the room with careful, deliberate steps. She paused, swallowing the lump in her throat. Ought she to call her guards? She drew another breath against her pounding fear, and then whispered, "Fang Zedong."

Silence.

Biting the inside of her lip, she marched to the door and flung it open. "Maids? I think there's a bug in my room somewhere. Will you please investigate it?"

Not waiting for their answers, and not bothering to acknowledge the guards that straightened, she set off down the corridor. Resolution pinched her brow, strengthened her steps, and *almost* rid her of her irritation as her guards followed her.

CHAPTER 24

SHANG WISHED HE'D had a chance to speak to Fen before the trial about his conversation with the emperor. She was nearly fuming as they walked out of the courtroom. He might have laid a hand on her shoulder if he didn't know that she would have thrown the touch off. Her fear was anger, her hurt was anger, her heartbreak was anger. It was a challenge to get past that barrier—Shang had only succeeded a handful of times.

He'd be more successful throwing a punch at her face than squeezing her arm in reassurance.

"I have something to tell you," Shang said under his breath to her. "It's *very* important. Follow me back to my room."

"If it's not about how we're going to be pardoned, I don't want to hear it," she snapped back.

"You'll want to hear this. But Meiling is going to be waiting for us outside, so you'll have to be patient."

"What do you mean, she'll be waiting outside? She was sent away—"

They walked out of double doors, and sure enough, there was Meiling. With a passel of guards, though the bevy of maids were nowhere to be seen. She was leaning against a beaded curtain, arms crossed. Her face, still wearing the ceremonial paint for the festival, was twisted in a scowl—not an expression she wore often. Half of her hair fell unbound to her hips, the other half was arranged with strung crystals like stars in an updo.

Fen shot Shang an incredulous look. "How did you know she was going to be here?"

Meiling's gaze sharpened on him, her brow furrowing with the same question.

"Because I know her," Shang replied.

And it is because I know her that I love her so dearly.

Perhaps Meiling read his unspoken thoughts. Her neck colored, and for a second, she glanced away.

If she will have you, she is yours.

Shang's heart had filled with hope to be thrice its normal size. If she wouldn't have him, he'd be that much more devastated. He didn't think he could bring himself to leave Suguan without her.

Fen cocked her head, eyeing Meiling like she was prey that had fought back harder than she expected. "You either have no self-awareness, or you have more guts that I have given you credit for. Or you're stupider than a headless dragon."

Shang exhaled slowly, reining in the sudden flaring of his temper. Why couldn't Fen say one civil word to the girl who saved her life multiple times on the road to Liafugen? "Guards have ears," he growled by way of rebuke, though he wanted to say much more.

Fen shrugged, her face darkening. "Not like anything matters anymore."

Meiling pushed off the wall and hurried to them, beckoning her grumpy guards to stay put. Their attention shifted to Shang, but he only lifted a challenging eyebrow in response. When she stopped in front of him and Fen, he was struck again by just how much shorter she was compared to them. She wasn't especially short, but next to Fen? She barely reached the shifter's nose. Much less his own.

He liked her height.

"I need to speak to you two," she hissed under her breath.

Fen shifted her weight impatiently to one foot. "We're *waiting*." The words, characteristic of Fen, bristled. The tone, however, lacked her signature malice.

That dragon-blasted shapeshifter actually harbored some genuine respect for Meiling.

Seven valleys, finally, Shang thought.

Meiling stepped closer, lowered her voice, and whispered, "I think you two should flee Suguan. So they cannot kill you."

Shang's gut plunged to the floor. *You two.* Not *we*. She wouldn't have forgotten his request from two nights ago that she flee with him. *It isn't a firm no,* he assured himself quickly. She didn't have all the information, and he hadn't officially asked her to be his wife.

Fen couldn't hide her shock when she burst, "Are you insane?"

Meiling held her ground. "I don't want either of you to be executed. Not on my behalf. Not when you are innocent. Please, you must consider it. I've listened to the trials, and I'm so afraid that you will be killed—"

"We do not run like cowards," Fen spat. "We will face what lies before us. I will not live in dishonor."

Shang winced at the unintended insult, even as he admired Fen's tenacity. Still, he needed to relay his conversation with His Imperial Majesty to them both. He was just opening his mouth when Meiling lifted her chin, defiance sparking in her lovely eyes.

"I can assure you that death is worse than life spent in dishonor."

Fen's eyes widened slightly as she realized the insult she'd dealt. For once, it hadn't been intentional. If anything, she looked chastened. Maybe she had more than just a little bit of respect for the princess.

Shang took both of their elbows and marched a few steps further from the watching guards. If he hadn't saved Meiling's life only yesterday, her guards might have come after him. Instead, when he glanced over his shoulder, they'd only tensed, but made no move to follow.

"I need you two to listen to me," he said, lowering his voice. "I was going to explain this in a more private place, but here we are. Meiling, I spoke to your father this morning. Before you did."

Meiling's eyes widened. Was that hurt flickering across her features?

"I was going to tell you. I didn't get a chance when you were called away," he added, and she relaxed. He had imagined telling her somewhere private, just the two of them, had dreamed that if she agreed to marry him, he would kiss her without a shred of guilt. Alas, he would have to tell her everything except the part where she was supposed to come with him and be his wife.

Fathers have mercy, the last person he wanted sitting in on that conversation was Hu Fen.

"You spoke to the *emperor*?" Fen hissed.

Meiling shushed her, and they shot glares at each other. If the moment weren't so serious, Shang might have been amused. He really did like Meiling better this way.

"He said he cannot get us pardons outside of the courts," said Shang, "but he—"

"What kind of powerless emperor is that?" Fen snarled, almost successfully hiding the utter dejection that stole across her face. "If he can't—"

"An emperor with a conqueror at his gates," Shang snapped back. "Now shut up and listen. He wants to smuggle us outside of the city before the execution."

Shang's arm shot out as Meiling wobbled on her feet. She grabbed hold of his biceps and front of his robes to steady herself as he slid his hand around her waist. "Forgive me," she gasped quickly, her pupils dilating, her chest heaving. His heart lurched, ducking his head closer to her, silently asking if she was alright. "I didn't know

Pa would"—she caught herself—"*His Imperial Majesty* would do that." Her voice was as unsteady as her feet.

His heart broke a little for her in that moment. The way her father belonged to this entire empire, not just to her and her family. How difficult it must be to be the daughter of someone who was forced daily to make some of the hardest decisions a person could ever face.

She had all but begged her father with tears for his life and Fen's life. And she had believed he would choose Zheninghai over her, protocol over true justice. He didn't blame her for fighting to control her emotion.

But her father was a better man than she even knew. She likely didn't have a clue how deeply he loved her.

Shang wouldn't have minded if she'd clung to him a while longer, but she straightened, found her balance, and drew together her composure as Fen demanded: "The emperor wants us to run? He wants to sweep us under the rug and *banish* us?"

"Would you rather be killed and your family starve?" Shang tried to keep his tone even, but he couldn't help the flare of anger. If Meiling wasn't here, he would have used much more graphic language. He understood now. Honor, reputation, and success were so much less valuable than he'd always believed. They were helpful and good, but they were empty promises by themselves.

If he was with Meiling, he could be a beggar in the streets and he'd still be happier than he could imagine.

"You have to choose what you want," said Shang, pouring the force of his belief into his words. "If you want honor, then walk yourself to your execution and face it without flinching. No one would call you a coward after that. But if your siblings, if your mother, if a chance for a future is what you want, then take the emperor's offer. Run. And don't feel guilty for one second."

A vein in Fen's forehead pulsed. She averted her gaze from his. Good—she was actually considering what he said. He turned back to Meiling, who stared up at him with enormous eyes and those beautiful lips he couldn't help but admire.

His throat turned a little dry. "You don't have to worry about us anymore."

Her brow lowered. That subtle fierceness returned. "I still want you pardoned."

"Then pray."

She scowled. "Why did you admit to things in yesterday's trials that were false? You did not answer me earlier."

"I answered the truth," he replied, frowning.

"No, you didn't."

He racked his mind for memories of yesterday's session, but details turned fuzzy. His attention slid away from the intensity of her scrutiny to fixate on the beaded edges of a scarlet curtain. "They always ask questions in a way that makes it sound worse. It does not mean it's not true. The only time I lie is to protect . . . *it*." He wasn't about to say *your magic* in a hallway where anyone else breathed but her.

Her forehead knit in consternation, and when she opened her mouth to protest, he stopped her.

"Please, just trust me."

He expected another scowl, another attempt to protest but instead she tilted her head to one side, a string of beads falling with her hair at the movement. "Are you leaving, then?"

Shang couldn't bring himself to answer.

She took it as an affirmative, his silence for sadness at their imminent parting. "When do you leave?"

"His Imperial Majesty said the timing was up to us."

Fen was studying her boots, her teeth clenched behind thin lips. Meiling glanced at her, then returned her attention to Shang. He wasn't expecting her to reach out and touch his elbow briefly, gently, her gaze liquid with sorrow. "Don't leave without saying goodbye."

With that, she turned and made her way back to her guards. Shang watched as she walked around the bend in the hallway, equal parts stunned, furious, and broken. Everything they'd been through, all the affection and care between them, and she could walk away just like that? She could accept him leaving that easily?

Then, just before she disappeared from view, she reached up with her long, trailing sleeve and wiped her eyes.

He exhaled, the intensity of his emotions easing until they were bearable. For once, her tears brought sweet, sweet relief.

CHAPTER 25

MEILING THOUGHT SHE'D cried all her tears earlier. As it turned out, she had plenty more to pour out on her bedquilt. This was the best news she'd heard all week, that Shang wasn't going to be executed. Pa would make sure it didn't happen.

So why was she so devastated?

Because he was leaving. Forever.

Would you come with me?

She wanted to. Everything in her wanted to. To run away with him, to hide with him, to escape the coming storm. And yet, whenever she went to practice those words, *"Let me come with you,"* her tongue cleaved to the roof of her mouth.

It felt wrong. She didn't know why.

Relief came in the form of her maids informing her it was time to prepare for the Academy dance. She was nearly ready when a servant came to deliver a message.

"Prepare yourself, Highness," the servant said after bowing and being instructed to stand. "You testify in court tomorrow."

Meiling stared at the servant, her jaw falling to the floor. He shuffled, and belatedly she realized he was waiting for her to dismiss him. She managed a vague wave since her throat completely seized up, preventing any sound from escaping. He left.

She was so lost in thought, in confusion, in wild, frenzied hope, that her maids addressed her several times before she blinked and looked up at them.

"The Crown Prince is here. He awaits you, Highness."

"Oh!" She scrambled to her feet, not bothering to check her reflection in the mirror.

Ma had done it. She had worked some sort of magic of her own, had woven some spell over Pa or the judge or someone powerful. Fathers bless her! They stood a chance, and Meiling could correct the wrongs. She could make everything clear for the judge that Shang and Fen were innocent.

Shang wouldn't have to leave.

Her heart wouldn't have to be broken.

Yun wore glittering royal blue, matching her own robes. Gold fire embroidery licked the edges of his garments, and when he walked, his robes split on the sides to reveal a peek at fire-orange trousers. The trousers were a little daring, but she doubted Yun knew that.

Nothing rattled on her head tonight. She did not know what ornaments were pinned in her hair, only that her head was much more secure than usual for formal events. Thankfully, the paint hid any lingering traces of her earlier crying.

Yun grinned at her, offering his arm. "Ready?" The fire danced in his eyes, lively and excited like a crackling, spitting campfire. His feet shuffled, and he tugged his robes straighter with his free hand. So much nervous energy.

"Don't burn me," Meiling said, trying to keep the mischief from twisting up her mouth.

"Only if you don't make me mad."

"So . . . don't set Hou on you?" she teased.

Yun's eyes widened with exasperation. "Did you hear what she did yesterday? Dragons, if she weren't a princess . . ." He shook his head and kept shaking it. "That girl should have been expelled from the Academy a dozen times over by now."

"Do I want to know?"

He genuinely considered it.

"Of course I want to know!" Meiling tugged on his arm with a laugh. "Tell me."

"She planted fire spits on three masters' mats, and another one under my head cushion—even though girls aren't allowed in the boys' dormitories. She's been insufferable ever since she learned she can make fire that doesn't burn." He growled under his breath, but it was half chuckle. "It's a good thing you don't have magic, sister. You don't have to deal with these things."

It was meant to be sweet, and so she smiled, but her gaze faced forward.

How little her own brother actually knew of who she truly was.

The event was held at a pavilion outside the Academy. She'd never been before and was immediately struck by the vast differences in clothing of the mingling attendees. There were enough people that no one was singled out, but they no longer wore the neutralizing white. The sons and daughters of wealthy, prominent courtiers were obvious, dressed in finery that rivaled Yun and Meiling's clothes. Social status was painfully obvious.

Horns blasted when Yun guided Meiling under the dripping garland of roses forming the entryway. Immediately, her throat closed at the sight of so many people, so many warm bodies and staring eyes.

At least Yun would never notice her hitched breathing.

He grinned, and when she peeked at him, found him making eye contact and nodding at different people. Friends? Or random fellow classmates?

Lift your head.

The strong voice in her mind urged her head up, made her fight her inclination to shrink closer to her brother and seek strength in his blazing warmth and surging power. He wouldn't notice if she curled in closer to him and lowered her eyes away from the darting stares, the averted eyes and uncomfortable shuffles away from her shadow.

She raised her gaze. Though it took everything within her, she made eye contact with the students. Their smiles froze, faltered, or disappeared entirely when she did so. But she refused to keep cowering.

She'd faced brigands. Fang Zedong. Torture, near-starvation, black dungeons, *mó guǐ*. Things these sapling youths could only dream of, could only discuss over the yellowed pages of ancient textbooks.

She could face a few hundred strangers. Right?

Anxiety pushed against her lungs, closed around them. *Tighter, tighter.* She shifted her gaze away from the people to study the candlelit pavilion and sunset stained paving stones of the patio. Roses spilled from bushes, yellow wintersweet blossoms woven into the wooden lattices. Laughter, both friendly and cheering, almost overcame the *guqin* music wafting from the corner.

Any minute now, she expected Yun to spot something exciting, deposit her in the middle of nowhere, and forget about her. But surprisingly, he led her through the parting crowds, giving princely acknowledgements as he went, and brought her toward a little dais in full view of the pavilion.

"Here," Yun said, giving her a hand so she could step up and make herself comfortable on the cushions. Food and drink were already spread on the table before her. Next to her, an empty cushion for him. "You don't know many people, so I made sure this was set up for you to have the best view of the dances. Unless, of course, you'd like to dance." He winked.

She gave him a feigned glare, making him laugh.

"Food. Drink." He swept his hand. "Anything you like. I will be back later."

He may not be considerate enough to stay here with her, to not abandon her amid strangers, but he *had* been considerate enough to make sure she was not entirely bored and comfortless.

She smiled despite herself.

And then she looked up as Yun's tall form was swallowed up in the crowds. The walls of anxiety closed in again. Her heart rammed at full speed in her chest as she frantically searched the hundreds of faces for someone familiar.

Where was Feiyan?

Of course, it was unlikely that Feiyan would be here. She would be curled up in the library, half asleep as she studied.

The music started, and she was glad she could feign interest in the girls skittering up the pavilion steps to take their place. They smiled and giggled, batting their eyelashes and twirling their skirts. They looked like regular girls, not magically gifted warriors-in-training.

Meiling focused her attention on the dance and decidedly *not* on the staring eyes boring holes into her head. They would wonder why she was here, why Yun had brought her at all. There would be more than a few disappointed girls wondering what was so wrong with them that Princess Meiling was the Crown Prince's preference.

Eight girls danced. She quickly noticed the best dancer in the group and was not surprised to discover by her clothes that she was a nobleman's daughter. The girl was much less concerned than the others about tossing simpering smiles at the audience and instead focused on letting her eyes follow her movements and bringing each graceful arc to completion.

She was beautiful, with a long, elegant neck and a tall, willowy form. Was she powerful too? Did her grace belie hidden strength and prowess? What sort of magic did she wield? Her obvious high birth indicated she was probably born of a long line of powerful wielders.

Meiling couldn't bring herself to watch any of the other young women. Her eyes were glued to the one. She soon forgot the judgmental stares and her own aloneness.

The dance ended.

The girls bowed and abandoned the stage as a new crop of giggles took their place. Her eyes still followed the one girl and found that she walked as elegantly as she danced. Languid, like a cat. She walked, chin high with the confidence of a thousand kings, and made her way directly to—

Oh dragons, Shang was here?

She sputtered on her tea and accidentally clattered the cup back down on the table much too loudly for a princess. She ignored her own flush of embarrassment, the extra eyes that snapped to her at the sound, and tried not to let her gaze widen with too much visible shock. Apparently, she'd been wrong to assume that because he wasn't a student anymore, he wouldn't be here.

Shang wore blue. He was far across the courtyard—which was why she hadn't seen him earlier—surrounded by a group of wielders. He was taller than those next to him except for the one man standing beside him.

Renshu.

That meant—that meant he had been cleared of Zedong's curses. Perhaps the rest of the prisoners were free and safe now. Relief like warm water ran down her spine. Her shoulders relaxed.

Fen was nearby, though not in Shang's direct circle. She was surrounded by her own group of friends, laughing with her head thrown back, and it made Meiling realize she had never considered how popular Fen or Shang might be.

From the looks of it, very popular.

The girl strode straight up to Shang and said something to him. He nodded back, smiling a little. Was it Meiling's own stupid, hopeless heart that made her think his smile was more polite than genuine? He leaned back, arms crossed with a goblet in one hand. He said something back to the girl, and the others laughed. Even the girl.

While she watched, a couple more girls strode up, and even from this distance, Meiling could discern their object of attention. Shang, however, hardly glanced at them before turning to Renshu and saying something with a smirk to him. Renshu leaned toward his ear and his reply made Shang toss his head back in full laughter.

The girls laughed too, though Meiling wondered if they had even heard the joke.

They had no idea that only two nights ago, he'd held her in his arms and told her he was a failure. Or that just hours ago, he'd been on trial for his life. One could not blame them considering the composure he kept.

How he managed it was beyond her.

When she had agreed to come to this, she had not thought she was agreeing to come watch Shang socialize among his friend circles. She had not thought this was going to be one huge reminder that she did not belong in this world. It was supposed to be a step toward moving past *everything*.

Shang looked up. Directly at her.

Immediately, instinctively, she dropped her head. Her white-knuckled hand clutched her empty teacup. The heat of the summer sun bloomed in her cheeks despite the winter cold.

Was he still looking? She had to know.

Her gaze darted up and across the courtyard. Something burst like a hundred fluttering wings in her belly when she found him staring straight back at her. A tiny, breathy gasp escaped her, but something about his eyes refused to let her blink away.

So she held his gaze, her heart pattering faster and faster, as Shang straightened, nodded to Renshu, and strode between the collecting audience of young female wielders.

He was coming here. To her.

Phoenixes *scorch* everything, now she would be even more conspicuous, now her own awkwardness and fear would be on display. He would bring attention to her distinguished disgrace.

And now, she knew. Now she knew she loved him and could never, ever have him.

Shang smiled at her in greeting, still carrying his goblet, and her mouth went dry as sand. He bowed deeply. As he rose, she blurted, “You shouldn’t—”

“The princess does not dance?” he asked, cocking his head innocently as another smile played on his features.

She sputtered for a moment, glancing around the courtyard to see the dozens of turned heads and raised eyebrows. She found her voice, though it came out sharper than intended. “I am not a showoff.”

He grinned and gestured to the edge of the dais. “May I?”

He did not presume to take Yun’s seat, but he still asked to sit beside her. She could only nod. Rebelliously, her eyes sought and found the tall beauty who had danced earlier and discovered her staring straight this way. Her mouth did not gape like her companions’, yet she still looked perplexed.

“One could never accuse you of being a showoff,” Shang said once seated. “But it is such a waste of your skill to let these other girls dance without you joining a single time.”

“My skill?” she asked, tilting her head and frowning. “You have never seen me dance.”

“Are you not a princess?”

Meiling pried her hands off her cup and stuffed them into her lap, smiling as she shook her head. “You know I am not versed in the typical accomplishments of a princess.”

“You evade me. I’d bet three months’ salary—nay, a whole year’s salary—that you are the finest dancer here. Yet unless you dance, others will think they are the best. They will think the princess does not dance because she is not good. But I know the princess does not dance because she is *shy*.”

Shang took a great draught of wine, as though oblivious to the effect his words had on her. He sighed and set down the goblet, planting a square hand on his knee. "Were that more people did not crave notice like you."

She could have sworn that his gaze flicked to the tall beauty.

Meiling *did* crave notice, but she'd learned that the notice she garnered wasn't the type she wanted. "Where's Feiyan?" she asked instead of responding, returning her attention to the delicacies laid on her table. Though she intently studied them, she did not see them at all. They were blurry distractions from the black eyes beside her.

"Probably studying." Shang shrugged. He cast a sidelong glance at her. "You look lovely tonight, by the way."

"What?" Meiling's head swiveled sharply, her gaze latching onto his. It was hardly a dignified response, but she was too stunned. He thought she . . .? A flush crept up her cheeks, so hot she was certain she was turning all sorts of telltale colors.

"I said you look lovely," he replied, eyes bright and full of something she dared not name. The faintest trace of amusement lined his handsome features. "Not to imply this is anything out of the ordinary, as I've always found you lovely. But tonight, you look especially so."

She was going to fall right off the dais. At least that would give her a reason for her flaming cheeks and an excuse to flee the premises. She ducked her head and clasped her hands much too tightly in her lap, dragging in a deep breath as she tried to regain her composure. "Oh. Um . . . thank you."

Mercifully, he shifted his attention away from her and nodded his head toward the pavilion. "Look, they are lining up for another dance. You should join them."

"Join them?" She balked, latching onto something other than his overwhelming compliment, and immediately shook her head. "I—no, definitely not."

"And let these idiots gloat? Show them why they ought to respect you."

The words were spoken nonchalantly, but when he took another sip of his wine, his eyes found hers over the rim of the goblet. That look—she knew that cool, calculating glint.

She watched the pavilion fill up as girls clamored up the steps and took their place. It was mostly full. Relief mingled with the wild hammering of her heart. "I'll do the next one."

"No, do *this* one. It's a harder dance, and the most skilled dancers will be lining up."

"It's too late—see?"

"It is not too late!" he scoffed and gestured with his arm toward the pavilion.

Meiling swallowed, her hands suddenly turning clammy and a cold sweat breaking out at the nape of her neck. She changed her tactic. "You have great faith in me."

"Of course I do," Shang growled. "Go join them!"

"I told you I'm not a showoff."

He rolled his eyes to fix her with a glare. "*Meiling.*"

Fine—fine—fine! With each breath practically a gasp, with her heart threatening to gallop straight out of her chest at every beat, with her legs turned to noodles, she stood. "If I embarrass myself," she snarled under her breath, "It's your fault."

Shang grinned and stood to offer her a hand down the dais. At his touch, her knees wobbled, which did not bode well for the impending dance, and she tried not to think about the warmth and strength of his hand holding hers, nor the rough warrior's calluses against her much softer fingers.

She did not look back at him as she made her way toward the pavilion, forcing her hands straight to her sides and her chin up. The music was already starting, but it was only the introduction. Her arms shook as she gripped her skirts to climb up the stairs, and it took all her strength not to let her shoulders sag when the last open spot was near the tall beauty.

The girl gave her a hesitant sidelong glance as she took her place. Only then did she look back and find Shang's gaze. She maintained her composure, despite wanting to glare at him. He gave an encouraging smile.

The dance started.

Suddenly, she desperately did not want to let Shang down. What if the girl next to her *was* better than her? Meiling never danced in public these days, and this girl looked like she was quite accomplished at public dancing.

But had this girl learned the name of a phoenix? Had she delved into the depths of minds and dreams?

Not that those things had anything to do with dancing, but somehow, they gave her the strength to close her eyes and lift her arms.

She danced.

That was when she heard it. The voice. The low, masculine whisper.

Dance among the wintersweet, daughter of Liena.

Meiling's eyes flared open, but she kept moving in time with the dance, with the music. As she danced, she tried to search the courtyard for the source of that voice. It was the only denial she could afford; she knew very well the voice wasn't in the courtyard.

She looked toward Shang and found his face . . . She couldn't guess what that face meant. His eyebrows were barely lifted, his eyes dark and rounded on the edges. His lips parted slightly.

She closed her eyes again.

How lovely you are, daughter of Liena. Enjoy your last days of beauty.

Open. Dusk burned against torchlight and the yellow flowers mingled with red roses. Closed—

Did you think I wouldn't come for you?

She almost choked, but a glance at the girls dancing with her revealed that whatever was spoken was to her alone. She should break out of the formation, curse Shang and his encouragement to dance, and hunt down that voice in her mind.

Why now? Why did Zedong speak now? She pursed her lips. Maybe she ought to listen.

Steeling herself against the chill of his words scraping in her mind, she closed her eyes. That familiar voice filled her once more. How far away it sounded.

Have your people accepted you like I did? Have they kneeled in reverence as you deserve? Will they let you prove your worth? Sweet Meiling, you know I never questioned your worth.

"Poisonous lies," Meiling seethed under her breath. The tall beauty next to her snapped her gaze down to hers, and Meiling met it with the searing furnace of anger now burning in her core. The beauty's eyes widened slightly.

Dance among the wintersweet, daughter of Liena.

What do you want with me? she shot back in her mind.

A surprised, rumbling chuckle answered her. She could almost see his grin, his close shaved beard, his cloak billowing in the wind behind him. Could almost feel the power emanating from him, that black magic encircling his mind—protecting him from her reaches.

Perhaps I could forgive your rebellion.

I cannot do likewise, she retorted.

The voice rumbled with laughter again. *How valiant you are when protected by the safety of distance.*

Why are you in my mind?

The music swelled to a crescendo, and Meiling knew her movements must be more jerky, more angry than graceful. She didn't care. Did not care if she proved herself the worst dancer on stage.

I thought you might miss me, sweet little Meiling.

Liar.

That raspy laugh again.

How are you in my mind?

I think you know how.

Had Zedong somehow . . . mimicked her magic? *Where are you?* She tried to keep the frantic note out of her mind-voice, but it permeated nonetheless.

You want me to tell you? And spoil the surprise?

The music ended. She found herself bent at the waist, still in her spot on the pavilion in the line of girls, one arm lifted with extended fingers. She was panting, dripping sweat, despite the dance being only mild exertion.

People blurred together, lanterns flickering brighter as the sun at last slipped behind the mountain. The courtyard plunged into night, and suddenly the smell of bodies and the fragrance of flowers cloyed in her nostrils, thick and nauseating.

She closed her eyes.

The voice inside her head was gone.

CHAPTER 26

MEILING SPARED ONE glance Shang's way as he stood and started toward her, a frown etched into his face.

This place was too full, too peopled, too . . . *distracting.* She nearly suffocated in fluttering silk as the girls dispersed from the pavilion, with more scurrying up the stairs in their wake. She barely had the presence of mind to hold her head high, to temper the speed of her steps, to *be* a princess.

Yun was nowhere to be seen.

She craned her neck, searching for him, trying to use the last bit of height before she stepped off the lowest stair and was lost to her own smallness. People—people—*people.* They were lambs for slaughter. Idiots! Dancing their way to their graves in their flaring and flashing garments.

Where was Zedong? Was he here already? He'd sounded so distant. What had he said?

Enjoy your last days of beauty.

As Meiling pushed through the crowd, taking the direction to the nearest escape from the courtyard, a wild hope bloomed in her chest. *Days.* Did that mean Zedong was still days away? Not minutes? Not prowling the palace even now?

Or did he only say that to relieve her urgency?

Why had he even bothered to talk to her?

She ducked under an archway of wintersweet, only the small, pale blossoms visible in the night by torchlight. Immediately, as she left the courtyard, cold blasted her. It knifed into her lungs, and she gasped, though not in pain. She welcomed the cold, welcomed the barrenness of the night after the engorged courtyard. Welcomed the silence with only the distant wafting of laughter on the wind.

Where was she even going?

Away. Away from the people, the voice—

Something hissed near her foot. She leaped aside, another gasp bursting from her lips. Then behind her—scuttling. Coming fast up behind her.

She broke into a run.

She tore deeper into the Academy gardens, deeper into the darkness. The sounds of crawling, scurrying bugs filled her mind, and as she ran, they seemed to coalesce into words.

I'm coming for you.

She wanted to scream, but if she screamed, Zedong's magic would find her and devour her whole. So she ran harder, chest heaving for the splintering cold air.

The gardens were left behind as she raced over a bridge, over a reflection pond full of lilies she wouldn't have noticed except for the white shining under the moon. She'd reached the Academy, the long set of buildings for lectures and training and dormitories.

Someone would see her running for her life. They'd think her mad. She couldn't care. She ran harder.

Something grabbed her shoulder, dragging her backward until she nearly screamed as a band like iron clamped around her waist and tried to pull her to a stop. When she fought, she was lifted right off her feet, her cry dying in a choking burst of panic. She struggled violently, throwing her elbow back until it connected with a rib. The grip on her loosened just enough that she nearly broke free.

Then her wrist was snatched. The world spun—

She landed hard with her back against the wall of an Academy building, wrists gripped and pressed into stone near her head. A whoosh of air escaped her open mouth. She looked up.

"Spattering blood curses. What are you *doing,* Meiling? It's only me."

She gasped again, both from relief and the need for air. "Shang," she managed, and her head sagged forward from her shoulders as he kept her pressed into the wall with hands that burned of ice. "You *scared* me!"

"Meiling," he growled, tightening his grip and leaning his face down closer to hers. "What are you doing? Why were you running like you have a qilin on your tail? Why did you leave?"

She tilted her face up, but shadows shrouded his face. Only his black eyes glittered in the night, so near her own. Her breath snagged. She had to break his gaze or lose her mind entirely. "Zedong was going to catch me. He was chasing me."

"No one was chasing you. Except me."

"It wasn't you." Meiling squeezed her eyes shut against the intensity of his. "Something else. He was in my mind—during the dance."

Shang released her wrists, letting her arms fall to her sides, and stepped back. When he remained silent, she peered up at him to find him looking off to one side, a muscle jerking in his jaw.

"He spoke to you? In your mind?" he asked, bringing his gaze back to her. Black eyes seemed to bore into her, no doubt looking for any evidence her words were false. "What did he say?"

"He told me to dance among the wintersweet."

The air between them froze, making her shudder.

"Anything else?" Shang ground out between clenched teeth.

She told him everything Zedong had spoken to her mind, including her speculation that he was not here in the capital already. She'd hardly finished speaking when his eyes flared wide and snapped sidelong.

"Someone's coming," he hissed.

Before she could react, he grabbed her elbow and pulled her after him to a shadowy crevice between buildings where the moonlight did not shine. She tried to arch her neck to see around him at what he'd heard or seen, but he dragged her into the darkness and set her against the wall. One of his hands planted above her shoulder, the other gripped her arm. His looming body was twisted, half shielding her and half watching for whoever approached.

"Why are we—"

He clapped an icy hand over her mouth, his exhale stirring the top of her hair. When she shivered, he glanced at her, then released her mouth. They huddled in the shadows as she finally heard the approaching footsteps. At the sound, she looked up at Shang's face.

He was so close she swore she could hear his heartbeat. But perhaps she heard her own, roaring with life and fear and heady emotion. She peered around his arm, trying to catch a glimpse of whoever was stalking the grounds at this hour. A straggler from the dance, like her? His tension radiated through the hand on her arm, filling her with his battle-readiness.

The footsteps stopped.

He gripped Meiling's arm tighter. Ice flared into her elbow. She jolted involuntarily.

The footsteps started again and continued until they faded into the night.

Slowly, the tension eased out of Shang. The air warmed, and the ice leaked from his hand. He turned his gaze from the courtyard down at her and seemed to startle when he found her staring up at him. His eyes widened almost imperceptibly as he registered their closeness.

But he didn't pull away.

If anything, he pressed closer to her.

"They're gone?" Meiling whispered, her voice cracking slightly.

The power of his eyes locked on hers was enough to make her melt and burn simultaneously.

"They're gone," he assured, his voice deeper than usual.

His eyes glittered like stars, the rest of him cloaked in shadow and darkness. A soft tendril of wind, whispering of winter, brushed her hot face. It was nowhere near as cold as his touch on her arm.

She couldn't break his gaze. She thought . . .

His thumb brushed her arm in a soft, tentative caress. Once, twice.

"Meiling." His voice was husky.

Her knees went weak, and her eyes must have been as wide as moons in their sockets, mouth open with disbelief and ragged, *desperate* hope. She meant to say something—his name, perhaps, but the sound died on her lips.

He let go of her arm, and slowly, hesitantly, he reached up with two cold hands. She felt the ice before it even brushed her skin, radiating in the air between his fingers and her cheeks. She closed her eyes as a tremulous, shuddering gasp escaped her lips when he cupped her face. Immediately, the ice vanished, replaced by warmth. Heat.

"Meiling, *oh* Meiling," Shang whispered, his voice so, so soft, but urgent. Painfully earnest. His next words came rushing out, as though they'd been pent up for some while. "You cannot know how deeply I love you."

Everything stopped.

It was like entire worlds died and were reborn in that mere second. They'd danced on this cliff edge for far too long, and now they were falling, falling, *falling*. She never wanted to land. Never wanted to feel solid ground beneath her feet again. This moment, this tiny piece of forever, was where she wanted to belong.

After one ragged inhale, he was speaking again, leaning his forehead against hers. "At night when I fall asleep, I dream of holding you in my arms, kissing your sweet mouth. I think of your beautiful eyes, like stars in an endless sky. Oh, Meiling, I want nothing in this world . . . Nothing but you."

Her lashes fluttered with disbelief and overwhelm as she gasped, "Shang."

Their eyes met. He leaned forward, lowering his face to hers. His mouth brushed her forehead first in a kiss gentle enough to make the stars weep. His second kiss, pressed to her cheek, sent tingles racing down her spine.

The softest brush of his mouth on hers—

And she couldn't hold back her own heart from spilling forth. "I think I have loved you from the day you told me your name, Tan Shangdi. I have loved you, and I love you, and I will never stop loving you." The rush—the pure *glory*—of those words sent her leaning closer, dizziness nearly overcoming her.

His reply was almost pained as one hand slid down to her waist, as he pressed her into the wall and let his breath caress her lips. "You don't mean that."

"I do, indeed!" she insisted, almost weeping and laughing simultaneously in her sincerity. Her entire body was shaking. "I didn't love you then as I do now, but Shang, *Shang,* I have longed for your regard, for your love—"

"You have it. All of it," he growled.

Then his mouth claimed hers with such force she might have been knocked off her feet without the wall behind her. For the first time they'd kissed, she was wide awake, yet she felt as though she were dreaming. Her hands moved to wrap around his neck, pulling him closer as their lips moved in perfect cadence. He groaned her name, a low, guttural sound that imprinted itself on her heart. She might have said his name in reply, but he'd already stolen her lips again, and there was something frantic and desperate about the way he kissed her.

As though he waited for the moment she'd be stolen away from him.

"Be my wife, Meiling, my darling, my own," he whispered urgently.

"Yes," she breathed, not considering anything but her own longings in that moment.

His reply was an exuberant, passionate kiss that filled her entire soul. And then he was murmuring over and over again: *"I love you. I love you. I love you. I love you."* Another jubilant kiss that was more like two grins crashing together. "I could say it thousands of times and it wouldn't be enough."

She dragged open her lashes to find his handsome face still so close, his shoulders blocking out the world beyond their wonder-struck bliss.

The world beyond.

Zedong, the trial, war.

Meiling froze. Shang's hand on her hip went still, his mouth halting just above the apple of her cheek.

She could barely get the horrible words out. "But you're leaving."

Shang took a deep breath, his broad chest expanding against hers. "Come with me."

He said it so simply. If only it was simple.

"Pa wouldn't let me go with you," she said to avoid the real question.

Shang cupped her face so gently it was almost as if he wasn't touching her at all. "That was part of our conversation this morning. He said I could take you with me if you wanted to go."

"What?" For the second time today, she was floored. "*My Pa* said that? He would let you take me away from Zheninghai? He agreed to never see me again?"

"He didn't want to, but he said you should have a say in your future. So he left the decision to you. If you want to stay, you can stay. But if you want to come with me, and be my wife, you are free to do so. We could go to the Southern Isles. You could see the world, Mei."

His soft voice was almost grating against the pounding behind her eyes. This should be an easy choice. She loved Shang—loved him so, so, *so* much. She would be safe with him. Far safer than she'd be in Zheninghai. She could make a home among people who didn't despise her.

So why did her entire being demand that she say no?

Saying no would mean giving Shang up forever. And she couldn't—she *wouldn't*—give him up. He'd only belonged to her for a few minutes. She couldn't say goodbye to him, to his strength and will and cunning and affection.

The pounding grew to a splitting pain.

"Meiling?" His voice was worried, and it faded in and out of her awareness. She squeezed her eyes shut. A new voice filled her mind, poisonous and deadly.

Go with him, darling Mei. I will let you have a few beautiful years with the man you love. Then I will come for you, for him, and your children. I will bring you back to Zheninghai. You will see the new society I have set up, and you will see your mother once again. The rest will be gone, but she will be mine. I will let her hold her grandchildren . . . before I kill them.

"Get out of my mind!" Meiling snarled, grabbing her head and digging her fingernails into her scalp. "Get *out*!"

At once, every last trace of Zedong's voice vanished. Shang had her by the shoulders, demanding to know what she'd heard in her head. Scorching rage filled her to the brim.

She was going to tear Fang Zedong to pieces for threatening her and her family like that.

And there it was: the buried part of her that had hidden for so long. The part that could kill and not be sorry.

She'd found it at last.

Her eyes flashed open, meeting Shang's hard stare. And though it was like a hundred knives into her heart, she didn't falter as she broke them both. "I won't go with you."

"Why?" he demanded, and there was a world of hurt and anger in that word. "Did Fang speak into your mind again? What did he say? Why won't you come with me?"

"Because Zedong isn't after Zheninghai, he is after revenge. Revenge against *my mother*. And I am part of that revenge. No matter where I go, he will come for me. Did I ever tell you why he kidnapped those wielders? It was partly for their magic, yes, but mostly it was to prove that he could capture, break, and destroy the strongest of my father's warriors."

"So what?" Shang snarled. "You are going to just *sit here* and wait for slaughter? I saw the emperor's plans for fortifying the city. They're good—very good—but I'm telling you, Meiling, they will not be enough. Fang is going to take this city. And you are just going to *wait* here for it to happen?"

"I know you think I'm useless, but—"

"You are *not* useless, and I've never once thought that you were. You are my *treasure,* Meiling." His voice broke, his brows slanting in pleading. "I won't make you come with me. But help me understand. You're powerful, more powerful than any of us know yet, but you're at your most vulnerable when you're wielding that power. All someone must do is find your sleeping body and they can kill you without a fight. If you're staying back to prove you're not useless, there are other ways to do that without throwing away your life."

"They don't *know* Zedong like I do. I've been in his mind. I know the boy he was and the man he is. No one in that palace understands him like I do. Not even Ma. And if I don't—"

"Why has fighting Fang Zedong fallen to your shoulders?" Shang demanded. "This isn't your responsibility, and it never has been. You owe *nothing* to Zheninghai."

"He just told me that if I ran away with you, he'd hunt down our children and kill them," Meiling shot back. Shang's eyes widened in stunned horror as she continued. "This is what I'm trying to tell you and this is what *no one* seems to understand: Zedong is coming to Suguan to destroy *me* so he can destroy my mother."

He stared at her, shellshocked, as though fully comprehending. Then, in a voice that was almost lifeless, "We need to break the connection he has with you. We have to get him out of your mind."

"I don't think we can. We were just kissing, which should have already broken the connection, but it didn't." Under any other circumstances, she might have blushed at the words. Now they only brought pain. "I believe he's mimicked my power through black magic—he had me working to understand the magic of the captive wielders—and perhaps mixing it with a mimic of Du Liuxian's evanescing magic to cross the distance? So what is there to do but listen and hope I can glean important information when he chooses to speak?"

Shang's jaw worked, and when he spoke, his voice was like death. "I will kill him."

Zedong probably wanted him to try. Which terrified Meiling almost as much as Zedong's threat to murder her children.

She was done letting him destroy what she loved.

CHAPTER 27

SHANG WAS SUCH a storm of emotion, there was no hope of building back his composure. He was sliced open, his heart bloodied and raw, and though the pain wasn't physical, he couldn't imagine ever healing.

To fall from such heights of exaltation to such depths of woe and misery . . .

All he wanted in this life was Meiling. Now he couldn't have her. What was he supposed to do now? He could escape to the ends of the earth and where would the solace be in that? He would never love again, that was for certain.

But he shouldn't be so selfish as to fixate on his own heartbreak. There were bigger things to worry about, and he needed to get to work. With this new information, he had a clearer understanding to aid in offering his suggestions to the emperor for city fortifications.

And if Meiling was determined to stay, then by all the fathers and lights above, he'd make sure this city had every chance of standing.

He couldn't have her. Very well. He would be what she needed.

Meiling seemed to sense his agony and the way he tried to compartmentalize it, because her face softened. Her fingers reached up, trailing down his cheek as though caressing the open wounds inside him. The determination in her gaze melted into sorrow, and what defenses could he keep against her? He closed his eyes and leaned into her touch.

"I have spent my life running, hiding, cowering," she whispered, "and I am *done* with it. I am *done* letting other people fight my battles for me. You mustn't believe that Fang Zedong isn't my battle. He kidnapped me. He tortured me. He manipulated and abused me. I watched him do horrible things. Don't you understand? I have believed so many lies about myself. That I am weak, helpless, useless, cursed. And if I run from Zedong, regardless of his threats, then I will only confirm those things. I couldn't live with myself, letting the opinions of others make me into a true coward. No, Shang, I *must* stay. But it doesn't mean that I am not devastated. It does not mean that I don't love you."

He wished he didn't understand. But he did. He hated that he did, that every time in his life he'd tried to hate Meiling, he couldn't do it. It would lessen the pain if he could blame her.

All he could do was love her more.

Loving her was life, and it was a bitter agony.

"You must go," Meiling begged. "Don't stay here for me. Please, Shang, do this for me." Tears glimmered in her eyes. "I need to know you are safe and alive."

Shang's heart shattered. It was a miracle he stayed on his feet. A miracle he did nothing but swipe away a tear sliding down her cheek with his thumb. He did something he so rarely did to her: he lied, and it burned like acid on his tongue. "Then I will go."

She offered him a shaky smile, her eyes glistening. "Thank you."

He tilted her chin up and kissed her. Slowly, thoroughly, memorizing the shape of her lips, savoring her taste. His kisses were confessions, things he'd longed to tell her.

I've wanted you in my arms for so long.

You are the most beautiful thing I've ever seen.

Then, his last kiss: *I love you, Meiling.*

The effort was monumental, but somehow, he found the will to pull away. His voice was gravel as he whispered, "I'll take you back." He didn't have to specify he meant to the palace; she only nodded and smoothed back her hair before slipping her arm in his.

They'd hardly made it three steps out of the darkness before something loud crashed nearby.

CHAPTER 28

THE CRASH WAS like the sound of someone stumbling through shrubbery. Meiling tensed, Shang's head whipping toward the sound, his body braced. Her fingers were almost numb, but her cheeks and neck still burned.

The crash turned into a whimpering cry. It struck Meiling as familiar.

"Oh!" she cried, bursting forward.

"Meiling!" Shang reached out and caught her again. But she twisted in his grasp.

"It's Feiyan!" she hissed, and immediately he released her. She ran out of the shadows, cold flooding where Shang's warmth had been only seconds ago. She shuddered, but she couldn't help being relieved at a distraction.

Another groan came from the edge of the garden. There was an arm. A leg. Sticking out of the shrubbery. "Feiyan!" She redoubled her pace until she fell to her knees beside Feiyan's fallen body.

The healer moaned when Shang—immediately in action—gripped under her shoulders and dragged her into the grass, out of the plants. He laid her flat, and Meiling quickly kneeled over her, grabbing her hands. *Cold.* She tilted Feiyan's head up and brushed the hair away from her puckered brow. Feiyan moaned again, and her eyes flickered open. Midnight eyes stared unseeing up at the stars.

"Feiyan, can you hear me?" Meiling's voice broke, and she gripped that icy hand tighter. "Feiyan? What's wrong? Tell me what's wrong."

Where was that flowing golden river? Where was the life? The vitality?

"Are you sick?" she urged, bending forward to press her hand to her forehead. Shang lifted his questioning gaze to hers. "She's very warm," she told him, gritting her teeth. "Of course she's sick, driven like a dog!"

"I saw her earlier today," he said, frowning down at her. "She looked completely fine. Tired, but nothing like this."

Feiyan's eyes flared open again, and her hand suddenly gripped like iron around Meiling's. Her gaze cleared, and a trickle of warmth flowed from her fingers. "My . . . my . . ."

"What? What, Feiyan?" Meiling prompted, squeezing her hand tighter.

"My . . . head . . ." Feiyan's voice broke, and her eyes rolled back.

"Feiyan? Feiyan! Her head? Does she have a headache?"

Shang, kneeling on the other side of her, said suddenly, "You said Fang Zedong was in your mind tonight. What if . . .?"

He didn't need to finish. "I need to fall asleep!" She kept Feiyan's hand clasped in hers while she glanced around the grass, searching the looming Academy buildings for a safe spot.

"There's hardly a private place around here," Shang growled, already pulling Feiyan up so he could lift her. "We can't risk someone finding you while you work."

"Feiyan's dormitory? What about the library?"

He shook his head as he heaved Feiyan's limp body into his arms. "The dormitories are full. Anyone can walk into the library unexpectedly." He pursed his lips and glanced sidelong at Meiling. "We could go to my room. It's not exactly . . . *appropriate*, but no one will bother us there."

"Qilins eat propriety," Meiling snapped. "Where is it? Hurry!"

Shang raised an eyebrow and seemed to suppress a smile as he nodded. "Over there. Follow me. And be quiet."

He shifted Feiyan, so she was slung over his shoulder, arms and hair dangling, and held to the shadows as they crept around the side of the Academy buildings. Meiling kept close to him, her hand hovering over Feiyan's back. She found herself glancing over her shoulder every few breaths, watching for any sign of pursuit.

Only the stillness of a winter night met her senses.

This felt oddly familiar, and if Meiling closed her eyes, she could almost imagine she followed Shang through the bowels of Zedong's fortress. She tried to focus on keeping her exhales soft and even despite her thumping heart. Tried to keep her teeth from chattering in her mouth. Tried to keep herself from readjusting her robes for another shred of warmth.

Shang loves me. He kissed me. He asked me to be his wife.

"Here." His low voice broke through her thoughts as he grunted and pushed open a door. Light flared from the room within, but he lifted his hand. The candles hissed and went out. He held the door open for her, and she strained to see by moonbeam until he shut the door firmly, ensconcing them in darkness. "I don't want anyone to see our silhouettes entering," he explained. "I'll relight the candles. Here, help me set her down."

She followed the sound of his voice in the pitch black until she found an arm—Feiyan's arm. Slowly, she supported Feiyan's back as Shang kneeled. Together, they laid her down on the floor. Once, she thought her fingers brushed his, but it was too dark to tell. She stayed with Feiyan as the floorboards creaked under his weight. She blindly stroked hair in the dark and held her friend's chilled hands as Shang shuffled around the room.

Light flared, soft and hesitant.

Enough for her to make out Shang's sharp profile, enough for flickers of light and shadow to play across Feiyan's closed eyes. Another candle flared, and she could look around the room.

It was sparse. Humble. A low platform bed was in one corner, a table in another, and a washstand on the far side. Now that she could see how small it was, it was a wonder that they hadn't banged their heads on the corners of the bed or table.

"We ought to move her to the bed," Meiling said, already trying to scoot her arm under Feiyan's shoulders. As if she could pick her up.

"The bed is for you. So you can fall asleep."

"It's big enough for both of us. Here, can you help me?"

Before long, they had Feiyan settled on the bed, her giving little moans every few minutes. Those moans were Meiling's lifeline; they assured her she was not too late. Quickly, she climbed up next to her and was about to lie down when Shang stopped her.

He held out a vial in one hand. "This is . . . It's actually for you. It was going to be a belated birthday present since . . . Well, since you were in a dungeon on your birthday. I was going to give it to you at a better moment . . ." He drew a deep breath and pressed the small glass bottle into her palm. "Here. It's a potion that will help you fall asleep. I thought it would be preferred to . . ."

"To knocking me unconscious?" Meiling said with a lifted brow.

Shang's eyes met hers before he quickly looked away. "One drop on your tongue is enough."

The potion worked quickly. Too quickly.

She was asleep before she'd even removed her finger from her mouth, giving her no time to thank him for his sweet consideration and remembrance of her birthday. Her spirit went hurtling into the ether, just in time to hear Shang swear and leap to catch her before her head slammed hard into the bedframe. Good thing she'd corked the bottle, otherwise it would be spilled all over Shang's bed.

She paused only for a heartbeat to watch him gently lower her head and shoulders to the cushion.

Then she dove into Feiyan's mind.

CHAPTER 29

MEILING STOOD IN a misty forest of pine trees.

She wore coarse trousers and a loose linen tunic. Pine needles cushioned and pricked her bare feet. Just beyond the clearing, she could make out the outline of a man. Not tall, but watchful. Strong. Imposing.

Feiyan's father.

She was familiar with this mind. She'd explored it before. There was no need to converse with the man hovering on the edge of every one of Feiyan's thoughts. Instead, she closed her eyes and reached out with her hands.

Immediately, when she touched the spider silk memory threads, she felt the difference. Something was wrong. Very, very wrong. She opened her eyes, her hand gripping a thread, and ran deeper into the forest.

At first, nothing looked off. It was only an insistent itch in her mind, her intuition filling her senses and telling her that something was not right. But the farther she ran, the more memory threads she touched, and she started to see things.

The threads were usually mostly invisible. Only if she touched a thread, would it glimmer like the tiniest sliver of a prism refracting the light. But with each step into the forest of Feiyan's mind, they started gleaming black. Slowly, they were more than mere snatches of ebony in the mist, but threads of pure midnight. She could see the weave and weft of the memories, could see how some fell slack, how some were tangled knots on the ground—disconnected from everything.

She stopped, surrounded by memories, and realized suddenly that her method of hunting in minds, of searching along the intact memory threads, was useless to find lost memories like the ones littering around her bare feet, scattered among the grass and pine needles.

But that was irrelevant.

She tore off again, trying to discover why the threads were so . . . *visible.* So black. She closed her eyes again, feeling the threads with her hands.

That was when she felt it.

The *humming* of the memories.

It was discordant, like bad music. But not just played incorrectly; music played *wrongly.* It ached in her ears, in her chest, making her furious while simultaneously making her want to weep.

The mist grew heavier around her. The change was so subtle she hardly noticed until she slogged through soot-colored smoke. It clung to her spirit limbs, not merely hindering her progress, but trying to haul her back. Trying to keep her from penetrating deeper into this mind.

Her chest tightened, and Meiling reached out to feel for her tether. The comforting, painful throb of her heartbeat through the tether soothed the fear rising in her throat.

This nightmare in Feiyan's mind was unquestionably the work of Fang Zedong.

The black clinging to the memory threads grew fatter. The smoke started reaching for her face, and she abandoned her physical projection of herself. Becoming little more than smoke herself, she moved faster through the fog, but it still tried to reach out to her and slow her down.

She reached a clearing. And balked at what awaited her.

It was just like the clearing she always saw when she first entered Feiyan's mind. The mist-shrouded pine forest clearing, though no father loomed on the edge. This was different.

Oh. This was the hidden, deeper, truer version of the first clearing. Feiyan's soul tether was anchored to this second clearing, protected. It was anchored into the soft ground, only two steps away from where she stood.

Crouched around the green-glowing tether that burned with the light of all that was Feiyan was something black. Almost formless, but not entirely.

The clearing was full of thick, dark smoke. The memory threads coalescing here turned to heavy, fat ropes of black, weighted down by sorcery. And in the center, something blinked back at Meiling.

Her heart stopped.

The black thing blobbed together, becoming more solid. Long legs scuttled in place, and the body of the *thing* crouched closer to Feiyan's tether, jowls clicking. As though it protected its meal. It had no eyes, but it watched her.

It was . . . it was a sentient curse.

And it was *consuming* Feiyan. Her mind.

Meiling's scream died into horror. Her traitorous self-preservation remembered the fox spirit's mind. What risk did she bear by approaching this . . . this *thing*?

What are you doing here? Meiling asked the curse.

It chattered its jowls, but otherwise did not answer.

How can I break you?

It screeched, legs clicking. But it stayed on Feiyan's tether.

She took a step closer, and the curse screeched again. It sucked more of the surrounding smoke into itself, growing bigger and bigger. It chomped something like a mouth and raised a long arm over its head.

It wasn't an arm. It was a tail.

With a stinger on the end.

The curse . . . It was a scorpion. A demon scorpion, sent from the fieriest layer of *diyu.* That tail darted out toward Meiling, and she barely had time to fly backward as the stinger struck into the ground where she'd been standing.

Black poison spread like spidery veins on the ground, crawling outward from the stinger. Pinchers struck next, the scorpion continuing to grow and grow until its tail loomed in the misty sky above.

Think, think, think!

How could she defeat such a curse? Such a wicked, evil, dangerous curse? The compulsion threads she'd snapped in the phoenixes were nothing compared to this.

All she'd done was scream, and the sound had sundered the magic in two.

Meiling opened her mouth and screamed.

The scorpion's tail came flying for her—whole and utterly unweakened.

She cried out as she flung herself to the side; the tail shook the earth as it struck. Poison seeped deeper into Feiyan's mind. Meiling gasped as the tail ripped away, leaving behind it a crater big enough for her to fit into. She scrambled to her feet and ran. That tail kept plunging into the ground near her, uprooting trees in its wake.

She'd seen success against black magic with three things—her own screams, other black magic, and . . .

The world tilted, and she fell. She fought the pull of the smoke on her limbs, tore against the fear clambering to rule her, and flung herself toward the sky. She had to get out of this mind—

She gave one glance back.

The curse-scorpion was the size of the palace, crushing Feiyan's tether beneath its weight. It towered over trees, its huge pinchers snapping trunks like twigs. And that horrible stinger came shooting straight for Meiling.

She screamed.

"Meiling! Wake up! Meiling!"

Her eyes flew open to find Shang's face right above hers. His pupils were completely dilated, both his hands clamped over her mouth. She blinked and tried to suck in a gasp of air through her mouth, but only received skin, not oxygen.

Panic squeezed her lungs.

She flung aside Shang's hands and leaned over the side of the bed, gasping.

Don't vomit on Shang's floor. Don't vomit on Shang's floor.

"Meiling? What happened? Are you hurt?" he demanded urgently, grabbing her shoulders to keep her from falling.

She'd escaped. She wasn't dead. Or hurt. The curse-scorpion had not killed her. Her heaving lungs calmed enough for her to roll back onto the bed and close her eyes.

Just for a breath.

A knock sounded on the door. "Shang? Are you in there?"

Meiling shot upright, panic on two accounts nearly blinding her. Shang had already turned toward the door, but she launched herself at his arm, ignoring his startled face. "Kiss her!" she gasped. "You must kiss Feiyan! Now!"

Shang drew back as though she'd struck him. "I will *not* kiss her. What are you talking about?"

"The Yanzhao Technique! We have no time! It might already be too late! There's a scorpion eating her mind, and it's the size of a mountain and you've got to kiss her to stop it!"

His confusion shifted into horrified bewilderment. He flexed his hand, set his mouth in a firm, stubborn line, and marched to the door.

"Shang!" Meiling cried, fury nearly overcoming every other emotion.

He opened the door halfway, reached out, and grabbed hold of the front of someone's robes—and dragged him inside. It was Renshu, whose surprised expression shifted to Meiling, then Feiyan in confused concern.

"Kiss her," Shang demanded, pointing at Feiyan. "Yanzhao. Now."

"Please, Renshu!" Meiling gasped. "It's an emergency."

To his credit, Renshu was only stunned immobile for about half a second. Then he crossed the room, taking up Meiling's place at Feiyan's side as she scooted away, and planted one hand on the bed beside Feiyan's head.

He hesitated for a heartbeat.

Oh fathers, Meiling thought with the realization of a lightning bolt. She'd forgotten what she found in his mind in Zedong's fortress—that Renshu had harbored a secret, unreturned affection for the healer for years.

Now she was making him kiss her.

He bent and pressed his lips to the healer's. He was careful, gentle, and Meiling looked away, the moment feeling too intimate to watch.

At least she hadn't had to watch Shang kiss someone else. He was standing now, turned away from the bed, holding his wrist in the small of his back. She slid to his side, peering up at his hard-as-flint face. His eyes drifted down to hers, his expression softening only just slightly; the rest of his face was stubborn as a mule. As though challenging her to be angry with him that he wouldn't kiss Feiyan.

Feiyan stirred.

Meiling spun around just as Renshu straightened and stepped aside, pulling out of the healer's line of vision before she opened her eyes. She tried not to notice the way he seemed eager to avoid her gaze, too.

Meiling hurried to take his place at Feiyan's side. She grabbed the healer's hand and squeezed it hard. Warmth flowed into her fingers. Her shoulders sagged with relief.

"Feiyan? Feiyan, can you hear me?"

"Meiling?" Feiyan rasped and blinked her eyes open. Fathers above, they were *clear,* no longer glazed or distant. It had worked. The curse was banished.

"Oh Feiyan!" Meiling gasped, clasping her hand with both of her own. "You're safe now. You had a curse in your mind."

Feiyan frowned, wrinkled her nose, and then sat up slowly. "No wonder I've been feeling like rubbish recently. A curse? What sort of curse?"

"It seemed like a parasite to me," Meiling said. "It was nasty. I couldn't get rid of it. Had to get Renshu to kiss you for me."

The look that crossed Feiyan's face was sudden panic mixed with shock. Her mouth opened, and her eyes darted beyond Meiling to find Shang's turned back and Renshu facing them, arms crossed as he leaned against the wall. The latter was mostly enveloped in shadow, but he still lifted a hand in greeting and smiled.

"I'm sorry it came to that," said Renshu, ducking his head in a nod. "Are you feeling better?"

Shang still hadn't turned around. Meiling wanted to elbow him in the ribs.

Feiyan tried to say several things but could never get past the first syllable. Face pale, she finally shut her mouth, nodded, and closed her eyes, leaning back against the bedframe.

Meiling swallowed, glancing between Shang's impenetrable back, Renshu's averted attention, and Feiyan's ashy skin. Her vision swam, and for a moment, she thought she was staring up into darkness and shadows as large, cold hands held her face. Tilting her head upward for a beautiful, impassioned kiss.

Silence was not usually a problem for her. But suddenly, she couldn't bear it. She opened her mouth and began chattering like a nervous, clucking hen. "When I first saw the curse, I wasn't quite sure what it was. Actually, that wasn't what I saw at first. Did you know your memories are little threads linked throughout your mind?

Well, normally they're *mostly* invisible, but they were black. Very strange. I found your—" She cut herself off before she betrayed Feiyan's hidden soul. Not that either of them would do anything with the knowledge, but it seemed like a private thing. Instead, she prattled: "The curse was guarding your tether. I think it was sending its magic out into your mind, but when I attacked, it seemed to pull it back in to make itself bigger and deadlier."

The color slowly returned to Feiyan's cheeks, but she stared up at Meiling like she had a few spare heads atop her shoulders. Shang was silent. Not even the creak of floorboards revealed his presence.

Renshu, on the other hand, frowned. "I beg your pardon?"

Meiling offered a lame, wincing smile. "I'm glad you're back, Renshu. I was afraid you'd be in the dungeons for a long time after the episode with Liuxian—and after you'd just been freed!"

Renshu's small answering smile was genuine. "Thank you, Princess Meiling. I, too, am glad to be back. And apparently just in time." His attention flicked to Feiyan briefly.

"Enough with the formalities. Where is the rest of this riveting, insane story?" Feiyan interrupted from the bed, drawing her knees up to her chest. "Tell me more about you attacking this parasite."

Meiling scratched her neck. "Well . . . I confess I didn't do much attacking. Once it coalesced, and I could see what form it took—a scorpion—it kept trying to skewer me with its tail while it mowed down the trees in your mind. It almost got me a few times. I barely made it out so—" She stopped herself before she mentioned the kiss again. "As I said, it was a nasty curse. I'm glad it's gone now."

When she looked over her shoulder, Shang stared at her in openmouthed horror. She cocked her head and glanced at Feiyan and Renshu, then back at him. "What?"

He clamped his mouth shut and shook his head.

"Where are we?" Feiyan asked as she scooted to the edge of the bed. "Unless the . . . uh . . . scorpion ate my memories, I am pretty sure this is not my room, nor the library, nor the infirmary."

Shang said nothing, so Meiling answered, "We're in Shang's room. He was so kind to lend it to us when we found you outside and had to carry you somewhere."

Feiyan seemed to pause slightly, glancing down at the bed, and then got to her feet. "Well, you all have buckets full of thanks from me. Will a bow to the mighty ice warrior and feral warrior suffice?" She swept one to Renshu—which was answered with a cordial nod—and another to Shang's back. "And one to you, the gentle and talented princess?"

Meiling ran forward and embraced her friend as tightly as she could. "I am so relieved you're well."

"*Well* might be a bit of a stretch, but I'm certainly *better*." Feiyan hugged her back with a squeeze, and it might have been Meiling's imagination that she hung on just a moment longer than expected.

You would have been Feiyan.

Meiling gave one more squeeze, then reluctantly pulled back from her friend. When she did, she found Shang had crossed the room to Renshu, and the two men were speaking in low tones to one another.

"I was concerned when you left the dance so quickly," Renshu was saying.

Shang said something back that was too quiet for Meiling to catch.

"Care to share with the class?" Feiyan chirped.

Renshu's mouth quirked in amusement, while Shang's cool eyes snapped up to Feiyan, then slid to Meiling and stayed there.

"Oh!" Meiling said quickly. "We'll leave. Sorry for intruding! Thank you for helping us!"

Shang heaved a quiet sigh, almost as if to say, *"I wasn't trying to get you to leave."*

Too late. She'd already spoken her misunderstanding aloud.

"Yes, we don't want to intrude on the best friends having a *moment*," drawled Feiyan, just before she banged her shin into the corner of Shang's table and swore. "Dragons curse it!"

Renshu and Meiling said at the same time: "Feiyan! Are you alright?"

But Feiyan was already waving her hand dismissively, obviously trying to swallow her grimace and paste a grin on top of it. "I'm dandy as a peach. Now, Shang, you really should sand down the edges of your table. It's a hazard to guests."

When Shang didn't respond, Renshu supplied a diplomatic, "I don't believe this is his permanent residence, but I'm sure he will—"

"Knowing Shang, he'll sharpen the edges of his table to slice into the legs of his enemies. More efficient that way."

Meiling winced. She needed to get Feiyan and leave—

"I won't be inviting my enemies into my home," said Shang darkly, his brow lowered.

"Well, this has been wonderful!" said Meiling with forced lightness. "Thank you, Renshu, for the kiss. For Feiyan, I mean. And thank you, Shang, for the help. And the room. And . . . and goodnight!"

With that, she grabbed Feiyan's wrist and dragged her out through the door. But before she could pull it shut behind her, a hand caught it. Meiling looked up to find Shang holding the door open, only half his face visible through the crack.

"The Crown Prince will be looking for you. Shall I escort you back?"

You—not *you and Feiyan*.

Her heart rammed in her throat. If she said yes, would he . . .? Would he try to kiss her again? In the darkness on the way back? Or would things be desperately awkward and serious? Somehow, with Feiyan standing here, it was like all her thoughts and motives were exposed. She couldn't quite bring herself to say it.

"Thank you," she said yet again, "but I think I will make it back just fine."

This time, he let her shut the door.

CHAPTER 30

THE NIGHT WAS restless.

Meiling laid upon her bed, staring up at the canopy overhead. This was the fifth time she'd woken up. And she *never* woke up once she fell asleep. She was always too busy floating around in the darkness.

Yet tonight, her tether kept yanking her back to her body, insistent as a kiss.

"I told him no," she whispered into the stillness.

She *should* be thinking about how to defeat Zedong in his own game. She *should* be thinking about what she would say when she testified at the trial tomorrow.

Instead, there was nothing she could do but trace her patterned ceiling and torture herself with questions of whether she'd made the wrong decision. It wasn't too late. She could go to him even now, to his mind, and tell him she wanted to escape with him. They could be married in secret first thing, and then they could escape together.

Then she wouldn't have to sleep alone anymore.

But every time she tried to imagine taking those steps, uttering those words, she couldn't.

Because as much as she wanted it, *she couldn't leave*.

"I told him no," she whispered again, this time with dull resignation.

When she fell asleep again for the hundredth time, she stayed in her room, floating to the moonlit windowsill. If this was her mind, her soul tether would be anchored right here. She'd found it when Fang Zedong had imprisoned her in her own mind back in his fortress.

She trailed a disintegrating finger along the stonework, expecting the grit of the grout between the stones, but feeling nothing. *So strange*. She stared down, stroking the stone and letting her mind balk at the lack of sensation.

A tendril of shadow broke away from her finger.

Meiling's gaze sharpened as it didn't evaporate, but instead slid along the stone, over the edge, and out the window. Becoming a little blur of black slipping away.

What?

She melted through the wall without a thought and flew fast, trying to keep up with the black that seemed to grow darker and longer by the moment. What was it? Not part of her.

The ground raced for her, but the snaking shadow curved along the wall, racing along the base. She chased after it. It must have a destination. Some place it was going. After all the events of today, she wasn't about to let a shred of Zedong's black magic escape her.

The closer she got, the louder the hissing grew. She could almost reach out and—

Meiling stopped. Looked around her.

She floated at the front entrance of the palace. At the top of a thousand stairs that flowed down into the city. Suguan winked at her, bleary-eyed and half-asleep. Drunken. The city sprawled so far, she almost couldn't see the sea from here. But there, towering above the rooftops of the city, was the pagoda they'd visited the other day.

The stars twinkled and seemed to laugh down at her. The moon was so beautiful tonight, almost full and nearly incandescent—illuminating the curved eaves of the buildings and the far strip of sea.

Behind her, guards stood at attention. Their glows mingled with one another, bright with soft, warm with cool.

Why in the seven valleys was she here?

She had not aimlessly meandered out here. In fact, she did not think she had been wandering at all. Hadn't she been . . . doing something? Following something? But what would she be following so late at night, if not a person? There was no one here she would have been following. There wasn't a single moving body. Even the guards were still as statues.

Bewildered, she floated back the way she thought she'd come.

This was just . . . It was a strange night. That was all.

The last parade. Meiling could do it. She'd done so many before, so many this week. She could handle one more.

Part of her wanted to gasp in relief—the last parade! The rest of her wanted to explode into a panicked frenzy. The last parade. The festival ended tonight. Shang would likely leave sometime during the night.

Today she would testify.

And *maybe*, just maybe, the judge would accept her testimony. Maybe they could get a pardon after all, and Shang wouldn't have to flee for his life.

Riding out with her family into the streets of Suguan was rather like a dream. Though her senses were full of the shouting, the overwhelming and conflicting smells of rich and poor, man and beast, and the rocking, jolting movements of her horse—it was like she was a layer removed from it all.

She kept her head high and her eyes higher. Over the heads of the people. She could not bear to meet their scornful gazes. And then she closed her eyes, just for a moment.

Did I not promise you so much more, little one?

Meiling nearly gasped, but managed to keep her composure even as her eyes burst open. When her heart calmed its sudden thunderous roar, she braced herself and closed her eyes again.

The sounds of the parade dimmed.

I will still forgive you and spare your life. If you will join me.

Forgive me? For what—escaping your murderous clutches? she snapped back. *Perhaps I ought to be telling you that I might forgive you, if only you would behave.*

That raspy chuckle was cut off instantly when she opened her eyes again. Despite how weak her legs had gone, despite the profuse sweat dripping off her hands into the leather reins she held, she was able to think clearly enough to notice what she hadn't last night.

Whatever magic Zedong worked was different from her own. She could block him out simply by keeping her eyes open. Which meant he might not be able to hunt in her mind like she had hunted in his.

He was still limited. Somewhat.

But it was not a good sign that he was *still* in her mind even after she was kissed by Shang. Was he coming and going as he pleased? It was the only explanation that made reasonable sense.

What was more dangerous: conversing with her enemy, or refusing to listen to any clues he might give her? Any hints about where he was or what he was planning?

If she discovered anything of use, no one would listen to her, but she could give the information to Shang. He would know how to get it into the right hands.

Where are you? Meiling prompted, closing her eyes.

Have you nothing else to ask me, Daughter of Liena?

Have you anything else to tell me? she retorted back.

My, you have indeed grown fiercer. Or perhaps this was in your mind all along. You only did not voice it. You are more like Liena than I thought. But also . . . more different.

I wish you would leave me and my people alone.

The soft tsking in her mind was louder than the cries and cheers of the people. *My sweet little Meiling, you know I offer salvation to you and your people.*

Salvation from what? she spat.

From themselves. Their own weakness. Aren't we all our own worst enemies? You, of all people, should know this, my soft-hearted one.

Meiling's reply sat on her tongue, lethal and fire-laced. It waited patiently, like a crouching tiger. She'd been in his mind; she knew what Fang Zedong feared. What haunted him.

But she kept her reply unspoken, caged it away for later. The truth of it burned in her chest. She saw what Ma had seen so many years ago. Saw it better than Ma, perhaps. For Ma had only seen the birth, the potential. She saw the road Fang Zedong had plunged onto.

Meiling saw his destination. It was far worse than what her mother had suspected long ago.

Meiling still could not be there for the beginning of the trial due to the parade. It gnawed at her every second she rode atop that horse, urged her to walk swifter through the palace—trailed by her relentless maids and guards—toward the courtroom.

Her heart was nearly exploding in her chest when she reached the doors, but she drew herself up higher and sucked in a deep breath. The doors opened.

Please let this be enough to save them.

The judge had this look about him. A mask of lazy indifference, or perhaps more like a bored willingness to hear her out—but behind it, he was ready to pounce. Meiling licked her lips, watching him follow her every movement. He waited for any mistake that could warrant him tossing her out into the hallway.

When she strode down the aisle and finally came into view of Shang and Fen, her heart tripped over itself. Fen's brows were raised, but not in mockery. Her face seemed to say, *"Let's see what you can do."*

Shang's eyes were fixed on her, so heavy that she struggled to peel her gaze away to face the judge.

It had to be enough to save them. It just *had* to be.

She swore her vows before the judge and the scribe to the right who shuffled his papers and bounced his spectacles. This done, she faced the judge. She willed her knees to strengthen, to not go wobbly on her. Willed her breath to be even, controlled.

She could *do* something. Finally.

The judge lifted his nose so he could stare down at her. "Princess Meiling, no magic," he seemed to emphasize the last two words. "You are here to testify to what?"

Her voice did not waver. "I am here to testify to the innocence of Tan Shangdi, ice-wielder, and Hu Fen, shapeshifter."

"Indeed," the judge drawled and let out a sigh of long-suffering. "Since they failed at their task, what makes you believe they are innocent?"

She squared her shoulders. "The journey proved far more perilous than anticipated. They were not given sufficient forces. They are not guilty of neglect and incompetence—I was there, and I saw how outnumbered they were."

"A warrior should not need even odds to win a battle," the judge replied. Purple robes spilled out from where he sat, and one hand stroked the fabric aimlessly as he stared at her.

Meiling had expected this, and so she carefully asked, "How many wielders are typically dispatched for a herd of qilins?"

"I'm not answering any questions, *Princess* Meiling."

She kept herself from glancing left toward Shang and Fen. Refused to twist her sash. Instead, she reached into her core, deep into that place where she'd discovered a fiery will. "Two or three wielders are typically dispatched per qilin."

The judge merely stared at her.

She stared right back. "Tan Shangdi and Hu Fen faced an entire herd of qilins by themselves. Not only did they survive, but they protected me. I was unhurt. Does this not prove their competence?"

"I answer no questions," he repeated impatiently.

Meiling gritted her teeth. She gripped the edge of her sleeves in her fists. "In the entire journey, not once was I injured. Though we were attacked by *mó guǐ* and brigands—" her voice was interrupted by scuttling overhead. Her head shot upward at the sound, but no one else flinched. Had no one else heard?

Get out of here, Zedong, she growled in her mind as hair raised on the back of her neck. If she didn't know better, she might have thought something had crawled up her spine.

"Though we were attacked," she repeated, "I was never hurt. Tan Shangdi and Hu Fen suffered injuries themselves, but never me. They protected me with their lives."

"Until the brigands cornered them. Then they bartered away the princess for their lives." The judge spoke like they were addressing some other princess. Hou, perhaps. But not Meiling standing before him.

More scuttling. It was closer this time. She tried to arch her neck to find it, but her vision started growing blurry around the edges.

"Princess Meiling," the judge snapped.

She whipped her head up to him, realizing belatedly that her mouth hung open stupidly.

"Tan Shangdi and Hu Fen did not protect you in the end."

A sharp pain in her mind made her wince, but she croaked, "That was not what happened."

"Stop mumbling!"

"That was not what happened," Meiling repeated louder, but more pain stabbed her head. Her stomach turned queasy, and she swallowed against the sudden rising nausea. Her knees almost buckled, but she forced them straight.

"Then enlighten us on what happened."

What happened? She breathed through clenched teeth against the pounding in her head. Lifted her eyes to the impatient judge. She clamped her gaping mouth shut and opened it again. "When?"

"When the brigands attacked, and you were kidnapped!"

At the word *brigands,* even sharper pain knifed through her brain. She barely kept herself from clutching her head and crying out. She gasped for air. Not caring how unladylike the gesture was, she reached up and wiped her brow with her sleeve. It came back sopping.

All she could manage around the pain was, "That wasn't what happened."

"You were not kidnapped?"

The world was spinning.

"I was kidnapped, yes," Meiling forced out.

"By whom?"

"By . . ." She tried. She swallowed; she opened her mouth. Closed it, opened it. But Fang Zedong's name—though it wrestled on the tip of her tongue—refused to pass through her lips. She squeezed her eyes shut, tried to force the syllables between her teeth.

She couldn't.

And then a voice filled her mind with a raspy chuckle. *I cannot have you betraying me now, can I? Perhaps it is beneath me, but I cannot help my interest in this handsome Tan Shangdi. This wielder who swept you away from me. You know me, my little Meiling, and how hard it is for me to forgive. Be sure that, when I come, I have a special death reserved for him. But I couldn't allow him to die a hero, now, could I?*

Somehow, amid the muddling confusion and dagger-like pain, Meiling found the clarity to respond. *You intervened in this to ruin his reputation before you take his life? What about Fen? She's done nothing to you!*

I didn't ask for her to be tried with him, Zedong drawled back.

Why—why—why can't I breathe?

Probably because you're dramatic.

The voice vanished into dark chuckles, and Meiling's eyes flew wide. She was standing in the courtroom, everyone staring at her with mingled confusion, concern, and predatory interest. Her legs wobbled again, but she stayed upright. Enough to stare blankly at those around her. At Shang's opened mouth and wide eyes.

"Princess Meiling? Princess Meiling. Princess Meiling!"

More pain launched into her mind, tying her tongue and closing her throat. And then, to her befuddled horror, her legs moved of their own accord. She turned around and, with a final attack of pain that almost ripped a cry from her mute mouth, she strode out of the room.

No, no, no, no, *no.*

Behind her, the judge still called after her. Disrespectful she was. Irreverent, cursed by the fathers. Destined for nothing. She was never allowed back into his court so long as he lived!

Meiling hardly heard his words. The doors closed behind her and her entourage, sealing them off forever. Though her legs kept moving and she could not speak, her tears flowed. They streamed down her cheeks in desperate fury and helplessness.

Cursed. She was cursed. Like Feiyan. Like Liuxian.

She had thought because Shang's kisses hadn't removed Zedong's voice from her mind, that she hadn't been cursed. And perhaps she hadn't been before he kissed her. Perhaps Zedong had implanted the curse after the kiss. It didn't matter.

She was cursed now.

It finally released its agonizing hold on her when her own door closed behind her and shut her into her own quarters.

Her tongue loosed, and she cried out, "I hate you, Fang Zedong! I hate you, I hate you, I *hate* you!"

She stalked to her bed and, flinging aside the quilt, practically flung herself down on the firm surface. Tears streamed relentlessly as she pulled the vial Shang had given her from her sleeve and stuck a drop into her mouth.

She fell into a deep sleep.

CHAPTER 31

MEILING STOOD IN a long corridor.

At one end, it branched off into other corridors, heading further into the dream. At the other end was a huge oval stained-glass window. Rose, emerald, sapphire, and silver poured through its sun-glowing panes onto the red trimmed rug running the length of the corridor.

Before her, flanked by life-sized statutes of blazing phoenixes, she faced a polished staircase. The colors were more vivid, more dazzling than the real palace. She might be dazed if this were not her own mind.

Tell me, Fang Zedong, where you are hiding your curse.

Laughter spilled from behind the stained-glass window, and the colors pooling on the floor momentarily flickered. Like something large and dark blocked the sunlight on the other side. Meiling stilled, watching the jewel-tones return. Her gaze darted down to both ends of the hallway. Listening. Feeling.

Resolve hardening like steel in her heart, she stepped toward the staircase. It climbed high, spilling out into a U to another floor of the palace.

Glancing down, she found she wore only her nightgown. Her feet were bare. Her hair hung long and free to her hips, its gentle waves cascading like a waterfall over her shoulders and down her back. She lifted a foot and planted it on the lowest stair. Chill flooded into her skin and she jolted.

Then she set her gaze and flew up the stairs. When she reached the top, she froze.

Back in her sleeping body, her heart lurched. She moved again, but deathly slowly. She closed her eyes again, sending her awareness out and ignoring the cobwebbing memory threads surrounding her.

Footsteps. Above her.

That stride was so familiar.

Oh no. Oh dragon-spitting *no*.

Her projection of her body shuddered with dread, but she increased her speed. Down the hall that curved around the staircase, she padded near silently toward another looming staircase. This one was . . . dark. It was as though the candles in this part of the palace had not been lit, and the staircase itself was shrouded in darkness. Only thin slivers of silvery light cast across random stairs.

Swallowing the fear that lumped in her throat, she did not slacken her pace toward that staircase. The palace around her grew darker, and when she stepped on the first stair, it was like stepping into another world altogether.

A world wreathed in night.

Circular windows lined the wall along the curving, winding staircase. Meiling looked out the lowest one, and her blood ran cold.

A full moon, big and liquid and almost painfully bright, showered moonlight through the glass. But when she looked down at the stairs, only threads of silver reflected back at her as though the moon was only the barest crescent.

She swallowed again, tearing her eyes away from the windows. The next stair groaned under her weight. She shouldn't weigh anything here. Even losing the projection of her feet and flying up the stairs resulted in the same creaking and groaning as she passed over each stair.

She'd hoped to have the element of surprise, but now . . .

Despite herself, she slowed. Her lungs tightened, her muscles bracing. She almost called up into the night bound staircase, to what—to *whom*—she knew waited at the top. But she pursed her lips shut and continued. Each inch, each stair, was agony.

The softest kiss of wind met her at the top of the staircase. It ruffled her nightdress, her hair.

There, wreathed in an icy-blue glow and emanating strength from his wide-braced legs, was Shang. He tilted his head, black eyes reflecting blue. His arms were crossed, and his face was serious. Hardly a shred of emotion.

Meiling lifted her chin and growled, "I never let you into my mind."

The stoic mask melted away at once, revealing a softened mouth, gentle brows, and an earnest gaze. "I love you, Meiling."

The declaration hit her just as hard as the first time. She grabbed hold of the cool, polished banister for support, but before she could insist that her mind belonged only to her, Shang had crossed the distance between them and drawn her into his arms. His lips found hers, the only part of him that was soft. And just like that, she didn't care how he'd ended up in her mind—didn't care that she wasn't sure he was even real. She'd craved his kisses like a starving man for sustenance. When she tilted her mouth to his, he responded immediately, tightening his grip on her and making a hundred promises with his lips that could never be fulfilled.

He broke the kiss first, but didn't pull away as he whispered, "You're cursed. We should hunt for it together." Silvery moonlight caught in his eyes. They glittered, strong enough that she was forced to meet them.

And she knew. She knew he wasn't real. Knew she hadn't let him into her mind. Really, she'd known the moment she saw him. She just hadn't wanted to believe it.

She worked her hands up to his chest and pushed.

His grip tightened.

"Let me go."

He caught her chin, tilted her face up to his, as though studying her closely. If he bent down and kissed her again, she'd let him. Even though she knew he wasn't real. She'd believe this fantasy simply because she wanted to.

He seemed to know it, too.

He withdrew his arms from around her and took off into the darkness. "I think the curse is this way. I sensed it when I arrived."

He expected her to follow, and she wouldn't have, except that she knew he was right. After all, she hadn't created this midnight wing in the palace of her mind. She frowned, stepping slowly after him. Not wanting to lose him in the darkness, she gritted her teeth and walked faster.

She followed him into a doorway and peered up warily at the hanging, splintered wood lintel. Each step raised her hackles more, but he never turned around to ensure she was following him.

"Watch your step," he called over his shoulder.

When Meiling looked down, she did a double-take and then crouched to get a clearer view in the dimness. Moonlight reflected on the floor in little pools of silver. "Is this . . . broken glass?"

"Yes."

She willed away her bare feet and floated over the scattered shards. Frowned again. She wanted to close her eyes, to try to sense what was nearby, to reach out for any hint of the curse. But she was too spooked to close her eyes.

Shang disappeared around a bend ahead.

Her heart slammed into her chest with a burst of fear. She hurried forward, but as she did so, her foot brushed something soft. She paused, biting her tongue, but she kneeled to see what was scattered across this length of rough floorboards.

She reached down and lifted up a handful of little . . . flowers? They were waxy between her pinched fingers, and the sweet fragrance filled her nostrils.

Wintersweet blossoms.

Her mind returned to that candlelit dance in the pavilion, with Shang's eyes on her. She did not need light to know these blossoms were yellow, tinged with a flush of maroon at the center.

One hand braced against the floor near her knee, the other holding the wintersweet. The blood drained from her face. An exhale escaped her lips. Not daring to say the words aloud, she cursed herself inwardly. *Stupid, idiot girl.*

She knew who awaited her around that bend, and it definitely wasn't Shang.

She fisted her palm and knocked it into her forehead. Honestly, she was growing *quite* exhausted from being baited by him.

Summoning her courage and feeling far more alone than she had a moment before, she stood and clutched the fistful of blossoms to her chest. Curse or no curse, this was her mind.

She stepped around the bend and stopped.

It was a small room, mostly empty save for a cushion lying in front of huge, open windows. The curtains wafted with the same breeze that now tugged at her hair, her nightdress. Through the windows, moonlight washed like snow onto that mat, and the man seated on it.

Fang Zedong smiled.

"You are a liar," Meiling seethed.

That smile tipped further, and he cocked his head. Just like Shang had done moments ago. "How else would I get you to come here, little one?"

"I'm not a dog," she spat. "I followed the curse."

He gave a full grin now, spreading his arms behind his head and staring with satisfaction at her. "Your mind is a beautiful place," he said, and swept one hand toward the darkened room. "I had to make this part of it a little more . . . livable. For me, you see. All that sunlight and those garishly blinding colors. Really, Meiling, I'd have thought your preferences a little more subdued."

"What have you done to my mind?"

He shook his head, lifting one eyebrow. "Your boldness exceeds that of a lion in your own mind. Tell me: why do you hide it around others, sweet one? Is it because they sweep you under the rug, tell you that you're unimportant? Just a princess to be stuffed into a library and hidden away?" He shifted forward, planting his elbows on his legs and setting his chin on his hands. "I know. I know they hurt you. Made you into this helpless . . . mess." He waved his hand. "Unable to save your friends—"

"That was thanks to *you*."

"—and unable to hold your own against the people who hurt you."

"Stop manipulating me. I'm tired of it. Get your mat, your broken glass, your midnight, and yourself, and get out of my mind."

He grinned. "How much more fun you are, sweet Meiling, when you are not as sweet as you pretend to be in the waking world. I'd spar with you all day if I didn't have more important things to do."

That was what Shang had called her once. *Sweet Meiling.*

She crossed her arms over her chest, shooting her most potent glare. "If you have so many *important* things to do, then why do you bother? Why do you bother with me, with Shang, with Fen, with Feiyan? Why did you send Liuxian to kill me? Why don't you focus on conquering Zheninghai instead of tormenting me?"

"Ahh, now *that* is the sort of question I love getting. One I'm delighted to answer."

She tapped her foot. Still glaring.

"You tell me, little one—or what does Liena call you? *My dove*—what is more effective revenge for her marrying that prince and bearing his brats than breaking her most cherished darling?"

"If you love her, you will not try to hurt her."

The light shifted in Zedong's eyes. They grew bluer, dilated, focused. "You know I am not a forgiving person."

"Love forgives."

"Love is blind," he returned evenly. "And stupid. Did I tell you I love Liena? Do you think I love her?"

"Why did you want to make me your princess?"

"Because I pitied you," he said with a piercing grin. "Because if you were to be my princess, I would have to successfully turn you against your family. Liena gave you powerlessness. I offered you power. I wanted Liena to see you choose me over her."

Meiling drove down her nausea. She braced her legs wider to keep her balance secure. To keep herself from toppling over. "Why are you telling me this?"

He lifted an eyebrow and leaned back on his mat. His eyes seemed to take on a light of their own. "Because I see your mind now. And you . . . you do not want power. Not one shred of it. You want your *people*. You'd be their slave, you'd crawl on your hands and knees, you'd debase yourself, you'd humiliate yourself to dust for the people you love." His smile shifted into a scowl, dark and hateful. "Forgive me if I'm not as interested in having you as my princess as before."

He was always tall, but when he stood, he was tall enough that his tight braids nearly brushed the ceiling. He assumed a casual stance, but his muscles seemed to twitch. Ready to pounce.

She faced him.

"Now you tell me," Zedong purred. "What would you give, little one, to save your loved ones?"

"It seems like you already know the answer," Meiling replied.

He strode closer to her, close enough to reach out and stroke the hair back from her forehead, making her flinch. "The power I was going to give you would have been enough to save them. You could have blocked my curse—the *second* one, the one I replanted after last night's kissing escapade—and given your testimony in today's trial. You could have stopped Liuxian from stabbing you, overcome that fox spirit's mind, punished the judge for not listening to you, forced your parents to do as you say instead of constantly limiting your potential. *So much,* Meiling, I could have given you. It is unfortunate that you will not be my heir."

"You made Shang and Fen lie in their own trial, didn't you?" Meiling demanded, fury making her step closer, caring little if it put her at risk. "You cursed them too. You've cursed everyone in this fathers forsaken palace!"

Zedong's eyebrows rose, and genuine merriment crinkled the skin near his lashes. "The conclusions you're jumping to are both fascinating and flattering. But really, I'd have thought by now that you would know I am not a brute force sort of man. I *could* curse everyone in this palace. It would take a while, yes, and use up quite a lot of spell resources. What would I gain from that, however? Little more than what I would gain from a few targeted curses and compulsions."

Shang was cursed. Fen was cursed. If Meiling didn't—

As though hearing her thoughts—perhaps he *did* hear her thoughts—his smile widened. It was almost pitying. "Your dear friends aren't cursed. Not yet, at least. It was only a temporary compulsion. Like what I set on Du Liuxian. This is the power of Wungfao—a force that does your bidding, that goes into the world at your behest. Have you seen magic capable of this? No, little girl, you have not."

"What has it cost you?" Meiling asked, lifting her chin. "To become the only person in the world to master black magic?"

Zedong's attention narrowed. "Nothing I haven't given up willingly."

"Then you didn't have anything of true worth."

"True, true." His smile sharpened. "The good I had was taken from me. But I will take her back. And I will be forced to break you, little dove, to show her that she should not have chosen power over promise." He slinked closer to her until she stiffened. He tilted his face down to hers, his rough voice becoming something low, melodic, and terrifyingly composed. "I'll kill your family, your friends, but I will spare you and her until the end. I will make Liena watch you grieve the man you love, your siblings, your father. Because nothing will hurt her more than seeing you suffering soul-deep pain."

"Get out of my mind," Meiling breathed around the tightness of her lungs. "Leave my mind. And stay *away* from my family."

She could hear the crinkling edges of his smile. "You are so like her. Nearly twenty-five years it has been. I've missed her. Speaking with you reminds me what it was like to kiss your mother."

He caught her flying fist before it connected with his face.

"Get *out*," Meiling snarled, barring her teeth.

He studied her, holding her wrist captive, clearly reading her intention in her face to hit him with her other fist. Something unexpected flashed in his gaze—and it was almost like he saw something different in her. A part of her that wasn't like her mother. A part of her that was wholly Meiling.

"Very well," he said at last with the longsuffering sigh of a martyr. He released her wrist, and she barely maintained her self-control to not attempt to hit him again. "I shall indulge you one last time. Come here, and I will kiss you."

"I'm not kissing you," she snapped, already tensing. "You can leave my mind without it."

"My curse is too deep, sweet Meiling, for me to simply call it away. Come, come. I'll only kiss your forehead."

She stared up at his towering form in the darkness and gritted her teeth. "You're not going to leave."

"Indeed, I shall."

"Why?"

He reached out and grabbed her face with both hands—like Shang had done last night—and drew her closer, ignoring her protests and twisting to get out of his grip. "Let's say I have more important things to attend to."

With that, he pressed his scalding lips against her brow.

She screamed.

CHAPTER 32

SHANG DIDN'T HEAR much else in the trial after Meiling left. He nearly threw caution to the wind and ran after her. Something was *wrong*, desperately wrong. All he could think of was Feiyan lying unconscious in the shrubbery last night. Meiling must be cursed too—either that or suddenly very ill. He needed to get to her and make sure she was alright.

The end of the trial came upon him suddenly.

"Verdict will be announced tomorrow," the judge said irritably, not even looking at them. Shang's focus snapped into place, and he didn't need to be a master at reading people's faces to know as well as he knew his own name what the verdict would be.

They'd lost.

When Meiling had walked, when she'd first begun presenting his case, Shang had let himself hope. Now, he just looked at Fen, at the ashen pallor of her skin, and couldn't help but feel a fool for thinking this case's outcome wasn't set from the beginning.

Shang bowed wordlessly to the judge and strode out of the courtroom with Fen on his heels.

"We're dead," she said once the doors had closed behind them, as though she couldn't believe it.

"We're not dead yet," Shang growled. He spun to face her, making her stop abruptly as he pinned her with his gaze. "Did you decide? About the emperor's offer?"

Fen's attention fled away as she chewed the inside of her cheek. A muscle flexed in her neck, a vein standing out on her forehead. Her hands fisted, and the words nearly killed her, but she got them out. "I . . . will go."

A sigh of relief gushed out of Shang's chest. He squeezed her shoulder, and then he was marching away as fast as he could, needing to get to Meiling.

At least one of the people I care about won't die.

He received strange looks from guards and servants the closer he got to Meiling's quarters—where he had no business being. It didn't deter him from striding right up to her door and facing her guards. "I must speak to the princess."

"She is getting ready for the celebration tonight and must not be disturbed."

Getting ready for the celebration? Then . . . then maybe she was alright? With her magic, perhaps she dealt with any issues on her own? Shang swallowed, nodding toward the door. "How is she?"

The guard looked at him, frowning. "I beg your pardon?"

"Is the princess alright?"

Suspicion twisted the guard's expression.

"Is she ill?" Shang demanded, fighting to control his tone. "I saw her not long ago, and she wasn't feeling well."

"She had a headache, but she has rested and is preparing for tonight. Now, if you please, you must leave. She isn't to be disturbed."

"But you are sure she is well?"

The guard leveled a fierce glare at him. Then, to Shang's surprise, he knocked on Meiling's door. At a quiet beckoning, he opened it a crack and asked, "Highness, are you well?"

Meiling's surprised voice called back, "Well? Oh, yes, I am quite well, thank you. Is something the matter?"

Shang closed his eyes as a relieved sigh escaped him. After responding that nothing was wrong, the guard pulled the door shut and with an arched, *"I told you so"* look, beckoned Shang to leave.

Shang wanted specifics. Was she fine physically, but was she trapped in a curse? Did she need help? But this seemed to be all he was going to get. It would have to be enough for now. Meiling was *fine*. At least fine enough to get ready and attend a celebration. He would see her shortly, then, and confirm she was alright.

Until then, he also needed to dress for the celebration.

The curse was gone. And so was her chance to save Shang and Fen.

Meiling stood, elbows propped up on the windowsill, staring out her window at the declining sun. Her maids awaited her call outside, but she couldn't tolerate them right now. Even if the grandest, largest feast concluding the Festival of New Lights was starting soon, and she had not even begun dressing for it.

She couldn't even cry. She could only stare, could only feel a growing sense of gnawing emptiness in her chest, her belly.

Failure burned.

What was there left to do? The trial was over; she could not present any more information. If the judge truly believed Shang and Fen had bartered her life in exchange for their own—which was utterly idiotic to even consider—then what good Meiling did for their case was nothing. Not against that mountain of fault.

Only a few months ago, Shang and Fen were the Academy's top graduates. About to step into their bright futures and illustrious destinies.

Now . . . Meiling bowed her head.

What would you give to save your loved ones?

Anything. Everything.

But everything wasn't enough.

Meiling beckoned her maids in and did not even try to lift her countenance for them. She sat mutely while they fixed her hair, paint, and pinned unnecessary baubles and accessories to her person.

All this time. From the moment she'd returned home, Zedong had been here. He had sent his magic to devour her, to prepare this place for his invasion. If she had recognized it sooner . . . If she'd recognized that scuttling as belonging to Zedong's black magic . . . She shook her head and pressed her palm over her face, closing her eyes even as her maids clucked about mussed paint.

Maybe she was the only one to see and hear the infiltrating magic because she had held, touched, wielded black magic while she was a prisoner in Zedong's fortress. Not even Shang had been able to detect it.

She'd tell her parents about the magic, but she was certain they would tell her to stop getting involved. As if it was her choice to be hounded and terrorized by their enemy. They would be sent into a frenzy of worrying and ensuring she was protected and safe.

But her blood would not be the first to flow.

Tonight, she would speak with Shang. Apologize for everything and beg his forgiveness and then tell him all she knew. He would get the information into the right hands. If he did not attend the feast, she would do whatever it took to lose her guards and find him, or she'd use her mind magic to speak to him.

She swallowed at her reflection and spared half a thought that she looked nothing like that girl who had been escorted out the west gate by two strangers all those months ago.

CHAPTER 33

THE FINAL FEAST was held outdoors, in an area not unlike last night's Academy dancing pavilion. Lanterns were strung across the pathways and courtyards, illuminating the sunset, and there would be fireworks later. Little fires were strategically placed to warm the guests.

Hundreds of people crowded, bustled, and laughed. It took Meiling fifteen minutes to locate a single member of her family besides Pa, who sat on his raised dais. Hou flung aside propriety to hug her, and then, with a flashing grin, scurried off with her friends. Yun acknowledged her much more politely, though his smile was warm. Oddly enough, she could not even find Ma.

She stopped her search for Ma when she spotted a surprising face. Forgetting everything else, she rushed over to Feiyan's side.

Feiyan did not wear Academy white. She wore simple green robes, but they were well-tailored for their simplicity. When she spotted Meiling coming toward her, she grinned and raised her goblet.

Meiling had to contain herself from embracing her friend and instead inclined her head politely to Feiyan's deferring nod.

"Highness." Feiyan's eyes gleamed with mischief. "How delightful to see you tonight."

"I did not expect you to be here," Meiling said eagerly, glancing around.

"You mean because I'm not the party sort? Well, regardless of whatever sort I am, apparently a healer's presence is *required* on the last night of the Festival of New Lights. Maybe just in case the fireworks go haywire." She smirked.

"I'm very glad you're here and . . . that you're well."

Feiyan's smile went over Meiling's shoulder and broadened. "We've got company."

Meiling turned around and was struck with a sudden mingling of joy and sadness at the sight of Fen, Shang, and Renshu approaching them. For a moment, she considered escaping for something to cure her parched throat, but no. She was done running. Even from this afternoon's embarrassment.

"Good evening, Highness," Shang said first and bowed. The others followed suit. "I hope you are well."

There was not a shred of malice or disappointment in his face, but there was a penetrating concern that sent her gaze fleeing to her toes even as she mumbled that she was, indeed, well.

"I would like to *officially* introduce you to my friend, Cao Renshu," Shang said. "Since the circumstances of your meeting have always been . . . less than favorable. He also graduated from the Academy this year and has been appointed to the Emperor's Guard."

Prestigious.

Meiling turned her attention up to Renshu, relaxing at the sight of his easy smile. "It is a pleasure to *officially* meet you."

She would never forget that dark, half-lit labyrinth, with claw marks gouging into the stone. Neither would she forget the sound of his echoing cries of pain back in Zedong's fortress.

Renshu's face split between a humorless grin and a grimace, clearly remembering the same thing. "Our first meeting was not exactly under the happiest of circumstances, unfortunately, so I'm glad to begin our friendship anew. I am also glad we are all back safely."

"All except Fen," Feiyan inserted with a smirk. "Who was probably polishing her buckles while we languished."

Fen narrowed her eyes and bared one snarling tooth, daring Feiyan to goad her further. "Don't forget how many times I've smashed your face in the dirt."

Feiyan grinned. "How could I *possibly* forget? Have you ever eaten dirt? You should try it sometime. I've been on a steady diet of dirt since I was five years old and look at how strapping I am!"

Renshu coughed to hide a laugh. Meiling glanced sidelong at Feiyan's sparkling midnight eyes, that wry mouth, and imagined her Academy training had, indeed, involved a lot of face- planting into the dirt.

Shang was not amused. His forehead wrinkled, as though he thought her joke in poor taste. Somehow it made it funnier, and apparently Renshu thought so too because his face split into a grin when he glanced at Shang.

Fen smirked as only Fen could, the way she'd once done at the antics of the panda cub they'd rescued ages ago.

Then it hit her.

She was standing and laughing with a group of friends. All of them knew about her magic—she'd been in their minds. All of them had seen her at her worst, most desperate places, but they were not offput by her reputation. They were here now, joking and bantering at a party.

She had never had this.

And she loved it.

"There's the worthless evanescer," drawled Fen. "I heard a rumor you were in Suguan."

"Hello, Kai. It's been a while," said Renshu.

Everyone turned toward the newcomer: a tall young man with a roguish tilt to his smirk who struck Meiling as vaguely familiar. He lifted one hand in greeting. "And there's the warm and fuzzy shapeshifter who loves me so much."

"You wish," Fen retorted with a huff.

"Actually, I don't. I have enough shapeshifters who adore me already. One more would be much too suffocating."

Shang was just standing there, arms crossed, saying nothing.

"Nice nose you got there, Shi Kai," said Feiyan.

Kai swiveled his head toward her, lifting both brows in surprise. "Um, thank you. I was actually just admiring your . . . ears."

Renshu snorted. "She means when she healed your broken nose years ago."

Feiyan shot a confused look at Renshu, as though confused he would know that.

"Oh! Yes, a great service to the collective common good of Zheninghai," said Kai, with a wink at no one in particular.

Shang glanced at Meiling as if to say, *"I can't take this man's ego much longer."* She waggled her eyebrows at him and giggled in response. His severe mouth cracked slightly.

Kai's attention shifted to her, and he flashed a dazzling grin. "Princess Meiling, we meet at last. My partner Delan was telling me he met you the other night. We tracked you for ages it seemed when the brig—" He cut himself off abruptly, glancing at the circle of people, as though unsure if everyone knew she'd been captured. "I'm glad to see that you are well."

Meiling spent all those long nights in darkness at Zedong's fortress, wondering if anyone would ever come for her. It struck her heart now: the realization of how many people she hadn't even known who'd been working to bring her back home.

Shang studied Kai, and Meiling could have sworn that twitch of his nose meant something along the lines of, *"Maybe he isn't a complete idiot."*

"It was a pleasure to meet Delan," Meiling said, smiling and fighting her unexpected swell of emotion. "As it is a pleasure to meet you, Shi Kai, and a privilege to give you my heartfelt thanks."

Kai stared at her, as though momentarily at a loss for words, either from what she said or what must be shining from her face. The bravado melted away from his expression, and when their eyes met, she saw the real Kai. The depth of spirit behind the swaggering confidence.

In that moment, it was like she felt the collective pulse of all their hearts in this circle. Shang, Fen, Renshu, Kai, Feiyan . . . and *her*.

Kai cleared his throat. "Of course. But really, most of the thanks should go to Delan and Aranya. They puzzled out what was happening long before I could have."

"Is that humility from Shi Kai?" Fen gasped.

"Do it again," said Feiyan.

While Kai was shooting glares at both of them—Renshu smiling wordlessly at the exchange while Shang sipped his wine—Meiling asked innocently, "Is Aranya the one you were writing love letters to the other night?"

Shang spat out his drink.

All eyes turned to him as he coughed. He waved a hand for them to ignore him. Meiling scratched her nose, using her long sleeve to hide her proud little grin.

"You're courting Sun Aranya?" Fen burst. "The tiny partial that was always finding excuses to leave campus? Seven valleys!"

"She was leaving to take care of her *grandfather*," Kai said defensively. "Who is a delightful man in his last days, so be respectful. But yes." A slow smirk spread across his face. "I'm courting Sun Aranya. And no, my fondness for her doesn't translate to other shifters, unfortunately."

Shang had composed himself, and when Meiling opened her mouth again, he took her elbow. "Walk with me?" He was all but dragging her away from the group before she could answer, exclaiming under his breath: "You little minx!"

"Minx?" Meiling demanded, huffing to keep up with his long strides. She couldn't hide her grin. "You thought it was funny."

"You think just because you have big eyes and long lashes, you can bat them at anyone and feign innocence and say the bluntest things—and no one will think anything of it! But you're wrong. I know when you're playing sweet and stupid. I've *always* been able to tell."

"Not true! I played sweet and stupid plenty of times when we were travel—"

"Yes, like the time you asked me to explain the different types of magic. Or when you tried to calm me down in Fang's dungeons by asking me questions about my ice. And a dozen other times. You think you're invisible, Meiling, and maybe once upon a time that was true. Not anymore."

They navigated through the crowds of people, the lanterns hanging low enough that he ducked around one or two. The further they walked, the sparser the people grew and the quieter it became.

"I cannot tell if you're rebuking me or not," said Meiling, hanging onto his elbow and smiling coyly up at him.

Shang rolled his eyes, guiding her around a cherry tree. "I'm not rebuking you. I'm telling you that you're not as subtle as you think you are."

"I'm not trying to be subtle. I think you're just jealous I smiled at him."

"You think I'm jealous of *Shi Kai*?"

"I can smile at you too, if it'll make you happy."

Shang stopped and whirled her around, catching her waist with an iron grip. They were near an overlook now, and no one else was nearby. The biting cold didn't have anything on the smoldering intensity in the black eyes he brought so near her own as he tilted her chin up. "Keep provoking me, and I'll be forced to punish you via kidnapping. You'll find yourself tied up in a hammock somewhere in the Southern Isles."

"Maybe Kai and Renshu will have to come rescue me then."

"You really are a little minx when you want to be," Shang growled, and then he kissed her.

She went liquid in his arms, softening against him. His hand slid from her chin to wrap around the back of her neck, his thumb stroking the feverish rhythm of her pulse beneath her jaw. When she broke for air, his lips chased hers, refusing to let her go.

She was the first one to start weeping. "I can't go with you."

"I know."

"I *can't*. I want to, I want to, *I want to,* but I can't."

"I know, darling. I know." His kisses trailed to her cheek, her jaw, the wet trails of tears down her face.

"I'm so sorry, Shang. I should have known Fang was intervening in the trial. Should have known I was cursed. Should have recognized his magic everywhere. He doesn't forgive or forget. *I should have known*."

"None of this is your fault."

"I ruined your chance at a pardon! Now you *have* to go, and I'll never see you again!"

Shang cupped her face in both his hands, his gentleness underscored by ferocity. "You have ruined nothing. Are you alright? Are you still cursed?"

"It's gone. I made sure of it."

He nodded slowly. Her cheeks, ears, and nose slowly froze in the winter night. She wondered if this was the last time she'd ever see Shang.

"I need you to tell whoever you tell," she managed around the lump in her throat, "that Fang Zedong has his magic all over this palace. Who even knows the minds he's infiltrated at this point? Someone needs to . . . to stop it." *Because I can't.* "Before he arrives."

Shang nodded tightly, his throat bobbing.

They were silent for a long moment, standing there so close together in the cold. She wanted to reach out to him, wanted him to wrap her in his arms so she could weep against his chest. Instead, she let him wipe away the warm tears from her face as she choked out, "He's been intervening in the trial from the beginning. Making you admit to falsehoods, ruining your chances of pardon. I should have seen it—"

"Meiling," he said at last. "Please. I don't want to talk about Fang. Or the trial. I only want to savor this time." His eyes found hers, and they flashed with a rare vulnerability. "With you."

Snow began falling then. Each snowflake was thick, fat, and surrounded them in a flurry of cold. She always loved the first snowfall, but now she couldn't help but think she would hate it for the rest of her life.

A snowflake landed on her nose. Shang kissed it away, then took her hand and guided her toward the overlook. The wall was too low for them to lean on, but they stood together looking out at the snow blanketing the city.

"If the snow comes down much harder, it'll cut off our visibility of the fireworks. But look, we can still see the fires on the beach." Shang pointed, and Meiling could barely make out the pinpricks of orange in the darkness.

He didn't have to say the rules of their remaining time together; she understood. No sadness or tears or discussing unsavory topics like Zheninghai's impending doom. Just the two of them.

Meiling wiped away the last of her tears. "I bet those celebrations are much wilder than this one."

"Indeed."

"Probably more fun, too."

He gave a short snort of amusement. Then his gaze shot to hers, bright and unexpectedly conspiratorial. "Should we join them?"

"Join them?" Meiling echoed in surprise.

"It'll be warmer."

"We're not *that* much higher at the palace," she said, laughing.

"You'd be surprised. Come, I know a shortcut to get there."

He held out his hand, a smile playing at the corners of his mouth. She placed her hand in his with a huff. "Of *course* you know a shortcut. Do I need to change?"

Shang's gaze swept over her. He shrugged, but there was that calculation in his eye—as always. "No. It would be good if they recognized you."

"You're sure?"

He leaned closer, reaching around her to pluck the pins out of her hair until it fell freely to her hips. "I'm sure." Then he took her cold hand and dragged her to the edge of the overlook where the wall ended.

CHAPTER 34

WHAT ARE YOU doing?" Meiling asked when Shang stepped over the wall onto the mountainside.

He flashed her a roguish grin. "Taking the shortcut."

Meiling pulled back. "I don't know if I like scaling cliffs."

"Sure you do," he replied, and grabbed her before she could retreat, dragging her to the wall.

"Tan Shangdi, if you're about to—"

He scooped her up with one arm, ignoring her thrashing. "Hold on to my neck!"

She did as she was told, but only because she didn't want to *die* when he balanced himself on the steep edge with only his feet and one free hand, and began sliding down the side of the mountain.

Meiling squeaked, wrapping both her legs around his waist so she clung to him like a koala. "You're going to kill me!"

He was grinning, apparently enjoying her terror as he half slid, half climbed his way at a dizzying speed down the cliff. "That would be slightly counterproductive."

"You're just trying to show off!"

"Absolutely. Are you impressed?"

"I'm scared out of my wits!"

"No, you're not."

"Shang!"

"We're almost to the bottom, darling." He gave her leg an affectionate pat. "Then I'll need you to use that charm and royal blood of yours to get us a horse from the royal stables. Unless you'd rather walk a couple of li to the beach in the freezing cold."

And with that, they were at the bottom. Shang straightened, hoisting her up, so she didn't slide, and then began walking into the streets of Suguan, skirting around the cliff toward one of the palace stables.

"You should put me down—people will think things!" Meiling squeaked, unwrapping an arm from his neck. She tried to disentangle one of her legs, but Shang only tightened his grip.

"I don't *care* what anyone thinks," he growled softly. "And you're cold. Come, let's have one night where we do whatever we want and don't care about the consequences."

Slowly, she wrapped her arm back around his neck, smiling. "Alright, then." She nuzzled into the space between his jaw and his ear and pressed a soft kiss there. Shang nearly stumbled, catching her tighter to himself as he corrected his balance, his cheeks turning scarlet. She couldn't help her giggle.

He pivoted suddenly, and her back hit a wall. The wall of what—she had no idea, and she didn't really care. Not when he was returning her kiss, his lips pressed against the very same spot. It sent a rush of tingles down her spine.

Then he pushed off the wall, and they were on their way again, his voice gravelly as he said, "No more kissing until we reach the beach. We'll never arrive otherwise."

"Would that be so terrible?"

At Shang's rebuking glare, she burst into another fit of giggles, and didn't overcome them before the sudden stench of horse manure nearly overcame her. He set her giggling self on her own two feet, and with a slight smirk and glittering eyes murmured, "Get us a horse, Highness. And try not to act drunk."

Seven valleys, she *was* acting drunk! The realization sent another peal of laughter ringing out in the stables as she tried to compose herself enough to ask the bewildered stable hands for a horse. Shang just stood there, shaking his head while she made an utter fool of herself.

But tonight, she didn't care what anyone thought. It was just her and Shang. Their one little pocket of time together. She intended to make every moment last forever, and she wasn't about to waste any of it.

Shang watched the travesty of Meiling trying to compose herself enough to order a horse with nothing but amusement. Eventually, he was forced to step in and interpret her half-choked request.

But that was only one battle of many on their quest to get to the beach.

He helped Meiling mount as he'd always done, and the incessant giggling eventually faded away as he swung up behind her. He slid an arm around her waist, satisfaction blooming in his gut as he at last had the freedom to pull her as close as he wanted. Then he bent forward, ignoring his own rule of no kissing until the beach, and pressed a quick kiss to her shoulder. When she tried to return it, he dodged with a laugh and kicked the horse into motion.

Meiling quickly forgot about fighting to kiss him back once they entered the main thoroughfare of Suguan. She gasped, goggling at the stalls, the brightly colored lanterns, the beautiful and conflicting music floating from every corner, and the celebration of the people.

"Wait! We must stop! I have always wanted to know if the candy from the streets tasted better than the candy at the palace!"

With a hidden smile, he let her slide off the horse and prance up to a stall with hard candy designs on a stick. She picked the one that was the shape of a panda face, and wound up talking to the stall owner until his rounded cheeks were split in a grin. Shang remained where he was, smiling as she began walking back to him and chomped down on the panda's ear. Immediately, her eyes went wide, and she spun back around to the stall owner. "This is the *best* candy I've ever had! How do you make it so good? Seven valleys, I need another one!"

Eventually, she pranced back with her half-eaten panda face and a second one in the shape of a *jiaun*. She handed it to him with enthusiasm. "This one is for you! I thought we'd share the panda—look! It reminded me of Bo!—but then I tried it and I couldn't share. This one made me think of you, since you're so good at shooting things."

He couldn't stop the small, rumbling laugh that escaped him. He'd never been happier in his entire life. And by the fathers, this *was* the best candy he'd ever tasted. Also, the best tasting *jiaun*.

"See?" Meiling demanded. "It's *amazing*."

He helped her back into the saddle, pulled her closer, and barely kept himself from kissing her again. They started off once more, but it wasn't long before something else distracted Meiling. He didn't mind. Watching her glow and sparkle made his pleasure complete. And just as he'd always known, the people of Suguan couldn't resist her any more than he could. She lit up the streets, making friends out of strangers at every turn.

She wasn't the same girl he escorted out of the west gate all those months ago.

It was so obvious now that he could never take her away from Zheninghai. This truly was where she belonged. She deserved to belong with the people she'd bled for. The people she'd loved before they had ever loved her.

He remembered what she'd said to him so long ago, that her dream was to experience the world, to not just observe it from a distance, but to feel it, smell it, taste and touch it. He couldn't take her to the ends of the earth to let her experience its height and depth and breadth, but he could let her experience Suguan in a way she'd never experienced it before. In this small way, he could make her dream come true. And perhaps in that fulfillment, she might find that the truth of her dream wasn't to see the world, but to fully belong in her own corner of it.

At last, they made it to the beach.

Their cloaks whipped in the wind, but Shang was so alive he didn't feel the cold. There was only a thrill when he pulled Meiling down from the horse and kissed her until she nearly lost her balance in the sand. She tasted like cinnamon candy. Each kiss grew harder and harder to pull away from, but he managed somehow. Her large, expressive eyes shone a little too brightly in the campfire light, and he wiped away one stray tear. She swallowed, then smiled bravely at him.

"That's my girl," he murmured, then kissed her forehead before taking her hand and dragging her toward the bonfires and rings of dancing people surrounding them.

She grabbed his elbow, pulling him to a stop. "I have a secret!"

He smiled down at her. "Care to share?"

"I've *always* wanted to dance in one of these dances—they're so different from what I learned at the palace!"

"That doesn't seem like much of a secret."

"No, no, the secret is that I used to fly out here when I was young, watch how they did the dance, and then practice in my bedroom by myself," she whispered conspiratorially. "You can't tell anyone!"

He chuckled, squeezing her hand. "Your wicked little secret is safe with me."

Men and women were separated at different fires as they danced and sang, but Shang had no interest in being parted from Meiling for the span of even one dance. Instead, he dragged her right into the ring of men dancing around one fire. They wouldn't mind the entry of a beautiful young woman.

It was the last night of celebration; who cared about propriety?

Shang didn't actually know the dance, but it wasn't difficult to pick up. Meiling burst into laughter at his side when she accidentally went the wrong way and cried, "It's backwards from the women's dance!"

The men laughed uproariously at each of her wrong steps, but before they knew it, she was dancing it better than them and laughing at *their* missteps—Shang's most of all.

"You're so graceful everywhere else," Meiling laughed, her long, lovely black hair flying everywhere. "But you dance like a horse!"

"A horse? What is that supposed to mean?"

"It's not a compliment."

"Why, thank you for clarifying."

It wasn't long before more women—mostly the young and bold ones—joined the men's circle too until it was big enough they had to split into two groups to stay near the warmth of the fire. No one dodged Meiling's shadow or seemed to care a whit about her supposed curse. When a villager called her Highness, she replied with a laugh that they should call her Meiling. So they did.

And when Shang was done sharing her, he pulled her out of the circle, built a little fire in a rocky alcove somewhat sheltered from the wind, and the heat of their kisses kept them warm from the falling snow. Triumph thrilled in his belly when the fireworks began bursting overhead and she didn't pay them any heed.

CHAPTER 35

DESPITE HER DETERMINATION not to waste a single moment, the cold eventually won out. Even when Meiling gave a chattering, teeth-clacking protest that she wasn't cold, Shang only smiled and lifted her up into his arms, carrying her to their horse.

Shang mounting up behind her on the saddle and holding her close did nothing to penetrate her bone-deep shivers. She gave a last forlorn glance to the beach, the bonfires, and the few people still dancing.

"I know I shouldn't ask," she said, craning her head toward his, "but when are you leaving?"

He tensed, just slightly. "At the right time."

"Don't leave without saying goodbye."

"I don't want to say goodbye."

"Well, I don't want to go searching for you, only to discover you're gone! That would crush my heart, Shang!"

"I know," he whispered, bringing his lips to the top of her head. "I know."

"So you will say goodbye? You promise me?"

His hot breath exhaled against her neck. He nodded. "I will."

"Good."

They rode in silence the rest of the way back to the palace. It had to be past midnight by now, and most of the children and their parents had retired, leaving the rest of the late-night celebrations to the drunkards, youths, and stall workers. She leaned against Shang, the rise and fall of his chest soothing her almost to sleep. With one hand, he guided the horse. With the other, he traced gentle circles on her waist.

They reached the stables, and Meiling's legs were frozen so stiffly they refused to work at first. The snow had stopped, leaving nothing but a light dusting and a promise of more in the coming months. Due to its proximity to the coast, Suguan didn't get much snow each year. Nothing to compete with the northern territories or Butagin. Still, they got enough that not everyone was excited at the first snowfall.

Shang helped her off the horse and guided her back toward the palace celebration. He stopped twice when they came across braziers and made her warm her fingers.

They reached the gardens and pavilion where the celebration was. Music and conversation wafted toward them. Meiling turned a mischievous grin up at Shang. "Shall we scandalize my father's court with my lack of hair ornaments? Maybe we should hold hands too—that'll scandalize them even further."

Her smile quickly faded at his serious expression. Her voice came out in a pained croak. "Now? Already?"

"Meiling," he whispered softly, brushing her hair out of her face, and her name on his lips was like its own goodbye.

"No—no, I'm not ready yet! I'm not ready!" The tears she'd suppressed all evening came with the force of a tsunami, and soon they were streaming in hot trails down her icy cheeks. "Shang, please, I'm not ready!"

His face crumpled. He pulled her to his chest just as his own tears slipped free. "We're never going to be ready."

"I can't," she choked, clinging to him. "I can't lose you. Let me come with you. Please, don't leave me here without you."

His hand fisted in her hair. "I love you more than I have loved anything in my life. There is no one in this world so good and noble as you. I'm sorry I was such a fool to not see it immediately." Then he tilted her face up toward his and kissed her hard. As though he was drowning, dying, like the sun was setting and carrying his last rays of hope with it. His voice broke when he whispered, "I'm not taking you with me, Meiling."

She tightened her grip on his neck, returning his fevered kisses as her heart broke into a thousand tiny pieces. Her tears turned to choking sobs. He kissed the wet trails running down her cheeks, but when she opened her eyes, he had trails running down his too. Laughter spilled down the path from the festival, and it seemed wrong that people were happy while her heart bled out in the cold. She clung to him, not willing to breathe even as her lungs cried out for air, too afraid this would stop and end forever.

Nothing mattered right now. Nothing except kissing Shang, except his arms around her.

Then suddenly, he pulled back, gasping, eyes raw, words strangled. "Meiling, I—"

Stabbing agony hit her chest.

She whimpered, choked on a frantic sob, and caught his face again. Tried to pull him back down to her, but he only drew her head firmly to his chest and held her against his pounding heart and heaving lungs. His arms were both comforting and restraining around her shaking, shivering body.

"This is why I didn't want to say goodbye," he choked, his breath on the top of her hair. Each inhale was like breathing around a freezing dagger in her chest. She squeezed her eyes shut, and the tears poured freely.

"Shh," Shang whispered gently, beginning to trace soothing circles on her back as he held her. It almost seemed like having someone to comfort was comfort enough for him. Meiling shuddered, though she was so much warmer in his arms. He was solid. Safe. *Home.* His heart thudded against her ear, but slowly, the racing rhythm calmed to something soothing and predictable. Hers, on the other hand, never stopped pounding with their imminent parting.

"There," his voice rumbled. "Everything will be alright." His knuckle brushed her cheek, wiping away her tears. He pressed a lingering kiss to the top of her head. "Everything will be alright."

No, nothing would be all right. But she wanted to believe him, so in that moment, she did. She decided that everything would be all right. Somehow.

He tilted her face up to his, and she memorized every line of his dear, handsome face. The sharp jawline, the harsh nose and prominent brow. Those piercing black eyes that softened only for her. He drew a deep breath, as though bracing himself. "We'll see each other again. This isn't a forever goodbye." He caught her cheeks in both his palms, his gaze boring into her. "I promise."

It was a lie. But part of her hurt eased at the comfort. "I'll see you again," she whispered on trembling lips. She braved a smile as more tears streamed free. "I will eagerly await that day."

He pressed one final kiss swiftly to her mouth. "See you later, my beautiful, darling Mei."

Then he let go and strode away. His tall, broad-shouldered form became nothing but a silhouette in the dark. And then he was gone, lost beyond the reach of the colored lanterns and the faint stars above.

Meiling wandered in a daze through the celebration. There was no sign of Feiyan, Fen, Renshu, or Kai. No sign of Master Dong or Delan. Hou had probably gone to bed, and Yun was likely doing something stupid with his friends. She ought to retire and work the chill out of her body. Instead, she kept walking through bright lights and laughter until she reached the overlook she and Shang had abandoned only a few hours before.

She sat on the edge of the wall and stared into the blackness of the sky and the dimness of the city below. Her hair blew around her face, and she huffed mirthlessly at the sight of her beads and hairclips on the ground.

Was Fen leaving with Shang? She hoped so.

"They'll survive," she whispered to herself. "Thank the fathers, they'll survive."

It was a hollow victory, but one nonetheless. She would forever have tonight to cherish in her memories.

"If only Zedong hadn't *ruined* my testimony," she snarled under her breath. Then Shang could have stayed. She closed her eyes, waiting for that dark voice to fill her mind. Almost *hoping* it would so she could rail against Zedong and let her grief become rage. The voice never came.

Still, unease prickled down her spine.

Meiling turned around.

And there was Du Liuxian.

He stared at her with that same empty gaze—the gaze he'd had when he stabbed her. His frame was bony as ever, his gray hair cleaned and trimmed but still unkempt.

She scrambled to her feet, putting as much distance between him and her as she could. Which wasn't much, considering the cliffside behind her. Her hands latched onto the cold brick of the wall and she searched for anything that could be a weapon. "What are you doing?"

He didn't say anything, but his body was shaking. He wasn't cursed anymore if he'd been released from the dungeons.

But that didn't mean he was in his right mind.

He took a step toward her, lifting one shaking hand.

"Don't come near me," Meiling snarled, her hand wrapping around a broken chunk of brick and raising it in threat. When he took another step, she opened her mouth and let out a scream.

Footsteps came racing down the path toward her.

She drew in a ragged breath, her fist trembling in relief. "Guards!"

Two guards rounded the bend first, followed by a handful of courtiers. Just as they did, Liuxian lunged for Meiling. She let out another scream and scrambled out of the way. The guards were upon him in an instant. But Liuxian didn't fight them.

He kept his gaze fixed on Meiling. He lifted his free hand—the one a guard hadn't restrained—and pointed one finger straight at her.

"Highness, you shouldn't be out here alone," the other guard said, coming to her side to escort her back to the celebration. The courtiers watched, talking among themselves, and when the man who'd gotten there first informed them that the old man had tried to attack the princess, they gasped.

But then Liuxian opened his mouth, his finger still pointed at her as the guard began dragging him away.

"She is a witch," he said, and his voice didn't sound crazed at all, but deeply bitter. "Princess Meiling has *magic*."

CHAPTER 36

"ARE YOU READY?" Shang asked Fen in a hushed tone. Her gaze shined with ferocity, and for once it wasn't anger at their situation, but a determination to protect her family. Even if it meant giving up everything else she'd spent her life working toward.

She nodded. They clasped hands tightly.

He'd always known saying goodbye to Meiling would gut him, but he wasn't prepared for the hit this goodbye would serve.

"You get through that gate and you don't hesitate, understand?" he said firmly around the lump in his throat. "The emperor has a man waiting for you. He'll escort you to the city limits. A horse will be tied there, loaded with provisions for the journey."

"If you stay, they're going to find you." Fen's face was deathly serious. "There might not be another opportunity to escape the city, and if you get caught—"

"I know."

"They'll kill you. And it won't be by beheading. If this is the best the emperor can do for us, he couldn't spare you from a deserter's death."

Shang's jaw flexed. "I know."

"And Meiling will hear of it."

He shot her a glare, trying to hide the way his gut clenched. "I *know*." If his plan failed, it would wreak such utter devastation he didn't think Meiling could ever recover. "I need to take this risk."

Slowly, Fen nodded and sighed. Then she closed the distance between them and shocked him with a bearhug. "It was an honor to serve beside you."

"Likewise," Shang managed, returning her embrace.

They pulled apart, and neither of them said those dreaded words of farewell. Instead, Fen gave him that snarling smile of hers, elongated canines and everything, and Shang gave her a deep nod.

Then they parted.

Shang's pulse thrummed as he snuck back through the Academy grounds to the palace and the celebration. If everything went according to plan, he'd lie low in the city until Fang attacked. Then he'd be there to fight and, if possible, spare Meiling from the bloodbath.

Because as tempting as the dream of the Southern Isles had been with her at his side, part of him had always known he couldn't turn his back on Zheninghai anymore than she could. They were in this together, and they were in it until the end.

Brutal as it may be.

He was skirting the edge of the lantern light at the celebration, searching the crowds for Meiling, trying to ascertain whether she'd gone to bed for the night, when he heard the scream. Coming from the bluff.

"Phoenixes scorch it," Shang cursed, breaking into a run. He pulled moisture from the air into his hands by instinct as he ducked under tree branches and leaped over benches to get there in time.

Two guards and an entire crowd of onlookers arrived before he did. He was just in time to survey the scene, to note with desperate relief the lack of blood, and run his eyes over a hale but frightened Meiling, when a voice he hadn't heard before sliced through the air with words he had dreaded for months.

"Princess Meiling has *magic*."

The words worked a shock over the crowd. Shang took his opportunity to spring into action, leaping out of the shadows and throwing himself between Meiling and the second guard.

"Shang?" Meiling cried in disbelief.

The guard acted on instinct, drawing a broadsword in a flash and stabbing it toward Shang. He dodged the blow, threw up his hands, yet still managed to stay between him and Meiling. "I'm not hurting her!" he said quickly.

"If you hurt him, *I will kill you*," Meiling snarled at the guard, fighting to put herself in front of Shang.

There was no telling who was more shocked by her declaration between Shang and the guard, but he stood down. At least for a moment, and that moment was enough for Shang to maneuver them a few steps back, trying to give himself more room to fight.

"What are you—" Meiling started to ask.

But everything descended into chaos when Liuxian began shouting at the top of his lungs. "Princess Meiling has magic! The emperor knows and has hidden it from us all this time! She's a witch!"

Oh fathers.

The secret was out.

Shang sprang into action.

Meiling wasn't sure if what she was experiencing was real or if she was trapped in a nightmare that wouldn't end. When the growing crowd of onlookers began screaming and shouting, and more guards ran to the scene, Shang shoved her behind him.

"Stand back!" he roared, drawing back his arm and sending a volley of ice toward the attackers. Large, deadly crystals sliced into the ground in a perimeter around them. He grimaced at the effort. People screamed, scattering briefly.

The first guard dragged Liuxian away, who still yelled at the top of his lungs about Meiling's magic, and shouted at the growing number of guards to restrain the people. The second guard approached calmly, stepping around ice bolts lodged in the ground, facing Shang. His face was grim. "We need to take Princess Meiling for questioning."

Her gut sank. They *believed* Liuxian. Or, at least, considered his accusations enough to act on them. She pressed her hand into Shang's taut back and fisted her hand in his cloak to keep her balance as the world tilted around her.

But wait—was Shang giving up his opportunity to flee the city to rescue her? He couldn't! It would cost him his life!

He didn't move, standing braced in front of Meiling as he faced the oncoming guard and the two more that followed a few steps behind him until they were cornered. Shang glanced at the wall, at the cliff, and seemed to be debating the possibility of grabbing her and sliding down like they'd done earlier. Until one guard slowly pulled a loaded *jiaun* from its holster at his hip.

"Will you arrest your princess like a criminal? What is this mob? This madness?" Shang demanded of the guards. "Why aren't you restraining *them*? The people who hurl unfounded accusations at the princess?"

"Stand down, Tan Shangdi. We are only taking her to verify she is not a brigand."

"Verify?" he cried, indignant. "You will drag the daughter of your sovereign away from a festival on the word of a madman?"

"Move aside. If she is innocent, she will be released. It's a simple formality." The guard's eyes narrowed, his steps growing more deliberate.

"You will *not* arrest the princess without the emperor's order. I will not stand down until the emperor sanctions her arrest. Stay back." His words were snarls, his hands full of ice.

Now that the crowd was controlled, more guards stepped forward. Further cornering Shang and Meiling against the wall of the overlook. She slowly stepped backward until her legs hit the wall, and she glanced quickly from Shang's tensed shoulders to the approaching guards.

Should she step around him? Offer herself up?

"I know what you're thinking," Shang growled under his breath to her. "Stay behind me. They're not taking you anywhere."

She had seen Shang in numerous battles and did not question his abilities. But five guards? With more running up the path toward them?

Then, a familiar voice thundered with the force of an earthquake, "Everyone, stand down *now.* Do not lift a finger against my daughter or I will kill everyone standing here!"

Her legs turned to water at the sound of Pa's voice, his running footsteps. He burst into view, taller and broader than any man present. Huge and powerful, with blazing eyes and fire swirling around his palms. Ma was right behind him, her face wreathed in panic.

Pa stormed between the guards, his golden robes glittering in the light of his fire. His eyes found Meiling's as she poked out from behind Shang. That look—all her blooming hope crashed and burned. Dread settled heavy in her stomach.

Pa's voice was much quieter when he spoke again. "Stand down, Tan Shangdi."

A jolt went through Shang, followed by the stiffening of his spine. His legs braced wide, his hands still full of ice. He did not move.

"Stand down," Pa ordered again, harsher than before.

Shang glared at the emperor.

"Shang," Meiling whispered. "It's alright."

He looked down at her, and the magnitude and meaning of that look made her swallow any further protests.

Dozens of people and guards watched the exchange between the fire-wielding emperor and the ice warrior, the air rippling and crackling with energy. It had gone deathly quiet, everyone waiting breathlessly for what would happen next.

Pa's shoulders rose and fell with a breath, his face hard, but far more open than Shang's flint-like mask. Quietly, he said, "She is my daughter, Shangdi."

Perhaps the onlookers would believe those words to be a claiming, but Meiling recognized them for what they were: a promise to protect her.

Shang's jaw flexed. But slowly, he stepped aside, his ice disappearing as his hands fisted.

"Come, little one," Pa said softly to Meiling. "Come with me to the council."

The guards didn't shift a muscle, and not a single titter raised from the onlooking crowd. Only the wind howled in the trees, stinging with salt. Meiling hesitated only briefly, meeting Shang's eyes. Then she went to her Pa, barely remembering to bow before him.

If they find out about your magic, our entire family will be executed.

Pa's fire vanished into smoke. "All dismissed." He stormed down the path, Meiling and Ma hurrying after him. When three guards started cornering Shang as though to restrain him, Pa bellowed, "Don't touch him. Back to your posts."

The guards dissipated regretfully, but Meiling couldn't bear to look back toward Shang. Even if it might be the last time she ever saw him.

CHAPTER 37

THE COUNCIL WAS full of old, stuffy men and a handful of grouchy women. It was a small room, lending it a sense of greater privacy. Everyone wore their festival finery and sat on cushions around the low table. They were already waiting, their backs straight and chins high enough that they looked as though they considered themselves each a sort of emperor or empress.

Pa sat at the head of the table and, surprisingly, gestured for both Ma and Meiling to sit on either side of him. His unnaturally warm hand rested on Meiling's low back. "Council."

"Emperor," they returned in one voice.

Meiling could hardly think as the questions started flying. She didn't answer any of them—Pa did. The numbness in her body spread to her mind, only to clarify suddenly a moment later.

"The Test will need to be performed on her to see if she has magic."

That hand on her back flinched, blazing hotter. So hot, she was afraid it would burn through her clothes. Her own heart faltered, and fear replaced the numbness. Dread. The Test was designed to be torturous, the pain causing hidden magic to manifest. It wasn't unlike slow slicing.

"The Test will not be necessary," Pa said through gritted teeth. "Princess Meiling has magic."

That easily, her secret was out.

She lowered her head. It was only a minor relief that she would not be forced to endure the physical and mental pain of the Test. More questions were hurled her way, Pa answering them until his voice caught. His hand pressed more firmly into her back, fingers curling around her arm.

So it was Ma who spoke. "Princess Meiling is a dreamwalker. Like the legend Zhou."

The council went silent as Ma's simple words echoed through the room.

Dreamwalker.

Despite the dread curling around her insides, something burned in her breast again, like it had when Shang had first told her about dreamwalkers. Something about the title resonated with a deep part of her soul.

They asked how and when she used her magic, and at this juncture Meiling was forced to speak. Pa's tightening grip reminded her to speak louder. Haltingly, between plenty of deep breaths and throat clearings, she recounted everything. If she were Shang, she would know condemning evidence from vindicating evidence. She would spin the tale. She would be clever about it. But she was not Shang, and so she only told them the broken, honest truth. Whatever they asked, even as they probed into her imprisonment in Zedong's fortress, she obliged them.

One especially old council member muttered, "Then there is only one thing to be done. She must stand trial, but the law is very clear. Magic is forbidden unless employed in the emperor's service."

Pa slammed his fist down onto the table.

Everyone jumped at the unexpected display of wrath, the sudden clatter of teacups. He was always so composed.

Not anymore.

"The princess is no traitor," Pa said, darkness threading his voice.

"But her magic has not been sanctioned," a woman insisted. "She is not in the records as a magic-wielder!"

"The law is the law for a reason!" someone shouted from the other end of the table.

The oldest member said in a low, gravelly voice, "And how did she use her magic while at the fortress? Was that for the good of the empire? Do we not have her to thank for Fang having our military plans? Countless people have died and will die because of her magic."

All went quiet.

Pa tucked her into his side and it took everything in her not to turn her face and bury it in his chest. And cry. She should feel shame, fear, anxiety, rage.

But she was empty.

Zhou—a god among men, legendary walker among the stars. Meiling—a curse to her people, a witch in her sleep. A *brigand*.

But she wasn't a brigand. She had seen brigands. Dozens of them. And she wasn't them.

"An investigation into the concealment of Princess Meiling's magic will also be necessary," the shortest man in the group said. He lifted his chin toward Pa, who stared evenly back.

"Indeed," Pa returned.

"To think," the oldest member mused, his glassy eyes shining between folded wrinkles, "that this mighty dynasty will end tonight. Just when we needed it most."

"You would depose me and leave our people vulnerable to conquer?" Pa snarled. "All for what?"

"I cannot follow a man who would lie to us."

A collection of heads nodded around the room, but that wasn't what set the empty hearth of Meiling's rage kindling. It was what someone said next.

"Perhaps Fang Zedong might usher in the new era that we need."

And then Meiling snapped. Deliberately, she rose to her feet. All eyes turned to her in surprise. Some looked to Pa, as though expecting him to restrain her. He didn't. Instead, he sat exactly where he was and watched her.

Her voice had never mattered before.

But she would speak now.

"Do you want to know about Fang Zedong's new era? I will tell you what you wish to know," she snapped, and her clear voice carried across the room. "He will rewrite our magic system with black magic, of which he is master."

"No one can control Wungfao! She lies!" someone argued.

Meiling turned toward that voice, that pinched face, and said, "Be quiet."

The whole room went deathly still.

"Black magic can be wielded," Meiling continued, lifting her chin. "I have wielded it."

She let that declaration sink in as she began walking slowly around the edge of the table, behind the seated councilmembers. Ma's face had gone ashen, but Pa leaned forward, waiting for her to continue.

"With black magic, Zedong can bind our own magic. Ask anyone who was imprisoned in his fortress. We were all bound. I wielded black magic *once*, in a desperate attempt to free myself from his trappings. But what I discovered was that black magic isn't like our magic. It is something to be partnered with, and you must sell your soul to gain its power."

Silent tears streamed down Ma's face, and she turned away.

Meiling couldn't stop her own sorrow from echoing her mother's. She didn't need to enter her mind to know that all these years, Queen Liena had cherished hope for her long-lost friend.

But that friend was forever gone.

"Fang Zedong intends to become the broker of magic, of power. You threaten to overthrow my father from his throne—only because you have your own power. You have your magic, your training, your seat on this council. And yet, each one of you knows that if His Imperial Majesty decided he wanted to decimate this council by fire and take forceful control of the empire, he could. But he *doesn't*." She flung a finger back to Pa, pointing, as she continued vehemently. "Because my father *isn't a tyrant*. He could have used me ages ago to blackmail those of you who refuse to work with him. Even now, I can enter your minds. Find your darkest secrets. And with a few words, I can destroy everything you've spent your life building. But His Imperial Majesty won't do that—and neither will I."

One of the women opened her mouth, but Meiling leveled a gaze of quiet fire at her. "Close your mouth. I am not finished."

No one in that room needed to obey her. No one needed to listen to what she had to say.

But fire burned in her belly, and she was done being cast aside. She was done being forced into the role of cursed princess. She was Lu Meiling, and she was a dreamwalker.

Lift your head. You listen to the stars sing while they sleep.

So Meiling did. She lifted her head. And when she spoke, everyone in the room listened.

"Fang Zedong is a man driven by vengeance and power lust. He does not forgive, and he does not share. If you overthrow my father, you are opening your gates to a tyrant the likes of which you have never seen before. I was his slave for weeks. If he conquers Suguan and Zheninghai, you will be dead, and your children will be his slaves. Ask me how I know this."

No one breathed a word.

"Because he told me," Meiling said with controlled vitriol. "Because I was in his mind, and he has been in mine. So choose for yourself tonight whom you will serve. And may our fathers have mercy on the souls of those who wish to destroy the good in our empire."

With that, she made her way back to her seat and sat down next to Pa.

He ducked his head as an enormous grin spread across his face. And then he lifted his head, refusing to hide the pride beaming from his expression. In that moment, Meiling turned back into a little girl as great happiness burst all the way through her body to the ends of her fingers and toes. She had found her true self, the buried part of her she'd suppressed, and in expressing it, she'd made her father so proud he couldn't help but make a fool of himself.

"Members of my council," Pa said loudly, "meet my daughter. Princess Meiling of Zheninghai."

All was quiet and still in the room.

Then arguments burst in fervor across the room, councilmembers turning on their neighbors, pointing fingers and pounding fists as they debated the dilemma before them with venom.

The door burst open, and as soon as the arguments had broken out, they stopped.

In the wake of silence, the young, pale-faced guard in the doorway cried, "The Academy is under attack!"

Pa lurched to his feet. "From Fang Zedong?"

The guard shook his head, eyes looking like he'd glimpsed a nightmare. "From *mó guǐ*!"

There was only one person who could command *mó guǐ*.

CHAPTER 38

WHEN THE FIRST burst of fire cut through the night sky over the Academy, Shang's insides bottomed out. A few women dressed in finery pointed and giggled, saying a few fireworks had gone haywire.

Shang didn't need to hear the beating of wings or see the gleam of scales in the sky to know exactly what was happening.

Fang Zedong was here.

And he'd brought an army of *mó guǐ.*

Chaos erupted in the council room. The Emperor's Guard flooded the small chamber. Some councilmembers ran out to fight while others hunkered down.

Meiling's focus snapped into place, and before anyone could grab her, slipped away from Ma and Pa, and dodged through the rush of guards. Pa shouted for people to get out of his way, and Ma's high-pitched voice called desperately for Meiling.

Gritting her teeth, she left them all behind and broke into a run toward the Academy.

Wielders—guards and otherwise—were running around her. There was so much shouting. The festival music had stopped, replaced instead with screams.

Children.

The Academy was full of half-trained children wielders. They couldn't begin to defend themselves from an onslaught of *mó guǐ*. Visions of phoenixes blasting into wielders scaling the wall of Zedong's fortress flashed across her mind. Meiling ran faster.

Her hand went to her sleeve, felt the vial of the sleeping potion there.

Good.

She was about to run out of a palace exit when someone snatched her wrist. She was whirled into a side hallway. Her heart leaped, and she looked up—

But it wasn't Shang who drew her away from the crowds of frantic people.

Meiling gasped. "Shuren!"

Zedong's illusionist quickly covered her mouth with his hand and shook his head. His beautiful face was hard as flint, his eyes wild. His voice was hardly audible. "Don't go near the Academy." He loosened his hand so she could respond.

"I can't stand on the sidelines while children are dying!"

"Find the healer and flee the city. Zedong is hunting for you and will kill you. He's planning to kill every living magic-wielder in this city. You must get out."

The blood drained from her face. "Kill every wielder?"

She should have known it. Zedong wouldn't waste his time trying to bind everyone's magic. He'd just kill the wielders, and with that, he'd hamstring natural magic in the empire. Then *any* magic in the empire had to come through him.

Shuren only stared back at her.

"What's wrong with you?" Meiling blurted, and she might have slapped him for how sharply he flinched. "How are you allowing this? Why aren't you fighting him?"

"He is too powerful! There is hardly anything I can do."

"You can defend those children."

Shuren turned away, his eyes flashing. He scraped a hand through his hair and growled low under his breath, "Flee the city. Get the healer out of this. I'm doing what I can."

Then he wrapped himself up in an illusion, disappearing completely from her view. She choked on air before shaking her head and darting back out of the hiding spot.

By the time she elbowed her way through the chaos to the Academy, smoke and flame rose in a billowing column into the sky. She coughed as the acrid scent filled her lungs. She pressed a hand to her chest and fought to keep her eyes open against the stinging smoke.

Worst of all—the sounds.

Screaming, shrieking, roaring, rending, blasting.

Wings beat in the air, jewel-like scales catching the fire of flaming phoenixes. Bells rang in the air, and it took Meiling several heartbeats to recognize the snorting of qilin.

Something swooped low overhead, and she threw herself to the ground as a screeching owl-like creature reached talons down toward the ground. Behind her, wielders shouted in attack at the *thing*. She pushed herself up on her hands, not bothering to brush the dirt off herself.

The hazy world clarified as a figure came running toward her.

A sob of relief caught in her throat at that familiar silhouette. She almost ran toward him but stopped suddenly at screams that sounded just behind her. She whirled as something slithered into the growing crowd of wielders.

Shang reached her and his face, already dirty and sweat streaked, was full of panic. "Get *out* of here! We need to find a place for you to hide!"

"A place to hide?" Meiling echoed as he grabbed hold of her arm to pull her back toward the palace.

Back toward the palace. The palace wasn't safe. If the Academy was under attack, the palace would be next. Shang would know that. Shang wouldn't—

This wasn't Shang.

Meiling jerked back, yanking on her arm. The grip on her only tightened, and for a second, her certainty wavered when confusion flashed across Shang's face. "Meiling—"

"Get away from me!" she screamed.

His face twisted.

And then a wolf tore into that face.

She stumbled back as silver blood splattered onto her, as the illusion of Shang flickered into a gleaming, silken fox body with nine twitching tails. Before she knew it, Fen was back in her human form, lips pulled back in a feral snarl, stabbing the *mó guǐ* with her knife. To . . . make sure it was dead?

"No time to burn the body," Fen barked as she tossed it aside and gripped the hilt of her bloody knife in her fist. She looked sidelong at Meiling and cocked her head. "For someone with no training, you have shockingly good instincts."

Meiling stared. And then blurted, "For someone who only guesses at fox spirits, you have a shockingly good record."

Fen grinned wolfishly. Meiling remembered what it was like to be in her body, her mind, to feel that thrilling rush of adrenaline. She could almost feel it now pulsing between them.

"Follow me," Fen said, taking off into a run.

"Weren't you supposed to leave?"

"I hadn't made it out of the city before I saw the dragons flying overhead."

She'd come back. And so had Shang.

They'd chosen to give up their freedom and their lives for Zheninghai.

Meiling followed, nearly losing Fen several times in the throngs of screaming bodies. So many of the surrounding people were young, wearing white. Many were singed, burned, or bleeding as they ran from the rising smoke of the Academy. It made Meiling wish she possessed fire magic and could unleash herself on these monsters.

But she didn't have fire magic, and she wasn't a trained warrior, so she had to be smart about this. Suddenly, up ahead, Fen cried out. The sound cut off abruptly, drowned out in the roaring overhead.

"Fen? Fen!" Meiling screamed, rushing forward and shoving aside anyone in her way. "Fen!"

Fen was climbing to her feet when she reached her. Slowly, she turned around. Meiling scoured the length of her for blood, for a blistering burn. When there was no injury, her gaze rose to Fen's face.

Her eyes had darkened. They fixed directly on Meiling. Fen raised her dagger.

"Oh fathers," Meiling breathed.

She couldn't even scream when Fen ran toward her, or when she was grabbed, slammed into the ground, and pinned by a girl in green and gold robes. They wrestled for the dagger, grappling in the dirt. Midnight eyes flashed with fiery ferocity.

The dagger skidded away, still in reach.

"Grab it!" Feiyan cried, gritting her teeth and grunting as Fen tried to elbow her in the face and scrabbled with her other hand for the dagger.

Why wasn't she shifting into a tiger? She could end Feiyan with one swipe.

Meiling didn't hesitate as she ran forward and barely managed to scoop up the dagger before Fen's reaching fingers could get a grip on the hilt. With one hard hit with the side of her hand to Fen's neck, Feiyan knocked the shapeshifter out. Fen slumped forward.

Feiyan got to her feet, standing over Fen. "Tell me how the dirt tastes when you wake up."

"She's cursed," Meiling choked, still clutching the dagger. "Zedong is turning our own on us!"

"I know. I saw it," Feiyan said grimly. Her gaze lifted from Fen's limp form to Meiling. "Can you break it?"

An earth-shattering blast tore through the world. Screams shattered into a burning night.

Meiling gasped as she was flung to the ground, bracing herself on flattened palms. She swiped away the hair falling in her face, darting a look toward where Feiyan similarly braced herself. Meiling looked up. Up to where the blast had come from.

Through the smoke, she could make out someone standing on a balcony overlooking the overrun Academy. His hands were lifted, stance wide, face twisted as he unleashed himself.

Unquenchable fire blasted from both his hands.

This was nothing like the red-eyed fire brigand of Zedong's making. She remembered those small fireballs he threw. Dangerous, deadly, but *nothing* like this fire that shot out with the force of a towering, raging waterfall.

Emperor Nianzu.

Pa.

Meiling stared, mouth gaping. She watched as Pa aimed his huge palms at the *mó guǐ*, in the air and on the ground, taking them down without a struggle. Even the fire-wreathed phoenixes had nothing on him. Their fire was swallowed helplessly, viciously.

One of the most powerful fire-wielders in the empire's history.

That was what they had always said about Pa. She had never seen it until now.

Someone shook her. She blinked, her vision focusing on Feiyan's face, the upraised palm to smack her across the jaw. Meiling flung up her hands just before Feiyan lowered hers. Her voice cracked. Sharp, fear tinged, smoke-filled.

"Can you break her curse?" Feiyan said again, her eyes flitting around the chaos to Fen lying at her feet. "Or should we tie her up and stuff her somewhere until this is over?"

Bonds could not hold Fen if she shapeshifted. One glance at Feiyan told her that she was just as aware of that fact.

"I'll try! I'll try to break all these curses." Meiling waved a hand at the *mó guǐ* being shot down from the air as they ravished the Academy. Her blood pounded in her ears, and her last instinct was to sleep, but she needed to. And fast. Before it was all too late. "And any other wielders who get trapped in black magic."

A familiar cry made her head shoot up and there was Shang in the thick of the fighting, his hair flying everywhere. He fought several one-horned qilins, their tinkling snort and baying cutting through the screams. Fire dribbled down their beards, sizzling as it went.

Pa's fire was picking off the *mó guǐ* he had a clear shot at, but these qilins had maneuvered themselves behind one of the angled walls. As she watched, they spat fire at the battling wielders running by, taking down countless.

Shang dodged the diamond sharp tip of a qilin's horn, only to be attacked by another. He rolled, barely avoiding being demolished by their fire. He leaped to his feet again, but there were too many qilins to engage, to distract from the other unsuspecting wielders fighting their own battles. Even from here, she could see how his eyes glittered with that calculating light. Calculating, but desperate. They flicked upward, to her Pa still on the balcony, mowing down *mó guǐ*.

An expression passed over Shang's face. Enlightenment. Fear. Determination. Meiling's lungs clenched in sudden horror. "Shang!"

But he was already in motion, too far to hear her. He leaped backward.

Straight into the line of Pa's fire.

She screamed. Shang roared—kept roaring.

The fire angled suddenly, seeming to reflect off Shang. Straight into the hiding qilins.

It happened so fast. Pa's fire choked out almost the moment Shang jumped into it, but it was enough. All that was left of the qilins were their ashes.

But Shang was still there. Still alive. The instant the fire died, a reflecting shield of ice gleamed red and blue in his upraised hands. The next moment, he stumbled to his knees, pressing a shaking hand to his chest, another to the ground.

His ice should never have been able to stand against fire like that.

"Whoa," was all Feiyan could say, gaping.

Meiling almost tried to run to him, to try to drag him out of the thick of the battle, but Renshu was there first, pulling Shang to his feet. And then Feiyan had her forearm gripped in her hand.

"Help me move Fen," she grunted, already pulling the tall girl's arm around her shoulder.

Meiling ran to help, but the moment she bent down, she happened to look up.

A cloaked form came tearing through the chaos, picking up people and flinging them across the field and into walls, trampling them underfoot, breaking bones with a quick snap of his wrists. Not *quite* killing them, but incapacitating them and leaving them writhing on the ground in agony. Her stomach turned with nausea.

He came running toward them. Young wielders parted like an ocean before him, screaming and trying to escape from his feral violence.

His hood flung back.

A long white beard, sagging skin, and a toothless grin.

The old man who she'd seen at the parade, who had come up to watch the trial, who had introduced himself as Fen's grandfather. The man whom Shang had threatened.

"Fen has no grandfather," Shang had said.

"Feiyan!" Meiling screamed, frantically trying to drag Fen out of the way.

Maybe he hadn't seen them yet—maybe they could still get out of the way.

"You!" Feiyan breathed, and fury roiled off her in churning waves. Almost as hot as Pa's fire must be. She dropped Fen without ceremony, whipping her knife out.

"No, no, no!" Meiling cried, shifting to loop her arms under both of Fen's armpits to drag her. This position was eerily familiar. "Don't be stupid!"

Feiyan squared off before the plowing brigand, but she spared a glance for Meiling. A grin—a devilish, wicked grin—split across her face. Her eyes danced. "I never back down from a fight."

Then she raised her arm, wheeled back, and flung her knife straight toward the oncoming, cackling brigand.

The brigand froze mid leap. His eyes, usually almost buried beneath folds of papery skin, bulged. He fell into a crumpled heap on the ground.

So . . . *fast.*

Feiyan eased, nostrils flaring and eyes narrowing. She stomped to the brigand, kicked him over to his back, and kneeled to yank her knife out of his heart. She wiped the blood on his own garments. "Be glad it was me," she spat to the dead body. "I don't deal agonizing half-deaths like you."

"Stop addressing unconscious and dead people," Meiling snapped, sweat falling down her brow as she dragged Fen. "Help me get Fen away!"

Feiyan was by her side instantly, and together they heaved Fen up. How much easier it was to carry her unconscious friend when the burden was shared by another!

"He's slammed me into a few trees myself," Feiyan continued, her eyes still burning with battle. She lifted a cocky grin. "Overgrown pile of bones."

"Feiyan!"

The healer only shrugged, that grin never disappearing from her face. Around them, magic flared and fire burned. The air shuddered with the weight of screams, battle roars, raspy death cries, feral howls.

Zedong's brigands were here, too.

Which meant the barbarian army could attack at any minute.

They were halfway to the palace when Feiyan's head whipped up, her gaze going past Meiling. That gaze went wide as moons and a scream unlike any other ripped from her lips. *"Meiling!"*

Sudden terror nearly paralyzed Meiling. Someone was about to stab her again. She was about to be—

She whirled, dropping Fen and instinctively throwing her hands over her face.

For a split second, her vision was full of a violent, twisted face she'd never seen before.

And then a broad back suddenly appeared. A slash of a broadsword. Splattering blood.

Shi Kai's grim face was streaked with red and dirt when he turned around. His left hand shot out and grabbed her shoulder before her knees gave out.

"Fathers!" Meiling gasped weakly.

"Don't go getting skewered after all we went through to get you home," he chided. Then he turned and yelled, "Delan! I need backup!"

Feiyan had buckled under Fen's weight. She struggled to hoist the heavier woman up enough to walk. When Meiling tried to help, her knees nearly turned the wrong way. Curse her wobbling nerves! But seven valleys, she'd *never* heard Feiyan scream like that. It was enough to scare anyone out of their right minds.

Delan was at their side in a minute, sweaty and panting. His tunic was burned at his side and Meiling prayed he wasn't injured badly. He hardly stopped shooting his *jiaun* for even a second as he demanded, "What?"

"Carry the shapeshifter," Kai shouted. "I'll cover you three."

And then he was just . . . *gone.*

Fen must have been the same height as Delan—possibly even taller—but the older wielder could have been made of bricks. He scooped Fen up as if she weighed nothing, tossing her over his shoulder like a sack of rice, all while shooting his *jiaun* and grumbling, "Dragon blasted evanescer thinks he can just order me around like a handmaiden!" Then he seemed to register Feiyan and Meiling, and his eyebrows raised. "With all due respect, Highness, stop being an *idiot* and get out of here!"

Then the three of them were running. Anytime a brigand or a *mó guǐ* came too close, Kai was suddenly there, cutting them down or forcing them back. Enough that they made it to the palace alive.

Stepping into the palace was like stepping into another world. A muted world. Smoke and ash floated on the air here, too, but less. The sounds of the dying and victorious and struggling, of waging war, echoed here, too, but quieter.

The palace was shockingly empty.

Her heart faltered at the sparse guards, the strange quiet. Premonition filled her from head to toe. But she didn't have time to worry about it. She ought to be thankful this was not a bloodbath, too. It was a mercy—a relief. Not something she should dread.

"You two need to take her from here," Delan said grimly, setting Fen down. With one last look, he ordered them with all the sternness of a father to stay safe. Then he disappeared through the doors back to the Academy.

"Hurry," Meiling choked as she and Feiyan lifted the shapeshifter between them. "Here, down this hallway."

Together, they half ran, half limped down the darkened corridor. The sconces burned dangerously low, shadows and flame dancing around the edges of drawn curtains. When Meiling gestured with her head to one of the doors, they burst through it to find at least a dozen maids in gauzy pink crammed into the space. They shrieked when the door opened.

Feiyan slammed it shut again.

They finally found an empty room. It was a pantry with dried herbs hanging from ties on the ceiling, sacks of rice and spices on the shelves.

Meiling practically flung herself to the ground as Feiyan laid down Fen, drawing out her vial and popping her finger into the opening. One drop of dark liquid rolled down her finger when she lifted it and popped the cork back on the bottle. She laid her head on the floor and stuck her finger into her mouth.

CHAPTER 39

MEILING LANDED ON waving gray grass. Overhead, the sky was almost as gray as the ground. In the distance, the outskirts of a town were visible. She hadn't recognized it the first time she had entered Fen's mind so long ago, but now she knew without a doubt that it was Fen's home.

No mountains in any direction. Fen had come from a small town, far away from Suguan.

She'd been one of the few exceptions of a powerful wielder showing up out of nowhere, with little magic in the family heritage. Shang was the opposite; he was the son of a powerful, wealthy lord. His job was to not be the weak link in a line of ice wielders. Fen's job? To make something of herself, be the one to lift her family out of poverty. It seemed that, no matter what, the pressure was always the same. *Our family is counting on you.*

Meiling needed to find the curse. *Fast*. She closed her eyes and reached out her fingers. Familiar memory threads greeted her. As she touched them, followed them, pictures flashed in her mind. Fen, fighting with her mother. Fighting with her father. Her siblings. Squatting in the dirt, digging her chubby fingers into the soil. Helping her family farm when she was only a toddler. Watching as her father hit her mother. Again and again.

Fen, feeling the shift in her body. Her anger channeled into some sleeping part of herself, the magic she hadn't known she possessed. She hated the small, helpless child she was. Wanted to be something bigger, fiercer, stronger. Something that could clamp fangs down into that hand holding her mother, something that could bite, claw, rend, *roar.*

So she had. She'd shifted into a full-grown tiger and torn her own father to pieces.

If she hadn't been so young, it wouldn't have been deemed an accident.

The pictures kept flashing. Fen, vicious and unforgiving and hard at the Academy, refusing to be less than the other students. Not because she cared about prestige, but because she hated being the child that couldn't intervene while her family suffered under the heavy hand of her father. Never again. That child was gone. A tiger stood in her place.

Fen's Academy life washed over Meiling. Bits and pieces. Enough to puzzle together how the young, angry girl transformed into the tall, strong, abrasive young woman.

Fen's tether was anchored on the edge of a glassy lake. The surface was so, so still. Unmoved, unrippled. The grass gave way to rocks and sand. On the other side of the lake was a copse of evergreen trees.

Around the tether that glowed with all that was Fen, a black thread of magic squeezed tightly. Meiling let out a relieved gasp. A simple curse, not like that parasitic thing in Feiyan's mind or the wicked thing that had been in her own.

She balled her fists and screamed with all her might.

The curse snapped.

Meiling flew above Feiyan and Fen's heads as they charged back into the battle, her body stuffed into a corner by the former.

The Academy burned. Night lengthened, deepened, but the world was caught in a hazy half-light that was more like a sun chained to the horizon, neither rising nor setting. Not only had Zedong managed to spell an entire army of *mó guǐ*, but he had unleashed his brigands on them, *and* he was apparently busy casting compulsion threads on the empire's wielders to turn them against themselves.

His barbarian army lurked somewhere.

But where was *Zedong*?

He'd planned his slaughter well. He possessed every advantage. But there was no space for thoughts like that, for trying to process the chaos and bloodshed around them. There was only room for the galvanizing fear and wrath driving her forward.

As soon as they reached the Academy, tripping over human and *mó guǐ* bodies alike, Fen and Feiyan disbanded. Meiling only caught a flash of claws and striped fur before Fen vanished into the smoke. Feiyan, however, ran to the fallen, hands outstretched. She grabbed a sprawled young boy's shoulder, paused, then squeezed it with a thick swallow and jumped up to run to the next. And the next, until she found those that still breathed. There she stayed, both hands planted squarely on the wounded's chest or directly on gaping wounds. Those sharp eyes of hers roved while she healed, one hand jerking to her knife whenever a *mó guǐ* got too close.

A dragon came diving for her. Too fast for Meiling to enter its mind and break its curse. She screamed soundlessly into the ether.

And out of nothing, a purple-glowing evanescer appeared and shot it out of the sky. Meiling's glimpse of Shi Kai was so brief she almost didn't recognize him before he'd evanesced away again.

Meiling hesitated, her vision filled with bodies. So many dead. So many *children* dead. Cavernous bodies empty of the glowing magic entwined with their souls. All around, glows faded slowly into nothing, or were snuffed out like a candle in an instant. Feiyan sprinted forward to kneel between an impaled guard and a gasping, choking little girl. The guard's orange glow dimmed rapidly while the girl's nearly white light sputtered dangerously.

In that heartbeat, Meiling was confronted with the choices the healer of Zheninghai faced every day.

How often salvation for one meant destruction for another.

Feiyan reached out and placed one hand on each of the two victims' chests. She bowed her head, her sapling green core shuddering as she gritted her teeth and sweat poured down her face. Magic, like molten gold with threads of emerald, flowed from her hands.

Bits of her own soul in every drop.

A cry wrenched from Feiyan's chest, pained and taut. The guard's soul flickered out entirely. *Not enough.* Feiyan brought her now free hand to the little girl's chest.

A silvery glow wrenched Meiling's attention away from the healer. A boy about fourteen waved his hand at a nine-tailed fox disguised as another Academy student, bidding it to follow him as he mustered his magic and courage to plunge into the battle.

She could almost see its snarling claws and teeth breaking through that illusion, grinning as it raced after the youth. Gaining on him. Her first instinct was to fling herself into the fox spirit's mind, but she caught herself in time and, instead, dodged into the boy's.

Darkness met her eyes. Not the darkness of night, or of a dungeon, but the darkness of a drawn curtain. The barest scraps of light escaped from beneath a large bamboo screen, not enough to illuminate the room Meiling now stood in.

It didn't matter. The boy's thoughts barreled over her, desperate fear laced with duty, with resolve to not flinch from the face of death. Bolstered by the friend at his side, he ran over his training in his head, telling himself to breathe and assess the situation before rushing into the middle of things.

Your companion is a fox spirit! Meiling screamed into that darkness. *Kill him!*

Roiling confusion met her.

She did not have time to explain, to answer his throbbing questions about why he was hearing a female voice in his head. Instead, she screamed over and over again, *Fox spirit! Fox spirit! Fox spirit!*

The boy was bewildered beyond belief. He slowed his run, stopped surveying the battlefield, and didn't notice the jewel-toned dragons arcing through the sky. He didn't even notice as a red-eyed fire brigand came running toward him, a fireball building in his palm.

The *mó guǐ* and the brigand were going to corner him.

She could almost feel the fox slavering behind him. The oncoming brigand raised his arm.

Brigand! Duck, you idiot!

Shockingly, he ducked and narrowly avoided a fiery demise. He tucked into a roll and leaped to his feet again, whirling so the brigand did not have access to his back. But the brigand was already railing past, red eyes aiming at a new target. The boy faced his running friend, and Meiling was suddenly hit with an idea.

His footsteps make no sound! Fox spirit! Fox spirit!

The boy, still bewildered, snagged on that realization: the silence with which his friend approached him over the uneven ground. Deeper realization—*finally!*—hit home.

His hand lifted, two fingers pointed at his friend's chest. His friend's eyes widened with horror. And though the doubt and fear were almost crippling, the boy shot his magic straight toward his friend's chest.

It was not wind, but like wind. A highly concentrated shot of air that blasted from his fingertips and went clean through the fox spirit's heart. Its illusion shuddered as the *mó guǐ* fell to the ground, revealing the glistening silver body. The sundered spirit tore into the ether, writhing and shrieking.

That was not the pride of accomplishment flowing through the boy's veins. Only terror that his death had been so near at hand, and desperate relief that he had not just murdered his friend.

Meiling left his mind to fly straight into a glittering amethyst dragon.

She blinked, and did not find herself in a mindscape. She was instead staring out of the dragon's eyes, seeing the Academy from above and all the running people. Out of the corner of its eye, Meiling saw her father still standing on the balcony, still shooting *mó guǐ* down from the sky.

I'm going to break your curse so you can flee, she said to the beast. *I don't want you to die. I know you are a prisoner against your will.*

No response.

Meiling had barely hunted the tether, struggling with the strangeness of accomplishing this without standing in a mindscape, and screamed to break the bond as Pa aimed her way.

Run! Get away from here! she screamed, almost choking on her own irrational fear.

Then she threw herself out of the beautiful amethyst dragon's mind and did not look back to see if it survived.

She broke curse after curse, releasing *mó guǐ* to flee the battlegrounds. She did not have time for the confusion lighting on the wielders' faces as the *mó guǐ* they battled suddenly turned and ran the other direction. There was only time to launch mind to mind, finding tethers in the span of heartbeats, and screaming herself hoarse. Whenever a wielder's glow flashed black, Meiling threw herself into their mind to break the compulsion forcing them to turn against their own.

She had just released an antlered qilin when the world cracked.

Meiling was thrown from the sky, landing and sinking into the dirt before it spat her back out. She lay stunned, confused, waiting for the rush of her heartbeat on the end of her tether, the inevitable tug it gave when she was afraid.

Nothing.

Dread, darker than midnight, thicker than blood, sank so heavily into her she convulsed.

Her tether.

She reached out a hand toward that familiar anchor, the one thing that kept her from being swept away from her body and into the frigid arms of death.

It was frayed. Ripped.

CHAPTER 40

HER TETHER HUNG intact by one fiber of thread.

No, no, no! she gasped, lurching upward to hold the nearly broken tether. It vibrated with the force of the souls being expelled around her. All the death. All the breaking.

Meiling wrapped her hands around that tether, trying to keep it from fully ripping. That was when something pulsed on the other end.

A heartbeat . . . Not *hers*.

One, two, three, four, five. That heart pulsed in an unfamiliar rhythm. Then, a name echoed through her tether into her soul. *Liena.*

Ma.

Spitfire.

Nothing could slow Meiling down as she burst into flight, tearing back through the battle toward the storeroom where her body was hidden. Usually, she would let herself be pulled back by her tether, but she could not risk that strain. She flew too fast for it to reel her in like a fish, following it and praying to all the fathers that her tether would not break fully.

Not before she could save her mother.

She broke into the dim room. Feiyan had closed the door behind them when they left, but it now swung open, listless on its hinges, letting the orange light leak through broken paper windows.

Two bodies lay on the floor now.

Oh, fathers, no, please, please no—

Slowly, Meiling's body rose. Her palms pressed into the dusty floor to heave it up, then her knees shifted. Her body stood, back to Meiling, and that head tilted down to look at its hands, then turned.

Meiling stared at herself. Her body. Her mouth curved upward in a cruel grin that had never, *ever* crossed her face before. She watched herself roll her shoulders and crack her knuckles and pop her neck.

Then that face—her face—looked up.

Blue eyes flashed from where her own had once been.

Fang Zedong, wearing Meiling's body, kneeled to pawn his own unconscious body for his knives, his broadsword which he strapped across his—her—back, and a pouch that clattered like it was full of marbles or rocks.

"I'm coming for you, Liena," he snarled, rising. "And we shall see what your answer will be this time."

He broke into a run, slamming the door open into the wall so hard the handle broke through the plaster. He drew his broadsword. The blade looked disproportionally large, gripped in hands so small. Her body should not have had the strength to wield it.

A lone maid rounded the corner of the hallway, and her eyes flew wide as saucers as Meiling's body charged toward her. "Highness—!"

Zedong plunged that blade straight into her heart and continued past without hardly blinking.

Meiling was screaming.

Screaming and drowning in blood and terror and pure horror. She fluttered to the girl's side, but she was already dead. There was nothing she could do. Nothing except race after Zedong and try to warn any other victims he tried to slaughter in cold blood with *her* hands.

She followed her mangled tether and the trail of blood after him as he tore into the palace.

This was why he leveled the initial attack against the Academy. To lure people away from the palace. To make the heart of the empire ripe for plucking. To take away the strength of her Ma's protection.

Her center hollowed out at the sudden thought.

Pa. Pa was gone, not with Ma. He was in the battle.

If there was anyone who could defeat Zedong's power of pure, black, wrathful magic, it was His Imperial Majesty. And Zedong knew it.

Ought she to warn Pa, or Zedong's immediate victims?

Guards rounded the corner, and in hardly a second, they were all lying in their own blood on the polished floors, constricted by black vines until they died. The vines slithered away and vanished as Zedong pulled his hand back from his pouch dangling at the waist of her body. Meiling's face split into a grin and sniffed. Drawing in the smell—the smell of death?

She couldn't warn Zedong's victims. Not unless she were to run ahead of him, and if she did, she risked losing him down another hallway where he slaughtered others.

She would fly back to Pa—

Shang burst through a door opposite Zedong, his garments burned and torn, his eyes blacker than night. Meiling's heart stopped.

He froze.

Zedong stopped too, and his grin widened. He leaned her body against the wall and crossed her arms. Batted her eyelashes. "Hello, Tan Shangdi."

Shang's eyes turned wild, frantic. His mouth opened, his throat bobbing in quick succession. "What did you do to her?"

Zedong gave a high-pitched laugh from her throat, using her voice. Then somehow, he switched, and it was his own voice that slithered from between those gloating lips. "I can slaughter you with hardly a thought. But *you* . . . I've been thinking about you and how I crave to savor your death. I'm a bit pressed with other priorities, so you can run along and amuse yourself with some more heroics. I hope you remember that this," Zedong gestured toward the slaughtered guards, "is *your* fault. Your mind was *so* helpful. It was the easiest thing I've ever done to march the long way here. I was so easily prepared for everything your emperor tried to hurl my way. So run along, before I change my mind."

Meiling dove into Shang's mind just as his thoughts echoed through the grand hall of his mind—*I cannot fight or kill him. Not while he possesses Meiling's body.*

Shang! she cried. *You need to run! Get out of here!*

Meiling? Shang gasped audibly, making Zedong lower her brows. Shang's thoughts were a jumble of trying to form a plan and hating the sight of Meiling's face and body twisted beyond recognition, beyond anything that was *her*. Torrential relief split those thoughts apart. *You're still alive.*

Shang bolted.

He's made himself invincible, he growled to her. *How did he do it? How are you alive?*

I do not know. My tether is breaking.

What? The breath slammed out of his lungs as he kept running, though not *away* from Zedong. His plan shimmered at the apex of the hall in his mind. Plaster fell from the ceiling as cracks tore up the pillars. *Your tether?*

She made no answer as he maneuvered the corridors like he knew every nook and cranny, trying to come up behind Zedong to follow him.

He's going for my mother. As she spilled what she had figured out about his plans, he blanched and swore aloud. *He kills so quickly*

I cannot warn the people in his path. I thought he was going to kill you. Her voice broke.

Shang slowed his pace, still moving swiftly but more stealthily. He bent, placing his hands on the hall framing, leaning just enough out so that he could see down the corridor.

Wind blasted him back. He reeled, overcoming his stunning much faster than Meiling could, and lurched to his feet. *Dragon's teeth, that cursed wind brigand,* he seethed. Then, *Don't let him out of your sight. I'll follow after I deal with this brigand.*

Meiling gave a quick, acknowledging *I will,* and left his mind. She was about to race down the hallway, leaving the blue-gray glowing brigand woman to Shang, toward the keep where she knew her mother must be and where Zedong would be heading.

But the flash of an angry red glow barreling down another hallway stopped her. She knew that color. She abandoned her pursuit of Zedong and the whooshing sound of wind long enough to throw herself into Fen's mind. *Fen! Shang is battling the wind brigand nearby—you can probably surprise her while she's distracted.*

I've been looking for that dragon spawn! Fen snarled back and spun on her heel to charge back where Meiling directed.

Neither Shang nor the wind brigand were prepared when Fen pounced on the brigand from behind, claws and teeth sinking in deep. Shang stumbled back, gasping as his hand moved toward his chest.

Meiling did not wait. She raced after Zedong and only heard Fen's growled, "*Finally*," behind her at the mauled corpse.

She stopped suddenly, an idea hitting her harder than a blow. She barely gave herself time to dart back into Shang's mind and spew, *I have an idea. You keep my mother safe until I can get there.*

With that, she was hurtling back the way they had come.

Back to the storeroom where Zedong's body lay.

CHAPTER 41

POSSESSING ZEDONG'S BODY was surprisingly easy. At first.

She'd hesitated only a moment, biting her lip, before dipping her toe into his body. It was like entering her own mind when the sun rose. She slid in as easily as a knife into its sheath.

It was standing up and maneuvering this body that was the challenging part.

She slammed Zedong's knee into the floor a few times, trying to stand, struggling with the long legs. Finally, she was on his feet. Standing.

Fathers above, she was so *high*. She ducked under the doorframe, certain she would have hit it otherwise. Falling must hurt so much more when one stood this tall. She would never again blame any tall person for being afraid of heights—qilins, but she positively *towered* over the entire world.

This was what it felt like to be strong and large. Muscles rippled in her arms, her legs—*his* arms and legs—and power coursed through her body. What an experience it must have been for Zedong to possess her slight frame. She almost laughed aloud, and she must be going mad with terror.

If she had a body like this, she did not think she would be afraid of anything.

Except falling. And heights.

Stumbling her way back through the palace, she lumbered louder than a bear and slammed doors when she hadn't even meant to close them.

"*Fathers,*" she gasped, and then gasped again at the sound of her voice, almost falling on her face. *Zedong's voice.*

Several wielders ran into view. Renshu and Delan were among them. With blood streaking his beard, Delan was shouting, "The barbarian army is attacking through the west and south gates! Send survivors you find to battle!"

Renshu was the one who first turned and saw her. His eyes widened, but only for the briefest instant. His usually kind face twisted into a feral snarl and he came charging toward Meiling, drawing his broadsword.

She had no weapons. *Nothing.*

Renshu had augmented strength. She had seen it all, sensed Zedong's magic struggling to contain the raw power in Renshu's soul as she hunted in his mind for information. Now, he was barreling toward her, battle lust and rage in his eyes.

She screamed, and the sound was entirely hers.

She threw herself to the side, breaking into a run down the hallway that went by the courtroom.

Meiling was fast. Faster than she had ever been in her life. Renshu was fast too, but if she had possessed her usual body, she would have been dead in an instant. Now she could keep a few moments between them, and maybe those moments would be enough to stumble upon Shang and Fen or anyone who knew her well enough to recognize her in Zedong's body.

A roar sounded behind her, and by the footsteps, it was clear Renshu was not the only one who pursued her. She dodged down another way, Zedong's boots nearly slipping on the slick ground. "Shang!" she screamed. "Shang! Fen! Help me!"

The impact hit her before the pain did. She looked down and found a furious red bolt through her shoulder. A curse bolt of blood magic. She stumbled hard to her knees near a door by a grand sweep of stairs as the pain dragged a cry from her throat. The life-sized polished qilin statutes stared down unblinking as she gasped.

Though her body was borrowed, she felt every torn muscle and flesh, every stab of agony, every drop of blood pouring down Zedong's shirt. No, no, she couldn't let this body die, not if she wanted to face Zedong, not if she wanted to protect her mother, not if she ever wanted her own body back from him.

So she snarled and forced herself to her feet.

They were almost upon her, but she wouldn't look back to check. She flung open the door and, with her newfound strength and height, wrapped her arms over the deer-like back of the qilin statue and pulled it off balance, toward her. She had barely enough time to run through the doorway before the statue smashed into it, splintering wood and cracking stone.

And blocking the door.

Renshu wouldn't have a problem moving it out of the way, but it bought her precious seconds.

She faced another staircase, and with a choking sob of pain, gritted her teeth and ran up two stairs at a time. She'd reached the top before her pursuers smashed through the blocked doorway. Her hand pressed just beneath that horrid curse bolt; she kept running.

A roar split her ears, the sound of a monstrous cat.

Fen.

The shapeshifter was nearby. Meiling gasped again as the pain shot down her spine. She ran toward the sound of a snarling wildcat caught in a vicious fight. She didn't care if she ran clean into the middle of the fray. She only had to get *away.* "Shang! Fen!" she screamed. There was not a trace of Zedong's wry, cruel, low voice in her throat. Her sobs were broken and feminine and desperate.

She stumbled into a decimated tearoom, falling to the floor as Shang landed the killing blow to the red-eyed fire brigand after Fen ripped him to the ground.

"Now for that dragon-eaten illusionist," Fen was snarling as she entered. Shang's head snapped up, but the shock in his eyes cleared almost immediately to recognition, then to panic.

"Meiling!" he gasped, glancing from her to the bolt through her shoulder to Fen, and then the door where the sound of pursuit echoed loud and close.

"Renshu—" Meiling managed as Shang kneeled by her side, almost looking like he didn't want to touch her as he reached out to grip Zedong's forearm.

"Fen!" Shang barked. "Slow Renshu and Hong down so they don't kill the princess!"

Meiling managed to ask the least important question. "Hong?"

"I recognize his curse bolts. But that doesn't matter," Shang growled, glancing over his shoulder toward the door as Fen raced out, before returning to her wound. "*Spitfire,* this is nasty. We need to find Feiyan."

"I don't need to save this body," she returned through clenched teeth. "I only need it to function long enough to kill Zedong."

"You're in tremendous pain."

"Will it kill me in the next twenty minutes?"

He frowned, but shook his head. "It's not a death wound unless someone pulls out the bolt. Then you'd bleed out quickly."

"Then there's no point in bringing Feiyan away from the dying." She used Shang to heave herself up into a standing position. It was so strange to be level with him, to stare him straight in the eye rather than craning her neck upward. "I . . . I need to find Zedong. If we can defeat him, his curses on the *mó guǐ* should dissolve." They *had* to dissolve. "And without him to rally the barbarian army, our forces could stand a chance at defeating them."

"Can't we just kill his body?"

Meiling shook her head as a shudder of pain swept through her. "My tether started breaking because he anchored part of his soul to my body. Killing his body will more likely make him be forced to completely occupy my body, severing my tether and killing me. Phoenixes *scorch* that Zedong."

"He's made himself invincible," Shang growled.

She looked at him then and was about to agree . . . until a frantic, wild smile split her features in realization. "*Almost.*"

Meiling stumbled to her feet, ran out of the tearoom—every step agony—and did not even look back when she heard Fen's snarls, or the pounding of feet. "Please keep people from killing me," she shouted back at Shang.

There was no time to wonder what was happening, or even to process the sound of Fen's shouts to "Find the healer!" No time to wonder about the army storming into the palace.

She only had to make it to Ma before it was too late.

With Shang on her heels, she shoved aside the pain and the trembling weakness spreading through Zedong's limbs. She ran toward the keep.

Ma wasn't in the keep.

Neither was Yun, but Hou was. She was whining at the guards to let her go out and fight, but thankfully, they were adamant and unflinching. The keep was full of huddling women and children—the women who were not wielders or who did not have battle magic. All members of Pa's court or very young Academy students trying to hide.

"Where is the queen?" Shang barked, Meiling standing back to not startle anyone with her stolen body and gory wound. It was an effort to keep her eyes open and clear against the pain.

"No one knows." The guard's eyes and faltering voice betrayed his fear and strain.

Shang cursed, and they tore off running again, Meiling leading the way. She almost stopped as an idea flashed in her mind, but she discarded it almost immediately. If she wanted to leave this body to scour ahead and follow the trails of sorcery that Zedong left in his wake, she would have to fall asleep and she had left her sleeping potion in her robes.

A wolf lunged into the hallway from a side door, and at first Meiling thought it was snarling before she realized it was grinning. Feiyan came running just behind her.

Relief poured into her soul like a river.

"Fen!" Meiling gasped. "Can you find the queen? Or Zedong?"

The wolf's eyes glittered with understanding and ferocious fire. She began sniffing the air and the floor.

"That's one wicked wound," Feiyan said, jumping over Fen's wolf form toward Meiling. "Fen explained what had happened to you after Renshu came to get me." Beyond the focus, the battle-heightened intensity flashing in her eyes, Feiyan looked exhausted. Far more drained than even Shang, who had expended so much strength to deflect Pa's fire.

Meiling jerked back, hand going to her wound as her gut twisted at the thought of those Feiyan must have abandoned to come to her aid. "No, leave it. I don't need to be healed. You're needed elsewhere, far more—"

"I'll take the edge off the pain," Feiyan insisted right as Fen howled and took off running.

"If you can do it while running!" Meiling cried, even as her hand reached out to grasp Feiyan's.

Feiyan gave a smirk as they ran to catch up with Shang and Fen. "You would never *believe* all the things I can do while running."

Meiling might have choked out a laugh, but her mind was suddenly consumed with Ma. What if she was too late? What if Zedong got to her first and took her as hostage to use against Pa? What if he made Pa surrender Zheninghai to spare Ma's life?

She couldn't let Zedong get to her first.

Fen stopped, pawing at the ground and jerking her wolf's head toward a towering set of double doors. The throne room. Meiling's heart stopped.

She saw your body. On the floor of the throne room.

Dead.

The four of them slowed, then halted.

"Are they both in there?" Shang demanded.

The wolf whined, pawing the ground and tossing her head. Affirmation.

"Fen, go get the emperor," Shang said, command lacing every word. Fen did not hesitate but shifted from her wolf form into a spotted leopard before silently bolting away, sleek feline muscles rippling with each movement.

"Do you want me to go first?" he asked.

Your dead body.

Meiling shook her head. Her heart thundered, but she could finally take a full breath now that the worst of the pain was gone. "I'll go first. You can come if anything goes wrong. Feiyan, will you be there for my mother? In case . . .?"

Feiyan didn't make her finish. She nodded tightly.

Shang's throat bobbed like he had something he wanted to say, but he kept his lips shut. Perhaps he couldn't bring himself to say sweet things to Zedong's face. Or perhaps he wasn't sure what he wanted to say.

Their eyes met.

She longed to kiss him one last time, to tell him she loved him so desperately she could hardly breathe. But if she didn't enter this throne room, no one would stop Zedong from using her mother to take control of Zheninghai.

If she died, she died for her people. For her family. For Shang.

Meiling savored that last second with his black eyes on hers. Then she opened the doors, exhaled the largest breath of her life, and wasn't afraid as she strode into the throne room.

CHAPTER 42

MA STOOD STILL as stone near the dais between dragon-wrapped pillars. Her shoulders were back, her chin lifted, her eyes blazing. Her hands did not clench into fists, but remained coolly by her side. The polished granite floor reflected her solid stance.

In the center of the throne room, bathed in torchlight, was Meiling's body, her back toward the doors. Facing Ma.

Fang Zedong did not turn when the doors opened, when smoke-tinged air swept in to fill the stale space. Either he had not heard them, or he simply didn't care. Not now that he was invincible.

Meiling paused, Shang and Feiyan on either side of her. Between her and Zedong, two tethers stretched taut, bridging the gap between their souls and bodies. Her own shuddered with weakness, threatening to break with the slightest movement. She could almost *see* how they glimmered in the air, hers golden-white, his stained with black.

Ma's eyes flicked to Meiling's. The only sign of her instant recognition in her otherwise impassive face was the way she held eye contact and then broke it.

"I said I would come for you, Liena." It was Zedong's unmistakable voice rumbling from Meiling's slight body. "Did you think I would go back on my promise?" Those words were oiled, smooth, poisoned.

Ma blinked slowly and exhaled through her nostrils. "I never doubted your return," she whispered. Somehow, despite her quietness, her voice carried through the cavernous throne room. "I am only surprised it took you over twenty years to do so."

"You left me little choice," Zedong growled. "Not if I wanted to return to you like this."

"Wearing my daughter's body?" Ma snapped, sudden rage twisting her features. "If you intend to make me love you, *this* certainly is not the way."

"I never said this was about love, Liena."

"Then what is it about? Why drag armies here, why slaughter innocents? What are you trying to prove?" Ma's voice turned pleading, her hands lifting slightly, palms upraised. "Zedong, what is all of this? I have *missed* you and *worried* about you for over two decades! And this is how you return?"

He snarled, and the way he stood in Meiling's body made it seem like it had never been hers. It was so wholly *not* her.

"This," he growled through clenched teeth. Low, deep, punctuated. "*This* is about—"

Meiling took a heavy, long-legged step forward. She let Zedong's voice flow through his mouth as she said, "This is about him proving that he is more powerful than the man you chose."

At those words, Zedong whirled. He fixed writhing blue eyes on Meiling wearing his body, on the protruding curse bolt. She savored how he was forced to look upward to meet her gaze.

His face—her face—was incredulous.

For someone with his nose in everyone's business, he should have considered this possibility. For someone who was grossly underestimated his whole life, he should not have underestimated her.

Zedong dragged his gaze from Meiling's eyes down his body. He continued dragging them until he stared at Ma.

Gone was Ma's regality. She stepped toward him, her face melting into that soft, loving woman who had tucked Meiling and her siblings into their beds every night since they were born. Her hands reached out to him, her face full of sorrow. "Zedong, oh my friend," she pled, voice full of heartbreak, faltering. "Please stop this now. Please talk with me, as we used to, and we can set things to right."

Her words hit Meiling like one of Shang's ice bolts.

Ma didn't see what Meiling saw. She saw her old classmate, the one she pitied, the one she had compassion for. The one she loved. The one she mourned all these years. She looked into the whirling vortex of insanity in his eyes and found hope for redemption.

But Ma hadn't been his prisoner. She hadn't seen him in over twenty years. Hadn't seen what he had become—or what he was capable of. Ma hadn't been in his mind. She hadn't seen how deeply he hated her. How fevered his resentment. How bitter his retribution.

Ma did not see that he wouldn't be pitied. Ma did not see that he would be worshipped for his might. She did not understand that he would destroy anything that threatened his strength and power.

Ma did not know that when Zedong took a step toward her, he meant to kill her.

Those careful plans of making Liena bleed last, all those years of patience, came to a screeching halt. Zedong raised his sword—and still Ma whispered, "Zedong, oh Zedong."

But Meiling saw. She saw it all.

The world narrowed to that blade, those hands. Feiyan and Shang were gone. It was just that one horrible moment when Zedong grabbed Ma—

—and slid his knife to her throat.

Ma went still. Betrayal flashed through her dark eyes. She didn't wince when Zedong pressed that blade hard enough that a ribbon of blood slid down to pool in the hollow of her throat.

Meiling refused to breathe.

Beside her, Shang and Feiyan had frozen.

"I missed you," Zedong whispered like a snake into Queen Liena's ear. "And now you're mine. As you were always meant to be."

Then he looked up at Meiling . . . and *grinned*.

White hot rage flooded her.

All of this—all this death, destruction, lies, and pain—for the chance to make her mother regret. This may have started with her mother, but it ended with her.

She would stop this.

Now.

"Fang Zedong," Meiling said, using her own voice. "As long as you live, you threaten me and all that I love."

Zedong turned back to Meiling, drawing his predatory focus off Ma for a second. His eyes flicked to either side of her, to her friends. "I see that you do not have the strength to face me alone, like your mother. She came here of her own volition. She answered my call."

"Because she is so good-hearted that she cannot see what you have become."

"You're afraid of me," Zedong said, mouth snaking into a smile. His blade teased Ma's vulnerable flesh, drawing another thin line of blood.

Ma didn't make a single sound.

Once, Meiling would have cowered before that smile, before those pupils that waxed and waned like a moon in a matter of seconds. That wide-legged power stance made even her small body look intimidating.

She wanted to throw his grin back at him, to smile fiendishly like she longed for his blood, like he longed for hers. But she couldn't.

Because she saw what he was, what he had been, and this was not about him at all.

This was about her family. Her friends. Her love. This was about the innocent people he slaughtered, the *mó guǐ* he had enslaved. This was about her *mother* in his grasp.

This was about Zheninghai.

She was not the blood shedding type. Not the warrior maiden. Not an accomplished magic-wielder. Not even a very good princess. It didn't matter anymore who she was or wasn't, what she could or couldn't do.

Only one thing mattered.

She was done letting Zedong hurt those she loved. Even if it cost her everything.

Meiling leveled his stare with one of her own. "I'm done being afraid." From anyone else, the words might have been snarled through clenched teeth or shouted loud enough to echo on the gleaming gold around them. But from Meiling, they were hardly more than whispers, yet they held the weight of worlds. "I'm no longer afraid of you. I . . ."

She swallowed, and the words that left her mouth were soft as snowflakes.

"I pity you."

Zedong realized what she was about to do as her hands reached out into the air between them. Fast as lightning, his fingers darted out, dropping his sword. Dropping Liena.

Their hearts thundered together in the air between them. Her hand closed around that flickering black tether just as his closed around her fraying white-gold one.

She snapped that tether. And screamed.

CHAPTER 43

IT HAPPENED SO fast Shang almost didn't recognize why the stolen eyes in Meiling's body widened with sudden terror as the true Meiling—the one wearing Zedong's body—reached out to grasp empty air. Something akin to lightning crackled in the air, and then horror slammed into him like a tsunami when Zedong let go of the queen and reached into the air.

The tethers.

Meiling was going to die.

His dearly beloved Mei was going to *die*.

"Meiling!" he screamed, breaking into a run even though he knew, he *knew* he wasn't fast enough. He couldn't stop it. There was nothing he could do. He'd failed her once and for all.

That didn't keep him from throwing himself toward her.

Feiyan's curse echoed in his ear like a death knell as she, too, broke into a frantic run.

But it wasn't just the two of them. A third person ripped through shadows and layers of reality.

The illusionist. *Shuren*.

The one Meiling had so vehemently protected.

Shuren dove toward Zedong, making to tackle him. He was too fast for Zedong to see until it was almost too late, but not fast enough. Not fast enough to escape the sudden glinting of a drawn knife in his stolen hand. Zedong plunged it toward Queen Liena—but it was Shuren who came between the blade and the queen even as Zedong yanked on air. On Meiling's tether.

Life slowed until Shang's heartbeat was a distant gong, thundering in slow motion. Feiyan screamed a name—*Shuren*. And that scream carried the weight of so much emotion. The weight of treacherous love and hatred and the loss of something that never should have been wanted.

He wouldn't have cared. Except that in one leap, Feiyan could be at Meiling's side—or she could be at Shuren's. One touch could be the difference between life and death.

But Shang couldn't make Feiyan leap toward Meiling. Not in the millisecond a choice needed to be made. His legs moved as though through a thick sludge in a dream. He'd never reach Meiling in time.

He'd spent the last several months devoted to her life, her safety. A hundred times, he'd put himself in harm's way for her. He defied what anyone believed possible to save her.

In the end, he failed.

In the end, he lost the only treasure he'd ever called his.

But Meiling wasn't his. Before, he would have said she belonged to her family, to Zheninghai, but now he saw the truth. She was her own. She didn't belong to anyone or to anything. Princess Lu Meiling of Zheninghai had carved her own path. Despite the dozens of forces that wanted nothing but to force her into a shy little box of curses, she had become a princess of legend. One that had decided to sacrifice herself for the people who had despised her.

Meiling had become a dreamwalker.

Shang hadn't failed her. He realized it now in this dark, horrible moment of his nightmares. Shang had loved her, had fought for her, had bled for her.

In the end, he'd given everything he had for her.

And it was *enough*. Not enough to save her, but enough for her to save him, her family, and Zheninghai. He had to let her give herself up—even if it destroyed him. Even if he wanted to shake the stars from the sky to keep it from happening. He had to let himself lose her.

So he let her go.

It broke him. It killed him. But he let her go.

Time resumed its horrific pace. Meiling screamed. The dagger pierced Shuren's heart. Zedong snapped air between his fist and teeth. Feiyan lunged.

The life vanished from Meiling's body, from Zedong's body, and they both crashed to the polished golden floor of the throne room.

CHAPTER 44

MEILING'S CRUMPLED BODY sent panic slicing through Shang's body. Feiyan had reached her half a second before him, her hands splaying across Meiling's stomach as tears streamed down her cheeks.

Shang dragged Meiling's limp form into his arms desperately, looking for any sign of life, searching with his fingers for any hint of a pulse. *None.* "Meiling, Meiling, Meiling!" he choked, his own tears an open floodgate, his voice utterly raw. "Please, *please* don't leave me. Come back to me, darling. Wake up! *Meiling!*"

"I'm trying to find her!" Feiyan cried, pressing her hands harder into Meiling's middle. "No, no, no, *no.* You can't be dead, you stupid girl! You *can't* be!"

The healer shook with effort; her face twisted in a grimace as she sent her magic into Meiling's body. Shang cradled her closer, denial and anguish warring in wretched turns.

The throne room doors banged open wide, and a distant part of Shang's mind recognized the emperor's furious strides and the way they suddenly came up short. The way a strangled noise came from deep in his throat.

Then those steps resumed, pounding across the floor until Emperor Nianzu slid to his knees and crawled to Meiling's side. Instinctively, Shang tightened his grip, refusing to let the emperor pull his own daughter from his arms. But Nianzu didn't try. He only reached out with a trembling, tear-wet hand to cradle the side of her face.

Shang bowed his head, pressing his forehead to Meiling's, and he wept like he had never wept before.

CHAPTER 45

EVERYTHING WAS BREAKING.

Meiling ran as plaster rained down from the ceiling. Her bare feet stumbled over the shards of a shattered stained-glass window. The knife-like edges plunged deep into her soft flesh, and it *hurt*. In a way it shouldn't in this world.

The banister smashed as a falling stone crashed into it. Splinters, big and small, went flying. The foundation under her bleeding feet shuddered, resulting in more falling debris and caving walls.

She ran.

The vivid colors leaked away from the rugs, the tapestries, the statues, the paint. The vibrant reds and golds leeched to gray. She flung up a hand to shield her head from the raining rubble.

She was dying, and she was trapped in her own mind as she did so.

Not with her Ma, with Feiyan, with Shang. Not with her Pa or her siblings.

She was alone to face the hungry jaws of death without eyes full of faces she loved, reminding her that the sacrifice was worth it, that she would do it a hundred—no, a *thousand*—times over again.

It was like being imprisoned in Zedong's fortress again, being beaten senseless and bludgeoned against the wall, knowing she was dying. It had been worth it then, and it was worth it now.

Zedong would never hurt her family again. Never lay another hand on her mother, never bind another *mó guǐ* to his control, never send his vile sorcery implanting in unsuspecting minds. It was forever worth it.

But the glass hurt her feet, the splinters dug into her palms, and the debris hit her head and arms hard. Hard enough to make her lose consciousness if she was in her body.

Meiling ran, ignoring the pain shooting through her.

She would be alone here while she died, but she was not going to die in the middle of the palace's maze of hallways, draining out on the polished floor and woven rugs.

Her legs were weak when she clamored up the shuddering stairs, and for a terrifying moment she thought they would crumble, and she would fall to the floor beneath. They held, and she found herself crawling on all fours to her chambers, gasping with effort.

The door was open.

She barely had the strength to enter, to close it behind her.

It would be a matter of minutes—no, less than minutes, mere seconds—until this entire palace of her mind collapsed to the ground and buried her beneath it. The rumbling, the echoing of her disintegrating mind seemed suddenly distant when the door to her rooms thudded firmly behind her.

Her room was shockingly intact, but that should not be a surprise. After all, this was the deepest part of her, this retreat from everything, where she had slept and dreamed and found the sweetest freedom. And at the core of it—

Her tether gleamed white gold at the window. It frayed, splitting quickly before her eyes.

She gathered the last reserves of her swiftly dying strength and hauled herself up to that window. She placed her hands on that anchor, feeling her life ebbing away. Her soul, her essence.

Her magic was dying, too.

She held her tether right at the base, right at the anchor, as it tore. The sounds of destruction grew louder, and even here in her room, in the most sacred part of her soul, the ceiling shuddered. The bones of the palace groaned. It shook beneath her hands.

No one would hear her last words, but she would speak them still.

"I love you, Hou. I love you, Yun." Plaster fell into her hair, striking as it landed. "I love you, Fen, Kai, Delan, Master Dong. I love you, Renshu. I love you, Shuren. I love all you people I met at the beach and in the streets of Suguan."

The rumbling grew louder. Loose objects in her room—teacups, beaded headdresses, hair pins, containers of facial paint and kohl—rattled on the hard surfaces.

"I love you, Feiyan."

Meiling almost lost her grip on her tether as an earthquake sent her wardrobe falling and smashing into the floor, her bed sliding across the room.

"I love you, Pa. I love you, Ma."

A sharp, stabbing pain thrust into her heart and went raking through her, devouring her. It took every ounce of remaining strength, every shred of willpower, to hold onto that gleaming white gold tether, to suck her life dry to the dregs.

"I love you, Shang."

She could barely force out the words around the pain, around the world breaking around her. But she'd done it.

Now, *now,* she could die.

A chunk of the ceiling fell onto her legs. She screamed as it broke bones and pinned her in place. Her room collapsed around her, onto her, but the pain started to fade, to grow more distant. With it, the noise dulled.

Meiling gasped, and she knew her lungs would never fill again. Her grip faltered on her tether. She should just let it go; she should just let her fingers slip off that sputtering, fraying tether that would soon fully snap.

She would just *let go . . .*

"Don't let go," a voice cried from all around. A girl's voice, broken with strain and frantic with pleading. *"Not yet. Don't let go. Don't give up."*

She did not have the strength to respond or to even draw another breath. She was being buried alive, suffocated. Any second now, the last fiber of her tether would snap, and that would be it.

"Don't you dare let go of your soul, Lu Meiling. Don't you dare."

But she was so tired, her lungs were empty, burning, and if she let go, she could be free from her pain.

"I know you're dying. I know you're ready to die, but we're not ready to lose you. I can't save you, Meiling, if you won't let me, if you won't fight as hard as I am. Your mother and father cannot lose you. Shangdi cannot lose you." The voice broke, "I *cannot lose you. Fight! Fight!"*

Meiling couldn't fight. There was nothing left, nothing more to give. Every ounce of her soul was drained, and her fingers began sliding off her tether as that last fiber began—

"Fight, Meiling!"

Shang. Ma. Pa. Feiyan. All those names, all those people she loved so dearly. She saw each of their faces flash before her. And suddenly, it was like they stood around her. Perhaps they did. Reached through the rubble, grabbed her, lifted her.

Meiling let out a cry and lurched upward, gripping her tether with both hands.

It was enough.

Honey warmth, glittering gold with threads of emerald poured into her tether just at the last instant, saving that thread from snapping entirely.

It was enough.

It was enough.

Meiling clung to her tether, clung to that warmth, and let oblivion wash over her.

CHAPTER 46

THE AIR WAS full of weeping. Shouting. Pleading.

It smelled of salt and smoke and blood.

It tasted paper dry.

Warmth—all around her. Flowing into her, holding her, touching her.

Her name. People were saying her name with familiar voices.

Meiling's eyes were crusted over, and after a futile attempt at opening them, she left them closed. Listened. Smelled. Drew breath into her lungs that had burned so horridly only a minute ago.

"Meiling?" It was a man's voice, deep and choked with emotion. With wild hope.

"Meiling?" that voice repeated, this time louder and more insistent. Something tightened on her arms, around her shoulders. "Meiling?"

Peeling open her eyes was the most difficult thing she had done in her entire life. They finally relented, finally gave way, and Meiling peered up into faces. Beyond them, stars glittered in a hazy night sky.

Her eyes focused, and she found herself staring up at three faces. Shang, Feiyan, and Pa.

She didn't know what happened next. It was too confusing, too overwhelming. Ma was there, and Fen showed up at some point. Even Renshu's head came into view once before disappearing. She was embraced, exclaimed over, and almost none of it registered.

It was not until a pair of warm lips pressed into hers, gentle and edged in desperate relief, that her vision and mind cleared. That kiss chased away the fog, enough for her to bring up her hands and plant them against Shang's chest and shove him away.

"Everyone is watching!" she cried.

Her first words back from the dead.

Fen snorted a laugh, and those other peering faces choked on their tears and smiled.

But Shang drew her back into his arms again, perhaps having waited for her parents to finish, and his face was ragged, his eyes raw. "The whole world could be watching for all I care. Now stop fighting me and let me kiss you."

At those words, she realized she didn't care either. She melted into his arms, into the warmth of home and love and goodness, and savored the kisses she had thought she lost.

A loud smashing from outside broke into the little cocoon of safety.

They were still under attack.

Meiling got to her feet with Shang's aid, and everyone seemed to study her—as though expecting her to collapse at any moment. She frowned and said, "Feiyan is good at what she does. You don't have to worry so much about me." She cast a pointed glance at Shang. "I'm not going to go into shock."

His black eyes glittered, but not in their usual way. They sheened over like he wasn't even listening to her words as he studied her face.

Suppressing the urge to close the distance between them, cup his face and comfort him with kisses, she turned away, looking for the one person who had inched away from the others.

There.

Feiyan sat on the ground, Shuren's head pulled into her lap. His eyes were open, unseeing, and wide with pain. Empty. Slowly, Feiyan smoothed away the hair from his face and, with a shudder, closed those eyes.

She trembled like a leaf swept up in a winter gale. Weak, drained to the bone. She rocked back and forth, holding him and not noticing his blood smearing on her.

Meiling's tears coursed down her cheek as she sat next to her friend and wrapped her arm around her shoulders. Feiyan lowered her head, a dry sob wracking her frame. She kept rocking, kept clutching the body in her arms.

"I couldn't save you both," Feiyan choked, tears dribbling off her chin and onto his face.

Meiling tightened her grip and, as if responding to the unspoken invitation, Feiyan leaned her head on Meiling's shoulder.

"He loved you," Meiling whispered.

Another broken sob. "I know."

"He wasn't a coward."

"I know."

Meiling remembered the illusionist's beautiful, lethal mind. That mind that covered pain with beauty, that longed for a deeper purpose than this gritty, unforgiving reality. She leaned her head onto Feiyan's and together they mourned, even as Ma stepped toward Zedong's body, only to turn away once more. Ma's frame shook with grief, with fury, and Pa stepped to her side and wrapped her up in his arms. Maybe at long last, she could find peace from the old friend turned enemy who had haunted her for over two decades.

Feiyan leaned down and pressed a trembling, dry-lipped kiss on Shuren's brow.

And then she fainted.

Pa rose. He drew himself up straight, setting back his shoulders, and ignored the wetness of his face. Gone was the fatherly devastation that had pained his features. He was His Imperial Majesty now. Meiling watched, waiting, as she held the unconscious healer and ran cold ice—courtesy of Shang—over her forehead and temples.

"Tan Shangdi," he rumbled.

Shang's bow was stiff and quivering, but regal and princely nonetheless. "Majesty."

"I charge you to assemble the survivors and lead the defense against the invading barbarians at our gates. They are weakened without Zedong, but keep your wits about you. Take him, too." Pa waved a hand at Renshu, who stood just inside the double doors with a bloodstained broadsword in each hand.

After a brief moment of looking stunned, Shang lowered himself to the ground and pressed his lips to the floor. "It is my honor."

"You," Pa said toward Shang, and then pointed at Fen and Meiling. "You, and you, are hereby officially pardoned of your crimes and accusations and whatever other nonsense. So help me, I will personally raze this city if anyone dares challenge me. And if what's left of the council after tonight gives me trouble, I'll show *them* trouble."

Meiling found herself staring at her father. He'd always been His Imperial Majesty, and her Pa. But she'd never seen the mighty fire-wielding warrior he was. It gave her a newfound respect for him. He turned to Ma, his tone only softening a fraction. "See to the healer. You,"—He pointed at Fen again—"take them to the vault and then return to the battle."

Finally, Pa's eyes met Meiling's, shining with a new light. Smoke curled up between his clenched fist. "And *you*. Come with me to the battlefield."

CHAPTER 47

MEILING PULLED UP short as she flew out of the palace.

The Butagin army poured through the gates, fighting the weakened empire forces. It seemed that everywhere she looked, there were bodies. She almost wished the night was completely dark so she would not see how many lives had already been lost, lives that were beyond saving. Instead, the smoke went up from the still-burning Academy and illuminated the world in a horrid, hazy half-light.

Pa had given her two sets of instructions before she left her body in the vault and came after him in her spirit. First, to enter the minds of the barbarian commanders to discover their next moves and report to Shang. Second, to not die no matter what.

Now, she looked back toward the palace to see him rushing out to another balcony, hands blazing as sweat poured down his face and now-tattered robes.

Then Meiling hurled toward the barbarian army.

She had not been given any instructions on how she was to know a commander from a regular foot soldier, but she imagined the commanders would probably wear some sort of distinguishing marker. So she flew quickly over the endless masses until she spotted a man who was shouting orders to the people around him.

She darted into his mind.

Meiling found herself standing in knee-deep snow, shod in decrepit boots and an old wool coat. The air was bitterly cold, even through the coat, and it was shockingly quiet. No sun shone, but no more snow fell, either. It was a silent world. The world after a blizzard, with snowdrifts and heavy-ladened trees. Not a single footprint was visible in the snow.

A barrage of loud, tense thoughts and the sounds of battle from outside ruptured the silence. She heard their language, recognized it as the same language the guards had spoken in Zedong's fortress, but as she listened, it reshaped in her mind so she could understand it.

The left flank needs reinforcement. Vanguard is breaking formation because of those festering gates. As soon as the idea came into his head, the commander was shouting aloud to someone, "See if you can rally any of Fang's brigands or *mó guǐ* to take down this gate!"

Meiling fought the urge to immediately leave and find Shang. Instead, she snapped her eyes shut and reached out for the memory threads. Then she ran along them, hunting for his tether so she could find his plans.

The memories flashing into her mind were bleak, full of winter cold and enmity toward their southern neighbors, the empire that had thrust them northward against their will. She saw him marrying a wife he had never met before, saw him losing both her and their first son to childbirth. There was him remarrying, hunting late at night to find *anything* for his family to eat. And there was his anxiety that he would lose his second wife and children, too.

She found the hope that Zedong had instilled in their hearts. Of better days and greener pastures, of sunshine and warm breezes. Meiling hadn't been the only soul he'd sought to manipulate for his own purpose.

Meiling stopped suddenly, the memories of the commander's life still flickering around her. She should keep going, should find all the information she could to give to Shang. But . . .

Hello, Commander, she said aloud. *I am Princess Meiling of Zheninghai and I am in your mind.*

He understood her. Somehow, being in his mind allowed them to speak despite their language barrier. He seemed to realize it too, in the back of his mind, though the rest of it was scrambling to understand, to—

It clicked. He remembered her. Zedong's pet. He remembered her unique abilities. He remembered how Zedong had used them to serve his own purposes.

What do you want? he barked in return.

I want you to call off your forces. I want you to persuade the other commanders to do the same.

You cannot be serious, he scoffed. *I do not care what gifts you possess. You cannot make me do anything.*

She sighed. She hadn't expected it to be as simple as batting her eyelashes and asking sweetly. But there had been enough bloodshed tonight, and she did not want this commander to die any more than she wanted her own people to die.

She would do what she had to do.

I have access to your military plans. I've been asked to give them to the strategist currently leading our forces.

The sounds of the outside world quieted as a solid pit of dread fell into the commander's stomach. Almost immediately, however, his mind began rationalizing how they could still win. After all, they had the element of surprise. They had an entire army while the empire's forces were battered and sparse after the *mó guǐ* slaughter.

Meiling sighed again, closing her eyes. And months ago, she never would have dreamed of uttering the words she did next. But she wasn't the same woman she was from months ago. She fought her own battles now, and when the people she loved were at risk, she would fight dirty.

I will give him your exact location.

His reeling mind faltered. His realization was not meant for her, but it was loud and echoed off the snowy caps of his mind. *Without me, my entire unit will collapse into disarray and fall.*

She would not beg. Instead, she said. *I saw the little daughter your wife just bore you, and . . .* She drew another breath, allowing the truthfulness of her words to fill her voice. *I do not want to give you away. I do not want you or any of your unit to die.*

He recoiled from the softness in her voice. *How coolly and viciously you threaten me.*

I have no desire to threaten, manipulate, or coerce you. But you are attacking my home and everything I love. If you wish to keep attacking, it will force me to divulge the information I know.

War raged inward and outward. Weighing, calculating, assessing the risk.

Fang was right to enslave your magic to his will, he said bitterly.

No, he was not, Meiling responded.

Silence—stiller than his frozen mindscape—filled the space between their words.

She saw his choice. Sacrificing himself and his unit, hoping the rest of the army could conquer the empire's capital even though he knew she would find their plans of formation. There was still a chance, given their strength of numbers.

Or *life.*

Life running away from a battle, life back in frigid mountains, but life. With his family, his children, his wife. *Life.*

I will order my unit to retreat. There was no lie behind that proclamation.

Very well. I will tell our troops to not pursue you.

With that, Meiling abandoned his mind. The commander turned and began shouting at his troops to retreat. She did not stay to watch, but instead scoured the darkness for that brilliant blue-white glow, flying around her father's fire as he annihilated men by the tens, fifties, and hundreds.

Shang was not leading the charge, but furiously dealing out instructions to others as he surveyed the battlefield. His eyes blazed as he shouted, tendons standing out starkly in his neck. He had that look on his face, like he had come up with a plan that *just might* work, if executed properly. As she hurtled toward him, his face lifted and spied the retreating unit. He blinked, frowning, and then she was in his mind.

Shang! she gasped.

What in the seven valleys did you do, Meiling? It was not an accusation; it was a question full of awe.

And confusion.

Don't send your men after them! I bargained with him and told him that if he continued attacking, I would reveal his plans. He chose to flee.

Him, and others, Shang replied.

She stopped, blinking into his sight, and found what he meant. Other units had turned and were wading their way back through the barbarian forces. It was causing such a chaos that more units splintered, and the air rang with conflicting charges to attack and retreat.

Meiling, he breathed.

She blushed, lowering her head as she stood in his mind. *I was not sure if it would work.*

You've given us the chance that we need to turn the tide. Can you deliver messages to my commanders on the front?

It would be my pleasure, she said with a smile. Much better than threatening enemies. *But I have to tell Pa not to kill the retreating soldiers first.*

Shang rattled off several complicated strings of instructions, and Meiling repeated them back to make sure she had them correct. Right when she was about to leave, he stopped her.

Meiling?

Yes?

Don't let anyone ever tell you again that you do not have battle magic.

She grinned and flew off.

CHAPTER 48

THE CARNAGE WAS suffocating.

Through the night, Meiling entered the minds of the stubborn barbarian commanders who refused to flee, giving everything she found to Shang and relaying his messages faster than any courier to those he could not reach quickly. She bounced between minds, hardly noticing what was happening until—

Meiling! Shang gasped when she returned to his mind. *We—we won! See? The rest of them are retreating!*

Indeed, when she blinked into his sight, the full army retreated out of the gates, and Pa's relentless fire sputtered into nothing.

Shang turned his head toward the city, toward the ocean, as if to show Meiling the rising sun staining the dawn pink and orange. He sighed, running a hand through the mess of his hair. Exhaustion made his limbs shake, and he desperately wanted to fall to the ground right there and sleep.

Instead, he kept himself upright and turned to look up toward the balcony where Pa was standing still, surveying the smoldering ruins of the Academy, the corpses filling the once-beautiful palace grounds. Pa looked down, caught sight of Shang. Reverence pulsed through Shang's blood and despite his knocking knees, he swept a bow to his emperor.

In return, Pa gave a deep nod.

Satisfaction and pride washed down Shang's spine, flowing into Meiling.

You did well, she whispered to him.

His cheeks colored at her words, another wave of pride sweeping through his soul as tender affection bloomed in his heart.

It is time for you to wake up, Princess Meiling. My . . . my love.

"You have *magic*?" Hou gawked.

"Where were you last night?" Meiling cried. "When I was dragged off to the council? Did you miss that commotion?"

"You were *what*?"

"Hou, leave your sister alone. She's had a very long night," Ma scolded, looking probably the worst Meiling had ever seen her, but there was no mistaking the relief on her face.

"You hid her magic from me?" Hou demanded, turning on Ma. That fierceness flooded her eyes, and she sat back in the vault, fixing a glare on their mother.

"Hush, my vicious warrior," Ma said, pressing a finger to Hou's lips. "Be glad you know now, because you were never intended to know."

Hou continued glowering, but Meiling clamored to her unsteady feet when people started filing out of the vault, exposing a sleeping figure on the other side. She hurried through the dissipating throng until she reached Feiyan's side.

Feiyan lay on her side, a few strands of hair falling into her face. Her green robes were torn, bloodied, and there was a bandage on her leg. Dirt crusted her face, and circles lined her eyes. Her lips were parted, and soft exhales brushed Meiling's hand when she held it against her mouth. Just to reassure her thudding heart that her friend was still alive.

"Thank you," Meiling whispered, brushing aside that fallen hair. "Thank you for being the best friend I have ever had and one of the best people I've ever known. You give of yourself until there's nothing left. I hope I can help you find rest."

This would be the next good she would do for Zheninghai. She would discover a way to give Feiyan the rest she needed so she could continue her work for many, many years to come.

"Sleep, my friend," she whispered, and rose.

Ma was watching her, tears gleaming in her weary face.

For a long moment, they stared at each other. The air between them was heavy with years of hurt and misunderstanding, with Zedong's life and lies, with the death and almost death of this night.

Then they were running until there was no space between them and they embraced each other. They could apologize. They could murmur promises of no more secrets. Could say how relieved they were that the other was still alive. There was so much they could say.

But Meiling shoved all those things aside and simply whispered, "I love you, Ma."

Ma gasped on a choking sob and clutched her closer. "I love you too, Mei, my dove."

After several minutes, a sudden thought seemed to hit Ma and Meiling at the same time. They jerked back, staring wide-eyed at each other.

"Where's Yun?" Meiling breathed.

They turned and broke into a run, careening out of the vault. Meiling's legs ached as she ran up the stairs, but she didn't care. Her heart skipped ahead several beats, her lungs heaving, and cold dread sliding down her back.

He must be alive; he must be alive. He must! He must!

By the time they made it outside, the entire sky was painted fiery orange and pink, the light filling the ruins and death all around.

And ahead—there was Pa, hurrying out of the Academy ruins with arms full of a heavy, tall boy. Pa's face was filthy and grimaced with effort and fear, but Meiling could only see that swinging, limp arm.

"Yun!" Ma's voice broke.

Pa nearly stumbled, but caught himself and heaved Yun down onto the cooled, charred grass. Ma sank next to him with a sob.

"He's alive," Pa spewed, reaching over Yun's body to grip Ma's shoulder tightly. The last of Meiling's tightly coiled fear disappeared, making her almost burst into tears of relief. "He's alive, Liena." His choked words almost seemed more for himself than for her. "All of our children are alive."

Yun coughed, rolled in the grass, and vomited right next to Ma. But Ma did not care. She only stroked his hairline and sooty face and crooned, "My brave boy."

"Should I send for the apothecaries?" Meiling interrupted, still standing and hovering. "Not just for him, but for everyone? Should we issue some sort of decree that the battle is over? That we won?"

That seemed to snap Pa out of his flooding emotion. He looked up at Meiling and nodded sternly, starting to rise. Then, he smiled suddenly and sat back down, waving a hand. "Have your Tan Shangdi send word out. He's proved himself competent in everything else. I am going to see to the care of my family."

Your Tan Shangdi.

Pa's eyes flicked past Meiling, to someone behind her. "Did you hear that?"

She turned and found Shang standing a few paces back. He glanced between her, Pa, Ma, and Yun on the ground, but nodded and bowed. "It is my honor, Your Majesty."

"I'll go with him and send for the apothecaries," Meiling said, spinning on her heel and hurrying toward Shang. His robes were singed, torn, and streaked with blood, his handsome face bruised, but the sight of his tall frame, his broad shoulders, and his strong arms—all hale and whole—nearly made her cry from happiness.

"Is your brother all right?" Shang asked in a low voice.

She nodded, not trusting her voice.

"I am relieved to hear it."

They had not walked far before Fen came jogging toward them, bloodied beyond belief even as her eyes glowed like never before. Meiling expected Fen to go immediately to Shang, but her attention was solely fixed on Meiling.

"Princess Meiling," Fen said, her voice raspy. She bowed, hands outstretched, and Meiling almost startled at the reverence. "Listen, I've been avoiding doing this for a while now, but after last night, I just can't anymore. I must ask your forgiveness for the way I treated you back on our journey to Liafugen, and thank you for all the good you did for me and Shang, despite . . . everything. I know you may not—"

Her words faltered slightly.

"I forgave you," Meiling said, smiling, "a long, long time ago."

Fen looked up, meeting her gaze with those eyes that betrayed how the adrenaline still roared in her blood. "Everything I assumed about you at first was wrong."

"You, me, and everyone else," Shang interjected, nodding toward the city bathed in dawn.

"It is completely understandable." Meiling smiled, gaze flicking between Fen and Shang.

Shang tilted his head, looking down at her, and the smile playing on his features and shining in his black eyes was brighter than the morning sun.

"I think it is time the world knew their princess was a heroine," he said.

His hand found hers, dragging her after him until they rounded the corner, out of sight of Fen and Meiling's family.

“But first . . .” Shang whispered. And then his arms were around her, fingers tangling in her hair as he kissed her with all the hope of a new dawn.

EPILOGUE

THE WORLD AROUND Meiling was quiet and red.

But this quiet was not the stillness after death, this red not the flow of blood. It was the silence that hummed of thrilling anticipation, an emptiness full of a single, throbbing heartbeat. And the red?

It was the scarlet of weddings.

The crimson of a bride.

She waited, alone, in an unfamiliar house, behind a series of locked doors. Her heart hammered against her lungs, and each breath puffed against her veil. Her bare feet were tucked beneath her as she kneeled on the mat behind the last locked door.

Ten months had passed since Zedong's attack and subsequent defeat. The Academy was being rebuilt, even as Meiling and Shang had been working together to create something new for the children of Zheninghai: schools for those without magic to increase opportunities across the empire. Education was its own power, its own magic, and Meiling dearly wanted that power in the hands of ordinary people.

What time he wasn't spending working his strategist appointment, Shang spent on preparations with the emperor, Master Dong, and Renshu for a separate military academy for students without magic. Trade had been reestablished with Butagin after decades of hostility, and the economies of both countries thrived as a result.

It had been an extremely full ten months, but the moment she had longed for was finally here.

Her hands shook. The roaring of blood filled her ears. The last skitters and patters of her Ma and her maids had long since retreated, leaving her to wait.

The emptiness stretched out before her, full and waiting to be discovered.

She waited and counted her breaths.

One, two, three.

Then, at long last, a distant sound pricked her starving ears. It was not as loud as she perhaps had expected, but it sent her heart racing even faster than before. *Thump, thump, thump,* was the ever-increasing drumbeat.

Another sound, this time closer. The creak of hinges swinging open.

Her skin was clammy beneath her gloves. She tried to keep her fingers from plucking at her sash, but her efforts were in vain. Nothing could calm her nervous movements.

The sound grew louder, paired with more sounds now. The sound of boots set in a purposeful stride against wooden floors. A stride she knew almost as well as her own name.

She reached up, gingerly touching her veil. Ensuring it was still in place.

Her thoughts were mush, muddled to the quivering of her muscles and the dryness of her throat. Only a few more minutes . . .

Those footsteps grew louder until the sound was all-consuming. Her breaths were tied to each thump, each stride, her very existence narrowing to the shadows moving under the door.

Air snagged in her lungs.

A sharp smash filled the quiet, though it was again not as loud as she expected. Through her filmy, shaking vision, she saw ice break through the lock on the door. It swung open, groaning with its own heaviness.

Her heart stopped.

There, standing in the doorway and silhouetted against the hallway behind him, dressed in his wedding raiment, tall and majestic, was Tan Shangdi.

Shang.

Her bridegroom.

Though her veil prevented her from seeing clearly, she would recognize his form, his stance, anywhere. She could tell those glittering black eyes from a li away, and even the gauzy red fabric could not conceal his thick swallow, his parting lips.

"Meiling."

His low, soft voice reached out to her across the space between them. Even her hands had stilled their fidgeting, her mouth open to speak. No words would come. She simply stared from where she kneeled on her mat in the center of this unfamiliar room and this unfamiliar house used solely for this purpose: the bridegroom's fetching of his bride.

Shang took one step, then another, toward her. She lifted her eyes to his as he came closer, her neck craning backward.

"Shang," she breathed.

He reached her, kneeled before her. He paused, as though suddenly hesitant. Then, moving deliberately, he reached for the edge of her veil.

"You cannot remove my veil yet!" Meiling cried suddenly, swatting his hands away.

At this, he smiled. "What if I promise to put it back?"

Somehow, his gentle teasing was enough to make her throat go dry again. This time, when he reached for her veil, she had no will to protest. One moment, the world was swathed in crimson film. The next, she stared into Shang's dark eyes. She saw clearly now what she couldn't see before.

His own hands shook like hers, his jaw clenching and relaxing in turns, and his too-bright eyes glowed with a well of unshed tears, even as he smiled so gently. His gaze was liquid with a plethora of emotions, thoughts, longings. Her lips parted at the sight, her lungs seizing up within her.

How she had ever thought a soul as deep as his to be stoic, she didn't know.

"Shang?" She reached out to him, to the hands that still held her veil away from her face. "Shang?"

His eyes closed just as a tear slipped free, just as his arms wrapped around her and his lips found hers. That tear slid and landed on the apple of her cheek, another kiss of its own.

"I never thought," he said as he pulled back, his shuddering breath caressing her face as he leaned his forehead against hers. "I never thought this day would be ours. I dreamed and hoped, but I never truly *believed* . . ."

"You never believed what?" she whispered.

He kissed her again, slowly, gently, ignoring Zheninghai customs. Kisses that promised thousands more over the course of a lifetime. When he spoke, his voice was an octave lower.

"I never believed you would truly be mine."

Meiling stared up at him, at his heart bared in his eyes. Never in her wildest dreams would she have thought that all those months ago, when Tan Shangdi had led her out of the west gate, that this was where they would be now.

"I love you, Shang," she said. They were the truest words she'd ever spoken.

He pressed one last kiss to her brow, a jubilant smile spreading across his face. There was a peace in his gaze, as though the striving and searching had finally come to an end. As though they'd both been searching for home all their lives, only to find it staring out of the eyes of the other.

Shang sat backward on his heels, pulling away from her, and reached down to something he'd set next to his knee. She followed the movements of his hand and let out a surprised, "Oh! You found them already!"

He held up her slippers, a wry little grin playing on his features. "You were the one to hide them, weren't you?"

"Me?" She feigned surprise. Brides were expected to hide their slippers from their bridegrooms, and he was to find them as another test of his competence, but often a mother or aunt would hide them.

He raised an eyebrow. "No one else except you would have hung them on a curtain rod."

She couldn't help the girlish giggle that escaped her. He smiled and held out his hand for her foot. A blush stained her cheeks as she obliged him, and he carefully slid each of the slippers onto her feet, first pausing to gently caress the arch of each foot. She couldn't help but shiver at the ticklish sensation running up her calves. He looked up, arching one amused eyebrow and catching her in his spellbinding gaze.

"Now what?" she asked, breathless, even though she already knew.

He smiled again, broader than before, and pulled her veil back over her face. In one smooth motion, he swept her up into his arms and turned toward the door.

"Now what?" he repeated, as her heart beat hard against her chest, as she wrapped her arms around his neck. "Why, we get married, of course."

Shang kicked open the front door of the house, still cradling her close in his arms, and immediately they were enveloped in the sound of uproarious cheering. Meiling was glad for the red veil covering the flush of her cheeks. Her old habit was to hide her face in Shang's neck, but this time she didn't, even as Shang whispered into her ear, "Listen to their cheers, little love."

Though he was supposed to carry her all the way to the awaiting litter, he set her down next to him, turning her to face the crowds. He held his hand against her low back, gently pushing her forward.

She stared into the courtyard that overflowed into the streets beyond. She stared at all of Zheninghai, at her people. Thousands of faces, full of strangers and familiars.

That was when she realized the difference. It hit her so suddenly that she nearly stumbled backward into her soon-to-be husband. It was almost more than she could bear, her eyes filling with tears, her heart nearly bursting with relief from a tension she'd borne all her life.

"They finally see what I see," Shang said.

Then he swung her back up in his arms and carried her through the cheering masses. She laughed, and before she knew it, she was squealing at each familiar face. There was her brother and sister, the former bellowing cheers so loudly the people near him had to cover their ears, the latter hopping up and down and clapping her hands even while fidgeting with the pink robes she had so vehemently opposed wearing. There was Fen, arms crossed, with a knowing smirk on her lips. Feiyan whooped at her side while Renshu clapped Shang on the back with a broad grin when they passed. A little further, and there was Lian Delan smiling with a beautiful woman on one arm, three young girls hanging from the other. Beside him was Shi Kai, bending down to kiss the girl he'd married only a few weeks ago: a lovely girl named Sun Aranya—technically now Shi Aranya—that Meiling was thrilled to get to know better in the coming years.

Waiting for them at the litter, with proud beaming smiles, looking younger, freer, and happier than they had in years, were Emperor Nianzu and Queen Liena. Meiling caught Ma's hand and squeezed it just before Shang swung her into the litter.

He hesitated, and then threw ceremony and custom aside as he climbed into the litter beside her.

"What are you doing?" Meiling demanded, laughing, as he drew the curtains shut—closing them in a little oasis of velvet, gold, and silk.

"Making every moment count," he murmured back, and kissed her all the way home.

Shang had been planning his wedding gift to Meiling for months. When he told her he had a surprise for her and escorted her out of the palace on horseback, she was absolutely convinced he was taking her for a stroll on the beach.

So when he took her to the harbor and led her aboard a ship, she was so stunned she could hardly speak—and then she was squealing with excitement and begging to know where he was taking her.

He only grinned and told her she was welcome to guess.

At that point, it was obvious.

"The Southern Isles?" Meiling gasped, and then ran to the bow as if she could see the Isles from here as they were casting off. Shang only laughed and shrugged.

As it turned out, Shang found he didn't care much for the tropical heat of their destination. It was a good thing he had a beautiful wife whose radiating happiness was worth every drop of sweat.

And radiate she did.

He rowed her out to coral reefs so she could nearly lose her mind with how beautiful the multicolored fish were. More than once, he was forced to caution her against touching vibrant coral that was close to the surface or moving so quickly she nearly flipped their boat. And then when they got back to their little hut, she made friends with everyone in the nearby vicinity.

Shang was in heaven.

At this moment, he was sprawled in a hammock near the edge of the water, watching Meiling play some horrible game with the local children that involved one person dumping a bucket of ocean water on every ninth person in the circle. They sang some rhyme as the person with the bucket marched around the edge of the circle and then they all screamed when the bucket was dumped.

Shang's lip quirked when he realized Meiling was going to get dunked next.

Sure enough, the child reached the end of the rhyme right behind her and Meiling let out a squeal when the water drenched her from head to toe. He couldn't help but chuckle as she peeled her wet hair back from her face and got to her feet. She'd finally gained back the weight she'd lost during the hardship of Fang Zedong, and it pleased him very much to look at her.

He wasn't expecting Meiling to come running straight for his hammock.

She clearly had one of two diabolical plans she intended to enact. Either she wanted to hug his dry self while she was dripping wet, or she intended to drag him into the horrible game.

"Come play with us!" Meiling cried when she reached him—and flung herself halfway into the hammock. Her wet hair smacked him right in the face.

Both plans, it seemed.

"But I'm so very content to watch you and your friends throw buckets of water on each other," said Shang, not at all minding a wet hug.

"I miss you though," replied Meiling, pouting.

He smiled. "I'm right here."

"It's too far away. Come on, the children are hilarious! And the water feels very good."

She could ask for the moon with that face, and he'd endeavor to give it to her. But that was the thing with Meiling. She asked for so little.

How could he not find every delight in granting any request she made?

So Shang swung his legs out of the hammock, smirking when she squealed and popped up on her toes to kiss him firmly on the mouth. Then he left his wonderful shade and braved the unforgiving sun.

Of course, when Meiling retrieved the bucket and filled it with seawater, she pointed to where Shang should sit in the circle: the ninth spot. The children began chanting their singsong rhyme as Meiling walked around the circle as though she wasn't sure where the bucket was going to land.

The children laughed uproariously when Shang squeezed his eyes shut with a sigh and let Meiling dump her sloshing bucket right on top of him. She laughed too—until he leaped to his feet and picked her up. Then she was shouting for him to put her down, all while laughter followed them to the lapping waves. He smirked as he held her tighter and shook the water from his hair.

"You said the water feels very good," Shang said. And then he dropped her right into the ocean.

She came up completely soaked, gasping in feigned outrage. "How dare you, Tan Shangdi!"

Shang only grinned at her, and then she was laughing too. Hardly a minute later, Meiling's passel of young friends came hurling into the water after them. Shang spent the better half of the hour obliging the children's requests to be tossed into the ocean, and the rest of the time he was counting heads to make sure no one had drowned.

At last, the children found some other game to occupy themselves on shore. Shang took that opportunity to scoop Meiling out of the water and carry her back to their hut. He kissed her until she fell asleep, exhausted from the hours spent outdoors. He held her close and watched as sunlight bathed her face. Somehow, he knew her spirit hadn't flown away when she slept.

She was right here, dreaming in his arms.

THANK YOU FOR READING THIS SERIES!
IF YOU ENJOYED IT, PLEASE CONSIDER LEAVING
A REVIEW ON AMAZON.

COMING SOON:

THE ASSASSIN BRIDE

*"The Neverseen King comes for a bride every hundred years.
I thought it was only legend . . . until he came for me."*

MORE FROM ANASTASIS BLYTHE

THE ZHENINGHAI CHRONICLES

Maiden of Candlelight and Lotuses
Guardian of Talons and Snares
Warrior of Blade and Dusk
Princess of Shadows and Starlight
Captive of Twilight and Treachery
Daughter of Darkness and Dreams

ABOUT THE AUTHOR

Anastasis Blythe makes her home in central Texas with her husband and their two adorable but rather whiny cats. When she's not writing, she is reading an unhealthy amount of fantasy novels, daydreaming about future books, and trying to keep up with the laundry.

If you would like free novels, regular behind-the-scenes updates on her writing, and an early peek at new book covers, join her community at Patreon.com/AnastasisBlythe.

Connect with Anastasis online at:
Website - AnastasisBlythe.com
Instagram - @AnastasisBlythe
Facebook - Anastasis Blythe
Goodreads - Anastasis Blythe

www.ingramcontent.com/pod-product-compliance
Lightning Source LLC
Chambersburg PA
CBHW020341310726
48979CB00015B/2461/J

9781960606051